## "WHY DOES IT MATTER TO YOU
## WHAT I DO OR WHAT I SAY?" ALYS ASKED.

The question seemed to take Nicholas aback, but he recovered swiftly and said, "I suppose that, having taken responsibility for your safety before, I am finding it difficult to relinquish it now. I feel much the same way I would feel were one of my sisters to behave so foolishly."

She did not want him to treat her like his sisters. "Oh, you enrage me! You treat me like a child, warning me to hold my tongue, to keep my opinions hidden behind my teeth. . . ."

Nicholas's lips pressed tightly together for a moment before he said, "There are dangers you cannot—"

"What dangers? What possible danger can there be here in the king's own palace? You speak nonsense, sir." Impatiently she moved to pass him, but he caught her arm and pulled her hard against him so his lips could claim hers in a swift, bruising kiss.

She knew his intent was only to teach her the danger of thinking she was safe in a palace filled with men. But when his lips and hands touched her, a fire unlike any she had experienced spread through her, softening, yielding, surrendering.

Nicholas did not prolong the moment but freed her within seconds, setting her back on her heels with a quickness that left her gasping. For a moment she saw a look she had never seen before in any man's eyes, one she was not at all certain how to interpret. But the look was quickly gone, followed by another she recognized only too well. He was amused.

With effort she restrained her temper. In as offhand a manner as she could manage, she murmured, "Is that also the way you treat your sisters, Sir Nicholas?"

A muscle leapt high in his cheek, but whether she had annoyed him or only added to his amusement, she could not tell. "Go to your duty, *mi geneth*. If there be justice in this world, her highness will order you whipped for your tardiness."

*Also by Amanda Scott
from Dell*

BORDER BRIDE

# AMANDA SCOTT

# THE ROSE AT TWILIGHT

A DELL BOOK

Published by
Dell Publishing
a division of
Bantam Doubleday Dell Publishing Group, Inc.
666 Fifth Avenue
New York, New York 10103

Copyright © 1993 by Lynne Scott-Drennan

The trademark Dell® is registered in the U.S. Patent and Trademark Office.

ISBN: 0-440-20725-8

Printed in the United States of America

Published simultaneously in Canada

January 1993

RAD    10   9   8   7   6   5   4   3   2   1

# 1

Shifting in her saddle, Lady Alys Wolveston wondered irritably if the sky meant to drip forever. Gloomy, dark clouds hovered overhead, and the drizzling, soaking, depressing rain just fell and fell. Would it never stop? Would the sun never shine on England again? Even her scarlet cloak brought no cheer to the day, though in general it could be counted upon to set off her golden hair and hazel eyes to excellent advantage. Sighing deeply, she pulled the heavy, damp hood lower to protect her face and huddled over the plodding mare's neck, having no desire to look at her half-score companions in misery or the bleak, rain-darkened moorland that spread for miles in every direction. She paid no heed to their route either, knowing that her escort from Drufield Manor would see her safely returned to Wolveston Hazard, her father's great gray stone castle overlooking the river Trent.

Beside her, she could hear Jonet mutter a rhythmic cadence, and knew that she was repeating her rosary. Again. As if a plump little woman swathed in gray wool and talking to beads could stop the rain. Swiftly Alys crossed herself and glanced about, wondering if by some movement or fleeting expression of countenance she might have betrayed the blasphemous thought.

"Mayhap," she said aloud in a casual tone, "our Lord sends a second flood to show us His displeasure."

"Then He would flood Wales for helping the usurper,"

snapped Jonet, "not all Yorkshire and north Nottinghamshire for defending our rightfully anointed king." Her pale blue eyes flashed.

"Hold your tongue," Alys said, keeping her tone even. She rarely spoke sharply to Jonet, who had served her most of her life, but she could not let this pass. "Such words are foolish now. One must be circumspect."

Jonet snorted. "This lot be loyal enough, I warrant. Old men and children for the most part, but loyal to their king."

"Richard is no longer king," Alys said, swallowing the lump in her throat as she thought of Anne's Dickon, dead now and named usurper by a man unworthy to kiss his boots. She remembered the good years at Middleham before King Edward had died, and before Anne's death. Dear, gentle Anne. At least death had spared her the pain and horror of her beloved Dickon's defeat. "Things will be different now," she said, more to herself than to anyone else.

But Jonet, still clicking her beads, said tersely, "Aye, and this weather be the least of our worries, I'm thinking. 'Tis to be hoped your lord father be safe and sure, not trembling in fear of his life like yon Drufield and his ilk."

"My father is known to be a scholar, not a soldier," Alys replied. "King Richard always said he would be better suited to run an abbey than a castle. Even King Edward used to laugh at him, though he scolded Dickon, Anne said, for not setting a more powerful man to be warden of Wolveston Hazard when Dickon was Lord of the North. But Wolveston is beyond the reach of raiding Scots armies, yet not so far afield that Pontefract, Tickhill, or Conisborough cannot provide us protection if the need arises, so Dickon let my father be. Mayhap the Tudor will do likewise."

Jonet shifted her weight awkwardly on her saddle. "The rain be easing. And to think 'twas at last bidding to be a dry day, if a cold and gloomy one, when we left Drufield Manor at dawn."

" 'Tis as well it was," Alys pointed out, "for Lord Drufield would have delayed our journey again had it not been so, and my lord father did command our swift return."

His order had come ten days before, on the heels of the dreadful news from Leicestershire that King Richard had been slain in battle and that Henry Tudor, the Lancastrian Welshman, with his French and Scots mercenaries, had emerged victorious. A fair copy of Henry's round-letter demanding that the nobles of the north bow swiftly to his rule had been carried by the same messenger and had included news of many deaths, including those of the great Earl of Northumberland, the Earl of Lincoln, and Francis, Viscount Lovell, whom Alys's brother Roger served. Alys remembered Lincoln and Lovell well. The first had been wise beyond his twenty-five years, a man who chose his words with care; the second, a gallant, merry gentleman, filled with gaiety, who could always make them chuckle at Middleham. How her life had changed, she thought, once Anne's Dickon had become king.

"Middleham may be in the usurper's hands by now," she said, again speaking her thought aloud.

"Aye, but 'tis naught to us if it is," said Jonet, adding bitterly, "Och, mistress, but I shall perish from this cold and damp. We ought by rights to have sought shelter long since, in Doncaster or Bawtry."

"And so I should have done, were Wolveston not so near that I can well nigh smell its hall fires burning," said Alys tartly. "I have seen neither stick nor stone of the place these two years past, and I do not mean to tarry longer. Geordie!" she shouted.

"Aye, mistress!" came the return shout from up ahead.

"How far now?"

"But two, mebbe three miles, mistress."

"There, you see," she said to Jonet.

"Aye, I see another hour of this wretched misery."

Alys chuckled. Jonet's family had long served her mother's family in Yorkshire, and Jonet had gone with Alys to Middleham, where she had been fostered by the Duke and

Duchess of Gloucester until two years ago, when he had become King Richard the Third of England. He had sent the pair of them to his castle at Sheriff Hutton, and then, six months ago, they had gone to Drufield Manor. Before being sent to Sheriff Hutton, Alys had expected to continue to serve Anne of Gloucester, to become a lady in waiting to the Queen of England, but that had never come to pass.

She still did not know the reason for Richard's sudden decision to send her away from Middleham. Anne had assured her many times over that she had done naught to offend, that Dickon was pleased with her, that it was, oddly, her own father who had commanded the change. Richard had agreed to Wolveston's demand without consulting Anne's wishes, or Alys's. After that, of course, there had been naught to do but obey his command. The reason for Alys's departure from Sheriff Hutton was much clearer in her mind. She grimaced, thinking of Elizabeth.

The sky had lightened, she noted, and the downpour was gentling to a drizzle. Perhaps it would stop for a time soon. It had been raining off and on, sometimes heavily, for nearly a fortnight. She was tired of rain.

Forty minutes later, the rain had eased to little more than a gloomy mist when there came a shout from Geordie, up ahead. "Riders, mistress! A score or more, approaching fast!"

At first she thought it must be her father riding to meet her with some of his men, but it quickly became apparent that the riders were soldiers in arms. Nearby, a particularly young member of her escort reached for his sword.

"Hold!" she commanded. "Observe their banner and beware." The oblong banner looked tattered, but it waved valiantly from the standard bearer's lance and, although its primary device, a golden wyvern, was unknown to her, it was quartered with a fiery red Welsh dragon on a field of green and white sarcenet. Such a device had recently been described to her, more than once.

"Sithee, m'lady, they'll be fer murderin' us," muttered the

lad to whom she had spoken, but she saw that he had taken his hand from his weapon, and was grateful.

"We are no threat to them," she said quietly. "I doubt not that once they have ascertained our destination they will leave us to go our way in peace."

The leader of her escort evidently agreed with her for he signed to the others to draw rein. The armed troop thundered up to them moments later, bringing their chargers to a standstill in a clamor of harness, trappings, and crashing hooves, some of them only feet away from Alys and Jonet.

When one man separated himself from the others and rode toward Alys on a muscular black horse with white pasterns and a narrow feathered stripe down its face, she straightened in her saddle and pushed her hood back a little, preparing to identify herself and demand safe passage for her company. The rider was a large man, tall in the saddle and unusually broad across the shoulders, even when one allowed for the bulk of the leather jacket and padding beneath his light, metal-plated brigandine. He wore a helmet, but the faceplate was up, and although he carried a sword at his side, his gauntlets hung by their thongs over the hilt and his horse was unarmored. When the rider drew up before her, he removed his helmet altogether, revealing thick, dark hair, curling tightly in the damp air.

His countenance was stern, even harsh, but that might, she reflected, be due to his prominent cheekbones, hawklike nose, and jutting, stubborn-looking chin. Though he appeared to be no more than five- or six-and-twenty, he was assuredly the leader of these men. Indeed, she thought, he looked like a man who would take the lead in any company, one who would demand his way in any debate, and one, moreover, whom only a man of great daring, or a fool, would venture to cross.

She raised her chin, looked him straight in the eye, and waited for him to speak. His eyes were deep-set and as gray as the day itself, she noted, and hard, like flints, making her wonder briefly if he might be older than she had first thought. But no, she had not been mistaken. Even as she watched, they changed, softened. His features softened, too. A small, brief spark of amusement lit his eyes, accompanied by a look of compassion that gentled his harsh countenance.

"Lady Alys?" His voice was deep with an unusual lilt in it, his accent gentle, not one she recognized but pleasant nonetheless and soothing to the ear.

"Aye," she said. "I am Alys Wolveston. How is it that you know my name?"

"We have been looking for your arrival these two days past," he said. "You are older than I had expected."

She lifted her chin an inch higher, carrying herself, albeit unconsciously, much as the late queen had done. "My age is of some consequence to you then?"

He shook his head. "Your father spoke of his little daughter. I expected to greet a *plentyn,* a child."

"I am eighteen," she said casually, as though she had been eighteen for a very long time, not a mere three weeks.

" 'Tis odd you are not wedded then," he said crisply.

She gritted her teeth at the arrogance of the man. "Who are you, if I may be so bold as to inquire?"

"I am called Nicholas ap Dafydd ab Evan ap Gwilym of the house of Merion," he said. "Englishmen who cannot wrap their tongues around our Welsh consonants do call me Nick Merion."

"Do they?" She frowned. "Does my father call you so?"

A shadow crossed the stranger's face. "Things are bad here, my lady. 'Tis why we rode out to intercept you."

"Intercept? Why, whatever can you mean?"

"There is sickness at Wolveston Hazard. You must prepare yourself for grave news."

"Sickness?" She had known there was sickness in Yorkshire, for letters mentioning that fact had been received at Drufield, but she had not heard of any outbreak at Wolveston, and his attitude frightened her, making her stomach clench as if it were trying to tie itself in knots. "What sickness? Not plague!"

"Nay, 'tis too early in the year for plague," he said. " 'Tis an ailment unknown to me, but 'tis truly terrible withal. Men grow ill, begin sweating heavily, and die within hours. 'Tis not unknown for a seemingly healthy one to drop down dead even as he speaks. Some say 'tis a new sickness altogether, come to England with the Tudor army, but I have seen naught of it before now. Many are dead or dying, my lady. Some, my own men, but English only, not Welsh, French, or Scot."

"My father? My mother?"

He grimaced. "There is no way to gentle such news, mistress. Your mother is dead. She died yestereve. Your father was healthy until this morning, but now he, too, lies ill. And your little brother died some few hours before your mother."

Alys sensed Jonet stiffening beside her and knew the older woman's reaction must match her own. Remembering that the man facing her was an enemy, she managed with effort to control her emotions, to keep the astonishment she felt from showing on her usually expressive countenance. She dared not look at Jonet, knowing the woman would never so far forget her place as to speak without being spoken to—not before a stranger, in any case.

Swallowing first so that she might command her voice, she said carefully, "My brother, Roger, and my woman's brother, who serves him, were with Viscount Lovell. We feared them both dead like their master on the Plain of Redmore, at the place Henry Tudor called Sandeton."

Merion shook his head. "The lad who died had not been at Bosworth Field, my lady, which is how the site is truly called. Though he was old enough to serve, the lad was gentle and soft, with more the look of a scholar about him, like your father, than that of a knight. I would judge him to have seen only twelve or fourteen winters, old enough to be fostered, certainly. I own, I was surprised to learn that he was a child of the castle, but the servants assured me that he was your brother Robert. Young Paul, you will be relieved to know, left Wolveston some weeks ago to join his foster family. We must discover his whereabouts. Do you know where he has gone?"

Alys shook her head, her thoughts racing as she murmured, "My mother and father were poor correspondents." The words were true enough, and she would not lie to him if she could avoid it, but again she sensed movement from her companion and could not be surprised. Her brothers Robert and Paul had both died eight years before. The most likely explanation that she could call to mind was that, for reasons of their own, the servants had sought to protect the identity of the son of a more prominent Yorkist family by claiming him as Wolveston's own. But why, she asked herself, would they lie about a second son, one who was safely gone? "I must see Robert's body," she said, not wanting to do any such thing but knowing that she must.

"I cannot allow you to enter the castle," he said. "The sickness spreads too quickly—we know not how—and I will be held to account for your well-being."

"Not enter my own father's castle?" Her eyes flashed. "Do not be daft! I must speak with my father before he dies, and I must see my brother's body. My mother's, too," she added as an afterthought. "I cannot imagine why you believe you may order me as you choose, for I do not know you and have only your word even for your name, which is an odd one, to be sure. To speak plainly, Master Merion, I have no reason to believe one word you have told me. You must explain yourself more clearly, I think."

"I am the king's man," he said quietly and with a visible effort to be patient. "I have been charged with ascertaining the loyalties of certain lords of the north. If your brother Roger did indeed fight with Viscount Lovell at Bosworth, then he is a traitor to the crown and will be punished if he lives. Wolveston Hazard is likely to become crown land."

"But Roger does not own the castle," she said, cursing her hasty tongue for having revealed her brother's loyalties. She had been so intent upon keeping Merion from guessing the truth—that her shock came not so much from hearing of the deaths in her family as from learning that somehow two new brothers had been added to it—that she had divulged the one piece of information that could mean Roger's death, if he were not dead already.

"Though women have been known to survive this sickness," Merion said in a gentler tone, "few men do. Your father will pass to his reward before morning, so if Roger is your eldest living brother, he will inherit, will he not? In Wales, where I come from, land is divided amongst all a man's heirs, but that is not the case here in England." He paused, eyebrows creasing thoughtfully. " 'Tis a better way, this, for land is power and therefore better left undivided. Nonetheless, your brother will most likely be named in a bill of attainder if he lives, my lady. That means he will lose his civil rights and titles, and—"

"I know what attainder means," she snapped. " 'Tis a sentence of death!"

"Not always," he said, "but until his fate is ascertained, I have orders to deliver you into the king's wardship."

Alys stared at him, fighting to conceal her dismay. "I am to become the king's ward?"

"Aye, mistress." He regarded her closely, as though he wondered if she would treat him to a display of feminine emotion.

But Alys was made of sterner stuff than that and, despite her whirling thoughts, retained her calm demeanor. "Shall I be allowed to return to Wolveston Hazard when all is safe again?"

"I do not know," he said. "My orders are to see you safe to London, nothing more."

She was surprised. "You had specific orders regarding me? I had not realized my own importance, Master Merion, nor that the Tudor so much as knew of my existence."

"His grace, the king," Merion said with gentle emphasis, "knows naught of you as yet, my lady. I was sent by Sir Robert Willoughby, who has been entrusted with seeing the

Princess Elizabeth and young Edward of Warwick safe returned to London."

Alys nodded. So Elizabeth had told the Tudor's men where to find her, and no doubt somehow had suggested to Sir Robert the desirability of her wardship. The Princess Elizabeth. How she would love that, Alys thought, to be acknowledged a princess again. "You have come from Sheriff Hutton then," she said. "No doubt the princess expressed deep concern for my welfare."

His look sharpened, and she gave him full marks for insight. He said gravely, "She was distressed, my lady, for she believed that although you might not have been allowed to leave Drufield Manor at once when word reached Lord Drufield of a Tudor victory, your father would soon command your return to Wolveston Hazard, and she worried lest harm should befall you on your journey. My men and I were dispatched at once. We rode here first, since we might otherwise have missed you, and when I discovered the situation at the castle, I was glad we had done so. I trust there has been no sickness at Drufield."

"No."

Before either could say more, a youth on a light chestnut gelding drew in close to Merion. "Sir," he said deferentially, "them clouds yonder be a-boiling up black and fiercelike again, I'm thinking. Best we get the ladies under cover."

Merion looked to the west where the clouds were indeed stirring ominously. He nodded. "We have pitched tents at the foot of the castle hill, my lady. We will take shelter there for the night and leave for London at sunup."

"Master Merion, I cannot—"

"Beg pardon, m'lady," said the young man at his side, "but he be Sir Nicholas Merion. My *meistr* be a knight banneret, his pennant tails cut off by the king hisself at Bosworth Field."

"Hush, Tom," said Merion gently. "Lady Alys did not know."

The younger man looked indignantly at the banner snapping damply in the breeze, then back at his master, but something in Merion's expression kept him from blurting his opinions aloud.

"I thought," Alys said, "that your banner was merely tattered, sir. For that matter, I suppose I thought it your master's banner, not your own, for your spurs are muddied and look black rather than white or gold as any knight's should be. I ask your pardon, however, if I have offended you."

"You have not," he said. "I do not expect a young *Saesnes* like yourself to know about such things as banners and spurs."

"What is that, a *Saesnes*?"

"Only an Englishwoman," he replied.

Annoyed as much by the unfamiliar term as by having had her knowledge challenged, she said stiffly, "You ought to have spoken of yourself properly, sir. A knight, particularly a knight banneret, does not call himself simply Nick Merion."

He grinned, the sudden change of expression altering his countenance dramatically, bringing light and merriment to his eyes and softening the harshness of his features. "I was told that highborn English girls are meek and soft-spoken, mistress, that they serve as near slaves in houses not their own until a marriage is arranged for them. At that time, or so I was told, they go from their foster home to their husband's home with little change in the order of things. Where did you foster, that they allowed you to retain your sharp tongue to so ripe an age?"

Alys stiffened and felt her stomach tighten painfully. "At Middleham, sir, for my mother was kin to Anne Neville. Later I was sent to Sheriff Hutton and from thence to Drufield Manor."

"Three houses? Could none of them tame you, mistress?" As he spoke, he turned and signed to his men to fall in behind them.

Alys would have been perfectly willing to let him ride on

ahead of her, but when he looked at her, clearly waiting, she
urged her mount alongside his, saying nothing.

"Well, *Saesnes-bach*?"

She wondered about the extra syllable, but the softness of
his tone and the twinkle in his eyes kept her from demanding
its definition. "I did not think you really required an answer
to so impertinent a question, sir. 'Twould scarce become me
to reply."

"Must I ask your woman to enlighten me?" he asked, gesturing toward Jonet, who rode directly behind them in the
company of another of his men, a large one. He kept glancing at the plump little woman as if he feared she might tumble from her horse.

Alys said, "Truly, Sir Nicholas, no one has tried to tame
me. I was quite happy at Middleham. I removed to Sheriff
Hutton two summers ago when King Richard commanded
that his lady wife join him in London. That is all."

"If you were in service to the usurper's wife, why did you
not accompany her to London?"

"I do not know," Alys replied honestly, forcing herself to
overlook his use of the word "usurper" to refer to Anne's
Dickon. "I was told only that my father did not wish me to
go. The matter had been decided before I knew of it."

"Odd," said Merion. "I had thought the ordering of a
young woman's future lay with the lord who fostered her.
Whom did you serve at Sheriff Hutton? The Princess
Elizabeth?"

Alys grimaced. "She was not known by that title when she
came to us, and I had been at Sheriff Hutton a good while
before her. The Earl of Lincoln was in residence there, but
the king was still my liege lord, and liege as well to Elizabeth
and Neddie—which is how we do call the Earl of Warwick."

"Then why did you leave? I had thought you must have
displeased the princess in some way, but mayhap that was
naught but my reading of your tone when you spoke of her
earlier."

Alys glanced around, but none of their large escort was

paying them any heed, with the exception of Jonet, who was, she knew, listening avidly to whatever she could hear. "I displeased Elizabeth," she admitted, "but she had no authority. My Lord Lincoln dislikes dissension, however, and thought it better for us to be apart." She would not—indeed, she could not—tell him about the scenes with Elizabeth. She could tell no one. They did her no credit. She added hastily, "I had hoped to return to Middleham at that time to serve the Countess of Warwick, my Lady Anne's mother, for she had always been kind to me, but I was sent to Drufield Manor instead."

Merion glanced at her but did not press her for more details about her relationship with Elizabeth. Instead he said, "And whom did you serve at Drufield Manor? I know little about your English nobility and do not recognize that seat."

"Lady Drufield," she said quietly, bringing a vision of that stout and querulous dame into her mind's eye. Looking at Merion, she encountered an expression of curiosity that was at once impertinent and yet compassionate.

He said blandly, "Not a woman whom you would desire to recommend to the Holy Church for sainthood?"

Alys choked. "Sir, you must not say such things!" She looked quickly around again, finding it well nigh impossible to stifle the laughter that threatened to overcome her. When she looked back at him from beneath lowered lashes, he was grinning again. "Truly, sir, you speak blasphemy."

"Not so. I believe I speak the truth. Will you deny that you heartily disliked Lady Drufield?"

"I cannot. She is precisely the sort of woman your informant must have had in mind when he spoke to you of English ways, for she would gladly have made me her slave. Nothing I did could please her. If I sat reading, she would berate me for idleness or for neglecting my prayers. If I wished to walk, she would say I wanted only to shirk my other duties. Often she said I had been spoiled at Middleham and that she would mend my ways. Indeed, she was a dreadful woman, through and through."

"Harsh?"

Alys nodded. "She spoke with a rod or the flat of her hand more often than not. There were other girls who suffered as much as I did, of course, though they had never fostered elsewhere and knew no other way. I had not been taught abject meekness from birth, you see, so my Lady Drufield thought it her duty to teach me. I . . . I wrote my father in March, begging him to let me come home. I was nearly eighteen then, after all."

"And he refused?"

She nodded again. "All I got for my effort was punishment. Father wrote to his lordship, describing in grave terms my lack of gratitude, my arrogance, and my boldness in complaining of my lot. He said I had got above myself, and he apologized to Lord Drufield for my behavior. The resulting interview was both painful and humiliating, as were the months that followed."

"So you were glad to leave."

Alys could not disagree. She looked at him. "I would have preferred a better reason for my departure, sir. I did believe I was to leave soon, in any case."

"Then you do expect to be wed?"

"Aye, to Sir Lionel Everingham. Do you know aught of him?"

He shook his head. "A Yorkist?"

"Of course he is a Yorkist! My marriage was arranged by King Richard nigh onto eight months ago, and I would have been wedded by now, were it not for the wretched Tudor. Now I do not even know if Sir Lionel still lives."

"Whether he does or not will not signify," he replied, "since all such betrothals will certainly be set aside. You will be in ward, after all, and I doubt that his grace, the king, will wish to leave your hand in Yorkist keeping. There is Wolveston now," he added with a gesture.

The castle, atop its low hill, loomed darkly through the gray mist ahead, and Alys gazed silently upon her birthplace. She had not lived at Wolveston Hazard since the age of nine, half a lifetime ago, but it was still her home. In truth, she had more feeling for the stone walls and the turrets than she had ever had for the people within. Her parents had both been cold people, her father more interested in his books than in his children, her mother not interested in anything much at all. If Alys had felt anything for them as a child, it had been fear of displeasing them, for punishment had been swift and harsh.

Life at Middleham had been far gentler, and she had experienced overwhelming sorrow at the news of Anne's passing. But she felt nothing now for her mother, little for her father, although she hoped to see him before he died, and hoped, too, that her tongue would not cleave to the roof of her mouth when she attempted to speak to him, as it always had done when she was small. She would have to be stronger now. There were questions to which she needed answers.

"I am sorry," Merion said.

She stared at him, then realized that he thought the sight of the castle had stirred her to grief. "I am alone now," she said slowly, "or nearly so. A week ago I had a family and other people to protect me. Today I have no one."

"You are safe, *mi geneth*," he said gently. "None will harm you whilst you are in my charge, and whatever you might believe of Harry Tudor, you will soon find him to be a good man."

Frowning, she said, "I do not know by what name you call me now, sir, nor do I care. Your Tudor is the true usurper—and a murderer withal—who has no right to the throne of England, as any man with sense, even a Welshman, must know to be true."

She heard Jonet gasp and was immediately aware of her own vulnerability, face to face as she was with the enemy, his own men gathered around them. Nevertheless, she kept her chin high and forced her gaze to meet his.

To her astonishment he smiled. "Do you know your eyes flash golden sparks when you are angry?" Before she could react, he added, " '*Mi geneth*' means only 'wench' or 'my lass,' nothing more. When did you come to believe that Welshmen have no sense?"

Alys opened her mouth, then shut it again, looking at him in bewilderment. "I did not say they do not."

"That is what you meant."

She heard the echo of her words in her mind and knew he had justification for saying what he did, but since she had no idea how to reply to him, she looked away and was silent.

They were approaching a cluster of tents. Several moments passed, and then at last, as they drew to a halt near the largest, she turned to him and said quietly, "I must make my apologies again, sir. I ought not to have spoken so."

"Will you be sorry if you are not allowed to marry this Sir Lionel Everingham?"

Her eyes opened wide and she spoke without thinking. "I do not know him. Richard arranged our betrothal, and I was present with Sir Lionel for the ceremony, but I have never spoken more than a word or two to him."

He nodded, apparently with satisfaction. Then he gestured toward the tent before them. "You will sleep here, my lady, with your woman. You will be perfectly safe." He dismounted.

Looking down at him, Alys said, "I would see my father, Sir Nicholas. He may be my only living kin. You must not deny me."

He shook his head. "You still have brothers, and I cannot allow it, in any event. The danger is too great. 'Tis why I ordered your escort back to Drufield." Having not realized he had done so, she glanced back to see that Geordie and the others had indeed departed. Before she could protest, Sir Nicholas said, "Nearly everyone inside that pile of stones has died, mistress. There is no one left now but a servant who looks after your father, and an old herb woman; and, although the cold weather allowed us to put off the burials until you could be here, we must leave tomorrow. We stay to bury the dead, no longer."

"But I—"

"No." He did not raise his voice, nor did he frown, but there was no mistaking the fact that that was his final word on the subject. She dared not press him further. Though he seemed to be a gentleman, he was unknown, and even at Middleham she had been taught the hard lesson of obedience to masculine authority.

She bowed her head submissively but decided at the same time that, one way or another, she would see her father. Before their departure, the Welshman must be made to understand that she would not allow him to deny her that final parting. Until then, however, it would be well to lull his suspicions, and while she bided her time, she would think.

# 2

Inside the large tent, Alys drew off her gloves and looked silently about her. Even the soft golden glow of the oil lantern did not improve the spartan furnishings or make the place look homelike. On the damp dirt floor, near the left canvas wall, lay a pallet of furs with more furs piled on a joint stool beside it. An open coffer stood opposite, with a wood prayer bench between—the sort known since Norman days as a prie-dieu. The only other furniture to be seen was a traveling washstand near the pallet. The lantern hung from a hook on the center pole.

"This is your tent," Alys said to Sir Nicholas, pushing off her hood to reveal her damp and tangled tresses.

"Yours now, mistress. One of my lads will take me in. Tom there is my squire and will gather my gear. Have you eaten?"

"Aye, some bread and butter at noon."

He frowned. "I'll have someone prepare a proper meal. 'Tis after five, but despite the clouds, it will not be dark for some hours yet, so mayhap you wish to rest a bit before you sup."

"Can someone bring me water?"

"To drink? There is a flask—"

"To remove some of the dust of the road from my person," Alys said tartly. She held out a muddy wrist. "My skin is not generally this color, sir, I promise you."

He chuckled. "Would you bathe then, mistress?" He gestured toward the little washstand.

She eyed it dubiously. "Is there no proper tub?"

"One might be fetched from the castle, I suppose, but you will catch your death of cold."

"I can scarcely be wetter or colder than I am right now," she pointed out, "and I would like very much to—"

"I'll order the water heated," he said, shaking his head in amusement. "I have no canopy or curtains, but like as not, the tent walls will protect you from most drafts. Nonetheless, you are not to wash your hair, Lady Alys."

"That she will not," put in Jonet, looking sourly at her mistress, "for 'twould never dry in this weather. The very idea! You can do what needs doing as well with yon basin, my lady, so there be no need to make Sir Nicholas's men tote water for the next hour only to satisfy a foolish whim."

Sir Nicholas smiled at Jonet. "I have no objection, and the task will not take so long as that. By the time they have found the tub and fetched it out, we will have hot water. 'Twill warm your mistress through, I'm thinking, and thus be no bad thing."

Alys nodded gratefully, then pointed out that her hair was already wet. "Washing can only improve it," she said.

*"Nage, mi geneth."* He felt it, his hand strong against her scalp. " 'Tis damp only, not wet through like 'twould be if you washed it. Your woman has the right of it. You rub it dry and then brush it out. I would like to see it dry," he added. "Though it is not dark, as I prefer a wench's hair to be, 'twill look like burnished gold and mayhap be even prettier than her highness's, for hers is too pale, like flax. Insipid, I thought it, though long and smooth as silk, withal."

His touch sent a flame of warmth shooting through her chilled body, and Alys, disconcerted by the sensation, stepped away from him and turned, her chin held high so that he might not guess the effect he had had upon her. "Thank you for your kindness, sir," she said evenly. "I look forward with pleasure to my bath." With a casual gesture of dismissal she turned to Jonet. "Have we herbs at hand to stir into the water?"

"Aye, my lady, when they fetch the coffers off the sumpter ponies. Best you get out of that damp cloak in the meantime."

Alys nodded, but before she could remove the scarlet cloak, Sir Nicholas said from behind, startling her, "Keep it on." To Jonet he added, "Damp or not, 'twill keep her warmer than she would be without it, unless you have another with the baggage."

Alys looked down her nose at him, no easy task since he was nearly a foot taller than she was. "I thought you had gone to order my bath."

He said steadily, "Have you another cloak, mistress?"

"Not as warm as this one, but my mother had a fur one, I think. Perhaps, since your men must go to the castle—"

"Your mother's cloak might be infected," he said. "Keep that one on till I find you something else. Then we can dry it by one of the fires. If the rain keeps off, that is."

"You worry so much about infection," she said, "that I cannot help but wonder why you will risk two of your men merely to fetch a tub for me."

He shook his head. "You forget that we Welshmen seem not to be at risk. I have a few healthy Scotsmen and—"

"Scotsmen?" She remembered then, vaguely, that he had spoken before of foreigners. "But the Scots are our enemies!"

"There are any number of them, however, and Frenchmen, too, who are not the enemies of the king's noble highness."

She scowled. "Mercenaries!"

"If you like. I shall send a Scotsman for your tub, shall I? Mayhap he will sicken and die to please you."

Pointedly she turned her back upon him, and a moment later a sharp but brief stir of cold air announced his departure. She heard him shout but paid no heed to his words, turning her attention instead to her companion. "It appears that we shall soon be bound for London, Jonet."

"Aye, mistress. I have never been there."

"Nor have I, as you know full well." She wrinkled her nose. "I wonder what it means to be the king's ward. I have no wish to find myself a slave to Elizabeth, but if wardship is like fostering, that is what will happen, for she told me once that she expects to marry that Tudor knave. 'Tis most likely she was lying, of course, just as she did when she said poor Anne's Dickon would wed with her, or the time before that when she told everyone he had gifted her with a Christmas gown when Anne herself had presented her with the fabric left from her own."

"The Tudor has named her princess," Jonet pointed out.

"Aye," Alys admitted thoughtfully, "and 'tis a grave risk for him to do so, for if she is a true princess, her brothers are likewise royal, and the Tudor has no true claim to the throne."

"Lord Drufield said Henry Tudor did lay his claim by right of battle, claiming God had thus clearly chosen him king."

Alys hunched a shoulder. "God cannot be so cruel. Our king was betrayed by men he trusted, and that is all there is about it. If the Tudor was chosen by God, why does he date his reign, as he did in his round-letter, from the day before the battle? I expect God to punish him for such a falsehood, do not you?"

"We know why the Tudor did that," Jonet said acidly. " 'Tis otherwise impossible to name loyal men traitors who did fight for their king. By claiming to have reigned from the day before, he calls them traitors to himself, but what God thinks of such can be known only in His own good time."

"I know what I think about it." Feeling another draft, Alys turned sharply to see that the squire, Tom, had entered the tent.

He bowed, touching his forelock. "I ha' come for m' *meistr*'s trappings, an it please you, m'lady."

Alys nodded, then looked at Jonet, not surprised to see a frown on her round face. Alys, too, wondered how much the lad had heard and whether he would repeat her words to his master.

When Tom had gone, hefting the heavy coffer before him, Jonet clicked her tongue.

"I know," Alys said before she could speak, "and you are right. I shall henceforth mind what I say."

" 'Twill be a new thing, that will," muttered her henchwoman.

Alys grinned at her ruefully. "I vow to you that I will mend my ways. Indeed, I have behaved right well these several months past, have I not?"

"Out of fear of her ladyship's swift right hand," retorted Jonet. "Not for else, I'm thinking."

Frowning, Alys said thoughtfully, "I disliked Lady Drufield, 'tis true, but I feared Anne's displeasure the more. So gentle was she that the slightest reproof—" The knifing pain in her throat and chest caught her unaware, as did the tears that welled into her eyes. She turned away, trying unsuccessfully to stifle the sudden gusting sobs that threatened to overwhelm her.

Jonet moved swiftly to her side and put a strong arm around her, hugging her but giving her an admonitory shake at the same time. "Lassie, do not," she said in the same way she had spoken when Alys was small. " 'Twill do thee no good to weep. She's been gone these five months and more, and 'tis as well that she has, for had she lived to hear how the villains desecrated his noble grace's blessed body after they murdered him, she'd ha' been wracked asunder by the shame of it. Thinkst tha' of that now, and dry thy tears. 'Tis naught but selfishness to dwell upon thine own grief."

Hiccoughing in her attempt to regain control of herself, Alys turned and laid her head upon Jonet's plump bosom, letting herself be held like a child. At last her sobs eased in their intensity and she straightened, brushing tangled hair from her tear-streaked face with the back of her fist, and said, "I have been wicked to think only of myself. You are right to remind me of what her pain would be. God in His mercy took her before she might suffer, and here am I, wishing she were with us yet."

"Let be now," Jonet said gently. "Sit tha' down on yonder stool, and let old Jonet do what she may to dry thy hair before thy bath be prepared."

Alys's hair was long, and because of her hood she had worn it unconfined by any other headdress. Once freed from the folds of the hood, it fell in damp curls to her waist, and as soon as the first of their coffers had been carried into the tent, Jonet unearthed a rough towel and began to rub. Despite her efforts, however, long before the tub had arrived and men began carrying buckets of hot water in to fill it, Alys was chilled to her bones. The water cooled rapidly, sending clouds of steam into the air, so as soon as there was barely enough for their purpose, Jonet told the men to leave the last two buckets and go. Then, rolling up her sleeves, she ordered her charge into the tub.

Quickly doffing her damp clothing, Alys moved to obey. The water felt much too hot for her chilled toes, however, and after dipping one foot into the tub, she jerked it out again with a cry of alarm. But Jonet was having none of that.

"Get thee in," she said, still speaking as though Alys were yet a child. " 'Tis only that thy feet be cold. Sithee, if tha' waits till it be cooler to thy toes, 'twill be cold to the rest of thy body, so tha' must be wick."

Moments later, her hair twisted in a heavy knot atop her drooping head, Alys sat hunched forward in the tub while Jonet poured more hot water over her shoulders and scrubbed her back with a rough sponge that soon gave her skin a rosy glow. The soap was perfumed with attar of lilacs, and the scent, mixed with that of the herbs in the water, quickly filled the tent.

When Merion entered, a heavy dark cloak draped over his arm, he paused at the entrance to inhale deeply before saying, "I came to bring this cloak and to see that all is well, my lady, but I believe I shall stay to savor the delights of your scent."

At the sound of his voice, Alys's head snapped up and she gave a gasp of dismay, swiftly covering her firm, rosy-tipped breasts with her arms. When Sir Nicholas's look of pleasure turned to puzzlement, she said with careful dignity, "I am not accustomed to entertaining gentlemen while I bathe, sir."

"But surely 'tis as much the custom in England as in Wales for all members of a household to bathe together," he said, still gazing at her and clearly deriving his pleasure now from more than attar of lilacs. "Has my informant misled me, mistress?"

"No," she admitted, pressing her arms more tightly across her breasts. "Such is indeed common practice in most houses, sir, but I was raised in the household of the Duke and Duchess of Gloucester, where I was permitted more privacy. Indeed, even at Drufield, I was accustomed to share my bathwater only with the other girls who fostered there. Men did not enter our chamber upon such occasions except to fill and to empty the tubs."

"Even as a duke, your liege lord behaved in a right royal manner, I'm thinking," he said, still looking directly at her, "and seems to have allowed those in his charge to do likewise."

Much though Alys would have liked to debate the subject with him, she felt too much at a disadvantage, too vulnerable in her present position. Jonet continued to scrub her back, ignoring their visitor, but Alys feared that she would rub the skin right off if she worked at it much longer. She looked pleadingly at the Welshman, noting the twinkle in his eyes and the way his lips turned upward at the corners. He was amused.

"I should take it kindly in you, sir, if you would be so generous as to grant me my privacy," she said quietly. "Truly, 'tis what I am accustomed to, and your presence does disturb me."

"Does it, wench?" His voice sounded lower, throbbingly so, and she saw the tip of his tongue dart to touch the back of his teeth. He had not turned his head away.

The warmth that began in her cheeks spread rapidly

through her entire body, heating it as the water had not done, stirring her nerves to tingling just beneath the surface of her skin. She could feel her heart beating—no, thudding—in her breast, and when he continued to gaze down at her, it was as though his large hands reached out to caress her, as though he touched her in places where even Jonet had never dared to touch her before.

"Please, sir," she whispered, unable to speak the words clearly. She looked away.

"Aye, mistress." His voice sounded hoarse. "I'll go."

A moment later he was gone, and she breathed a sigh of relief. No man had gazed upon her naked body since she had left Wolveston nine years before. In fact, she could not remember the last time one had done so, but she was as certain as she could be that the looking had never stirred such feelings in her as she was feeling now. Even now that he had gone, the tingling continued, though it seemed to have focused itself in one particular area of her anatomy. She squirmed in the tub.

"Straighten up now, Miss Alys," Jonet said, "so that I might soap the rest of thee."

"I'll do it," Alys said quickly, taking the sponge and rapidly soaping her breasts and stomach, then rinsing herself. "The water turns cold, Jonet. Fetch my towel. And stop talking to me as though I were four years old."

"Aye, mistress."

Jonet hurried to do as she was bid, and Alys stood, keeping a wary eye on the door, fearing that Sir Nicholas, or even one of his men, might enter again. No one did, however, and she was soon wrapped in a large rough towel. At her command, Jonet unearthed a French surcoat from one of the coffers, and with that over her linen smock and woolen overdress, she was nearly as warm as she would have been in her own cloak, or in Merion's, which still lay in a tumbled heap on the floor where he had dropped it.

"Shall I call in the lads now to empty the tub, my lady?"

"Aye," Alys agreed, "and we will go stand out by the fire."

Lifting the front of her skirt, which had been hemmed long enough to puddle fashionably about her feet, even in clogs, she turned, pushed aside the flap with her free hand, and stepped outside.

She half expected Merion to take exception to their joining the others, particularly since she had refused to wear the cloak he had brought her, but he just smiled at her. She was grateful then for the darkening gloom, because her cheeks warmed again the moment he glanced at her and she found it difficult to think of anything but the moment inside when he had stood gazing down upon her naked body like a hound eyeing a favorite bone.

Looking at him from beneath her lashes, she noted as she had before that he was a handsome man and strong. His shoulders were broader than any she had seen since King Edward had died, and he was easily as tall as Edward had been. Indeed, had Merion's hair been golden instead of dark, one might have mistaken him for a Plantagenet. She remembered that Anne's Dickon had been dark, but he had not been a typical Plantagenet in size either.

"Your supper is ready," Sir Nicholas said, breaking into her reverie. "Since the rain seems to have passed us by, will you eat here by the fire, or do you prefer privacy for dining also?"

There was no taunt in his voice, and she smiled at him. "You must think me foolish, sir. In faith, I cannot think why your entrance discomfited me so. 'Tis certainly a foolish custom to waste hot water when there are others about who might make use of it. No doubt the ways at Middleham were extravagant."

"No doubt," he agreed, smiling back. "I'll warrant that everyone there did not sleep in the same room either."

"Goodness, does that old custom still prevail in Wales?"

He chuckled. "It does in many a household, just as I make no doubt it does here. But since what you really mean to ask is if that custom still obtains in all Welsh homes, I will admit that it does not. My parents demanded a certain privacy unto themselves even before it became fashionable to do so, and since our house is a large one, it was possible for my mother to have her solar and my father to have his private chambers as well. Their sleeping compartment is kept to themselves alone."

"As was my Lord Richard's," she said, subdued again.

"And your parents' also, by what I have seen."

"I believe so," she said, "but such is commonly the way of things now amongst the privileged in England."

"Aye." He was silent for a moment, then noting that young Tom stood nearby with a pair of rough wooden trenchers in hand, he signed to the lad to serve Alys and Jonet.

One of the other men brought a pair of joint stools for them to sit upon, and Alys sat down and removed her gloves to eat. The food was common, being no more than a thin meat stew served with chunks of stale bread, but she ate with relish, using her fingers and sopping up the juices with her bread. When she had finished, she washed her hands in the pail of water Tom brought for the purpose, dried them, and replaced her gloves.

Sir Nicholas waited until she had smoothed them, then handed her a mug of ale. "Down that, mistress. 'Twill warm you well."

"Aye, it will that," she agreed, sipping cautiously. It was a heady brew, so she took her time, enjoying the warmth of the fire, determined not to drink enough to make her sleepy. A few moments later, however, she realized that it might serve her purpose better to let it appear that she could scarcely keep her eyes open, and yawned behind one dainty hand.

Night had fallen, and one of the men began plucking a lute. A breeze moaned dismally up from the river, adding an odd harmony to the lute's song, and beyond the glow of the cook fires, through the mist still surrounding the camp, Alys could see the soft silver glimmer of a waning moon above the dark shape of the castle at the top of the hill. The eerie moonlight, though doing nothing much to illuminate the landscape, cast ghostly highlights upon the shadows of men moving beyond the firelight. It was a good thing, Alys decided, that she was not a fanciful person.

Half an hour later, she stood, handing her empty mug to one of the men and gathering her skirts. "The day has been a long one," she said to Sir Nicholas. "If you will excuse me—"

"Go with my blessing, mistress," he said. "In fact, I shall escort you to see you safe within your tent."

She gestured toward Jonet, who had got to her feet as soon as Alys had done so. "My woman will see to my needs, sir. You have no cause to disturb yourself."

"As you say, mistress, but I will walk with you all the same. I have a mind to see that my sentries are well placed."

A chill raced up her spine, and she realized she had been a fool not to think of sentries. "Do you fear we shall try to run away?" she asked, trying to keep her tone light, even teasing, but certain he would hear the rasping catch in her voice. "I have not got so much courage as that, sir, I swear to you."

If he heard the odd note in her voice, he attributed it to simple fear, for all he said was, " 'Tis not to keep you in, *mi geneth*, but to keep others out. I am commanded to keep you safe, and my men as well, so I have posted guards. I should be a fool not to do so, since we are the enemy to many in these parts. My men will keep a good lookout, however, so you need have no fear."

She said nothing more, and gathering her skirts with one hand, allowed him to place her other upon his forearm to take her back to her tent. The ground beneath their feet was not smooth, and she had no objection to letting him think her dependent upon his strong arm for her footing. Jonet followed, and if she was surprised by her mistress's meekness, she said nothing about it.

Inside the tent again, Alys discovered that a second pallet had been brought in and that both had been piled high with furs. She thanked Sir Nicholas for his thoughtfulness but was careful to give him no excuse to linger once he had said good night.

Alone with Jonet, she turned the lantern up and looked at her thoughtfully.

"I know that look," Jonet said warily. "Prithee, what mischief can you be brewing up for yourself now?"

For a moment Alys toyed with the notion of lying to her, of telling her she had no thought of mischief. She could play the indignant innocent with the best of deceivers, she knew, but she knew also that Jonet would always see through such an act, and in a twinkling. Hearing a muffled footstep outside the tent, she held a finger to her lips, then turned toward her pallet, saying, "Just fetch me that small coffer near the prie-dieu, will you? I want to say my prayers before my eyes refuse to stay open."

Rifling the contents of the coffer, Alys found her rosary and knelt at the prie-dieu. Instead of praying, however, she motioned Jonet closer and murmured, "I must go and see my father, despite the Welshman's orders. There is mystery afoot, Jonet. You heard what Sir Nicholas said. My brother Robert dead and my brother Paul gone to his fostering but a fortnight past."

"Aye, and the poor lambs cold in their graves these eight years and more. What be the meaning of such, my lady?"

"I do not know, but I mean to find out. I never take sickness easily, as you know, so I have little to fear by being inside the castle walls. In faith, I have more fear of what demons may lie between this tent and the castle, but I warrant I can get inside without mishap."

"I shall go with you."

"That you will not," Alys said, raising her voice in her dismay. Lowering it again, she hissed, "I need you safe within this tent to deter any who attempt to enter. I have already made great play of my need for privacy, and though I confess I had not realized how useful that would be, I do not think anyone will disturb us. Still, if they do, I depend upon you to protect me. Tell them I visited the necessary or anything else you can think to tell them. Only do not mention the castle."

"When will you go?" Jonet asked, capitulating much more easily than Alys had expected.

"As soon as the camp is at rest. The difficulty between now and then will be to stay awake. That ale nearly finished me, and I am nigh to sleeping here on my knees."

"Then sleep, mistress. I will waken you."

Alys regarded her doubtfully. "How do I know that you will not let me sleep till dawn?"

Jonet said with dignity, "You may trust me as you have always done, Miss Alys. I have looked after you since you were a child, and I have not betrayed you yet. Moreover," she added with a crooked smile, "I have as much wish now as you have yourself to know the answer to the riddle, and though your father will not speak to me, he may speak to you."

A shiver raced up and down Alys's spine at these innocent words. "I hope he may," she said. "He spoke to me in the past only when I had misbehaved and was to be punished. Even though he now lies dying, I fear my tongue will fly to the roof of my mouth and cling there like it did then, and my lips will grow too stiff to move. He used to demand that I recite my misdeeds to him, and when I would be unable to obey, he would punish me all the more for what he called my 'stubborn insolence.'"

"Well, 'tis certain sure he will not like it that you have entered a house of sickness," Jonet said wisely, "but if he is as ill as the Welshman says, you have no need to fear his wrath, and mayhap he will tell you what we want to know. But sithee, child, come now and sleep whilst tha' may."

Alys nodded, then rapidly said her prayers and stood, letting Jonet divest her of the fur-lined surcoat and her overdress. Then, still wearing her linen smock, she crawled beneath the furs, and no sooner had her head touched the pallet than she was fast asleep.

She resisted when Jonet attempted to waken her some

hours later, but her henchwoman was persistent, stifling
Alys's protests with one hand while she shook her with the
other. At last Alys stirred and sat up, rubbing her eyes. The
lantern had been put out, and there was scarcely any light
within the tent. Nonetheless, she kept low when she climbed
from the pallet and donned her overdress, fearing, however
unreasonably, to cast a shadow that would be seen from outside. Not caring in the least now for fashion but only for ease
of movement, she tightened her belt at her natural waist and
bunched the top of her skirt up over it so that the long front
hem would not trip her when she walked. Then she picked
up Merion's cloak from the floor, the icy chill in the air
making it impossible to disdain its protection any longer, and
stepped toward the entrance.

Jonet stopped her with a warning hand to her elbow. "Sentry," she whispered.

Nodding, Alys turned to the rear of the tent and dropped
the cloak to find an exit. Silent effort was required from both
of them, but they found it possible to lift the rear wall of the
tent enough to enable Alys first to make sure the way was
clear and then to roll out. She refused even to contemplate
the damage done to her gown by the muddy ground beneath
her.

Once outside, she took the cloak when Jonet pushed it out
under the canvas, and got carefully to her feet. The fires in
the central clearing had died to beds of glowing embers now,
and the camp appeared to be asleep. Even as the thought
crossed her mind, however, a movement to her left froze her
in place. She held her breath until the sentry had passed the
opening between her tent and the one next to it. As nearly
as she could tell, he had not so much as looked her way.

Moving as swiftly as she dared, she stepped away from the
circle of tents, remembering that the horses and no doubt
another sentry or two were on the opposite side. The mist
had thickened overhead, and the moon no longer shone at
all. Alys paused only long enough to don the cloak, which
was long for her and brushed the ground; then she hurried

on. The farther she moved from the camp, the darker it became. She could hear the river now, however, and knew she had only to keep it on her right as she moved uphill, away from the firelight. The dense, black bulk of the castle was barely discernible ahead, but it was enough.

She stumbled over uneven ground more than once, and stiff bracken fronds tried to attach themselves to the hem of the cloak, forcing her to lift it higher, lest the noise of her passage draw attention. She wondered how many sentries there were and if there would be guards at the castle gates. There would be, she decided. That was not a detail Sir Nicholas would have overlooked. The postern gate would be safest. It was the way she had obtained entrance to the castle in childhood days when she had slipped out unbeknownst to anyone else to explore the countryside. Not that she had never been caught then, but it was a safer way than the main gate would be, and it was possible that the Welshman would not have seen the trick of the smaller gate and would have thought it safely locked and bolted.

She had to follow the curtain wall by touch for some distance because she misjudged the exact location of the gate, which was set a few feet into the wall, but she found it at last, and saw that it was unguarded, although noises from the yard told her that there were guards inside. As she approached, she saw through the narrow slits in the iron-and-timber gate the glow of a fire some distance away, surrounded by low heaps that she soon identified by their snores as sleeping men.

Moving slowly and with great care, she drew close to the gate and put her hand upon the main bolt. There was a small knob behind, which when turned upright, allowed one to draw the bolt from the outside, unless a counterlock had been tripped within. Her father's steward had shown her the trick of it when she was but six or seven and too small, he had thought, to make use of it. But Alys was nothing if not resourceful. She had used her knowledge many times before her departure from Wolveston.

Once the bolt was drawn, she moved even more carefully lest the gate's hinges betray her by squeaking, but quickly realized when the gate moved in silence that they had been recently oiled. She wondered then if someone might have prepared the way for her brother, in the event that Roger successfully eluded the Tudor armies and made his way home.

It was hard to breathe now, for the worst lay ahead. She had to cross a corner of the yard, and she knew that where many slept, some would be wakeful. Moreover, there might be roaming sentries as well as those who slept or guarded the main gates.

The postern door, several feet away, was unguarded, and she slipped quickly inside. Clearly, the soldiers believed that no one would try to enter a castle of death, and blessing their confidence, she paused a moment to catch her breath, hoping now only that she would remember the way to her parents' bedchamber well enough to find it in the dark.

She found the spiral stairs and made her way up them more by feel than by sight, passing the main floor to the next, where she could see a glow coming from a chamber at the end of the gallery overlooking the great hall below. The moment she saw the light, she was certain it came from the room she sought, and hurrying now, hoping that whoever was within would be friend, not foe, she moved swiftly to the doorway and looked inside.

# 3

A high, curtained bed stood against the right-hand wall of the room, and a fire burned brightly on the hearth opposite. At first there appeared to be no one inside other than the occupant of the bed, but then a rustling sound drew Alys's attention to the inglenook beyond the hearth, and she saw a scrawny, elderly woman on a floor cushion, her knees hunched to her chin, dozing. Alys did not recognize her but decided she looked harmless. Alys entered the room and shut the door behind her.

The old crone opened her eyes and lifted her head but showed no sign of alarm until Alys moved toward the bed. Then she said in a high-pitched, croaking voice, "Dinna uncover 'im, m'lady. He mun be kept full covered."

"You know me?"

"Aye, tha' dost be ahr young Lady Alys come home again."

"And you?"

The old woman straightened a little but made no attempt to stand up. "Goody Spurrig, m'lady, from over t' Browson village. I be the herb wooman. Nane other'd bide wi' the auld lord."

"I thought there was a servant with him."

"Gone."

Alys had pulled back the bed curtains, and although she glanced over her shoulder at the blunt response, she said nothing before turning back to gaze for a long moment at the man who had awed her so in her childhood. All that was visible of Lord Wolveston now was his face, glistening with sweat but drawn and gray, even in the little light provided by the fire.

"Will he live?" she asked the herb woman. There was silence, so she turned.

The woman shook her head.

"May I speak with him?"

"Aye, gin tha' canst wake him."

Spying several wax tapers on a table near the hearth, Alys shrugged off her cloak, letting it fall to the floor, then moved to light a candle at the fire. Going back to the bed, she held the taper so it would light his face but not drip wax on him or set the curtains ablaze. "Father," she said urgently. "Father, my lord, it is Alys. Please, sir, you must wake up."

His eyelids flickered, then lifted, revealing dull gray eyes that shifted rapidly back and forth before focusing at last on her face.

"Father? It is Alys, my lord. I have come home."

"Alys?" The voice was no more than a rasping croak. The frail body stirred beneath the heavy blankets. "Bless thee, child. I sent for thee, did I not?"

"Aye," she said. Then, glancing over her shoulder once more, she said, "Leave us, dame. Tell no one that I am here. Do you swear?"

"Aye," muttered the crone, getting stiffly to her feet. "B'ain't nane left t' tell."

"Go."

She shuffled stiffly to the door, opened it, and went out. Alys waited until the latch had clicked into place before turning back to the figure in the bed. "My lord, pray tell me what has happened here."

"Dead, all dead." His eyes widened, the pupils flicking wildly, first right, then left. "Soldiers . . . sickness . . . mustn't stay. Safe, Alys is safe. Saw to that. Get the lads, get them safe . . . to Alys . . . no, to Tyrell. Alys at Drufield. Saw to that.

Good, my liege. Loyalty binds—" He broke off, gasping, then repeated clearly, "Dead, all dead."

"Father, please, look at me," she said with a hint of impatience in her voice. "It is Alys, my lord, and I am here, not at Drufield. I am to go to London, sir. The soldiers you speak of are the Tudor's men. I would not have been let to stay at Drufield even if I were still there and had wanted to do so."

"Find Roger. Must find Roger." His eyes focused on her again. "Where is Roger, wench? Send him to me at once."

"I know not where he is, sir. I have had no word of him or of his man, Davy Hawkins. Indeed, I had hoped that you would know. We were told that Lincoln and Viscount Lovell had been killed, so Roger and Davy, too, may be dead."

He stirred restlessly. "Not dead. Message. Keep safe."

She had barely been able to hear his words. "You had a message, you say? What was it, sir? Who must be kept safe?"

He still looked at her, but now she thought his look was full of cunning. "Brothers, Alys. Thou hast brothers again."

"Aye," she retorted, glancing swiftly over her shoulder at the closed door. "So I have been told. My brother Robert died less than two days ago, they tell me, and they say that my brother Paul left the castle a fortnight past. How can that be, sir, when both Robert and Paul died of the plague eight winters ago?"

"Dead, all dead." His eyelids fluttered and the eyes behind them drifted out of focus.

"Father," she urged, "you cannot sleep yet, sir. What do you know of Roger? Who was the lad they called Robert? Who is Paul? Is there someone hiding here at Wolveston now?" The possibilities stirred by that last thought were frightening. "Who must be kept safe, sir?"

"Safe?" The pale eyelids opened wide again. His body moved, the body she remembered as being gigantic and fearsomely powerful, but which now was frail and helpless beneath the great pile of blankets. "Keep Alys safe," he murmured, "at all cost." He paused as though he were lis-

tening, his eyes narrowed, stern. Then he said quickly,
"Agreed, agreed, but my daughter must be kept safe, out of
it all. Send Tyrell . . . no, not Tyrell, he is known, too well
known. I'll not see him, your grace. 'Tisn't safe. Safe, safe
. . . Alys . . . all must be safe."

The last words came in a singsong rhythm. She knew that
he was delirious and wondered if he had said anything at all
to the purpose. He was talking to someone else, not to her,
and his words made no sense. "Father, who are these brothers of mine—false Robert, false Paul? Who are they? Of
what must I beware? Please, you must tell me. I go to London, to the enemy. Must I go in fear? Help me, Father!"

"Forgive me, Father, for I have sinned," muttered the
figure in the bed. "Have mercy upon this miserable sinner."
His eyes were closed now, his lips barely moving with the
last words.

"Father, look at me," Alys begged desperately. She dared
not touch him; she did not wish to die. Yet she wanted to
shake him. She could see that the old herb woman had been
right. He was dying. Time was fleeting. "Speak to me! Tell
me!"

His eyelids lifted and his eyes focused again, briefly but
sharply. "Go now," he murmured much more clearly than
before. "Thou must not take the sickness. But go warily, lass,
lest thou drawest the Tudor wrath unto thyself." His eyes
closed.

"Father! No, that is not enough. Tell me!" But it was no
use. Though he still breathed raggedly, the muscles in his
face had slackened. There would be no waking him again.

Alys wondered if the old woman knew anything that might
help her, but dismissed the notion when she recalled that
the crone had come from a nearby village. If there were
secrets here, as it seemed there must be, Goody Spurrig was
not party to them.

Suddenly chilled despite the heat in the room, she moved
to the fire, snuffing the candle and setting it down on the
hearth, then rubbing her hands together, trying to think. Ab-

sently noting the caked, drying mud on her skirt, she drew
a fold up and flicked at bits of dirt with a fingernail while
she pondered, and after a time she sat down by the hearth
and rubbed at the muddy patches more carefully, still trying
to focus her thoughts.

If someone were in hiding at Wolveston Hazard, how safe
could he or they be? There were soldiers everywhere, looking for stragglers from the Yorkist army. Ought she to search
the castle? What if she found someone? What would she do?
The servants were all gone, she remembered. Even the manservant who had cared for her father. The crone had said he
was gone. Perhaps he had died; perhaps not. But who would
feed the ones in hiding if such there were? Ought she not
to look?

The fire was dying. Looking around, she saw a small pile
of logs beneath the window, which she had not seen before
because the bed hid them from view from the doorway. She
got to her feet and carried two to the fire, putting them on
carefully so as not to send sparks flying; and only when she
had finished did she realize something was missing from the
room. She had been thinking, then moving about, and for a
moment she could not imagine what she missed. Then she
recognized the silence.

His harsh breathing had provided a background for her
thoughts. She had paid no heed to it, but it had been there.
Now it was not.

Fearfully she got to her feet again and moved toward the
bed. His lips were parted, but there was no movement, no
sound. She reached to touch him, then snatched her hand
back when a frisson of fear shot through her body. Backing
away, she felt a surge of panic, overwhelming, terrifying
panic; and whirling, she ran to the door only to stop with
her hand on the latch. Frozen, she fought to regain control
over her emotions, to think.

Remembering that there might be men hidden in the castle, she knew she dared not give any alarm that would bring
soldiers running. For that matter, she dared not raise any

alarm at all, not because of the men who might be hiding, but for her own sake. What Sir Nicholas would do if he discovered that she had slipped away to be at her father's deathbed did not bear contemplation.

For the first time she gave thought to the fact that she had exposed herself to death. It had been easy to keep the thought at bay while her father lived, while she needed to speak with him. Her determination to see him and to get information from him had outweighed every other consideration. But, alone with his dead body, she had been nearly overcome by a fear deriving from something far older, more primitive, and much more powerful than mere concern for possible fugitives. That same terror of death still urged her to run screaming from the room.

Forcing herself to stare at the door, not to look back at the corpse in the bed, she made herself breathe slowly and deeply, a technique Anne had taught her. Anne had discovered it for herself after years of coping with her father's sudden whims, whims that had often resulted in drastic, undesirable changes in Anne's life. Alys had never known the formidable Earl of Warwick, for he had died when she was three, but she was certain that should she ever encounter him (if she were unfortunate enough to displease God and be sent to Warwick's undoubted place of unrest), she would know him at once, so much had she heard about him from Anne and his long-suffering countess.

From Warwick, her thoughts flashed instantly and of their own accord to the present earl. Neddie was less than ten years old, nephew of the late king, and no doubt now in Tudor hands. This sharp reminder of her changing world steadied Alys as the careful breathing had not. She could not run screaming from this place of death. She had to devise a plan, to make decisions.

First she decided she would find the old woman and tell her Lord Wolveston was dead. Then, while the crone did whatever needed doing, Alys would search. That thought came to a dead halt, however, when she remembered how ill-lit the castle was. She dared not light torches, nor could she carry one from room to room, and certainly not down into the murky depths of the place. Reluctantly, she admitted to herself that even if she might have done so undetected, she did not have the courage to do so alone.

It was chilly by the door. Without looking at the bed, and without really thinking about what she was doing, she moved back to the hearth to warm herself. Once there, she looked down into the fire as though she might find answers in its leaping flames. Her conversation with her father repeated itself in her head, but his words still made no sense. She was calm now, her fears gone, kept at bay so long as she did not look at the bed, so long as she kept her mind on other things. She decided at last to get the old woman, and found herself hoping she had not gone far.

The fact that Goody Spurrig might have gone away altogether occurred to her as she lifted the door latch, bringing a fresh wave of fear that threatened to undo all her calm, but the fear proved groundless. The old woman was hunkered down near the parapet wall opposite the door, her black gown making her appear wraithlike in the glow of firelight that spilled onto the gallery's stone floor when Alys opened the door.

"I think he is dead," Alys said quietly.

"Aye, he was near," the crone agreed, rising with difficulty and moving toward her.

Alys stepped aside to let her pass into the room. "Will you tell them below?"

"Wi' the dawning. No need afore that. They care not."

Alys nodded. "You say there is no one else in the castle?"

The crone shrugged. "Nane as I know, m'lady. Ain't seen no one. Best tha' goest now. He hath no further need o' thee."

"Aye, or ever, I suppose." Alys turned back to the door.

"Thy cope, mistress." The crone picked up the heavy dark gray cloak from the floor where Alys had dropped it.

Alys stared at it, feeling an inexplicable desire to laugh.

She would, she thought, make a poor conspirator. She had forgotten all about Sir Nicholas's cloak, had not looked toward the bed, and thus had not seen it lying nearby. She took it and draped it over her shoulders. It was heavy and still damp from the mists. Even so, it was enveloping and made her feel warmer.

"I will go now. Thank you, dame, for your care of him. I shall see that you are properly rewarded."

The old woman's eyes gleamed, but there was skepticism there, too, making Alys determined to see that Sir Nicholas provided recompense for her loyalty.

Fifteen minutes later, she was back on the hillside, hugging the heavy cloak about her, wondering if she had really ever been hot. It was almost cold enough now to be winter instead of early September. She had encountered no difficulty in leaving the castle the way she had entered it, and now, ahead and below her, she saw the golden glow of three small fires, the encampment. She hoped she would be able to recognize her tent. It was the largest, she thought. But suddenly she was not certain, and the panic that had lain dormant within her leaped at the thought.

Hurrying, hearing unfamiliar noises with every step, she glanced around, fearing that ghosts or worse might fly out at her from the dark mists. One noise up ahead sounded like a shout, but she could not be certain because the murmuring of the nearby river muted the sound. Holding up her skirts, she moved as quickly as she dared, hoping she would not stumble over the treacherous bracken, would not kick against a stone and fall.

The change of light ahead alerted her. She had been watching the ground, using the glow from the fires as her beacon without actually looking at them, to see shadows of higher shrubs, of rocks and other obstacles in her path. But suddenly it was easy to see where she was going, far too easy. She stopped in her tracks and looked up.

There were torches now, lighting shadows that moved around the three fires, and more torches moving toward her, their light casting shadows of men approaching on foot. Recognizing what had happened put no strain on her imagination, and her first impulse was to run toward the river, where she knew from her childhood there were places she could conceal herself at least until daylight. Every nerve in her body screamed at her to run away and hide, to do anything rather than face Sir Nicholas. He would be angry. She did not know why she was certain of that; she just was. And though she did not know exactly why she feared his anger, she did fear it. That he was a man was enough. Masculine displeasure was something to avoid.

But Alys was no coward. Though it took effort, she stood her ground, watching the small procession draw nearer and nearer, as if he had a string attached to her, she thought, knowing even as the thought flitted through her mind that it was a foolish one. He was moving up the hill toward Wolveston, and she stood in a direct line between camp and castle.

A moment later the searchers were upon her. She stood straight, knowing she must look very small to them. Certainly, Sir Nicholas loomed over her. In the torchlight now surrounding them, she saw that his eyes blazed with anger.

"Where have you been?"

"If I told you I had been walking in my sleep and somehow wandered up the hill, would you believe me?" she inquired softly.

He grunted, his right hand catching her upper arm in a bruising grip. When he turned, pulling her with him, the men parted before him, letting them pass. She saw their faces, grim faces, the men as displeased with her as their master was.

Alys swallowed, wanting to speak but unable to do so as long as he forced her to hurry along at such a pace. A moment later he seemed to realize that she was having nearly to run to keep up with his long strides, for he slowed a bit.

"You are hurting my arm," she said.

"You deserve more than a sore arm," he retorted.

"My father is dead."

Sir Nicholas halted abruptly, turning to face her. "I am sorry for your loss, my lady, but I told you there was nothing you could do to help him. You ought not to have disobeyed me."

She glared at him, having nothing to say, wanting only to defy him and not knowing in the least why she should wish to do any such thing.

He returned her look for a long moment, then turned away, urging her forward again, though at a slower pace than before, and his grip no longer bruised her. When they reached the encampment he did not take her to her tent as she expected him to do, but led her toward the central fire.

To her horror she saw that a whipping post had been erected there. Even as the fear shot through her mind that she was the intended victim, she saw that two soldiers were forcing a third to the post, a mere lad, thin, with tousled russet hair. In a twinkling he was secured, his arms stretched over his head, his back bared. When Alys saw the larger of the other two—a truly enormous man—reach for a whip, she shuddered and turned away.

Sir Nicholas's grip tightened, and he forced her to turn back. "You will look," he said grimly. "This is your doing."

"Mine! How dare you?" she demanded, glaring up at him. "How can such a dreadful business be aught to do with me?"

"That lad yonder is Ian MacDougal," he said. "Since he is only a Scotsman, I do not expect you to feel remorse, but you will watch because he is being punished for his carelessness on your behalf." He looked directly into her eyes. "Ian was guarding your tent, Lady Alys. He has a weakness for pretty young women, and he trusted you. Had he fallen asleep, I would order him hanged. As it is, he will merely be flogged."

Horror engulfed her mind, making her dizzy, and with the first crack of the whip she cried out and tried once again to pull away, but Sir Nicholas would not allow her to do so. When she shut her eyes at the second stroke, swaying against him, he muttered curtly, "You may shut out the sight, wench, but if you try to cover your ears, I'll order your wrists tied behind you. It disappoints me to find you such a coward that you cannot look upon the result of your own misdeed."

Alys winced at his tone, then winced again when young MacDougal screamed at the third stroke of the whip, but Sir Nicholas's words echoed in her head, and she could not ignore them. Her misdeed, he had called it. The young Scotsman was being cruelly punished because of her, his dreadful suffering the direct result of her own disobedience.

She could not regret her visit to the castle. That was something she had had to do. But she could and did regret this. Never before had her actions resulted in such dire consequence to someone else. Because the lad had trusted her to remain where she was, because he had thought it unnecessary to watch the back of her tent as well as the front, he was suffering untold pain. The fault was her own, just as Sir Nicholas had said it was. She could not look, could not bear to watch the whip slashing against Ian's bare back. But she would not attempt to stop her ears. She deserved to hear his screams. In faith, she deserved more than that, and when she remembered that Sir Nicholas had said a sore arm was little compensation for what she had done, she wondered if he would extract greater payment from her when Ian's awful punishment was done.

The screaming stopped at last, and she opened her eyes in time to see Sir Nicholas sign to the man with the whip to stop the punishment. Ian hung by his wrists, limp, having passed out from the pain. For a moment Alys was afraid Sir Nicholas was only waiting for him to regain consciousness before ordering the punishment continued, but the two men moved forward and the smaller one drew his dagger from its sheath and cut the lad down. As she turned away with Sir Nicholas, she saw them lifting Ian gently between them. His back was marked with stripes, clearly visible even by firelight, and she saw that some were bleeding.

She said nothing until they reached her tent, but then she

turned to face him, drawing on courage she had not known she possessed. "Do you intend to punish me, too, Sir Nicholas?"

He was silent long enough to stir the horrors again before he said quietly, "By the rood, I ought to do so. You endangered your own life by your foolish actions, and thus, since I am responsible to the king for your well-being, you endangered my future and that of my men. But I have no right, for all that, to punish you, being neither father, brother, nor true guardian." He paused before adding very gently, "In future, mistress, I do advise you to take more caution."

He would have turned away then, but repressing the chill stirred by his words, she stopped him. "You will bury them all—my family—in the morning before we leave here?"

He gave her another steady look. "Do you think us barbarians, that you must ask such a question?"

"No, sir, but I would look upon their faces before they are set to rest. In faith, I must."

"As God is my witness, you will not. It is not safe."

"By heaven, sir, I have stood by my father's bed! If I am to contract the disease, I will do so whether I look upon my mother and brother, or do not."

"Nonetheless . . ."

"You do not understand," she said desperately. "Their souls will not rest if I do not speak a proper farewell!"

His eyes narrowed. "Not rest? What mean you by this?"

Thinking swiftly, she said, " 'Tis custom hereabouts. If the dead are not bade proper farewell by at least one of their close kin, they will walk. No one will step near Wolveston then, for fear of the haunts. You must allow me to do this, Sir Nicholas."

He hesitated, then pushed aside the tent flap and motioned to her to precede him inside. Jonet, sitting on her pallet, scrambled to her feet and stepped forward.

"My lady, you are safe then! I knew not what to think, what with all the commotion."

Merion answered, "She is safe enough. Tell me, Mistress

Hawkins, is it true that the people hereabouts will believe the castle haunted if certain customs are not observed?"

Alys held her breath, but she need not have worried.

"Aye, sir," Jonet replied wide-eyed. "There must be a proper burial service, with a priest and all, and a member of the family to bid the dead a proper farewell beforehand."

He nodded. "I will see to it then."

A moment later he was gone, and Alys rushed into Jonet's arms. "I was afraid you would stare at him in wonder or deny the nonsense outright," she said. "You said just the right thing."

"Aye, I was listening. Only ran back right before he opened the flap, and feared he'd see I was nigh out of breath from the terror of being caught." She held Alys away from her. "What was your purpose, mistress? 'Tis a dangerous thing you mean to do."

Alys nodded. It would be dangerous all right, and not only because she might be exposing herself again to the dreaded sickness. If Sir Nicholas discovered she had lied to him, he might not be as forbearing as he had been tonight. She was trusting Fate, which was never a wise course to follow.

"I have to see my *brother* Robert," she said now.

"Then his lordship did tell you naught."

"He was delirious. He said much but little that made sense. He said, I think, that either Lincoln or Viscount Lovell still lives, and maybe Davy, or even Roger. 'Tis possible, in fact, that someone is hiding right there in the castle."

"Then the sooner we be gone from here, the better," Jonet said practically, helping her off with the heavy cloak and then moving to deal with belt, shoes, and laces.

Alys realized she was right. The fugitives, if indeed there were any, would be all the safer for their departure with the soldiers. "Sir Nicholas said we would leave directly after the burials," she said.

Some moments later, tucked beneath her furs, she tried to relive in her mind the events of the night, but her imagination failed her. Her head ached, and she felt tired enough to sleep for a week. When she did sleep, her slumber was troubled and she felt hot under the furs, throwing half of them off by morning.

Jonet woke her early, exclaiming over her flushed complexion and the dark circles beneath her eyes, but Alys ordered her to cease her fretting. "You only make my head ache worse," she snapped. "Leave be. We will be gone soon, and I shall sleep better tonight, and better than ever when we reach London."

The mist was gone when they emerged from the tent, and the sun shone brightly upon the landscape, purple and green now with heather and bracken. Wooded areas to the south, outskirts of the vast, legendary Sherwood Forest, made darker splashes of green, and although Alys had never traveled that way, she knew that beyond the forest lay Newark and Nottingham Castle, the latter long a stronghold of the Plantagenets but probably now, like the rest, in the Tudor's hands. Nearby to the east flowed the river Trent, wide, deep, and blue, hurrying north to join the Humber. Beyond sprawled the fens and marshlands of Lincolnshire, but the sight, though she once had loved it, held no interest today.

Breakfast was only dried meat and ale, for there was no more bread, but she didn't care. The thought of food was an unwelcome one. No doubt, she thought, her stomach still writhed at the evil she had brought upon young Ian the night before.

Thinking of him now, she gathered both her strength and her courage and went to find Sir Nicholas. "Where is Ian MacDougal?"

"In the tent I shared," he replied briefly. "He will remain there until we are ready to strike camp."

"Is he a prisoner?"

"No, but he is too stiff to be useful. He is still in pain, as you might guess." He peered suddenly into her eyes and frowned. "Are you well, my lady? You do not look so."

"I am well enough," she retorted, conscious again of her aching head and her fatigue. "Have you sought out a priest?"

"Aye, there are two monks from the priory at Bawtry who are caring for the sick in nearby villages. One has agreed to speak the service for the dead. He will be along soon."

"I want to see Ian MacDougal first."

Sir Nicholas nodded. "As you wish. Tom will take you." He shouted for his squire.

After one look at Ian, a wiry lad with russet-colored hair, who lay on his stomach with his bare back still exposed for the simple reason that he could not bear anything to touch it, Alys sent for Jonet. "Fetch your herbal salve," she commanded. Then, to Ian, she said, "It will soothe the pain and make you better."

He managed a wan smile. "I niver thought tae see the day when I'd bid a bonny wooman tae keep her hands from me, but i' faith, I canna bear it. Ye mustna touch me, mistress."

But when Jonet returned, Alys ordered her and Tom to hold Ian while she smoothed the salve directly onto his wounds with her own hands. Though she was as gentle as she knew how to be, she knew how much she hurt him, and so heavy was her guilt that every gasp and groan sent a slice of pain through her own body.

"I am sorry, Ian," she whispered with tears in her eyes. " 'Twas my fault. I am as sorry as I can be."

He protested weakly, and although she did not know whether his protest was at her words or at her touch, she did not stop until his wounds were covered with the aromatic salve.

"He can wear a shirt now," she said to Tom. "Not armor or a jacket, but the day promises to be warm, and by nightfall he will be better able to endure the weight of heavier material."

Tom, who had watched her every move with undisguised curiosity, went at once to fetch a shirt. When he returned, Alys stood to leave. "Sleep, Ian, if you can, till it is time to go. Riding will be unbearable if you are still exhausted."

"Aye, mistress," he murmured. "I thank you."

She left, discovering when she emerged from the tent that preparations had begun for the burial of her family.

Three rough coffins were being carried from the castle to the graveyard on a nearby rise, above the river. She hurried to find Sir Nicholas, cursing the headache that still haunted her, wishing for more energy, knowing the day would be a long one.

The wood coffins had been placed next to three hastily dug holes in the muddy ground. A brown-robed monk stepped up to the first of them, making the sign of the cross above it. Sir Nicholas, beside him, motioned to Alys to come forward.

"I do not approve of this," he said, "but the priest agrees that you ought to look upon your dead."

" 'Tis the right of the living," murmured the monk.

"Aye, and it may be her death as well," Sir Nicholas retorted. "Men who die of the plague are buried rapidly, often without ceremony, in order to protect the living."

"This sickness is not the plague," the monk reminded him, "and even those who die of plague have the right to a proper burial, my son."

"I have agreed." Merion signed to one of his men. "Open her ladyship's coffin."

Alys stepped forward, not really wanting to look upon her mother's face, but knowing she must if she was to see the boy who was said to be her brother. When the coffin lid was raised, the figure that was revealed meant little to her. She had scarcely known her mother, and she was able to look at her face with little emotion. Alys had brought her rosary, and silently she prayed, made the sign of the cross, and stepped back.

The second coffin was opened. She stepped forward and stared down in amazement. To the best of her knowledge she had never seen the boy before, but his blond good looks were more familiar to her than her mother's face had been. She had seen King Edward more than once, and she knew Neddie, who was the son of Edward's second brother, the late Duke of Clarence. If this boy was not as much a Plantagenet as either of them...

Her thoughts froze her in place. When she realized who the boy might be, she told herself she was mad to think such a thing, but the thoughts that tumbled over themselves, racing through her mind, made her dizzy. Conscious of Sir Nicholas standing beside her, she knew that she must do nothing to arouse his suspicions. She must click her beads and move her lips, no matter that her muscles refused to obey her. Tears spilled from her eyes, her headache raged, her skin felt as though it were aflame, and her breath came in short, ragged gasps. Her face felt numb, her hands and feet, too. One moment they burned, the next they tingled with pins and needles.

When she collapsed, Sir Nicholas caught her in his arms.

# 4

Her body was burning up. Her head ached, and her stomach felt as though knives were cutting her from within. Worst of all was that she felt too weak to move, even to open her eyes. There were voices, low but angry, both of them, arguing about water.

Water. Alys tried to speak. She would give her best gown and girdle for a sip of water. It was no use. She could not move, and she seemed to have no control over her voice.

"Nay, tha' mustna!" The crackling voice was familiar but not so much so that she could identify the speaker. "Sithee, t' sickness mun be sweated from 'er."

The voice took her back to her father's deathbed, to an echo of the puzzling words he had muttered. He seemed to be in the tent now, straight and strong as he had been before she went away to Middleham. She tried to call him, but he faded when a voice said, "She is delirious; she will die without water." The voice was not her father's. It was Nicholas, Sir Nicholas, the Tudor's man, the enemy. Without opening her eyes, she could see him, could almost feel the crispness of his curls beneath her palm.

Why could she not move her hands? It was as though she were tied up, her arms bound to her sides, her feet so heavy she could not stir them. A cold, damp cloth touched her lips and blessedly cool water trickled down her parched throat. Then the cloth moved over her cheeks, her forehead, cooling them. She slept.

Her dreams were no comfort. Monsters threatened her, and dark, bottomless chasms opened beneath her feet when she walked. A black tunnel loomed before her, and from its depths a distant light beckoned. A voice called to her, Elizabeth's voice. But Elizabeth was at Sheriff Hutton with Neddie—gentle Neddie, now the rightful Earl of Warwick. But he would never be what his formidable grandfather had been, nor even his father. He was not guileful like Clarence was. But Neddie and Elizabeth were not at Sheriff Hutton. She remembered now. They were . . . somewhere.

There were monsters again, and the heat, the dreadful heat. She had to move, to get away from it. Someone was holding her. She struggled, fighting this monster who would force her down into the flames, and then suddenly she was free, but it was as if she were falling, still struggling as she plunged and whirled, down and down. The heat was terrifying. Then she was caught and someone held her again, this time someone stronger than she was. So strong, in fact, that it was useless to struggle anymore.

The voice calling to her had weakened while her thoughts were diverted, but she could hear it again now and was tempted to follow it, to step into that dark tunnel, to see what lay beyond. Anything would be better than the flames, and the pain.

"No, Alys." Only two words, but the voice unmistakable. Anne's voice—gentle, sorrowful, firm. The tunnel faded. She became aware of other voices, nearer at hand. One was Jonet's, another Sir Nicholas's. There were at least two others. Oddly pleased with herself for recognizing the fact that there were four voices, Alys slept again, heavily and without the dreams.

The next time she awoke, she heard something altogether different. Someone was playing a lute and singing in a deep, pleasant voice, in a lilting language she had never heard before. Curiosity lent her strength, and she forced her eyes open.

At first she saw only the warm orange glow from the oil lamp, casting dark, dancing shadows on the walls of the tent. It was enough to remind her of where she was, and she wanted to see who was singing. Her mind suggested a name, but the very thought of it was absurd. He would not sing to her. And her imagination boggled when she tried to envision a graceful lute in his hands.

But it was Sir Nicholas, sitting on a joint stool by her pallet. The lute looked ridiculously small in his large hands, cradled against his broad chest, but his expression was gentle. When her gaze met his, she saw his satisfaction, but his voice did not falter, and she was glad. He had a wonderful voice for singing, deep and full. She could not understand a word of the song, but it comforted her, and she wanted him to go on and on.

When he fell silent at last, she said in a raspy voice that sounded completely unlike her own, "What was that?"

"A Welsh ballad," he said quietly. "Only a tale of a boy and his sheep, but I liked it when I was a lad and fond of roaming, when I could, with the shepherds in the hills near my home. My mother used to sing it to me. How do you feel?"

"Hungry," she said, "and thirsty."

"Good," he said. "We have broth keeping warm over a fire, and young Ian rode to Bawtry Priory to fetch bread for you."

"You made Ian go?" Indignation put energy into her voice.

"He wanted to go," Sir Nicholas told her, getting up and setting the instrument aside. "Your young Scotsman does not trust the English monks to give any of the other men fresh bread. He's always had an eye for the lasses," he added with a wry smile, "but I think you have become rather special to him. Rest now. I'll send someone with your broth."

She dozed again, but the sound of others in the tent soon roused her, and she made no objection when Sir Nicholas

knelt to raise her so that Jonet could put cushions behind
her. When he let her lie back again, she sighed, exhausted.

"I am as limp as a rag," she muttered, "and my skin feels
as if it might crack, like a hide that has been dried in the sun."

"Both feelings will pass," he said. "I shall leave you to
Mistress Hawkins now. Let her feed you." He said the last
as though he thought she must be commanded to allow Jonet
to serve her, but before she had time to protest, he was gone.

Jonet said quietly, "We thought we had lost thee."

"I do have the sickness then," Alys murmured. "I thought
that must be it. But why did I not die?"

"We thought tha' didst, just before yon fever broke. Tha'
wert wild wi' it," she went on, her renewed distress evident
to anyone who knew her by the stronger hint of Yorkshire
in her accent. "Tha' fought me till I couldna hold thee. That
were when Sir Nicholas came and said he'd look after thee
himself. He said women sometimes do survive, though men
rarely, and he meant to see thee through. But then, after the
wildness, tha' wert so still we thought thee gone. He shouted
at thee, bellowing thy name, and commanding thee to live.
And when tha' didst stir, I thought the lad would weep like
a wee bairn. Though he did no such thing," she added more
briskly, recollecting herself.

"I suppose you think him kind," Alys said, "but he did say
before that he will be blamed for aught that happens to me."

"Aye," Jonet agreed, but her tone was dubious. " 'Twas a
dire sickness, my lady, terrible to behold. Before you grew
so wild, we had that herb woman here—the same as stayed
with his lordship—but Sir Nicholas sent her away when she
said giving you water would kill you. He said he could not
believe it would do any such thing. You were crying out for
it so, and you were so hot! He just wanted to cool you, I
think. He *is* a kind man, mistress, for all that he be a Welshman and at one with the Tudor." She held up a horn mug.
"Drink this now."

Alys sipped slowly. She could taste herbs and the flavor of

beef, and it was good. She wanted more, but Alys shook her head. "He said you must not drink too much at once, or drink too fast."

"He also said there was bread."

"Aye, and so there be, but you are not to have it till we see you do keep this broth within." Her voice sounded weary, and Alys looked at her. Jonet's expression was haggard and careworn, and her eyes were dim, lacking their usual sparkle.

Fear leaped within her. "Jonet, are you ill?"

"Nay, my lady, only a wee bit tired. He told me to sleep, but 'tis not likely I could do so with my lamb ailing, and so I told him. But he is not a man to cross, I can tell you. The way he spoke when I refused to lie down made the blood freeze in my veins, so I did not dare argue when he ordered me to go away."

"He ordered you away?" Alys sipped again.

"Aye," Jonet told her. "To begin, he let me lie down on my pallet yonder, but when he saw I was not likely to sleep there, he sent for one of his men to take me to another tent and see me laid down. 'Twas a lout name of Hugh with a lot of other names after, like Sir Nicholas has, and the biggest man I ever laid eyes upon. An ugsome brute. Sithee, when I tell you he be the same as flogged poor Ian . . . well, I shall say no more, but if I were a more timid sort nor what I am, he'd fair have raised the gooseflesh on my skin, and that be the truth of the matter."

"But what did he do?"

"He took me to another tent, yonder, and fetched out blankets, making it clear he meant to cover me with his own hands. But I was not going to allow that, I can tell you. I told him that he could take himself off, but he just stood like Goliath and said he would wait till I slept. Called me his wee minikin, too, as if I were six and not nigh onto five-and-thirty years of age. Have you ever heard the like?"

"Well, if he did not harm you," Alys murmured sleepily,

"I suppose he must have . . ." But she lost the thread of what she had been going to say, and her voice faded away.

When she awoke the next time, she felt stronger, and when Jonet asked if she might fancy more broth and a bit of bread, she agreed instantly. Jonet signed to someone behind her, and Alys saw Ian MacDougal standing in the entry.

"Wait," she said when he took the horn mug from Jonet and turned with it toward the entrance, to fetch her broth.

He turned. "Aye, m'lady?"

His soft brogue reminded her of his antecedents, but they no longer mattered. "I do thank you, Ian, from my heart," she said. "Sir Nicholas told me you rode to fetch bread for me. I know your back cannot be healed yet. 'Twas most kind of you."

He flushed rosily in the lamplight. " 'Twere nobbut a pleasure, m'lady," he muttered, ducking out on the words.

"That lad has kept close about the tent these two days past," Jonet said softly, "fair begging to fetch and carry."

"Two days! Have I been ill so long as that?"

"Aye."

Alys shifted her position. Her strength was returning, but she still felt as weak as a newborn lamb. And when the covers moved, she instantly became conscious of a noisome odor, and gasped when she recognized its source.

"Jonet, I stink like a summer jakes!" She raised a hand to feel her head, grimacing with distaste. "My hair feels like damp bracken, and it's as tangled as a bryony hedge. I want a bath."

"Well, you'll not be having one yet a while," Jonet said sourly. "You nearly died, as I'll thank you to remember, so you must eat up the bread when Ian brings it, and drink your broth, and mayhap we can begin thinking of baths in a day or two."

"But I want a bath now!" Alys knew it was unreasonable, but the desire to be clean was suddenly overwhelming. Her body was sticky, the bedclothes damp and clinging. She wanted fresh ones, and though she knew the chance of get-

ting them was small, that only made her want them more.
When Jonet calmly moved to the entrance of the tent to take
the refilled mug and the bread from Ian, then dismissed him
and turned back, Alys said sullenly, "I will neither eat nor
drink again until I have had a bath, Jonet."

"Do not be difficult, Miss Alys," Jonet said with a weary
sigh. "Tha' must eat, and tha' hast not got enough strength
to fling those pillows at me, so do not be thinking tha' wilt."

"I will do as I please! Stop treating me like a child!"

"What goes on here?" Sir Nicholas entered, followed by
the largest man Alys had ever seen. Dark-haired and dark-
eyed, wearing leather breeches and boots, he was a good bit
older than Sir Nicholas, and larger. The pair of them filled
the tent.

Paying the large man no heed at all, Jonet turned in relief
to Sir Nicholas. "She insists she will have a bath, sir. I have
told her that she is not to have one, but she has been like
this from a child, I fear, and when she sets her mind—"

Alys cut her off with a snap. "Do not babble at him, Jonet!
Men never notice how things smell, so he cannot understand
how I feel. In faith, he does not care a whit about me, and
he cannot want to hear your foolish, whining prattle. Just
order up a tub and have it filled the way we did before,
and—"

"Just when," Sir Nicholas inquired mildly, "did you decide
that I do not care how you smell? I can assure you that I
prefer attar of lilacs to attar of sweating sickness, if you do
indeed need to hear such an obvious fact spoken aloud."

She glared at him, and he turned to Jonet. "Go with Hugh
now and have your dinner. I will attend to her ladyship."

"No!" Alys cried. "Jonet, I command you to stay!"

Jonet hesitated, but though she ignored the large soldier
when he gently touched her arm and held the tent flap open,
when Sir Nicholas frowned at her, she went without another
word.

Alys gritted her teeth when the flap fell into place again,
leaving her alone with Sir Nicholas. He picked up the horn

mug from the table where Jonet had set it and moved toward
her, drawing the stool close to her pallet and sitting down.

"Can you sit up unaided?" he asked.

"I do not know." She continued to glare at him.

"I can make allowance," he said evenly, "for a temper
made uncertain by illness, but you ought not to speak so
sharply to Mistress Hawkins. She has worn herself out with
worry over you, so this fractious mood of yours must distress
her sorely."

She opened her mouth to tell him her moods were no
concern of his, but his words had struck home, and she shut
it again. Her chest ached suddenly, and her throat hurt, and
she did not think either of these new pains stemmed from
her illness. When her eyes filled with tears, she shut them
tight, but she could not stop the tears. They trickled silently
down her cheeks.

When she felt his arm move beneath her shoulders, lifting
her, she had all she could do to keep from flinging herself
onto his chest and sobbing until she could sob no more. The
urge startled her and steadied her, and when she opened her
eyes at last, she found it was no longer difficult to meet his
gaze.

"I should not have spoken so," she muttered gruffly. "I
know not why I am in such a foul humor. I have not treated
Jonet so since I was a child. I pray you, forgive me."

" 'Tis not my forgiveness you require, *mi geneth*. Here,
drink your broth."

He held the mug and she sipped from it, watching his face
over the rim, wishing he would smile. No doubt, she assured
herself, that wish was also born of her illness, for there could
be no other good reason for it.

There was little conversation between them after that, but
the silences were comfortable, and she felt no need to break
them. Nor did Sir Nicholas seem inclined to do so. When
she had finished her bread and broth, he helped her lie back
again, then picked up his lute and began idly to pluck the
strings.

Jonet's return twenty minutes later was heralded by the sound of her voice. That she was in a militant mood was made clear to Alys, if not to Sir Nicholas, by her complete lapse into the broad Yorkshire speech of her youth.

"Tha' hast got above thysel', tha' great club-fisted gowk! There be no call for thee ta traipse after me like a kitchen cat prayerful o' scraps. By the look o' thee, tha' art well-enow fed no ta go beggin' fer sich, nor fer other 'n far grander favors!"

"True, my little prickling, but I would see you safe inside," the big man said cheerfully as the flap was drawn back.

"Safe!" Jonet came through the opening with her hands on her hips, turning as she entered to snap up at him, "Sithee, tha' great shuttle-brained maggotpate, I'll be the safer for thy space than for thy presence, as I'll thank thee t' remember!"

"Is Hugh annoying you, mistress?" Sir Nicholas inquired.

"Aye," snapped Jonet. Then, seeing the frown on Sir Nicholas's face, she recollected herself and added quickly, "Not to say *annoying*, sir. 'Tis only that he will follow after me wherever I go and does prate the grandest absurdities to me. Why, not ten seconds past, he told me I reminded him of a sea beet! Now then, sir, I ask—"

Sir Nicholas chuckled. "A sea beet, Hugh?"

Big Hugh had bent to follow Jonet into the tent, and when he straightened again, Alys was amazed anew at how he dwarfed all around him. "Aye, Nick," he said in his deep bass voice. "Is her dress not the same soft lavender as that wee flower? Ah, but the sea beet is a sweet thing, and useful. I disremembered that when first I compared our Mistress Andras here to one."

Sir Nicholas choked back a laugh, and Jonet, more indignant than ever, said sharply, "The name is Hawkins, addlepate."

Alys, seeing that Sir Nicholas was still struggling to contain his laughter, demanded, "Why does he call her Andras?"

He grinned. "Andras is a goddess—in sooth, a fury—to

whom the ancient Welsh felt obliged to offer human sacrifices."

Jonet's plump bosom swelled up then till it looked as if it might burst, but she primmed her lips tightly and gave the men a fine view of her back as she moved to straighten Alys's covering. Alys grinned too, but when Jonet fluffed the covers, freeing the fusty odors again, her grin altered abruptly to a frown.

"Please, Jonet," she said, "we must contrive a way in which I can be made clean again, or by which the bedding can be aired and refreshed with herbs. I am sorry I was sharp with you before, and that I laughed, but I am dreadfully uncomfortable."

"My poor lamb," Jonet said instantly. "I shall order new moss gathered and set fresh bedding to air by the fires at once. That dismal rain has truly stopped for a time, and the men even seem to think we will have sunshine tomorrow. Perhaps, if it grows warm then, we can see about getting you clean again."

Sir Nicholas said quickly, "You will not bathe so soon after your illness, mistress, so do not think it."

"I do not want a bath so much as I want someone to wash my hair," she retorted. "It hurts my head and offends my nose."

"That may be attended to as soon as it is safe," he promised her, "but not before. You will do better to sleep now."

But even though he played the lute and sang for her again, she did not want to sleep. She was uncomfortable and sullen, and disinclined to exert herself to appear to be anything else. "Why do you allow Hugh to call you Nick?" she demanded suddenly.

"He is my second in command," he said. "His family has long served mine, just as Mistress Hawkins's has served yours. He was in charge at the castle that night," he added in a different tone. "He would like to know how you got inside, as would I."

"I will not tell you," she said, adding quickly, "He was here in the camp when . . . when we returned. Jonet said—"

"He had come down to report to me. You must have just missed encountering him on your way up the hill."

She fell silent then, and to her relief, he did not press her to tell him how she had managed to enter the castle. When Jonet brought fresh bedding, Alys would not let her replace the furs and blankets, or the pallet, insisting that fresh ones would only smell like the old ones in less than an hour. Even Sir Nicholas could not debate that point, and he soon left, recommending again that she ought to sleep.

By the following day, Alys was much recovered and determined to have her hair washed and her body bathed. When Jonet refused to assist her without Sir Nicholas's permission, she came as near as she had since early childhood to shrieking at her. But Alys was older now, and wiser. She pleaded instead.

"It is perfectly warm," she said. "Now that the rain has stopped and the sun come out, I shall not be surprised if the men do not begin to complain about the heat. There can be no good reason for my not having a proper bath and washing my hair."

"There is one very good reason," Sir Nicholas said gently as he opened the flap and stepped inside the tent.

Alys glared at him. "You mean because you have forbidden it, I suppose."

"An excellent reason, is it not?"

"I do not agree, sir. I am not accustomed to having my every move dictated by a Welshman. In faith, I am not accustomed to arbitrary orders of any kind."

"Ah, but you have forgotten, *mi Saesnes-bach*," he said. "Had you not already told me about Lady Drufield, I might have believed you, but since you did . . ."

"What does that mean?" she demanded. "I remember the first part means Englishwoman, but what is the rest, the *bach* part?"

"Only that you are small," he said, giving her a direct look as he said it. " 'Tis a point worth remembering, mistress."

There was a note in his voice that sent a shiver up her

spine, but she ignored it and gazed steadily back at him. "In England," she said, "gentlemen do not employ such terms when they speak to ladies. They show proper respect."

"Do they?"

She nodded, determined not to let her gaze falter.

He shrugged and turned away. "I suppose that is entirely possible. Nevertheless, you will not defy my orders, nor will you command your woman to do so." He flicked a glance at Jonet, who kept her head down and made no effort to return his look. "I came to tell you I will be away from camp for several hours," he said. "I am taking men to Conisborough to see if the sickness has struck there as well."

"How many are you taking?" Alys asked swiftly.

"Only a half dozen," he said. "You will be safe here."

"I have naught to fear amongst my own," she retorted, "but you will need more than six to see you safe to Conisborough."

"The castle is in our hands now," he said, "as are Barnard Castle, Middleham, Beverley, Pontefract, and most others of any strength. If I need more men, I shall have them right swiftly, and there has been no time for the rebels to reorganize, in any case. You will not be rid of me so easily, mistress. Remember that and behave yourself." He glanced again at Jonet. "Are you well, Mistress Hawkins? You have lost much of your color."

She straightened. "I am perfectly stout, sir."

Alys managed a smile. "She is concerned lest you decide to leave her large guardian behind to plague her, sir. He follows her rather closely, as though he does not trust her to look out for herself, but she does not like to complain to you."

"Hugh stays," he said. "If I am gone, I want him here."

"I should have thought that taking only six, you would want him along. He is big enough to count for another half dozen."

Sir Nicholas smiled but shook his head. Then, after another speculative glance at Jonet, he left them.

Alys sighed. "I hope you will not refuse to fetch me a damp cloth at least, Jonet, to cool my brow. I swear I shall not be answerable for my actions if I am not to be allowed that much."

"I'll fetch it, my lady, and send for warm water to wash your face. There be fires still, and young Ian will oblige us."

Ian brought warm water willingly and seemed inclined to linger until Alys asked him how his back was. Flushing, he insisted it was all but healed, and balked at allowing Jonet to examine him. Alys was having none of that.

"Remove your tunic and shirt, Ian, and let Mistress Hawkins see, or I shall complain to Sir Nicholas that you are obstinate."

The lad grimaced but obeyed her without another murmur. Nor did he complain when Jonet fetched the salve. As she rubbed it into his flesh, she said to Alys, "He would not allow me to look this morning or yesterday, and though it had ought to be done each day, I did not like to complain of him to Sir Nicholas."

"Well, I shall have no such scruples," Alys said firmly. "Do you hear me, Ian?"

"Aye, mistress." He put his shirt on again and laced it, then donned his tunic, apparently in no hurry to leave. "Be there aught else ye would ha' me do, mistress?"

She was tempted to order a tub of hot water, but a glance at Jonet decided her against it. "Not now, Ian, but ask me again after we have eaten. Perchance there will be something then."

"Aye, mistress." He left them.

Jonet brought her a cloth damped in the warm water. " 'Twas kind of you not to rebuff him, my lady. Yon lad seems to feel himself under an obligation to you."

"Well, he need not," Alys retorted, uncomfortable that Ian should feel such a thing. Scrubbing her face, she muttered, "Had it not been for me, he would not have been flogged at all."

"Aye, but he fails to see the matter in that light. He knows he failed in his duty, and accepts his punishment. 'Twas your care of him afterward that matters, for I warrant no one has done such a thing for him before. A Scotsman, he be. Heathen savages, the lot of them. Your kindness to the poor laddie—"

"Enough, Jonet. Help me." Alys did not want to hear about kindness. The whole conversation served only to remind her of Ian's screams and her own guilt. Once she felt a bit cleaner and Jonet had helped her change to a fresh shift, she sat wrapped in an herb-scented robe and watched the woman strip her pallet of its rank-smelling covers and replace them. But when Jonet straightened with the bundle of old bedding in her arms, Alys saw the deep lines in her face, the dark hollows beneath her eyes. "In the name of heaven," she said sharply, "you must rest."

"We shall both do so after we have eaten," Jonet agreed.

But it was more than an hour before Ian and another man brought their dinner, and by then the novelty of fresh bedding and fairly clean skin had worn off and Alys was more conscious than ever of her filthy hair. Jonet had plaited it and twisted the plaits into a coil at the back of her head, but Alys had refused a covering, insisting that it would only add to the weight of her hair and bring back her headache. Jonet had not argued. She looked as if she had a headache of her own.

She admitted it after they had eaten, and made no effort to argue when Alys ordered her to her pallet to sleep.

"Aye, m'lady, I can do with some rest," she said wanly, obeying at once. She was sound asleep when Ian returned twenty minutes later to collect their dishes.

"Will there be aught else the noo, mistress?"

She glanced at Jonet, but the woman was so deeply asleep that she had not even stirred at his entrance. Alys looked speculatively at Ian, wondering if his master had thought it necessary to leave the lad with specific orders regarding what she might or might not do.

"I must wash my hair, Ian," she said, striving to sound

casual but firm, and watching him closely for the slightest sign of hesitation. She did not doubt from his recent behavior that he would do whatever she asked of him; however, she would not allow him to disobey any order that Sir Nicholas had given him.

But Ian showed no such hesitation. He glanced at Jonet. "Shall I wake her then?"

"On no account," Alys said. "She must have her sleep, so you will have to help me. Can you fetch more hot water and help me do it here? I shall need a tub for the rinsing, too. In the usual way of things, I should do it outside, even at the river, but I doubt I am strong enough yet for that."

"Och, ye mustna gae ootside, mistress," the lad said, "but I ha' niver helped a wooman wash her hair afore."

"I will tell you what to do," she promised, casting another look at Jonet to reassure herself that she was deeply asleep.

When Ian had gone for the water, Alys got up quickly and hurried to find a clean skirt and a front-lacing bodice, so she would be decently clad when he returned. She also unearthed her French soap and herbs for the rinse water.

The business of washing her hair was not by any means a silent affair, for when Alys discovered that she still lacked the strength to hold up her arms long enough to accomplish even the simple task of unplaiting her hair, Ian had to help her, and afterward when it was all she could do to hold herself over the tub, he poured buckets of water over her head and lathered it with her soap. It was not long before they both forgot Jonet. The first time Ian poured water down Alys's neck instead of over her hair, she let out a shriek of laughter and commanded him to pay more heed to his actions. But Ian lacked a certain deftness required for the task, and by the time he was finished, both were soaked and giddy with laughter.

Ian handed her the thick linen towel she had put ready near the tub. It, too, was damp, but she managed to catch most of her long hair in it and to wrap the towel around her head, sitting back upon her heels to look up at him.

"I shall treasure Jonet more than ever after this," she said, adding with a guilty glance at the sleeping woman, "She must be worn to the bone to sleep like that." Turning back to Ian, she chuckled again, for his leather sleeves were soaked through and the entire front of him was in a like condition.

He looked down at himself, shook his head, and said, "I washed one o' m' dogs once when it coom in covered wi' muck, but I doot I were sich a mess after as what I am the noo, mistress."

She laughed. "Ian, I must go outside to dry my hair in the sun. Can you fix a sheltered place for me to sit?"

"Aye," he said, turning to go. But before he had taken a second step, he stopped, stiffening.

His body blocked Alys's view, and she craned her neck to see around him, gasping when she saw Sir Nicholas standing there.

Glaring at her, he said, "Leave us, Ian. I will deal with you later."

"No!" Alys leapt to her feet so swiftly that her head swam, and she reached out distractedly to steady herself. When Ian moved to help, Sir Nicholas pushed him aside and grabbed her, but the moment he touched her, she found her wits and snapped, "Ian did not disobey you! You never told him—"

"I know I did not," he said. "I shall not make the same mistake again. But I did tell Mistress Hawkins, so how—"

"She is asleep."

"Nonsense, how can she—" He broke off, letting go of her to kneel swiftly by Jonet. His next words came over his shoulder like whip cracks. "Ian, get the Lady Alys out of here, and send Hugh to me. This woman is not asleep; she's unconscious!"

"No!" Alys cried, eluding Ian to fly to Jonet's side.

She could not evade Sir Nicholas so easily, however. He swept her up into his arms and carried her from the tent. "Hugh," he bellowed as he ducked through the flap, "to me!"

Helplessly, Alys sobbed against his shoulder.

# 5

Alys scarcely heard what Sir Nicholas said to Hugh when he came, but when she realized that Sir Nicholas was taking her away from the tent, she struggled wildly to free herself, terrified about Jonet's illness, but it did her no good. She even tried to pull his sword from its scabbard, thinking she could force him to release her, but the sword was too long, too unwieldy. He did not even attempt to stop her from tugging at it but carried her quickly to another tent, where he set her abruptly on her feet. When he turned to leave, she grabbed his mail-clad arm. "Wait! Don't leave me here. I must be with her."

"You will not," he snapped. "You are still weak from your own illness, and for all I know, you can get it again, from her. I will send someone for the herb woman, but you are not to go near Mistress Hawkins. If I must, I will set one of the men to guard you to see that you do not leave this tent. Do you understand?"

Tears spilled down her cheeks. "You cannot do this. Jonet will die. She is exhausted from looking after me, so she cannot fight the sickness. I must help her."

She thought she saw compassion in his eyes and hoped he would relent, but his voice was hard when he said, "Then you pray for her, mistress, for only God can help her now. There is a prie-dieu yonder." When she opened her mouth to argue, he added implacably, "You might give thanks first that I have no time right now to discuss your defiance of my orders. Just how did you propose to dry your hair?"

She raised a hand to the towel still wrapped around her head. In her agitation over Jonet she had forgotten her wet hair. Frustrated but wary, she bit her lip and fell silent.

Sir Nicholas glanced around the dimly lit tent. It was smaller and more Spartan than the one she had occupied with Jonet, lacking such luxuries as a washstand, stool, and thick pallets. And although it was warm from the sunlight outside, there was no place to sit but upon the prie-dieu or the ground. He said, "I will send one of the lads to help you."

"I can do it myself," she muttered, "outside in the sun. I will just get my brush from the other t—"

"No."

"But—"

"I will send Tom back with your brush. You find a place near the cook fires where you are in plain sight. And you had best have that tunic off before you go. It is wet."

Her arms snapped protectively across her breasts. "No!"

A glint of amusement lit his eyes. "I see. Tom will bring some of your things over. See that you are decently clad before you step outside, *mi geneth.*" He was gone.

Her bosom swelled with resentment before memory of Jonet's illness swept over her again and the sobs came, wracking her body. She sank to the floor, giving way to a despair she had not felt since Anne's passing. All her life it had been Jonet upon whom she depended, Jonet to whom she had gone as a child when she had hurt herself or been punished for her misdeeds. Jonet had wiped her tears and tended her hurts, bathed her, dressed her, and heard her prayers after tucking her into her cot at night. And now Jonet would die, for the sickness was terrible. She knew as much from her own experience. Though she was young and strong and rarely ill, she had nearly died. Jonet was old—well past thirty—and weak from worry. Jonet's death would be her fault, for not only had she pushed her to journey in a single day from Drufield to Wolveston through the dreadful rain, but then she had fallen ill, and Jonet had neglected herself to care for her.

Alys was still sobbing when Ian entered, carrying an armful of her belongings. "He ha' sent Tom for the herb wooman," he said, and when she did not reply, he stood for a moment, watching her, before he said, "Shall I gang awa' again, mistress?"

She struggled to control herself. "No, this towel is soaked through, and so is my bodice. I must put something else on, and I must dry my hair. He will blame you if I become ill again."

"Nay, mistress, he willna," Ian said. "He did say he kens weel it were nane o' my doing. He's a fair mon, is the master."

She looked at him. "You like him." When Ian nodded, she sniffed and said, "Well, I like him, too, when he is not being as stubborn as a"—She hesitated, because the saying was *as stubborn as a Scotsman*, and that would not do— "as any other Welshman," she ended, eyeing him apologetically.

Ian smiled. "There disna be a Welshman breathing who's as stubborn as me auld dad, mistress. Master did find yer comb and brush," he added, holding the articles out to her before he set her bundles down. "He said I wasna tae linger."

Taking the boar's-bristle brush and tortoiseshell comb, she forced herself to ask the question, "How fares Mistress Hawkins?"

"They canna wake her," Ian said gently.

Dropping comb and brush, Alys rubbed the tears from her cheeks, jumped to her feet, and rushed to the opening.

Ian barred her way. "You canna gae to her, mistress. I'm tae stop you, an you try."

She stared desperately up at him, making no attempt now to stem her tears. "I must."

"Nay, ye mustna. Goorthfan Gower's looking after 'er."

She blinked, bewildered. "Who?"

Ian flushed. "That's how it sounds when yon Welshmen say his name, mistress, though I niver heard the like, m'self. The big 'un. I ha' heard Mistress Hawkins call him Hugh Gower, which be a sight easier tae say, but I darena call him so. She disna fancy him, but he did say he'd look after her at least till the herb wooman cooms, and belike till we depart, wi' the dawnin'."

"At dawn?" Alys was dismayed. "We cannot leave her!"

"Master said—"

"Fetch him!"

"But—"

"Do not argue, Ian. Fetch him. Now." She yanked the damp towel from her head, letting the sodden mass of hair fall to her hips. Lifting her chin as she shoved wet strands back over her shoulders with her free hand, she said, "You tell him that not a step will I take outside this tent until I do speak with him. If I die of an ague through not getting out into the sun to dry my hair, the blame will rest squarely upon his shoulders."

Ian left at once, and Alys paced the floor impatiently. There were no more tears. Crying would not help. She needed her wits about her if she was to convince Sir Nicholas to stay.

He came at once, and his mood was clearly precarious, for he was frowning and the first words out of his mouth were curtly spoken. "What is it? Why are you not yet out drying your hair? The sun will soon be too low to do you any good."

"There is a breeze," she told him. "My hair will dry." Then, drawing a long breath, she said firmly, "Sir Nicholas, Ian tells me that you have decided we are to depart tomorrow. I have not yet regained my full strength, and in any case, I cannot possibly leave with Jonet still so ill."

His mouth tightened. "We must go. The king will be in London by now and expects my lads to be close behind him. We are already days late leaving, and as it is, your state of health will prevent our traveling as rapidly as I should like."

"But we cannot leave her! Who will look after her?"

"The herb woman will care for her. We cannot take her, my lady. She would carry the infection wherever we go."

"I will not go without her, Sir Nicholas."

"I have explained that you have no choice. The king—"

"I do not care a rap for your Tudor usurper. I love Jonet!"

"I can make allowance for your affection," he said sternly, "but I warn you, have a care for how you speak of the king."

"Why?" she cried, unable to stem her tears any longer. "Will you execute me for treason when I tell you I hate him?"

"*Nage, mi geneth,*" he said more gently, "but 'tis a habit too dangerous for me to allow you to indulge yourself in it."

"I do not know how you will stop me!" Dashing a hand across her eyes in an ineffective attempt to clear her vision, she added fiercely, "I won't let you take me from her!"

Still blinded by tears, she did not see him move toward her, was not aware that he had done so until his hands came to rest upon her shoulders. Then, certain he meant to shake her, she braced herself, but he did not. Instead he did nothing at all for so long that she became aware of the warmth of his hands on her shoulders, the nearness of his large body to hers. Her breath caught in her throat, and her tears ceased.

The silence lengthened. She could smell the leather of his brigandine and hear muted sounds from the men outside, sounds that soon faded until she heard only his breathing. His hands tightened. She licked suddenly dry lips, and her hands moved of their own accord to his chest, where she felt the small, overlapping metal plates beneath the outer covering of his brigandine. A memory stirred of Neddie, expounding upon new-learned knowledge, trying to explain why the plates overlapped upward instead of downward— something to do with the way a man's chest was formed— but Sir Nicholas's chest, hard beneath her palms, was entirely too close to allow her mind to catch the fleeting memory. He still did not move or speak.

She darted a glance at his face and found his expression puzzling, for he was looking at her almost as though he had never seen her before. His lips were parted; his eyes, like deep-set dark gray pools in the dim light of the tent, had lost their harshness. But as the thought crossed her mind that he must be at a loss for what to say to her, he shifted his weight and the flintlike expression returned. Briefly, his grip on her shoulders tightened, bruising her; then she was free.

He said, "There is no point to continuing this conversation, for I must obey my king's orders just as you must obey mine. Mistress Hawkins will remain behind. Has she family hereabouts?"

Alys nearly mentioned Davy, then remembering with regret that Sir Nicholas was the enemy, and the Tudor's own man, she realized that she could not do so. "Her sister Mary lives in Doncaster, I think," she said gruffly.

"Then we will arrange with the Bawtry monks to get word to her. That must suffice." And with that, he was gone, leaving her to stare after him in dismay. Jonet's sister was older. What if she had died? What if she was away or just could not come? And who would care for Jonet till Mary came? But she had no power over him. Though he had clearly weakened in those few brief seconds, she had no idea why he had done so, and it did not matter, anyway, because he had recollected himself all too soon.

She had to think, and the best way she could imagine to do so at the moment was to proceed with drying her hair. Removing the wet bodice, she found a simple red woolen loose gown in one of the bundles and slipped it over her head. Tying the ties at the neckline, she fastened a colorful tapestry bodice over it, lacing and tying it at the waist with gold cording. There was no need for girdle or belt, and the day was warm enough so that she needed no other wrap.

Outside, she found a sheltered place to sit near the cook fires, settled herself, and began to draw her brush slowly and carefully, as she had been taught, through her tangled, damp tresses. It was a tedious, difficult procedure, one she was accustomed to having someone else—usually Jonet—do for her, and soon her right arm was too tired to wield the brush. She rested it in her lap and wondered what on earth she would do on the journey, not to mention in London, without Jonet.

The breeze was gentle. It scarcely stirred her wet hair. She raised her brush again, not caring now about the new tears wetting her cheeks. She tried changing hands, attempting to brush with her left, but it was not even as strong as the right. After three strokes, she quit in frustration.

"Give me the brush, *mi geneth,*" Sir Nicholas said gently behind her, "or it will never be dry."

She looked up in surprise. He had changed out of his mail chausses into tawny hose and leather buskins, but he still wore his brigandine, and though he had removed his sword and baldric, his dagger was suspended through a metal ring at the brigandine's waist. Wordlessly, she handed him the brush, and if he was not as efficient as Jonet, he was stronger, and he made little work of drawing the brush through her long hair. She was certain he must have things he would rather be doing, but when she suggested that one of his men might replace him at the task, his response was brief, spoken with a curtness she had come to recognize as his way of saying he did not want to discuss the matter.

Her hair was still damp when the evening meal was served, but the night was warm, and she did not fear catching a chill. Before she retired to her bed, she plaited the tresses as Jonet always had, and if the job was not as neat, at least it was done. Alone in the empty tent, she listened to the sounds of the men in the camp, prayed for Jonet, and racked her brain for a way to convince Sir Nicholas to stay at Wolveston until Jonet was well or, God forbid, until she died; but, when morning came, Alys had not even thought of a way to convince him to let her see Jonet.

The camp awoke earlier than usual. Sir Nicholas wanted

to be away by dawn's light, and at that time of year, the dawn came almost on the heels of the dark. There was a fog, but he made it clear that he had no intention of allowing it to delay him.

Alys had no immediate chance to debate his decision with him, for he sent his squire and Ian to wake her.

"How fares Mistress Hawkins?" she demanded, sitting up and clutching the covering close about her.

"She still lives, mistress," Tom said.

"Then I would see her," Alys told him. "I'll go at once."

Ian said, "Nay, mistress, the master ha' said you mun be ready when the others be, or he'll coom hisself tae dress you."

She did not doubt him, but the thought of simply riding off and leaving Jonet was nearly too much to bear. "I do not know how I shall get on without her," she said, choking back tears.

Tom stammered, "*Meistr* knows you be not accustomed to looking after yourself, m'lady, and he did say we are to help you as much as you do let us—Ian and me—even though you be not accustomed to menservants in and out, like most folks be at home. He did say, in sooth, that you do be accustomed to bathing with only other womenfolk about." His expression showed his doubt at such an unusual inclination for privacy.

She smiled wanly. "I was raised in a royal household, Tom, or as near as makes no difference. I was fostered at Middleham, the home of our late king when he was yet Duke of Gloucester and Lord of the North. Things were different there. But perchance your master will find a village woman to accompany me to London."

He shook his head. "Many in the village do be sick, mistress, and he will allow none to go with us, for fear they will carry the sweat south."

Ian added, "Like as not, a village wooman'd no be able tae keep up wi' us, mistress. The Welshman rides swift."

"But I have been ill," she reminded him.

"Aye, but ye're a bonny guid horsewooman, as we saw for ourselves, mistress. A village wooman—"

"Oh, take yourselves off," Alys snapped, exasperated, "but mind, you tell your precious master that if he thinks he will force me to ride breakneck to the Tudor's waiting arms, he had best think again, for if he tries it, I shall make it a point to expire on the way, if only for the pleasure of knowing my death will displease the usurper." When both young men stared unhappily back at her, making no move to obey her command, she glared at them. "Go! Tell him!"

"Methinks," Tom said cautiously, "that we shall tell him you are well nigh ready to depart, m'lady. I have no wish to measure my length upon the ground, and I have no doubt that if I were to speak so rudely to the *meistr*, that would be my fate."

She looked at Ian.

His face, even in the gloomy light of the tent, appeared to have turned nearly the same bright red as his hair, but he said staunchly, "If ye do wish such a message taken to him, mistress, I will do yer bidding, though I have a mither and father at home in Pitlochery who will sairely miss their only son."

She had been ready to tell him that she certainly wanted him to bear her message, but his mournful tone and the heavy sigh that accompanied his words made her bite her lip instead. She knew she was close to tears and had no wish for them to linger. "I would not endanger you, Ian. I will tell him myself."

Relieved, they left her to dress herself, and that was an ordeal, for her traveling dress laced up the back. It seemed as if wherever she turned, her desperate need for Jonet was there to aggrieve her. Twenty minutes later, when Ian called to her to ask if she needed assistance, she replied tearfully and without the least thought for modesty, "Indeed, I do. I cannot manage these cursed laces. Come and see if you can do them up for me."

He came at once and attended to the problem, making no

comment about her tearstained face, and turning afterward to tie up the sumpter packs she had not yet bound. Swinging several of these to his shoulders at once, he stepped toward the entrance.

Alys said gravely, "I do not deserve such kindness from you, Ian, but I thank you for it."

He smiled over his shoulder at her. "You were kind tae me, mistress. I dinna hold it tae your account that the master had me flogged. I didna do m' duty, and he might ha' been a deal the harsher. I willna fail him again, nor will I forget yer kindness or that o' Mistress Hawkins."

When the tent flap fell into place behind him, Alys stood for a moment, staring at it. She had begun to think she might simply slip away during the commotion that always accompanied preparation for a journey. Believing she had only to get to the river where, especially under cover of the fog, she could count on finding one of her old hiding places, she had briefly hoped that such a plan might allow her to stay behind with Jonet. But the thought that someone else might suffer for her actions, as Ian had done before, deterred her now.

Donning her scarlet cloak and her gloves, she stepped outside the tent at last, and saw at once that her plan would not have succeeded. Sir Nicholas was not hurrying thither and yon, shouting orders to his men, as she had thought he would be, but was sitting at his ease upon one large pack, leaning against a pile of others, watching her tent. He lifted a hand in greeting when he saw her, and got to his feet.

"I have bread and ale for you, *mi geneth*," he said. "The fires were quenched earlier, but I would not have you starve."

"Yet you would tear me from the only person who loves me when she needs me most, and . . . and force me to wait upon myself, as well," she added abruptly, certain he would mock so desperate a need for a simple waiting woman. She lifted her chin. "I am not accustomed to such treatment, sir. I shall look a sad sight by the time we reach London, but no doubt that is how the usurper would have all his captives treated."

"You may be grateful that you are not to be treated as most of his captives were treated," he retorted grimly.

Her face paled and her throat went dry. "We heard only that the battle was short, that many did die. Were there so many taken captive? Were they ill-treated?"

He was silent for a moment, then said more gently, "Most did flee at once when it became clear that our forces must prevail."

She ground her teeth, then snapped, "Once it became clear that our rightful king had been betrayed yet again by that toad Stanley is what you ought properly to say!"

Sir Nicholas shrugged. "Richard was a fool to trust a man married to Henry Tudor's mother. And Northumberland did not fight either."

She sighed, feeling the great sadness fill her again. "I know. How glad I am that Anne did not live to see that. She always said her Dickon believed other men could be trusted as he himself could be. His motto was *loyaulte mie lie.'*"

"Loyalty binds me."

She nodded. "He never spoke a word he did not mean. Anne said it was that trait which did make him a great man. But she did say, too, that he thought other men believed as he did in the chivalrous codes of knighthood when they no longer did so. The Stanleys and Northumberland did not. Their word was not good."

"The battle would have gone to us, even had they not stayed their hands," Sir Nicholas said. "Our forces were superior."

"I did not know the Tudor commanded a greater army," she said sorrowfully. "I thought our troops outnumbered his."

"They did," he said, "but the French guns made ours the stronger force. Alack, a woman cannot be expected to understand such matters, but the French artillery is accounted to be the greatest in the world, and their troops well seasoned."

"I do understand," she said, narrowing her eyes. "The usurper's men—your men—did not fight like knights, but like villains. Instead of engaging the enemy fairly, you cut them down where they stood, as though they had been but blades of tall grass in a meadow and your guns the scythes of summer."

"The world is changing," Sir Nicholas said, guiding her toward her palfrey, "and men must learn to accept the changes. In truth, the French guns were only one part of the whole. Had Richard's men not been discouraged by Norfolk's death after the first charge, the course might have been altered. But our men, instead of turning and running as they were meant to do when Norfolk's men charged down the hill, did stay and fight."

"While the Stanleys and Northumberland sat and watched."

"Aye, but even so, in the hand-to-hand fighting the honors were equal. Had we fallen, Northumberland and Stanley would have charged in on the winning side, all the same, but it would have been Richard's side. You must not blame them for doing what English nobles have done for the past thirty years in the wars between Yorkists and Lancastrians. Most have been steadfast only in their pursuit of self-interest, an attitude I doubt will change anytime soon, but his grace, the king, will soon make it clear to them all that their interest lies with him."

They had reached their horses, and he lifted her to her saddle. Traveling, she rode astride, which was safer than riding sideways on a lady's saddle, so it took her a moment to arrange her skirts. Beneath her, the animal stirred restlessly, a familiar movement and one that steadied her. She straightened her gloves and gathered her reins, nodding at Ian, who held the palfrey's bridle. "You need not hold her now," she said.

"Aye, get thee mounted, lad," Sir Nicholas said.

A few moments later, the entire cavalcade was ready, and with a last sorrowful look back through the thickening mist at the tent where Jonet lay clinging to life, and another in the direction of the hillside where the graves of her parents and her "brother" lay, Alys turned away, stifling her tears and trying to force her thoughts ahead, to London. But there was still one more item of unfinished business here.

"We must first go to the priory," she said to Sir Nicholas.

"We ride due south," he said.

"But I have not paid my mass pennies! Even in Wales, surely masses must be purchased for the good of departed souls!"

"Why do you think such things might be different in Wales?"

"I did not say that." But she knew that once again he had somehow fixed upon a vague thought behind her words rather than on the words themselves, that he had chosen to debate her prejudices rather than her accusations. She glowered at him.

He returned a steady look but did not speak.

With a sigh, she said, "I suppose I do believe things are done differently in Wales. After all, when we say a man is wearing Welshman's hose, we mean that he is wearing none at all. Is your land not the harsh, wild place I have been told it is?"

"In some ways it is, but we have our priests and bishops just like anyone else, and I was thoroughly educated at the Blackfriars' school in Brecon. Your masses have been purchased, *mi geneth*. I gave that monk enough coin to protect the souls of your dead for at least a year."

She was grateful but bewildered. She could not understand him. He was not like knights she had known from her childhood, for he did not hesitate to be ruthless and displayed little tendency to treat her as she had been told a true knight treated a lady. Yet he could be gentle, too, and considerate. He had sung to her to help her get well, and he had looked after the dead, going beyond what reasonably might be expected from any enemy, first in waiting until she could be present to bury them (and that despite the fact that he had had no wish to allow her to go near them), and then in seeing to the good of their souls.

"I do thank you," she said at last, quietly.

He nodded, then turned in his saddle to shout an order for a group of men to ride ahead with Hugh, and for other small groups to spread out along their flanks. He kept Alys beside him, and for a time they rode in silence.

At last, with her fears for Jonet threatening to overcome her again, and hoping to delay them with conversation, she muttered, "Mayhap you are right that Richard ought not to have trusted anyone wed to the Tudor's mother, Sir Nicholas, but he ought to have been able to trust Northumberland."

Sir Nicholas shrugged. "I do not know what led to the earl's decision. Belike 'twas no more than that he reckoned to do better with Henry, but in faith, when Richard recognized treachery, he might still have fled in order to return another day. Instead, he tried to snatch triumph from disaster by attacking Henry Tudor himself."

"He did? We heard nothing of that."

"Aye, he did. He had courage, your Dickon, and one must always admire that quality in a man. With only his household knights mounted beside him, he charged at our Harry across the bare heath, right past Stanley's troops. Before Stanley could recover from his shock, Richard cut down Harry's standard bearer, who rode next to Harry himself. But then Richard was unhorsed when the Stanleys recovered and fell on him. He died, and with him gone, the battle was done."

She swallowed a lump in her throat. "We heard that his body was desecrated, that the Tudor forces did mock him and do godless things to him, that they did not bury him in consecrated ground."

Sir Nicholas looked away, but she saw the muscles in his jaw tighten. "I had naught to do with that, nor did my men."

He said no more, but by his grim look and tone she knew he hated what had happened as much as she did.

She said, "We heard, too, that Richard's crown, retrieved from a thorn bush, was placed upon the Tudor's head. He has no right to it, no proper claim! Why, there must be thirty nobles in England with a stronger right than his."

"Henry Tudor has God's blessing," Sir Nicholas said calmly. "He rules by right of battle."

She did not reply immediately, because the road had turned to follow the course of the Trent, swollen beyond its banks by the weeks of rain, and he had reined his mount in sharply to move between her and the tumbling water. When he was beside her again, she raised her voice over the noise of the river to ask, "Is the Tudor such a great soldier?"

"Nay, he is no soldier at all," he replied, his deep voice carrying easily to her ears. "In a head-to-head fight, your Dickon must have bested him easily. Our Harry is a politician, albeit a right canny one, who gathers his forces wisely. After they nearly felled him at Bosworth, he swore to keep to the rear henceforth, and let his leaders fight his battles. His uncle, Jasper Tudor, is a great soldier, and the French commander is another. That pair will be well rewarded."

"As you were," she said.

"Aye, though they may get land, too, and wealth."

Their pace slowed, for not only did the river define the eastern boundary of the road now, but a scattering of trees to the west had thickened to become the dense, fog-shrouded wilderness known as Sherwood Forest, narrowing the track and forcing the men behind to reposition themselves in pairs. There was no sign of those who had ridden ahead, and Alys decided that the men who had been flanking them must have fallen well behind.

"Dickon was a good king," she said sadly a few moments later. "People respected him more than they will the usurper."

"Richard of Gloucester was the real usurper," Sir Nicholas

retorted. "He stole the crown from his own nephew, whom he did swear to protect."

"He did not steal it. Anne told me it was thrust upon him. She explained it all. Dickon did not want the crown. His task was to protect the realm, and when he learned that his brother's children were bastards, that they *could* not inherit, he had no choice but to claim the crown himself."

"That tale was a myth," Sir Nicholas said scornfully, "made up to suit his purpose."

"It was nothing of the sort," she snapped. "Edward was pre-contracted to Lady Eleanor Butler, daughter of the Earl of Shrewsbury, when he married Elizabeth Woodville."

"A very secret contract," Sir Nicholas pointed out. "So secret that none save one man knew of it."

"But Edward's marriage to Elizabeth Woodville was likewise kept secret," Alys said. "Only when he knew the Woodvilles would tell the world, when he knew there was another marriage in the making, with a French princess, did he confess what he had done. And men do say," she added, blushing, "that his reason in both cases was the same, that neither lady would submit to his passion without promise of marriage, and so he gave each one the promise she wanted to hear. 'Twas his way. But though Lady Eleanor did respect his wish for secrecy, Elizabeth told her family, and the Woodvilles forced him to acknowledge her his true queen."

"Why did Lady Eleanor not speak up then?" he asked.

"Edward was king by then, and unlike the Woodvilles, who are naught but underbred Lancastrians, Lady Eleanor was the daughter of a proud Yorkist family. She entered a convent, having no wish to force Edward to acknowledge her, or to live in the world to which he aspired. And, too, she had no wish to create a scandal that would endanger York's proper possession of the throne."

"But she was most conveniently dead, was she not, when all this information was sung to the public ear?"

"Aye, she was dead, but the information came from none other than the Bishop of Bath and Wells, who officiated at the pre-contract. And Edward had locked him in the Tower, which made men wonder, for the bishop was a staunch supporter of York and a man of great integrity. Once the truth was out, men knew why he had been locked up. Indeed, Anne said that a great many things became clear once the truth about Edward's actions was known."

"I warrant that she thought so," Sir Nicholas said dryly.

Alys opened her mouth to utter a scathing retort when with no more than a single shout of warning, a troop of armed horsemen erupted from the forest, swords drawn, lances at the ready.

Sir Nicholas dropped his visor, used the same hand to smack her palfrey on the rump, while he drew his sword with the other. "Ride on!" he shouted at her. "Take to the forest!"

By the time she had yanked her startled palfrey to a halt and turned back, he was in the thick of battle.

# 6

Horses screamed, men shouted, and a trumpet blared, the sounds mixing with the thunderous crash of hooves and clangor of swords and lances on shields and armor. The roar of the river was lost in the din. The horn blew more frantically, and Alys could hear Sir Nicholas's shouts above the others', but she could not understand what he said. Only when she heard another voice screaming orders in English did she realize he had shouted his in Welsh. At least she supposed it had been Welsh. It certainly was not French, for she could speak a little French herself.

She drew the mare a short distance further away from the battle but made no attempt to flee, for she could not imagine that either side would do her harm, since the attackers must be Yorkists. Peering through the mist into the melee, she fancied she recognized one or two who had visited Middleham or Sheriff Hutton, though it was hard to recognize anyone for certain when one could not see the devices on their surcoats. For that matter, only a few of the men seemed to bear such devices.

Suddenly, a group of the attackers broke from the skirmish and charged toward her. Before she had time to think, one man reached out and grabbed her bridle. The palfrey plunged and struggled to be free of him. "Tha'rt wi' us, lassie!" the man shouted. His mail was rusted, and he looked fierce and wild, and in any case, Alys had no wish to ride off with a group of unknown men. Remaining in the Welshman's charge was preferable to that. She slashed at the man's arm with her whip, but the stroke had no effect through his mail sleeve.

"Nay, lass, none o' that!" he exclaimed, snatching the whip from her hand. Kicking his horse to a faster pace, he forced her palfrey to follow. Then suddenly, glancing ahead, he wrenched his mount to a halt again and released her rein, shouting at his men to look out. " 'Ware riders! Get thee gone!"

The group Sir Nicholas had sent ahead with Hugh, having heard the clarion call of the trumpet, had turned back and could be seen now galloping toward them, growing clearer as the leaders emerged like ominous but substantial shadows from the mist.

No sooner did the attacker bellow his warning and release Alys's mare than he and his men seemed to vanish into the forest, but when one of Sir Nicholas's men wheeled his horse to follow, the Welshman snarled at him to hold. Then, giving spur to his destrier, he galloped up to her, reining in with such violence that the stallion reared, pawing the air with its sharp hooves, sending shudders of terror through her mare.

Not turning tail instantly at the sight of him had taken most of Alys's courage, for Sir Nicholas alone, bearing down upon her out of the ragged skirts of fog, had looked more dangerous than the entire rebel force. But when her mare began to tremble, she straightened in her saddle, her anger lending color to her cheeks. "Control your mount, sir," she snapped.

" 'Tis not Black Wyvern you need fear, *Saesnes*," he retorted, "but me. I commanded you to ride on, to take shelter in the forest, but you dared yet again to defy me. You had best learn, and right quickly, to obey when I give a command."

"Those men would not have harmed me," she said, hoping she sounded more sure of that than she felt.

"You know them then?"

"No," she replied swiftly, telling herself it was so, that she had not really recognized anyone.

He looked long at her, then said, "Those rebels no doubt hoped to use you as a pawn against Harry Tudor, but they were fools to attack a larger force, or else mighty desperate. In either case, you ought never to have trusted them."

"I did not!"

"You did not run, though I told you to do so, and I saw no sign when they approached you that you resisted them."

"They took me by surprise!"

"They could not have done so had you obeyed me."

"I am not such a coward as to ride away and hide!"

"You will learn, *Saesnes.*" He raised his mailed fist, and she gasped, thinking he meant to strike her, but she realized even as the fear ripped through her mind that he was merely signaling to his men.

While they regrouped and moved up behind, Alys saw by the expressions on a number of faces that they must have heard every word that flew between Sir Nicholas and herself. She grimaced but was glad to see that other than one soldier whose arm was wrapped in a bloody rag no one appeared to have been badly injured in the brief but hard-fought battle.

When Sir Nicholas gave the signal to ride, Alys scowled at him and muttered for his ears alone, "You have no right to command me, sir. I am not one of your men."

Making no attempt to keep his voice down, he said, "I have been patient with you, Lady Alys, but you will do well to test my patience no further. You were foolish not to obey me. I will do you the courtesy to believe you did not know them, but that means only that you could not have known they meant you no harm. They might have decided that a lady's dainty ear—or her finger or hand—sent to our Harry would encourage him to agree to any demand they might choose to make. 'Tis not unknown for rebel abductors to begin with a lock of hair and proceed from there."

Paling, and distractedly jerking her rein so that the mare

danced nervously in the road, she cried, "They would not dare!"

He grabbed her rein, halting the mare and demanding grimly, "And why would they not?"

She opened her mouth to tell him she believed that at least one or two must have known her brother, but she caught herself before the words were spoken, swallowing them, and after a long, uncomfortable moment, said only, "They would not, that's all."

"Only a liar or a fool would make such a statement," he said. "I do not know which you are, but I'll tell you one last time that you'd best obey my orders. I have only your safety in mind, nothing more, but while I am responsible for you, you must do as I bid or suffer the consequences. Where is your whip?"

She bit her lip at the transition his thoughts had made but answered steadily enough, "That villain snatched it when I tried to strike him with it."

His expression softened. "I see. I wronged you then, by believing you did not resist. Still, *mi geneth*, you will do as I bid next time, for your own safety. If you persist in defying me, I will have no choice but to order your hands tied and place you in charge of one of my men, who will lead your mare and, if we are attacked again, take you instantly to cover."

Instead of cowing her, the threat, coming as it did on the heels of what amounted to an apology, helped steady her, for she could not believe he meant it. No man would treat a lady so. She smiled, looking at him from beneath her thick lashes. "I was glad to see Goorthfan Gower and his men." She tried to match Ian's pronunciation but clearly failed, since Sir Nicholas looked bewildered. "The one you call Hugh," she explained. "Is Goorthfan Gower not his proper name?"

Amusement lit his eyes. "Welshmen do not have surnames as you English know them. In legend *Gwr Gwrddfan* is a strong, tall man, a giant. Tales are told in Brecknockshire, where our homes lie, and in nearby Glamorgan, of a giant called Gwrddfangawr. The men began to call our Hugh the same, because of his size. But you and I do not speak of him now, mistress, only of you."

"Ought we not to ride on, sir?" she asked with an innocent air. "You have spoken often of your wish to travel swiftly."

"I want your word of honor that you will defy me no more, Lady Alys, and I will have it before we ride another league."

"My word of honor, sir? Do Welshmen believe—No," she interjected quickly, realizing that he would only twist her words if she asked such a question. Smiling again, albeit wryly, she said, "Would you really trust my word, sir?"

"May I do so?"

She nodded, serious now, holding his gaze with her own. "If I give it, you may trust it. I know that women are not held to that same high standard by which knights abide, but—"

"In these modern times, *mi geneth,* even knights can no longer be trusted to abide by that standard."

"That is not something about which to speak lightly, sir!"

"I do not speak lightly, mistress, but I do speak truth. I said before that the world is changing, and that manners and morals change with it. One cannot say if such changes are right, but they come to us, and the Lord does naught to hinder them; and so, though 'twas once true that the word of a knight could be trusted, your Richard found, to his misfortune, that that is no longer the case. Harry Tudor uses change to suit his own good. No doubt, when it was expedient, Richard did the same."

"That is not true! Richard was an honorable knight."

"So honorable that none can say what became of the nephew who by rights should have sat upon the throne in his stead, or of that lad's younger brother. So certain are men of their fate, in fact, that none do question it."

Alys opened her mouth, then clamped it shut again.

"Well," he prompted when she remained silent, "have you naught to say to that, mistress?"

She had much to say and much to do to keep from saying it, but the conversation had now taken a tangent too dangerous to explore, for she knew both too much and too little. In truth, she had her suspicions and little else, but since she dared not make those suspicions known to him, she could say nothing. Her thoughts tumbled over one another, without order or sense, and suddenly, for the first time since her illness, she remembered the possibility that there had been men hiding at Wolveston, and she wondered if they had been among the recent attackers.

He was watching her. She bit her lip, regarding him again from beneath her lashes, trying to read his expression, wondering if there might be any way to make him see her side of the matter. Certainly, if that was too much to hope, she ought still to be able to win his good offices by employing the same tactics that had served her before now, both with Plantagenet men and others. She looked down and said quietly, "I do not understand what you want me to say, sir, but you must not speak so to me of Richard. You are no doubt a wise man, strong and brave as a lion—"

"Such woman's prattle does naught to soften me," he said with sudden harshness. "Not even a wench with hair like a raven's wing and eyes like shiny coal would move me with such simpering wiles. You will learn that I do not easily lose sight of my intent. I will have your word now."

"I thought you liked my hair." She was pleased with the retort, thinking she had learned to use his own device against him, to twist debate as he did himself. "You did tell me once that it is like burnished gold and prettier than Elizabeth's."

His stern look did not waver. "Shall I call Ian up here, Lady Alys, and tell him to bring bindings?"

Believing now that he would do it, she swallowed and said with as much dignity as she could muster, "I will not defy you again, sir, not before we reach London."

He nodded without comment, and they rode on in silence.

Without conversation to distract her, Alys had to fight to keep from thinking about Jonet, no doubt dead now. She

found the effort to maintain a calm demeanor was exhausting, and soon realized that she had not fully recovered from
her own illness. When the fog lifted at last, and Sir Nicholas
increased the pace, any inclination she might have had to
initiate more conversation disappeared. But despite his continued silence and the fact that his attention seemed fixed
upon the road ahead, she knew he was watching her. Determined though she was not to let him suspect her growing
fatigue, she nearly exclaimed aloud in gratitude when at last
he signaled to his men to slow again so that some could
dismount and lead their horses for a time, to rest them. She
was having all she could do by then to remain upright in her
saddle.

Knowing that to occupy her mind would help her stay
awake, but wanting to dwell neither upon Jonet nor upon
Sir Nicholas's preference for dark women over fair, or on
the humiliation she would experience if she tumbled to the
ground before all these men, she forced her thoughts ahead
to London. Elizabeth would be there before her, would in
fact—if the Tudor held by the vow he was said to have made
at Rennes Cathedral two Christmases past—soon be Queen
of England. Remembering Sir Nicholas's suggestion as to the
most likely fate of Elizabeth's brothers, Alys realized that
Elizabeth had said nothing about either of them at Sheriff
Hutton. That was not so odd in itself, since Elizabeth preferred to speak only of herself, but as best Alys could remember, no one else had ever mentioned the two young
princes either.

"You are silent, *mi geneth*. Art weary?"

"Aye, a little."

"I thought it must be so, for I had expected you to speak
again by now in defense of the Yorkist usurper. You have
not so much as attempted to deny that he murdered his
young nephews."

It was as if he had looked into her mind, but she refused
to allow him to disconcert her this time. She said calmly,
"King Richard would never have harmed them, sir. He had

been charged with their care and that of the realm by one whose regard he sought and to whom he owed his greatest fealty. He would have protected his brother's sons with his very life."

Sir Nicholas said gently, "It will perchance be better for them if that is not found to be the case, mistress. This country wants peace, but there are rebels who would rally in support of a Yorkist heir if they thought he could supplant our Harry. I doubt he would harm Edward's sons by choice, but if the boys do live, Harry might find himself left with no other recourse."

She said, "They can be no more of a threat to him than they were to Richard, for they cannot inherit. They are bastards."

"I have been told that your Parliament can alter that fact."

"So, too, might they set aside the bill of attainder that prevents Neddie—the Earl of Warwick—from inheriting. You must know he is the son of Richard's elder brother Clarence, but Richard did not harm him. He sent him to Sheriff Hutton with Elizabeth. If you fear for Richard's nephews, sir, you must also fear for Warwick, and verily, the Tudor has no cause to harm him. Neddie is no knightly warrior but only a soft and gentle boy."

"Like your brother?"

"My brother?" But as she spoke, she remembered that he had described the dead youth at Wolveston in just those words. Despising herself for a fool, she kept her countenance with effort and said with another casual shrug, "I do not think them at all similar. My brother was no doubt a scholar like my father, who detested war. Neddie is . . . Well, not to put too fine a face on it, sir, Neddie is a bit simple."

"What about your other brother," Sir Nicholas asked, "the one who had already left Wolveston? Do you still insist, *mi geneth,* that you know not whither he has gone?"

Alys shot him an angry look. "I do not wish to speak of my brothers, sir, and you are unmannerly to ask me such questions. In point of fact, I scarcely know them." That, at least, was true, and she was glad, for she found it uncomfortable to lie to him. But she truly did not know Roger well, since she had met him only on a few occasions since leaving home. Daringly, she added, "I believe you question me only because I have made you think of things you had rather not have pondered. You did not know our king and yet have you attempted to blacken his name, only to justify your own allegiance to his usurper."

"Why must I justify my allegiance? You do little enough to justify your own, and do you not honor Richard for his unswerving fidelity to his brother, King Edward? I should think you would understand that such loyalty needs no justification."

She was silenced for a moment, because she understood that men frequently believed such things. Her own loyalty, regardless of what he might think, was not so easily commanded. She believed in Dickon because Anne had believed in him and because she had loved Anne. But perhaps it was likewise with Sir Nicholas. After all, the Tudor was also a Welshman, though he had spent most of his life in France. Perhaps Sir Nicholas's true loyalty was to Wales, and to the Tudor only because all Welshmen believed he might be depended upon to benefit Wales.

"Well?" he prompted.

She smiled. "Perhaps you are right, sir." It was always better, she knew, to agree with a man until one had marshaled one's thoughts with care. One accomplished two things thereby. One pleased the man in question, thus disarming him, and gave oneself a chance to think of a new and better argument. Then, when the time was ripe, one still might have the last word if one was careful and a bit lucky. A woman in these perilous times had few weapons with which to protect herself against masculine power and authority, so it behooved her to make careful use of the two greatest ones she did possess, her wits and her allure.

With these thoughts in mind, she turned the subject, but it was not long before the conversation died again. She was finding it harder to keep her seat, and Sir Nicholas seemed reluctant to stop the cavalcade to rest properly. Her replies to his comments became monosyllabic, and although the fog had lifted, the scenery around her began to blur. Her eyelids were heavy, and kept drooping, until suddenly and without warning, she slept.

When she awoke, the first thing she noticed was that the sounds around her had not changed. There was still the rhythmic clatter of hoofbeats on the road, the tumult of the river to her left, and the steady murmur of men's voices behind her. She was also still mounted, although her saddle seemed to have grown more supportive. Even as the thought crossed her mind, she realized she was no longer riding her palfrey, or riding alone.

When she realized that she leaned against a broad masculine chest, her head nestled comfortably in the hollow of his shoulder, she started, straightening as best she could to look about her in bewilderment.

"You ought to have told me how tired you were, *mi geneth*," Sir Nicholas said behind her. "I should not have liked it much had you fallen beneath the horses' hooves."

"I am sorry to have troubled you," she replied tartly, straining to turn and look at him. "I suppose it was too much to expect you to stop this procession while I rested."

"There was no need. You are not ill, merely exhausted, and that is not to be wondered at."

"I can ride my palfrey now," she said stiffly.

"I think not. You will do better to rest while you may, and Black Wyvern can carry us both easily. You are no weight at all for him compared to a full suit of armor."

"I am surprised he will consent to carry me at all. He cannot be accustomed to skirts."

"He does as he is bid," Sir Nicholas said with meaning in his voice. "Moreover, he is fully accustomed to trappings of all sorts. Though we do not burden our horses with all the colorful but unneeded ornaments that the English do, we do, even in Wales, have tourneys and ceremonies for which such trappings are worn."

"But you do not wear armor now either, though you travel in enemy lands," she said, voicing a question she had wanted to ask since she had first laid eyes upon him and his men.

She felt him shrug, the plates of his brigandine feeling rough even through her cloak. "We are a cavalry troop," he said. "It behooves us to move swiftly, and heavy armor slows the horses. Therefore do we wear as little as safety allows, much as foot soldiers do. War is not like a tournament these days, *mi geneth*. The victory goes to those who can deliver their blows and move away again with speed to strike again. Moreover, if a man falls from his horse, he does not want to be spitted by his enemy like a tortoise flipped over in his shell."

She encouraged him to tell her more about the methods of war, and an edgy truce was begun between them that lasted until they reached London. The days of travel soon fell into a routine that made them seem to pass swiftly, and the nights passed quickly, too, for Alys no sooner swallowed her supper than she took to her pallet and slept like one dead. She rode her palfrey in the mornings, gaining strength with each passing day, and after the midday meal, she rode with Sir Nicholas, who made no more mention of placing her in charge of anyone else.

He told her of his childhood in Wales, of his studies at the Blackfriars' school in Brecon, and some of his adventures as a soldier. She liked the sound of his voice. With her head against his chest, she let its deep vibrations lull her, and often she slept. Her grief for Jonet faded when she was with him like this, and she felt secure with him in a way she had never felt before. A little unsettled by these feelings, she told herself she merely looked upon their conversations as highlights of what otherwise would be a rather dreary passage of time.

They crossed the Trent at Fiskerton ford to join the Great North Road south of Newark. Although Alys had never been so far south before, the rolling green hills and the rivers soon began to look alike, as did the villages through which they passed. Each had cottages, common, manor house, and tithe barn. And each had its curious citizens, who turned out to watch the cavalcade. Men bowed and touched their forelocks and women made their curtsies, but Alys, knowing they recognized the red dragon on Sir Nicholas's standard and bowed to the Tudor, ignored them. She was tired of travel and longed to be clean again, to enjoy once more the caressing softness of velvet or silk against her skin.

Even Leicester failed to impress her. She had seen York, after all, a vast city of ten thousand people, so she was not likely to widen her eyes at a town of fewer than one thousand folk. There was a fair in the town, however, and she laughed to see the jesters and wished she might visit the stalls and perhaps purchase a new ribbon or two. She was riding with Sir Nicholas at the time, and she glanced over her shoulder at him, but his face was set, his eyes narrowly watching the crowd of people in the streets, no doubt on the lookout for unfriendly faces.

There did not appear to be any. After all, they were south of the Trent now, in a land where people had long been easily swayed from faction to faction, preferring peace to principle. If there was any expression to be seen, it was curiosity, and Alys soon realized it was directed at her, not at the soldiers. The people had seen many soldiers, but rarely had they seen a cavalcade accompanied by a lone young woman in a scarlet cloak.

"I hope they never learn my identity," she murmured to the man behind her. "I would acquire a most undesirable reputation."

"They will not do so," he said calmly. "It is one reason we do not stop in the villages through which we pass, or at houses of religion. I do not want the lads chatting with strangers, nor do I want any of them made vulnerable to an assassin's blade. Had I provided you with waiting women before now, I'll wager they'd have been more trouble than their presence was worth."

"They would have slowed us, to be sure," she agreed, repressing a sharp pang at the inevitable thought of Jonet.

"Aye," he replied, "and more. My men will not trouble you, mistress, but women of a lesser station might tempt them. I want no additional worries on this journey, but I trust you have not been put to a great deal of trouble."

"No, sir," she said. "Your squire and the Scotsman make admirable maidservants." When he chuckled, she was pleased, for there was a warmth and intimacy in the sound that she found soothing. Shifting in her seat, she settled more comfortably against him, having long since given up any attempt to sit bolt upright when they rode together.

The villages were coming closer and closer together, with less expanse of open countryside between them. On the morning of the ninth day of their journey, Sir Nicholas sent Hugh with a party of four men to ride on ahead of them.

"You anticipate danger, sir?" she asked.

He glanced at her, smiling. His helmet was lashed to his saddle, and his gauntlets hung from his sword hilt. "Look yonder, my lady, betwixt us and the sun."

She had been riding with her eyes on the roadway because the sun shone bright enough that day to hurt her eyes. But she obeyed him now, squinting into the brightness. They had come to the top of a rise, and there, just to the right of the brightest rays of the sun, she could see the towers and walls of a city, with a wide silver ribbon of river beyond.

"London?"

"Aye, London." His voice throbbed with pleasure, his eyes gleamed with anticipation, and she realized that, like herself, he had never been there before.

Reaching the gates of the city took longer than she thought it would, and the nearer they got, the more her excitement grew, for it was as clear as could be that this city was much, much larger than York. She had heard that it was the greatest city in Christendom, and now she believed it, for so large was it that it had spilled over its walls to the fields beyond, to sprawling villages unlike any others she had seen. There were not only cottages dotting the land but shops and great houses as well, and large gardens with trees and bright flowers that could be seen from the road. The cavalcade passed between hedgerows and elm trees, beyond which they could see pleasant meadows with rivers and brooks meandering through, and people walking or riding.

Just before they reached the city gates, the party Sir Nicholas had sent ahead joined them again, and after speaking with Hugh, he turned to Alys and said, "Harry is at Greenwich. We are to join him there."

"Where is Greenwich?" she asked, disappointed to think she would not see London after all.

Sir Nicholas grinned at her. "Downriver, *mi geneth,* but we ride through the city, for the only nearby bridge across the Thames is here, and 'tis too wide a river for swimming or for ferrying so many horses. Art fit to continue riding alone?"

"Aye," she said firmly. Not for the world would she ride through London on his saddlebow. But he did not debate her decision and when she glanced at him several moments later, she saw that he was as fascinated by all he saw as she was herself, though he took more pains to conceal it.

London bustled with humanity, for it was ten times the size of York, larger even than England's second city combined with the next three largest in the country. But, for all that, it had not lost its country flavor. Alys remembered York as a pretty city of cobblestones and people, noise and clatter. London was certainly noisy, for besides the shouting of people and the clatter of horses, there was also the clamor of church bells and the cries of street vendors. Houses were built flush to the streets, and many of the streets she saw were narrow, with upper stories hanging over them, just as in York, but there were trees around and behind the houses, and the air was fresher than she had expected it to be, for there was a breeze from the river.

There were birds, too, and flowers and trees everywhere, for they passed pleasant squares of houses built around central gardens. And even when the streets grew more crowded, as they neared the great river Thames, she caught an occasional glimpse of a tree beyond a garden wall. They did not have far to ride, for the city was built in a wide half-moon crescent along the river, measuring a mile and a third from the Tower to Westminster and little more than half a mile from river to northernmost gate.

The river was as fascinating as the rest. There were ships drawn up to great wharfs and others riding at anchor, all towered over by the huge five- and six-story warehouses that crowded the banks. The noise and bustle were greater than ever, but once they had crossed the stone, shop-flanked bridge to Southwark, the populated area soon merged into meadows and woods. Behind them, back across the river, they could see the Tower of London against the horizon, until a turn in the river hid it from sight.

The road took them along the riverbank, where late summer wildflowers made colorful splashes in the green and golden meadows that punctuated otherwise dense woodland on their right. They saw several great houses, and then suddenly, ahead, lay the stone battlements and towers of the palace of Greenwich. The drawbridge over the moat was down, and soon they were clattering over it into the outer court. Alys barely had time to look about her before Sir Nicholas lifted her down from her saddle and they followed a pair of retainers in royal livery into the hall. So far, her impression was that Greenwich was a fortification built to withstand siege, so the hall came as an astonishing surprise.

It was magnificent, gilded and hung with exquisitely worked tapestries. The floors were paved with terra-cotta tiles bearing the monogram of Queen Margaret of Anjou, the spirited wife of Henry the Sixth, whose palace it had been before the York kings had taken possession. The windows were glazed with expensive glass, and sculptors had adorned the pillars and arcades with Queen Margaret's emblem, the ox-eyed daisy called the marguerite.

"His noble grace will see you at once, Sir Nicholas," one of the lackeys said. "The lady is to come with us."

Panic surged in Alys's breast, and without thinking she clutched at Sir Nicholas's sleeve.

Placing his hand comfortingly over hers, he said calmly to the servant, "Where do you take her, sirrah?"

"Why, to the ladies' chamber, sir. His noble grace, the king, will send for her later, after she has rested."

Not wanting the Welshman to guess that she was still afraid, Alys removed her hand from his sleeve and raised her chin, looking at a point beyond the lackey's shoulder. But Sir Nicholas must have sensed her unease, for after a momentary silence he said gently, "Go with him, Lady Alys. I swear by mine own honor that no harm awaits you here."

Comforted more than she would have liked to admit by these simple words, she said, "I do not fear harm, sir." Then, to prove it, she said firmly to the lackey, "I shall want to order a bath at once." Looking back over her shoulder, she had the satisfaction of seeing a delighted grin on Sir Nicholas's face. Its warmth supported her up a broad stairway and along a wide stone gallery, but her poise nearly deserted her when she saw two armed men ahead, flanking a pair of tall doors. They flung them wide at her approach, and panic rose again when the first person she saw upon passing through them was Elizabeth of York.

Without rising from the elegantly carved and gilded armchair in which she sat, Elizabeth said with sweet, albeit right royal, dignity, "Why, Alys Wolveston, how pleasant it is to have you with us again. We hope we see you well."

# 7

Gritting her teeth, Alys made a deep curtsy. Elizabeth's voice had been gentle, filled with concern and goodness. Alys glanced at the other two women in the room, wondering if they knew Elizabeth as she did. She did not know either of them.

The elder, a plump woman with several chins quivering above the neck of her gray-fur-trimmed green dress, had risen to her feet when Alys's name was announced and stepped forward now to greet her. The younger woman, slimmer and garbed in lynx-trimmed rose velvet, also got up but remained standing beside Elizabeth. All three wore simple cap-and-band veils over their hair, instead of the butterfly headdress that had been the fashion for years.

"Lady Alys," the older woman said, "I am Lady Emlyn Lacey, and my companion is Lady Beatrix Ffoulkes. We are pleased to greet you. Her highness has spoken of you frequently and has been looking forward to enjoying your company, however briefly."

"Briefly?" Rising from her curtsy despite the fact that Elizabeth had made no sign that she might do so, Alys looked at her, certain that she detected a glint of malice in Elizabeth's pale blue eyes. Repressing the anger she felt to see her so elegantly garbed in sable-trimmed blue damask, and showing no sign of mourning the uncle she had professed to love, Alys said carefully, "I had been given to understand that I was to be taken into the king's ward. Is that not the case after all?"

"Certainly it is," Elizabeth said more gently than ever, "but surely you do not think that that means our lord king will keep you always in his company, Alys dear. You are to be housed in the Tower, I believe, just as dearest Neddie is, until his sovereign highness has decided how best to dispose of you."

"Dispose of me?" Alys raised her eyebrows, hoping Elizabeth could not see how the words frightened her. "If he does not want me, why did he not leave me in peace in north Nottinghamshire?"

"Do not be tiresome, Alys." Some of the gentleness had gone from Elizabeth's voice, but with a glance at the other two women, she added in her normal tone, "You must know you will be safer in London than at Wolveston, though I trust you were not so foolish as to linger in the city today but passed straight through it."

"We did, but why should that concern you?"

"There is talk of a new plague there. 'Tis why I am housed here at Greenwich instead of at Westminster Palace with my mother. And after taking such care to remove ourselves from harm's way, we would not wish you to infect us."

"I know something of this plague," Alys said, repressing a shiver at memory of her illness, and of her grief for Jonet. "Indeed, I have suffered it myself and have—"

"Do not talk nonsense," Elizabeth said almost tartly. "It is said that strong men fall dead in the streets—men who but moments before were in a state of perfect health. Even the Lord Mayor has died. You cannot have had it and survived to boast of it. You say so only to make yourself interesting."

"If you like," Alys said with a shrug. "In any event, I cannot infect anyone. We rode straight through the city."

"Where are your women?"

"I have none." She hid her sorrow. She would give Elizabeth no new weapons to use against her.

The corners of Elizabeth's mouth tilted up. "Poor Alys.

How very dreadful for you to have traveled so far without proper maidservants to attend you. I had assumed you would be provided with a suitable litter and a host of your own servants."

"There was no litter to be had, and most of my father's servants had died of the sweat. Those who did not were gone from Wolveston, but I was served well enough. My escort was led by a Welsh knight who serves the king. I was quite safe with him."

"Who is this knight?"

"He is called Sir Nicholas Merion."

Elizabeth dismissed him with a gesture. "I do not know him, so he is of no importance. You will want to change to a more proper dress, I'll warrant, before the Lady Margaret sees you."

"The Lady Margaret?"

"The king's mother, of course." There was a flicker of annoyance in Elizabeth's expression, but Alys could not determine whether it was aimed at her for not realizing of whom she spoke, or at Margaret Beaufort, Countess of Richmond and wife of the traitor Sir Thomas Stanley.

"She is here?"

"Of course. Where else would she be? In truth, it was she who decided that I should remove from Westminster to Greenwich, where I should be safer from the sweating sickness."

Alys was surprised, not because Elizabeth had left her mother, or had been allowed to leave, but because she had somehow supposed Margaret Beaufort would be in the north with Stanley. But, of course, the woman would prefer to be with her son. She had fought as hard as anyone to see him on the throne, so it was not odd that she would want to enjoy the benefits of his hard-won position. What was odd was that Margaret Beaufort should express such concern for a daughter of the House of York, unless the rumors of an impending marriage were accurate.

"It is true, then," she said, speaking her thoughts aloud. "You are to wed the king."

"I told you so, months ago," Elizabeth said, not attempting to conceal her satisfaction. "He made a vow, after all, on the high altar of the cathedral at Rennes. Surely you do not think Henry Tudor the sort of man to disregard a sacred vow."

Since under the present circumstances Alys could scarcely express her true opinion of the Tudor, she said carefully, "I cannot say what manner of man he is. I have never met him."

"Well, you may certainly believe one thing," Elizabeth said complacently. "I shall soon be queen of all England."

"It is settled then? When are you to be married?"

"As to that, the date has not been determined, for Henry is not yet crowned king. 'Twas thought best to delay his coronation until the sickness has passed, for he wishes to be crowned with all due pomp and circumstance at Westminster Abbey."

"Perhaps God wills it otherwise," Alys said daringly, "and that is why He has visited such dreadful sickness upon the land."

There was a long silence. The two waiting women glanced at each other, but neither spoke. At last, quietly, Elizabeth said, "You'd do well to guard that unruly tongue of yours, Alys, for the sort of impudence in which you delight will not be tolerated here. Henry is king by God's will, through right of combat. His coronation is a ceremony to please the people, nothing more."

"How can you say he is king by God's will?" Alys demanded, her good intentions overwhelmed by Elizabeth's self-righteous attitude. "He killed the rightful king! And he cannot marry you, in any event, for you are no proper princess. Your father was not properly wed to your mother!"

"That is a lie," Elizabeth said, rigid with fury, her eyes flashing. "My uncle merely used that lie as an excuse to steal the crown from my brother Edward."

"Then what of Edward?" Alys snapped. "We hear naught

of him or of Richard of York. What of them? If 'twas a lie and your family all legitimate, then one of them is rightful king, not your precious Tudor!"

"They are dead," Elizabeth said. There was no grief in her voice, only certainty. "No one speaks of them, and when it was suggested that my uncle might have killed them, he failed to produce them, to prove they lived."

"You know perfectly well that the accusation, made as it was in the French parliament, was naught but French spite against France's greatest enemy; and even so, 'twas merely an observation on the frequent fate of those who aspire to the throne. No one in England paid it any heed, for even Richard's worst enemies knew him to be too honorable ever to do such a thing."

Elizabeth shrugged. "No one hears from them now, so they must be dead. My mother says they are not, but that is because she does not want Henry Tudor to feel too secure upon his throne, for fear he will change his mind about marrying me if he believes my brothers are safely dead, that he will then marry some foreign princess instead of fulfilling his vow to unite the houses of York and Lancaster. But I know he wants me in any case, just," she added with a challenging look, "as my Uncle Richard did."

White-hot anger washed over Alys, blinding her to the dangers of her position, and she had taken two steps toward Elizabeth with no other intention than to murder her, swiftly and painfully, when she was halted in her tracks by the sight of Elizabeth rising swiftly to her feet and sinking into a deep curtsy, her attention riveted not on Alys but on a point some distance behind her. Ladies Emlyn and Beatrix were also bowing low, and Alys required no great astuteness to know that someone of importance had entered the ladies' chamber.

She turned slowly, half-expecting to find herself face to face with the Tudor himself. Instead, she beheld a slender, fragile-looking woman in her mid-forties, dressed in dully red, sable-trimmed velvet, with a white coif and a banded, black-velvet hood. The woman held a jeweled rosary in her right hand, a satin-covered prayer book in her left. Her hazel eyes were hard-looking, like agates, and shrewd. Her voice was like ice when she said, "I shall do you the courtesy to forget what mine eyes have just beheld. You are Lady Alys Wolveston, I warrant. Do you not know how to behave in the royal presence?"

Sinking swiftly to a curtsy as deep as any of the others, Alys told herself firmly that it was no business of hers to suggest that the only person with any cause whatever to claim a royal presence just then was male. It likewise did not strain her intellect to deduce the identity of the newcomer. "Forgive me, Lady Margaret," she said calmly. "I did not hear you enter, or hear your name announced."

"I do not require to be announced," declared the Countess of Richmond. "You may rise, all of you, and explain to me what has transpired in this chamber that Lady Alys Wolveston dares to approach the Princess Elizabeth without due courtesy."

Alys suddenly felt the same way she had felt on certain occasions in her childhood when she had been called to account by her tutor or by Anne herself. Fighting an impulse to look down at her toes, she held her head erect as she straightened, and kept silent. Elizabeth likewise made no attempt to speak, and the silence lengthened until Margaret Beaufort broke it.

"I trust," she said quietly, "that the Lady Alys will recite a few extra decades of her rosary when next she attends to her devotions. Perhaps our Lord, in His infinite mercy, will then see fit to guide her to behave in future with proper submission." Then, without missing a beat, she turned to Elizabeth and added, "I have ordered silks and canvas for you and your ladies. It is our wish that you work some altar cloths for the chapel here. And I have asked your lady mother to allow your sister Cecily to join us. I would not have it said that you were separated from your family by any will of mine or of his sovereign highness. Your mother, too, if she desires it, is welcome to join us here."

"She knows that, your grace," Elizabeth said in a tone of gentle submission. "In faith, she would be the first to express gratitude for your kindness to me, to all of us, but I know that you, of all people, must understand her desire to remain mistress of her own establishment insofar as that is possible."

Alys blinked, controlling her countenance with difficulty. She knew Elizabeth Woodville only by reputation, but she felt a sense of growing respect for Elizabeth of York that she could so easily (and without turning to stone on the spot) describe in bland terms her mother's well-known, implacable obsession for power. Elizabeth Woodville, as Edward the Fourth's queen, had exerted every effort on behalf of herself and the huge Woodville family, gaining honors and positions for them far beyond the station God had allotted to them; for Elizabeth Woodville—as everyone but the Woodvilles themselves had known—had been no great prize for Edward the Fourth to marry, which was why he had kept his marriage secret until he was forced to acknowledge it.

And now that Alys came to think of it, Margaret Beaufort was known to be as hungry for power as Elizabeth Woodville; however, Margaret's ambition was centered in her son, not in herself. If the Tudor had any claim to England's throne, it was only because Margaret had had the same claim before him. But the Lancastrian claim was a faulty one, relying upon the feminine line, and two illegitimate connections at that. The Yorkist claim was both legitimate and masculine. Realizing suddenly that if Edward or Richard Plantagenet were still alive Henry Tudor would be the last man to assume that their illegitimacy barred them from the succession, Alys felt an icy shiver of fear race up her spine.

While she had allowed her thoughts to distract her, Lady Margaret had said something else to Elizabeth, but now she said directly to Alys, "You will be taken to a chamber to refresh yourself and prepare to be presented to the king. He might not see you today, but you will await his convenience.

That he has expressed a desire to see you and to speak to you personally is a measure of his compassion and mercy toward his enemies."

There was an ominous note in Margaret's voice on the last three words, one that prevented Alys from saying anything more than "Yes, Lady Margaret."

"We will hear mass in an hour," Margaret said to the others in a tone of dismissal. As she turned away, the ladies all sank quickly into deep curtsies again.

When she had gone, Alys felt a sense of profound relief and glanced at Elizabeth, wondering if she felt the same. But there was nothing to be read in the princess's expression when she straightened to her full height. She was taller than many women, certainly taller than Alys, and very slender. She wore a blue cap-and-band headdress, and as she turned toward Lady Emlyn, Alys saw that her shining flaxen hair was unconfined beneath the short veil at the back. The fine, straight, silken tresses hung like a sunlit sheet to the backs of her knees. Alys remembered with a glow of satisfaction that Sir Nicholas had said it was too pale.

"Emlyn," Elizabeth said, "prithee, be so kind as to go with Alys and see that she has all she needs to make her comfortable. With no waiting women of her own, she will feel sadly discomposed in such strange surroundings."

For once Alys had no wish to dispute a point of Elizabeth's making. Even before the appearance of the awesome Lady Margaret, the great palace of Greenwich had seemed a foreign place, a place of strangers who wished her, if not ill, at least no great good. Swallowing hard, and despising herself a little for wishing she need not leave Elizabeth, who was at least a familiar enemy, she turned to follow Lady Emlyn from the room.

After that, things moved more swiftly than Alys expected, for the king did not keep her long, awaiting his pleasure. She was scarcely bathed, brushed, and gowned in tawny velvet— a dress that she suspected was sadly out of fashion—her hair oiled and arranged beneath a gauzy butterfly headdress, before the summons came. Lady Emlyn led her across the entire width of the palace to the doors of the presence chamber, then abruptly left her.

Alys was taken into the royal presence by an armed yeoman, which surprised her, for she knew the Plantagenet kings had been surrounded by gentlemen, not soldiers. The yeoman's dress was elaborate enough for a royal palace, however, for he wore green trunks and hose and a white damask tunic embroidered with green vines decked with silver and gold spangles. A red rose, the device of Lancaster, was embroidered in the center of the design, both front and back. Inside the presence chamber, along with a large, murmuring crowd of elegantly attired nobles and gentlemen, there were other armed yeomen wearing the same uniform. The new king clearly did not feel safe, even in his own palace.

Henry Tudor sat in an estate chair on a raised dais. Having imagined him a cross between the magnificent Edward Plantagenet and the devil (with possibly a Welsh touch of Sir Nicholas thrown in), Alys had expected a tall, broad-shouldered, dark-haired man; so Henry, with his long pale face, gray eyes, and straight, shoulder-length light brown hair came as a shock. Though he was royally gowned and bejeweled, and seemed to be above middle height, he looked more like a scholar than a king. His elbows rested on the arms of his chair, and he slumped a bit against its back. His hands, clasped beneath his pointed chin, were thin and pale, not those of a trained knight but more like her father's hands had been. His nose was long and pointed, his lips thin and colorless, and there was a red wart on his right cheek.

Silence fell upon the white-and-gilded chamber, and Alys realized that the yeoman had spoken her name. She sank into her curtsy, bowing her head, hating herself for bending her knee to the Tudor, but unable to contemplate the consequences of refusal. In that moment, she understood defeat as she had never before understood it. And once again she was glad that Anne was dead and had never had to submit herself to the usurper.

"You may rise." Even his voice sounded thin. King Edward's voice had been loud and generally merry. Dickon's voice had been more controlled, firm rather than imperious, except when he spoke to Anne. Then it had always been gentle, even when he had had to deny her wishes. Henry's voice, in her opinion, was that of a rather lazy priest, certainly not that of a king.

She straightened, hoping her headdress was straight and that the skirt of her tawny gown was not caught up somewhere it ought not to be, revealing more of her emerald-green underdress than was seemly. She was hot in the crowded room and would have preferred to have worn damask or brocade, but the occasion had called for the most elaborate gown she had brought with her, velvet or not. She had not thought much of fashion at Drufield Manor, for such thinking was not encouraged by Lady Drufield. But now that she was at court, she would have to find a way to acquire some fashionable new gowns. Perhaps Henry would choose to be a generous guardian.

He had said nothing further. He merely looked at her as though he examined some oddity or other. Not wishing to appear to challenge that look, Alys dropped her lashes a little and allowed her gaze, thus veiled, to wander.

The Tudor was flanked by two yeomen guards and backed by the three standards he called his own—the Cross of St. George upon white silk, the fiery red dragon of the Tudors on white and green sarcenet, and the Dun Cow of the Warwicks—but Alys's gaze swept past them to the attending gentlemen, their splendid clothes making her more aware than ever of her outdated gown and headdress. But then her eye was caught by a familiar smile, and she found herself staring at Sir Nicholas.

If not for the smile, she might not have recognized him so quickly, though he stood in full view. He had put aside his brigandine for a pale gray hip-length robe, lined and turned back with pale rose velvet, its hanging sleeves trimmed with the same. The pourpoint beneath it, worn over his white shirt, was a darker rose. His hat, worn over a cap of emerald green, was a soft, rose-colored beaver surmounted by black and white ostrich feathers. He had cast off his leather chausses in favor of pale rose-colored hose, buff pedules turned down to show their ochre lining, and black shoes. Thinking he looked truly splendid, Alys forgot to keep her eyes veiled and allowed her widened gaze to sweep over him from top to toe.

"We trust your journey was not unpleasant," the Tudor said.

Snapping her head back around to face him, Alys felt heat flash to her cheeks, but she managed to say with tolerable calm, "No, your grace. It was not unpleasant."

"Sir Nicholas Merion looked after you well then."

"Yes, sir." The warmth increased, for she knew Sir Nicholas was watching her, perhaps even laughing at her. The last thought brought with it a strong desire to say that he had mistreated her, just to see what the Tudor would do, but Nicholas had not done so, and she would not lie about that. Indeed, she had no wish to speak further of him, so instead she asked, "What is to become of me now, your grace?"

The king frowned and said curtly, "You are of small import at the moment, Lady Alys. Your father is dead, and your brother is under attainder for his role in the recent unpleasantness. I may yet choose to show him mercy if he submits to me. The Earl of Lincoln, Sir James Tyrell, and many others have already done so. But until then—in faith, until we can arrange to have your unfortunate betrothal to the Yorkist Sir Lionel Everingham set aside by the Church—you will reside in the Tower. At present you have no fortune but what I choose to settle on you, so I must consider if your wardship shall be bestowed elsewhere, and if so, whether the bestowing must result in loss to our treasury."

She nodded. His meaning was clear enough. The likeliest fate she might expect was to become what women so often were, a pawn in the game of power. Anne had lived her life so until she had married Dickon. Anne's father had exploited her to further his own ends, unheeding of her wishes, and it had been little more than good luck that she had ended as Dickon's wife, though she had loved him from her childhood.

At least, Alys thought, she knew now that Roger, Lincoln, and Sir Lionel had survived Bosworth—and a man named Tyrell, as well. She remembered her father saying that name. But if Tyrell was the Tudor's man now, he would be no use to her. Until the king decided what to do with her, she would have no real freedom to act on her own, though she would be housed in a royal castle and treated in a manner befitting her station. The Tower of London had been one of Edward the Fourth's primary residences, and she knew that both he and Richard had frequently held court there. The Tudor would no doubt do the same, so he had chosen to treat her well. He might easily have gifted her to one of his soldiers instead, for she was but one of the spoils of war.

Her audience with him was over shortly after it began, and she returned to the bedchamber allotted to her use only long enough to collect her scarlet cloak before she was taken by barge back up the Thames to the Tower. The barge landed at a wide stair, where a yeoman helped her disembark, and together they crossed the royal wharf and entered through the Cradle gate. The Tower of London was a great deal larger than either Wolveston or Middleham, and she had time to notice only a few gray-white stone buildings and a broad green central lawn before she was taken inside. A short time later, having gone up two pairs of stairs and through a number of chambers and halls, she was ushered into a comfortably furnished sitting room. The yeoman bowed, turned on his heel, and left.

Alys turned from the door and crossed the room to the nearer of the two tall narrow windows. Peering out, she saw that it overlooked the central area and the green lawn.

"Goodness, who are you?"

The rich feminine voice startled her, and she whirled in

surprise to discover a pretty, dark-haired, violet-eyed young woman a little larger than herself. The stranger's head was tilted to one side, and she examined Alys with open curiosity.

Alys, pleased to find that she was not entirely alone, replied in a friendly way, "I am Alys Wolveston. Who are you?"

"Madeline Fenlord. Ought I to know you? I do not recognize your name, but I am shamefully ignorant, or so my father often tells me. To be sure, I have noticed that he mentions the fact only when I disagree with him, but that happens frequently."

Even at Middleham, where Alys and her companions were permitted freedoms generally not accorded to young women, she had known no one who would speak so blithely of filial disobedience, and she regarded Miss Fenlord with blank astonishment. "Goodness, do you dare to disagree with your father? I should never have done so with mine."

Madeline grinned, showing a row of even white teeth. "I am here because I am not only an unnaturally disobedient daughter but a grossly indulged one, and I confess, I was hoping you were just such another, for if you are properly submissive and obedient, we shall scarcely have time to get to know one another before I shall find myself alone in these apartments again."

"You need not fear that," Alys said with a sigh. "I am to stay until my betrothal has been set aside by the pope, which may take months. You see, I have been taken into the king's ward."

Madeline's head tilted the other way, reminding Alys of the way a bird examines an insect before snapping it up in its beak, and she said thoughtfully, "Your betrothal is to be set aside, is it? You are a Yorkist then, or your intended is one."

"Both," Alys said, "although the king did say that many have already submitted to him. Perhaps Sir Lionel is one of them."

"You do not sound as though you are too dreadfully concerned about him," Miss Fenlord observed.

Alys shrugged. "I do not know him, so I have little feeling one way or another."

"I understand completely. 'Tis why I refused to marry the last man my father selected. He is the son of another Devonshire knight, but I knew naught of him save his name, and that cannot recommend him, for 'tis Sir Humphrey Twaddleham. Only think!"

"I do not know the name," Alys confessed.

Madeline chuckled. " 'Tis not that it is unknown, for that would not sway me. 'Tis merely that I have no wish to spend my life as Madeline Twaddleham, like a rhyme sung by a jester."

Alys laughed. "How dreadful, to be sure! I was to have become Alys Everingham. There is naught to complain of in that."

"Perhaps not, though the fact is that I do not wish to marry any man. I think men are, in general, both stupid and childish, and I have no desire to entrust my fate to one."

Alys's jaw dropped. "But what will you do?"

"Do not look so alarmed. I shall not die for lack of a husband, you know. My father indulges me delightfully, as do my brothers. I had four of them. My sisters all died young."

"And your brothers? You say you had four?"

Madeline's brow clouded. "My eldest brother, Jack, died when he was seventeen, fighting for King Edward at Tewksbury."

"Then you are Yorkist too!"

Madeline's smile flashed again. "Generally, although my brother Robert was with Buckingham and the Lancastrians at Shrewsbury. Willie and Alexander are only boys, but Will is a staunch Yorkist. My father is hoping he and I will soon come to our senses. Father believes King Henry is here to stay. In faith, he hopes he may be, for he believes he will bring peace to England, especially if he has the good sense to marry Elizabeth Plantagenet, though Father is skeptical about whether he will or not. Thankfully, Henry Tudor, immediately upon his arrival in London, accepted Robert's service with the late Buckingham as a sign that our family had seen the light early. He was saddened, however, by Father's refusal to force me to wed Sir Humphrey, who chances to be one of the Tudor's strongest supporters."

"Another excellent reason to refuse him," Alys said tartly.

"Do you think so? I confess, I had not thought about that. My father, you know, refused to become involved in the wars. We were a trifle out of the way in Devonshire, so no one demanded his allegiance when it might have proved awkward to grant it, and thus he managed nicely, except for losing Jack, of course. But Robert cares more for the land than Jack did, so perhaps that was why God spared him." She paused, then added with a twinkle, "To refuse Sir Humphrey because of his being Lancastrian would not be tactful, I fear. Indeed, it might be the very thing to make the king command the marriage, and I doubt I can depend upon Father's continued indulgence of my wishes if that were to occur."

"But why has your father not commanded it? I do not understand how you can refuse to do as you are bid."

"Well, I could not, of course, if he did command me," Madeline agreed. "But when Father consented to hear the first suit for my hand—there have been many, for I inherited my mother's fortune when she died after Willie was born—I told him I would enter a convent if he commanded me to marry any man. That was merely to prevent him from threatening to send me to one, you see. I know that is a favorite ploy of fathers, for I have a friend at home in Devonshire who was tricked in just such a way and who lived to regret agreeing to her marriage."

"Goodness," Alys said, "but surely, if the king decides you must wed, you will have no choice but to obey."

Madeline shrugged. "I have to take care, of course, and I confess I was not prepared to find myself in the Tower. Father brought me to London because I begged him to do so, and we were here when the king entered the city. Father went to him at once, of course, to swear fealty, but the king was a trifle skeptical about my family's loyalties, and invited him to leave me as a royal guest until such time as they had shown he could truly trust them. Thus, you find me a prisoner here like yourself."

"A prisoner! But we are not prisoners," Alys protested.

"Oh yes, we are," Madeline informed her flatly.

# 8

Alys soon found that Madeline was right. Though their accommodations were comfortable, they were not allowed to leave the rooms allotted to them—a pair of small bedchambers, the sitting room, and a tiny stool closet. They were waited upon by Elva Dean, a kindly maidservant of Madeline's, who slept on a pallet in her bedchamber, and by two middle-aged menservants, who brought their meals and who were clearly their guards.

The first few days were not so bad, for the two young women found much to talk about. Alys described her life at Middleham, Sheriff Hutton, and Drufield, and learned much in return about Devonshire. She rather envied Madeline her early childhood, for it became clear that she had been greatly indulged by a devoted father and loving brothers. That they continued to indulge her was just as clear. Madeline regarded her present condition as a royal hostage with complacency, assuming it would soon be over. That her father or her brothers might do anything to endanger her safety simply did not occur to her, so secure was her certainty that she was of primary importance to them. Alys wondered what it would be like to know oneself so well beloved as that.

Madeline had not been so carefully educated as Alys, but she could read and write, and had been taught such domestic accomplishments as a husband would expect her to know. She could play more skillfully than Alys could upon the virginal and lute, and she had spent considerable time in London, so she was able to tell Alys many interesting things about the city.

The second day, when they were sitting companionably by the sitting room window, watching yeomen march on the green, Madeline said suddenly, "I tell you, the Tudor is wise to have created his yeoman guard, for his reception in town was not at all what he must have wished. Father and I were there when he was met by the Lord Mayor and aldermen, all wearing scarlet robes. There were a great many citizens on horseback, too, and trumpets were blaring. There were a few cheers but no great outcry of delight, and while many people expressed the hope that he will bring peace to England, others expressed strong doubts that he can do so."

"He does not know anything about being a king," Alys said flatly, certain by now that she need not guard her tongue with Madeline. "He has no experience of government."

"No, how can he? He lived in Wales, of all places, till he was fourteen, and then was carried off to Brittany by his uncle, Jasper Tudor, out of fear for his life if he remained. He cannot have learned much statecraft in Brittany, for surely they do everything differently there. One can only hope, I suppose, that he will acquire some good advisers."

"But who?" Alys demanded. "One cannot doubt that by now he will have executed anyone who served Richard or Edward, and—"

"Ah, but he has not," Madeline said. " 'Tis said that he has kept most of them, declaring that they may continue in their positions until they give him reason to doubt their good faith."

"Has he said so, in truth? How very odd."

Madeline smiled. " 'Twas good sense to set my father and my brothers to oversee collection of the royal rents in Devonshire. They won't betray his trust, and would not, even were I not his hostage, for they hope he can bring peace to England. Doubtless, others want the same, so mayhap the king shows great wisdom."

"He cannot be very wise if he intends to wed with Elizabeth of York," Alys retorted with a grimace.

Madeline chuckled. "He has not done so yet, nor has he repeated his vow to do so. At present, she is safely under the Lady Margaret's thumb, where she can do him no harm."

"When I was in the ladies' chamber at Greenwich, Lady Margaret told Elizabeth that her mother was welcome to join her there." Alys made no attempt to hide her amusement.

Madeline shuddered dramatically. "No one could envy poor Elizabeth with those two fighting to dominate her."

"At present they appear to desire the same thing, however," Alys said thoughtfully. "They both want her to marry the Tudor."

"But first she must be declared legitimate."

"Yes." Alys looked at her new friend, and an expression of understanding passed between them of matters neither wanted to put into words. Alys had told Madeline a great deal, but she had said nothing about what had happened at Wolveston, only that she had become ill, and that Jonet had, too, and that Sir Nicholas had brought her to London without her waiting woman. She had not mentioned the dead youth with hair like sunlit gold, but she knew Madeline was thinking now, as she was, of possible ramifications if the Tudor were to declare the daughters of the House of York legitimate before the fate of their brothers was known. She had no wish to dwell upon that mystery, however, for to do so was frightening, and just thinking about the princes reminded her of Neddie. She knew he must be terrified to be a prisoner, and she could not even get a message to him. She had tried after she had seen him once, walking on the Tower green with a guard. He had looked small and so vulnerable that she had wanted to reassure him. They were both in the enemy camp, after all, a dangerous position in any case, but even more so if yet another faction arose to support a Yorkist claim.

Alys did not confide her worries to Madeline, who seemed blithely unaware of the danger, nor did she say much to her about Sir Nicholas, answering questions briefly when they were asked, and mostly, she knew, making him sound like an avuncular sort of man who had looked after her, and even bullied her. But though she did not speak of him, she thought about him often, telling herself one moment that he was only a Welshman, and one of the Tudor's own, that he was ruthless and brusque, possessing none of the chivalrous qualities she had been taught to admire. The next moment she would recall his dark curls, the way his gray eyes lit with laughter, and the sound of his voice the time she had awakened to hear him singing to her. And when she remembered the touch of his hands on her body, the memory alone was like a gentle caress. She felt an odd warmth, not just in her cheeks, but radiating all the way to her toes, making them curl in her shoes. Having never acquired the habit of confiding her deeper feelings to anyone, she did not discuss these thoughts, her fears, or any odd sensations with Madeline.

On the tenth day of her stay in the Tower, the growing monotony of their daily routine was broken when the elder of their two guards opened the door with no more ceremony than the scrape of his key in the lock, poked his grizzled head through the aperture, and said with brisk kindness, "You've a visitor."

The door opened wider, and to Alys's astonishment, she beheld Ian MacDougal standing beside the guard, bearing a covered basket and an expression of grim purpose. "I willna be but a few moments wi' the lass," he said to the guard. "I shall rap on the door when I be ready tae depart."

Alys stared at him. His manner made him seem older than she remembered him, but once the door was shut behind him, Ian grinned, looking as boyish as usual, and said, "I was told tae mak' yon guards look upon me as a bit of a stern fellow."

"But how came you here?" Alys demanded, delighted to see him and stepping quickly forward to greet him.

He held out the basket to her. "I ha' fresh white bread

and berries, m'lady. The master did think ye'd be glad o'
them."

"Goodness," Madeline said, stepping up behind Alys so
hastily that she caught her foot in her hem and nearly
tripped, "I can smell the bread. It must be warm from the
oven."

"There be jam as weel," Ian said, eyeing her with rather
more approval than Alys thought was seemly.

"This lady is Mistress Fenlord," she said firmly. "Ian is
one of Sir Nicholas's men. But you have not said why you
are here, Ian. Surely, Sir Nicholas did not send you to me."

"Aye, that he did," Ian replied. "He ha' thought ye were
wi' the Princess Elizabeth, and when he coom tae hear that
King Harry ha' sent ye here instead, he recollected that ye'd
nane o' your ain servants by ye, and were fain tae lcarn how
ye were bein' treated. He bethought hisself that ye'd require
a waitin' wooman, and sent me tae discover an that be so."

Alys was pleased to think she might have her own servant,
but a second thought made her shake her head. "Four of us
living in these few small rooms would be too many. Mistress
Fenlord's Elva serves both of us easily enough for the present." Seeing his expression sharpen at mention of yet another
female on the premises, Alys tried to imagine what his reaction would be if he saw Elva, who was comely enough but
old enough to be his mother. Quickly, lest her amusement
show itself and either offend him or stir him to less acceptable liberties, she added, "What we really lack, Ian, is news
from beyond these walls. What can you tell us? Is Sir Nicholas still with the court at Greenwich?"

"He is, but Harry ha' set a date fer his crowning. 'Tis tae
be the end o' next month, and he'll be coomin' tae the Tower
in a fortnight, like all English kings ha' done afore their
crowning. The procession is tae be a grand one, they do say,
from here tae Westminster Abbey, and the master will ride
wi' the king, and is tae be made a Knight o' the Bath afore
the grand ceremony."

"A Knight of the Bath?"

"Aye, 'tis a splendid honor," Ian told her with as much pride as though he were receiving it himself. "They say t' master will wear a long blue gown wi' sleeves lined in miniver, after the manner o' prelates, wi' a knot o' white lace on his shoulder, an' white cords and tufts hangin' doon that the king hisself will remove tae signify that he ha' performed a great service. Och, I wish I could see it, but yon Welsh fool Tom is tae squire him."

"Where is the ceremony to take place?" Madeline asked.

"Here at the Tower, mistress."

"Perchance we shall be allowed to watch," Alys exclaimed, more delighted than she had expected to be at the prospect of seeing Sir Nicholas again. She hid her feelings, telling herself it was only that he was someone she knew, nothing more.

"Och, nay, mistress," Ian said. "They canna allow females, for though the knights will coom tae the ceremony clad all in white and silver, they say there be a night-long ritual when they mun bathe and pray tae prepare for the installation. 'Tis all part and parcel tae be naked then and gowned after."

While he talked, Madeline had placed the basket on a table, and she bent now to examine its contents. Sighing contentedly, she looked up with a smile and invited Ian to taste some of the bread and jam he had brought them.

Clearly taken aback, he recovered quickly and said, "Och, I canna, mistress, though I do thank ye kindly for the askin'."

"There was naught of kindness in my invitation," she told him. "I am famished, and the good smell of this warm bread is like to deprive me of my senses if we do not taste it at once."

His eyes twinkled. "Och weel, there isna any reason tae wait longer, mistress, for I ha' stayed beyond m' time. But I shall coom again, ye ken, for the master ha' said I'm tae tak' me orders from the Lady Alys until he ha' told me different."

Alys felt a rush of warm gratitude. "Tell Sir Nicholas I do thank him for his concern, Ian. I had not expected such kindness from him, though you need not tell him I said that," she added, blushing, "only the part about being grateful."

Ian grinned and said he would remember.

"And come again soon," she said, adding with a laugh, "not only for the bread—though I do confess, the food they give us here is worse than I had with the soldiers—but also for the news you can bring us. We have talked each other out, and although the Lady Margaret Beaufort has commanded that we hear mass each morning, the priest who speaks it and who hears our confessions will tell us naught of worldly matters. And although Elva is allowed to leave these rooms, she dares not venture beyond the castle walls lest they refuse to allow her to return to us. Thus, we have been reduced to making up tales to entertain one another. Verily, Ian, we are like to die of boredom. Do you think you can perhaps procure a pack of cards for us, or dice, or even a board and markers to play Tables?"

Ian's eyes had glinted again when she mentioned Elva, but he thought for a moment, then gave it as his opinion that he might be able to acquire something to entertain them. "For I tell ye true, mistress, King Harry likes a game or twa hisself. Plays tennis and Tables, and gambles the night away over cards, for all they say he be a close mon wi' his money. Like as not, I'll find something o' the sort tae bring ye. Will there be aught else?"

She could think of nothing just then, but by the time he returned, less than a week later, she and Madeline, with Elva's assistance, had thought of a number of commissions for him. He met Elva that day, but if he was disenchanted, Alys thought he would recover swiftly, and was sure of it when, during that same visit, he chanced to mention a comely kitchenmaid he had met. He brought them a pack of cards that second visit and an intricately decorated Tables board complete with ivory markers on his third. The next time he came, a fortnight before the king's coronation, he brought a package containing colorful wools, two rolls of tapestry canvas, and several carefully drawn patterns, including the red Welsh dragon and the cross of St. George.

Alys, examining these and noting that he had left nothing to chance but had also procured for them a well-supplied sewing box, looked up at him with a teasing grin. "Never tell me that Sir Nicholas sent these, Ian, for I should not believe you."

"Nay, mistress, 'twas the Lady Margaret sent them. Yon louts ootside your door had them and was arguin' over which was tae tell ye o' her command tae mak' kneeling cushions fer yourselves. When the king cooms tae reside in the Tower, ye're tae be allowed tae attend mass in the chapel, and her ladyship's yeoman did say his mistress commanded him tae say it would be a grand gesture an ye were tae add tae the chapel's decoration."

"I'll warrant she did," Alys said dryly, "but I shall not kneel upon the Welsh dragon. I might put my foot upon it—"

"Alys!" Madeline's eyes were alight with laughter, but her next words were nonetheless cautionary. "You must not speak so, lest someone hear you who will carry word to her ladyship, or worse, to the king."

"The Tudor cannot think we love him," Alys said grimly.

"No, you unnatural girl, but I have no wish to spend the rest of my maidenhood in these three paltry rooms. If agreeing to kneel on the wretched man's dragon will get us out of here—even if it be only for one mass—I tell you, I will stitch both our cushions myself. When does the king come to the Tower, Ian?"

"In ten days' time, mistress. He dines with the Archbishop of Canterbury at Lambeth Palace and rides from there in a grand procession. The next day will see the installation o' the Knights o' the Bath, and his crowning follows on the Sunday."

The two young women noted an increase of activity on the green in the days that followed, and they were able to observe from their window the arrival of the royal procession. However, if they hoped to view any part of the ceremonies that followed, they were disappointed; and, when they accompanied their guards to the chapel for mass that Saturday morning, expecting to meet ladies and gentlemen of the court at worship, they were thwarted again, for they were taken to a private pew before any but a few Tower retainers had entered, and were not let out again until the others had departed. They could not even look around during the service, because magnificently carved privacy screens prevented them from seeing anyone but the priest in his pulpit.

Alys was more disappointed than she wanted to admit, for she had hoped to catch a glimpse of Sir Nicholas in his robes of the Bath. Thus, she was elated when one of their guards put his head inside the door, an hour after they had left the chapel, to inform them that if they wished to watch the royal procession leave for Westminster they had best make haste. Having expected to see, at most, a colorful gathering of people and horses on the green, they agreed with alacrity to accompany their guards to the castle ramparts, from which they could see the entire procession as it passed through the gates, into the streets beyond.

The day was a splendid one, clear and sunny, and the procession as grand as anyone might have wished. The two guards were unable to identify anyone except the king's noble grace and two men preceding him, the new Lord Mayor of London and the Garter King of Arms. The king, bareheaded and clad in a gown of purple velvet edged with spotted ermine, and a richly embroidered baldric, was borne in a litter beneath a royal canopy supported by four knights on foot. Crowds lined the street, shouting and clapping, and long before they dispersed, Alys and Madeline were back in their sitting room. Not until the following day, after Henry Tudor had been anointed and crowned King of England, when the procession returned for the coronation banquet, were they able to discover what had transpired at Westminster.

Elva brought them the news then, for little else was being talked about in the castle. When she returned to them after an absence of nearly two hours, both young women fell upon her to hear whatever she might tell them. Swelling with a sense of her own importance, she accepted a seat on a back stool with every indication of being about to narrate a long and fascinating tale. "They do say that 'twas all most wondrous and the words spoken over him was the same as spoken over King Richard and his Anne."

"But how could that be?" Alys demanded. "He has no queen."

Elva waved a hand in a dismissive gesture. "They did say that all the bits about the queen was left out, but the rest was all the same. And they do say old Archbishop Bouchier had all he could do to splash the holy oil on the king's highness, and struggled to hold onto the crown till it rested on his head. He's right ancient, is the archbishop, but there was others there to see to the rest of the ritual. Even"—she paused for effect—"the Bishop of Bath and Wells was there. He did lead the whole business. There be a word for that, mistress." She looked inquiringly at Madeline, but it was Alys who responded first.

"He officiated." Her expression was thoughtful.

Elva nodded, pleased to have been so quickly understood, but Madeline frowned, saying, "It was the Bishop of Bath and Wells who proved King Edward was never properly married to Elizabeth Woodville, was it not? Because of him, Elizabeth of York was declared illegitimate. Can it be that the Tudor means to remind everyone now that she is no fit queen for him?"

Elva had no answer for that, nor did they expect one from her. She went on, almost as though she had been present in the abbey herself, to describe how Jasper Tudor, the king's uncle and newly created Duke of Bedford, had borne the royal crown, and how Thomas Stanley, his father-in-law and newly dubbed Earl of Derby, had carried the sword of state. She described the consecration and crowning, the taking of the oath, and the aftermath when Henry, king now by grace of God, accompanied and supported by his entourage, had emerged from the abbey and shown himself to the crowds still lining the streets back to the Tower.

At the banquet yet to come, she told them, the king's uncle would appear on horseback trapped with ermined cloth of gold, and the hereditary king's champion would ride his horse into the banquet hall to challenge all comers just as he had done for King Richard two years before. Here she paused again, as aware as her mistress and Alys were of the extreme irony of such a challenge.

"It don't hardly seem right," she added with a sigh.

"None of it seems right," Alys agreed.

When the coronation festivities were over, the king and the court returned to Greenwich, and what little news the two young women had of the world outside the Tower walls came from Elva, who had made a number of friends among the retainers there, and from Ian, who not only continued to visit, but who informed them that he had taken lodgings close by the Tower gate.

"But what of Sir Nicholas?" Alys demanded anxiously.

"He ha' gone into Derbyshire, mistress, tae look into reports of trouble there fer the king's highness."

"Without you?"

"Aye." He gave no further explanation, and Alys was reluctant to demand one, fearing that he was somehow at outs with his master. It occurred to her that perhaps, being Scottish, Ian felt less loyalty toward the Welshman than his own followers would feel. In any case, she was grateful to him for his loyalty to her. Just knowing that there was someone nearby who cared about her made Sir Nicholas's absence and the lack of news regarding herself and Mistress Fenlord both easier to take.

They heard much about the doings of the king in the weeks that followed, but very little of what they heard interested them, for it was all political and had nothing to do with either Madeline's family or the setting aside of Alys's betrothal; therefore, there was nothing to suggest a possible end to their confinement. Even Ian, with Sir Nicholas no longer at court, had few means by which to pursue answers to these entirely personal questions, although he informed them cheerfully that since he had made a number of feminine conquests among the palace maids, he could expect to hear some news or other before long.

When they received a large parcel at the end of November, containing bolts of splendid fabrics and accompanied by a message from the Lady Margaret informing them that seamstresses were soon to assist them in making new gowns for themselves, Alys commanded the messenger to wait while she composed a careful note of thanks and an even more carefully worded request for enlightenment as to their future. A reply came with unexpected swiftness, advising them both to place their faith in God and the king's sovereign highness, and to remember that curiosity was an unbecoming fault.

Despite the fact that so far Ian had succeeded in bringing them only information that was widely available, Alys pressed him to do better, with the result that he returned three days later, not with news of their own fate but with word that Lady Margaret was as set as ever on seeing her son wedded to Elizabeth of York.

"Why do you say so?" Alys demanded. Since she and Madeline had spent the entire morning after mass being measured by two tight-lipped women sent by Lady Margaret, who spoke of nothing but fit and style, frustration lent sharpness to her tone.

Ian grinned. "One o' Lady Margaret's own women ha' a bonny wee lass servin' her, and the women do talk amongst themselves, ye ken. The lass ha' told me the king can hear the Lady Margaret when he shuts his ears tae the rest, and the princess, she says, hasna much tae say at all. They do say, too, that 'tis passing strange but the king be pardoning most o' them as fought agin him from the north." He wrinkled his brow, trying to remember what he had heard. "Only Norfolk, Surrey, Lovell, and some few other northern knights ha' actually been attainted, as yet."

"The dead ones, then," Alys said sadly.

"Nay, mistress, not all are dead. Lovell lives and ha' taken sanctuary, they say. Others, too."

"Francis Lovell lives?" Her brother had been with Lovell. "Roger Wolveston," she said quickly, "have you heard aught of him? He would be Lord Wolveston now."

"Nay," Ian said. "I dinna recall hearin' the name, so I doot the lassie or anyone said it. I'd ha' recalled Wolveston."

She sighed. For a brief moment she had felt a surge of hope that if her brother truly did live, he might have submitted to the king, and she might no longer be kept in ward.

Ian said slowly, "They do say, mistress, that there be dunnamany attainders against them that did fight but ha' not yet submitted, and too, that Harry's patience is no wi'oot limit."

"If they submit soon, he will pardon them. Is that it?"

"Aye, so they say. But mayhap the pardons willna gi'e them back their lands, ye ken, only their lives and freedom. They say Harry ha' but three wishes—tae rule England, tae gather wealth for his coffers, and tae bring peace and prosperity t' the land."

He reported more as the days passed, and Alys and Madeline feasted on the rumors, hearing one day that the king would not wed Elizabeth, the next that he would. No one mentioned the princes of the House of York. Few people, Ian said, seemed to care about them. Most were opposed to more fighting and seemed inclined to support a union of Lancaster and York.

Matters came to a head at last in December, when Parliament demanded that the king honor his vow to wed Elizabeth of York. A tentative reminder that permission had not yet been received from the pope was dismissed as inconsequential. Parliament, speaking on behalf of the people, insisted on the wedding, and relief was expressed everywhere when Henry Tudor agreed, announcing at last that it would take place in little more than a month.

Two days afterward, Alys and Madeline received word from the Lady Margaret that the king had appointed them maids of honor to his bride. They would remain lodged in the Tower until after the wedding, when it became appropriate for them to take up their new duties, but they would be released in time to take part in the festivities at the palace of Westminster.

Madeline received the news with her customary optimism and good cheer, giving it as her opinion that the Tudor must have seen for himself by now that the men in her family— so long as it was in their best interests, and hers—were entirely to be trusted. Alys's feelings were mixed. Release from the Tower meant she would be likely to see Sir Nicholas again, which would be pleasant, and at court she would more easily discover her brother's fate. But glad though she was to know that their confinement would end soon, she could not look forward to serving Elizabeth of York. The very thought set her teeth on edge.

# 9

The long-awaited ceremony was over, and the bride and groom, having walked the short distance from Westminster Abbey, entered Westminster Hall to a blare of trumpets and a thunder of cheering and applause from the multitude gathered to greet them. The palace of Westminster, built by Edward the Confessor and thus even older than the Tower of London, had been used by William the Conqueror as a place where he might be seen in his glory with all the trappings of state about him, to remind potential troublemakers of the king's power; and the grandeur of Henry Tudor's wedding procession made it clear that he intended to make similar use of it. The high gold crown he wore, his rich clothes, and the colorful, enthusiastic crowd of supporters surrounding him and his bride were intended, unquestionably, to create a sense of awe in the minds of all beholders.

The hall was the largest in England, perhaps in all Europe. Its soaring hammerbeam ceiling, adorned with carved and gilded angels and boasting open arches seventy feet across, was a marvel of engineering, and provided a magnificent canopy for the grand assemblage below. Around the perimeter, trestle tables had been set up for the feasting, and the royal table, draped with white linen and bowed beneath the weight of the gleaming silver plates and vessels, stood on a dais at the far north end. Not until the king and his bride stepped onto the dais could Alys or Madeline, standing on tiptoe together near the center of the crowd, see either of them clearly.

The king wore a long purple gown over a doublet of vermilion silk shot with gold thread. He continued to bear the heavy state crown of Edward the Confessor on his head. No one looked long at him, however, for at his side, Elizabeth of York stood proud, serene, and beautiful in a close-fitting kirtle of pale blue damask that matched her eyes. It was worn beneath an open white cloth-of-gold gown, trimmed with ermine and nipped in above her hips with a loose belt of gold plates set with sapphires, rubies, and diamonds. Her flaxen hair, beneath a jeweled golden caul and coronet, flowed straight and shining down her back to her knees. Though it hung loose as befitted a virgin bride, she had followed the newest fashion by having it combed tightly back from her forehead but with a little left showing at the front edge of her caul. Neither her forehead nor her eyebrows had been plucked bare, as had been the custom for so many years.

Alys, sighing, said, "She is lovely."

Madeline chuckled and said in an undertone that just reached Alys's ears, "All brides are lovely, but I do not think that fact alone a sufficient reason to emulate them. No husband can be counted upon to treat me as kindly as Father does."

"You wait," Alys retorted. "You will have no more choice than anyone else. All women marry unless they take an oath of chastity or become nuns, and I have known you long enough now to be certain you will do neither. Therefore, you will marry."

Madeline shrugged. "Mayhap you have the right of it, but I have been of age for seven years now and still am unwed, though I know of at least one heiress who was married for the third time when she was only eleven, a full year *before* she came of age."

Alys shook her head in amused exasperation. "Yes, and Anne Mowbray was married to Prince Richard of York when she was six and he only two. But fortunately, neither of us is so great an heiress as that. Indeed, my wardship would be a good deal less bearable if I were, because the Tudor would use it to his own benefit by awarding it to one of his supporters, who would use my fortune as if it were his own until duty commanded him to see me properly provided with a husband."

Madeline grimaced. "If my father ever threatened to sell my wardship to anyone, I *would* enter a convent, for I have heard awful tales of such things. When a girl is sold like that by her parents she has no recourse until she reaches her majority. Then she might be permitted to sue her guardian for disparagement if he has forced her to wed below her degree. However, she can say nothing even then about what he might have done with her fortune in the meantime. I think it is disgraceful that wardships can be bought, sold, and fought over like precious jewels while the poor ward is passed from nobleman to nobleman with no more say in the matter than a bolt of cloth. Father would never use me so."

Before Alys could point out that any female who attempted to foretell what a male might do was asking for trouble, a familiar, albeit quite unexpected, masculine voice sounded behind her.

"Lady Alys?"

She turned sharply, and found herself face to face with Sir Nicholas Merion. His eyes widened at the sight of her, and when his gaze swept her like a caress, she called down blessings upon Lady Margaret's seamstresses. Her gown of sable-trimmed, emerald-green velvet over an underdress of gaily embroidered white satin, fit her slender body like a second skin from her shoulders to her hips, where it flared gently to soft folds around her feet. Green-satin slippers peeped out when she lifted her skirt to walk, and her hair was concealed beneath a simple matching veil. She knew the costume became her, but she had not known it would please her so to see appreciation in his eyes.

She had not thought of him for nearly a day, nor had she

expected to see him, for when Ian had last mentioned him, only days before, it was to say that he was in Shropshire and that Ian did not know when to expect his return. He was dressed as magnificently as any man present, in tawny velvet and blue brocaded satin. The hard muscles in his thighs flexed beneath his tight tan hose when he shifted his position, and feeling telltale warmth leap to her cheeks at the pleasure of seeing him, Alys hastily found her voice and introduced Madeline, whose gown of violet-colored damask Sir Nicholas did not appear to notice.

When he bowed over Madeline's hand, Alys bent closer to him so that he would hear her over the noise of the crowd and said, "She has been my fellow prisoner, sir. I must tell you we were released from the Tower only today, for these festivities. 'Twas said the order to free us came from the Tudor, but 'tis my belief 'twas the command of the Lady Margaret, for she commands the very air we breathe here, does she not?"

Sir Nicholas straightened and glanced hastily around, muttering sternly, "Will you never learn to keep your tongue behind your teeth, you foolish wench? Should such words as those be repeated in the wrong quarter, you would find yourself right speedily back whence you came." His deep voice carried easily to her ears, though she doubted anyone else could hear him.

Nothing daunted—in fact, rather pleased to have aroused him again—she replied sweetly, "I have no objection to returning to Wolveston, sir. Perhaps I shall even be so fortunate as to be accorded your escort for the journey."

"Believe me, mistress, I did not mean Wolveston," he retorted. "Nor would such a journey be pleasant, for I have no wish to spend more time as a lady's maid or guardian."

"Why, how unfair, sir, when 'twas not you but your squire and one of your Scottish mercenaries who did attend me."

He fixed her with a basilisk eye and said with calm intent, "I approached you just now, mistress, because you appeared to be without escort, and now that the marshals have begun to seat everyone, I had thought to offer to accompany you to table. However, if you would prefer to look after yourself—"

"On no account would we prefer such a fate, Sir Nicholas," Madeline interjected, laughing and sweeping her train up over her arm in a broad gesture that threatened to flatten a gentleman moving past her. Unaware of his peril, she added merrily, "Before Alys can be so absurd as to send you away, pray allow me to inform you that we were hustled from the Tower before we had dined and have not been offered a single bite since our arrival at Westminster. Therefore, since I at least am in danger of perishing from starvation, you may certainly take us to table."

Sir Nicholas had not taken his eyes from Alys, and he continued to hold her gaze with his when he said gently, "Does my suggestion meet with your approval as well, my lady?"

Something in his expression stirred the imp that lurked beneath the surface of her well-practiced ladylike demeanor, and she said saucily, "A man who truly desired to escort us would have been more chivalrous in his approach. Such a man would have paid us compliments before he begged the honor of our company."

"I'll warrant he would," he replied calmly, still looking directly into her eyes.

Her bosom swelled with indignation. "If you do not wish to escort us, Sir Nicholas—"

"I did not say so. On the contrary, I said—"

"Have mercy on a starving woman, the pair of you," Madeline exclaimed. "I shall swoon from hunger right here on the spot if I am not instantly granted sustenance."

With a glint of amusement lighting his eyes, Nicholas turned to her at last and said, "Forgive me, mistress. Will you take my arm?" Holding out his right forearm, he glanced at Alys again when Madeline had placed her hand upon it, and said dulcetly, "Do not get lost in the crowd, my lady. If you stay close behind us, 'tis possible you may yet get your supper."

Rendered speechless, and sorely tempted to stay where she was just to teach him a lesson, Alys nevertheless had no desire to be left on her own in the increasingly boisterous throng. Snatching up her skirts, she hurried after them, repressing a compelling urge to grab hold of Madeline's skirt. She did not want to lose them in the crowd before a marshal could find places for them at one of the long trestle tables.

The whole company was seated at last. Throughout the hours of feasting they were entertained by jesters, singers, players, and musicians, who performed in a clearing in the center. Alys enjoyed them all, but she was conscious the whole time of Sir Nicholas beside her, talking mostly to Madeline. He made no effort to engage Alys in conversation, although he made an occasional polite comment and checked from time to time to be certain she had what food she needed. The gentleman on her other side spoke to her often, and politely passed sauces when she required them, but the hours passed slowly. She was glad when at last it was time for the royal couple to depart.

When the king stood and extended a hand to his bride, Madeline, who had been conversing gaily throughout the evening both with Sir Nicholas and the gentleman at her other hand, said suddenly, "Are we all expected to follow them, do you suppose? At home, when we have a wedding, everyone crowds around the marriage bed to drink toasts, shout advice, and fling gloves at the bride and groom. The first man who hits the groom's nose is said to be the next to marry, and the same is said for the first lady to hit the bride anywhere at all."

Speaking across Sir Nicholas, Alys said tartly, "The same customs prevail in the north, Madeline, but one does not throw things at royal persons. 'Twould be unmannerly."

" 'Twould be treason," Sir Nicholas said, grinning at one and then at the other. When they had risen to their feet with the rest of the company, he added, "The king has decreed that there shall be no unseemliness tonight. All men are to be barred from the bedchamber as soon as his bride arrives. She will be brought to him by her women—only the married ones, of course—and he will receive her in his shirt, with his gown wrapped around him. She, too, will wear a gown. Then the bishop and chaplains will enter to bless the royal marriage bed, after which every man but the king must leave the room. Harry has also decreed that there shall be no posset-drinking in the bedchamber."

"Goodness," Alys said. "I hope he will not be disappointed if his orders are not obeyed. Many of the men are ape-drunk already, and I have never heard of a wedding where there was not a great deal of drunken foolishness to be tolerated. If the men are barred from the bedchamber, surely they will dance and carry on in the gallery and pound on the door of the chamber."

"All will be as the king commands," Nicholas said calmly, raising his cup when everyone else did to drink a toast to the bride and groom.

"I suppose it will," Alys replied with a sigh, setting down her cup. "Do you go with the king's men to the chamber, sir?"

He nodded, looking at her a little more sharply. " 'Tis part of my duty to see his orders obeyed. You look tired, my lady. When do you take up your duties with the princess?"

"We join her ladies in waiting on the morrow."

He was silent for a long moment, gazing at her as though he would speak again, as though, she thought, he meant to warn her to behave herself. The thought irritated her, but when she stiffened defensively, intending to give as good as she got, he merely nodded again and disappeared into the crowd, leaving her with her emotions in a tangle. One moment she hated him, the next she was annoyed when he paid her no heed. She reminded herself that he was only a Welshman, a henchman of the enemy, but this time, the familiar phrases seemed to have no meaning.

Knowing that it would be unwise to remain with the revelers without a gentleman to protect them, she and Madeline retired soon afterward. They had each been assigned a tiny chamber on the ladies' side of the palace, and they arrived first at Madeline's, where Elva was waiting. Alys reluctantly bade her friend good night. Though she was glad that all the ladies in waiting did not sleep in a common room, as the girls at Drufield had done, she was not looking forward to the loneliness of a solitary bedchamber after weeks spent in Madeline's company.

When Alys turned away, Madeline said, "Shall I send Elva to help you when she is finished with me?"

Looking back, Alys shook her head. "I have been assigned a chambermaid who will undress me. Elva can stay with you." Suddenly she missed Jonet more than she had in months, and turned swiftly away again, her eyes stinging with unshed tears.

The maidservant who awaited her in her own chamber, farther along the gallery, had taken the liberty of lighting a tallow candle and the little room was filled with the acrid odor, and full of shadows as well, for the candle cast but a dim glow, and was neither welcoming nor as comfortable as the rooms she had shared with Madeline in the Tower. Still, it was better than what she had had at Drufield, where the two other young women who fostered there and shared her bedchamber had made no secret of the fact that they disliked her as much as their mistress did.

When she entered, the maid scrambled up from the pallet on the floor where she had been sitting. "There be water for washing on the stand, m'lady," she said in a hushed voice.

Alys scarcely had had time to note more than the girl's plump figure and fair complexion earlier, for she and Madeline had dressed at the Tower and, upon their arrival at Westminster, had been shown to their bedchambers only long enough to note their location before being hustled down to the hall where the festivities had already begun. Alys had not even had a chance to learn the chambermaid's name. She asked now.

"I be Molly, m'lady, Molly Hunter. I'm ter see t' yer clothes and ter fetch and carry fer ye. They did say ye'd no servants o' yer own. Ladies in waiting mostly have dunamany servants, 'n some even have ter send some away. 'Tis a pity ye've none, but I'll do what I can fer ye."

"Thank you, Molly. Will you sleep here?"

"Bless you, mistress, but I've me own pallet in the servants' hall. I'll be back here come mornin', afore prayers."

Alys nodded. She had mixed feelings about the arrangement. She did not really want the girl to stay, but neither did she want to be left alone. It was the first time she had ever had a bedchamber all to herself, although she knew it was no longer such an odd thing for a person to sleep alone, not so odd as it had been in her father's youth, at all events.

Taking what comfort she could in knowing that Madeline was not far away, she allowed the maid to undress her and prepare her for bed, then dismissed her. Blowing out the lone candle was difficult, however, for it plunged the room into a blackness far beyond what she expected, and she realized then that the only window was high up in the wall and very small. With a sigh, she lay down, pulled her quilt up, tucked her hand beneath her cheek, and let the tears come. Not long afterward, she slept.

Molly woke her early in the morning with a ewer of water for washing and an offer of ale and beef to break her fast. Alys assented gratefully, and when the maid had gone again, jumped out of bed, shivering when her bare feet touched the stone floor, and raced to splash water on her face and to wash her hands.

When Molly returned with a wooden trencher piled with beef and bread, and a mug of ale, she placed them on a low boxlike table she dragged away from the wall. Ladies in waiting were not provided with such luxuries as chairs, but there was a joint stool, and Alys, wrapped in a warm pink woolen robe, sat upon the stool to eat, watching while Molly searched through her things to find appropriate clothing for her.

Her belongings had been unpacked and placed in a large chest near the wall opposite the door. Molly first shook out an apple-green wool kirtle; then, placing that carefully on the narrow bed, she got out a darker green velvet gown trimmed with lynx. Both were garments Alys had had for some time, but their lines were simple, and the colors became her, so she made no objection to Molly's choice, merely asking her to find a clean smock as well, since she had slept in hers and it was no longer fresh.

When she was dressed, she sat down again on the joint stool to let Molly attend to her hair. This task was simple, requiring only that what little showed look smooth and neat and that her headdress be clean and modest. She knew from experience that Elizabeth would take exception to any garment more grand or more costly than what she wore, and she had no wish to draw the princess's ire at this, the beginning of their new relationship. Thus, when Molly unearthed the wire frame for her gauzy butterfly headdress, she did not object. That the style was going out of fashion would render it acceptable in Elizabeth's eyes, but it was becoming to Alys and would serve until she could get settled in and try to acquire some new things. Since she was not by any means certain of how that last task was to be accomplished, she thought it best to tread softly for a time.

When she was dressed, Molly advised her to go along to the princess's chamber as quickly as possible, lest she be late for morning mass.

Alys sighed. She had always thought herself properly devout but was beginning to think that the custom prevailing at court would require her to spend a good deal more time on her knees than she was accustomed to spend there. She doubted that the notion was Elizabeth's. She did not remember Elizabeth as being more than ordinarily pious in her habits.

"Hears mass three times a day, does the princess," Molly said. "The Lady Margaret said it were right and proper, but even the servants be a-hearing God's word dunamany times a day now, m'lady. Can't scarcely get our work done between, we can't."

Reminded, Alys made certain she had her rosary tucked up her sleeve, swept up the train of her skirt over her left arm, and set off to find Madeline. That young damsel, gowned in lavender, had only to fasten her gold belt beneath her plump bosom before she was ready to go. The pair of them, seeking the aid of a yeoman guard, soon located the ladies' chamber, where they found an elderly priest preparing to say the mass. Kneeling with the other women on the hard floor, Alys regretted leaving behind at the Tower the cushion she had stitched for the chapel there. She would, she decided, have to make another, and right speedily.

While the priest's voice murmured the Latin phrases, she let her gaze wander, inspecting the room and the other women. Only one other wore the butterfly headdress. Most wore the simple cap-and-band favored by Elizabeth and Lady Margaret. The latter was not present, a fact for which Alys was intensely grateful.

Elizabeth knelt at a prie-dieu beside her elaborately carved armchair. Another woman knelt beside her, also at a prie-dieu, and the smooth golden-blond hair showing beneath the front edge of her headdress made Alys nearly certain that she was the queen dowager, Elizabeth Woodville. Alys had never seen her before, but her features were enough like her daughter's to make it a near certainty. The woman chose that moment to open her eyes and look at Alys, who had forgotten to keep her eyelids lowered. Blushing, she quickly returned her attention to her prayers.

When the priest had gone, the ladies arose gratefully to their feet and began chatting to one another. Alys soon learned that not only was the woman beside the princess indeed the queen dowager but that the princess's sister Cecily was also present. Alys thought Elizabeth looked tired, but the princess conducted herself as she always did, with an air of gentle distance and quiet elegance, taking no part in the conversation around her but sitting in her chair with her slim, fair hands properly occupied with her stitchery. Even when her gaze drifted, attracted by an overloud voice or laughter, her expression remained serene. She seemed to pay no heed to Alys, for which mercy Alys was grateful.

There was nothing in the ladies' conversation to displease the princess, for nearly all of it concerned the wedding festivities—the splendor of the groom, Elizabeth's beauty, the magnificence of the banquet. And Alys soon learned that although it was more common for a king and queen to dine separately with their attendants, there was to be another feast that day.

She soon tired of standing, but since there were more ladies than joint stools or cushions, her only choice other than to stand was to sit upon the floor. She glanced across the room at Madeline to see her shift awkwardly from foot to foot. Clearly, there were details about being a lady in waiting that one had to learn, such as how to find a stool or cushion of one's own. Perhaps the stool in her chamber would do, though she would have to find someone to carry it for her. To carry such an object herself would be both unseemly and demeaning.

Though she was interested in learning more about the women with whom she would serve, she soon found their constant chatter tiresome compared to the talks she had had with Sir Nicholas, and she even yearned for the peace she had known at the Tower. Her back began to ache, and her legs grew tired, and she was soon bored, but nearly three hours passed before she found relief.

Madeline returned to her side then with a weary sigh. "I am as hoarse as a crow," she said. "Do these females never cease twittering? Even Elizabeth must long for the time when she had to make do with only two ladies in waiting."

"I would not wager a button on that likelihood," Alys said. "Elizabeth will not willingly deny herself anything that adds to her consequence. She has waited all her life for this."

"You know her as I do not," Madeline admitted, "but I must say, she still appears to be as I thought her before, quiet and gentle. Surely she is not as bad as you remember her. Might not your previous opinion have arisen from a natural, childish hostility toward another living beneath the same roof?"

"We cannot discuss that here," Alys said, feeling oddly betrayed by Madeline's casual words. She had not described every detail of her prior relationship with Elizabeth, but she had said enough to think that Madeline understood she had reasons for her opinion. "Here is the priest again," she said. "My knees are already bruised. We simply must get kneeling cushions."

Madeline chuckled. "No doubt Lady Margaret will willingly procure the materials for us if we will but promise to bequeath our results to her favorite chapel when we pass on."

Alys smiled. One could not long remain vexed with Madeline. A silence fell upon the room. The mass had begun. To their relief, when it was over, the queen dowager announced that the princess intended to retire to renew her energy before the evening's festivities. The ladies were dismissed.

The irrepressible Madeline, tripping along some moments later at Alys's side on the way to their chambers, said, "I'll warrant she got no sleep last night. The Tudor looks a bit chilly, but no man is cold on his wedding night."

Absently Alys nodded agreement. She had been wondering if she was expected to remain in her chamber until Elizabeth chose to send for her. The prospect was not an appealing one. Madeline's thoughts had obviously taken a similar course, for when they reached Alys's room, she suggested using the time to explore at least the ladies' side of the great palace.

Alys had no objection, and they spent the afternoon locating the privy gardens, garderobe towers, and other sites of interest. They both knew the court would soon leave Westminster, for huge as the palace was, no royal residence was big enough to support for long the hundreds of people in a royal retinue. They would move to Sheen or Greenwich, or maybe, as spring drew near, some palace farther from London. It was common for a king to make a circuit of his residences each year, staying at one till the moat and the garderobes—more commonly called the jakes—became too noxious to bear, then moving on to the next.

By the time the two young women returned to their chambers, it was time to dress for the evening festivities. They had enjoyed their freedom, however, knowing that later, when their routine became more settled, they would spend much more time with the princess and have little free time of their own.

The gathering that night was held again in the huge hall, but there were fewer people present, so the place no longer seemed to be bursting at the seams and the marshals were able to seat everyone without commotion. Alys and Madeline sat with the other ladies in waiting, near the high table. Again, there were jesters and minstrels, acrobats and players, but Alys soon became bored, and her gaze began to wander.

Sir Nicholas was at a table some distance away, seated with other gentlemen and ladies of the court. He did not look her way, and since she did not want to be caught staring at him, she looked at the others at his table instead. She thought one might be Sir Lionel Everingham. Her gaze froze on the man next to him. She could see only his profile, a strong chin and aquiline nose, but he turned toward her a moment later, and she was sure.

"What is it?" Madeline demanded when she gasped. "You look as though you just saw a ghost."

"Perhaps I did," Alys muttered. "If that is not my brother, Roger, at that table yonder, then it is someone exactly like him. But if it is my brother, why has no one told me that he is here? And if he is here, why has he not sought me out?"

"Marry, do not continue to stare at him. He will see you."

"I want him to look at me."

The gentleman was involved in a conversation then, but several moments later he looked up and Alys managed to catch his eye. For a moment he looked puzzled, as though he thought he ought to know her but did not recognize her. Then, politely, he smiled and nodded before turning back to his conversation.

"Goodness," Madeline said, "if he recognizes you, he does not appear particularly delighted to see you."

"I am not sure he knows who I am," Alys said with a sigh.

"When was the last time you saw him?"

"More than a year ago, I suppose, and then briefly, but he ought to know me." She relaxed, then smiled when a new thought entered her mind. "Since he is here, he must have submitted to the king, so surely I will be released to him and will not have to continue to serve Elizabeth."

She was able to indulge this hope only until she managed to confront her brother, after the tables had been cleared and removed, when the company began to mingle again.

"So it is you indeed, Alys," Roger Wolveston said with satisfaction when she stepped in front of him. "Everingham said that it was, but you have grown up since last I saw you."

"Thank you," she said crisply. "No one saw fit to tell me that you were here at court. I was told only that you had been at Bosworth with Francis Lovell."

"True enough, but one need not speak of that awful day in such company as this," he said sternly, glancing around the hall. "I have sworn fealty to the king, and he has been gracious enough to restore my title and estate. I am Lord Wolveston now."

"In faith, I am glad to hear that. We knew he had pardoned some, but I feared he would punish many who fought against him."

"Some he did, but he pardoned most of us from the north, where it is said he seeks to gain friends. He even named Tyrell Sheriff of Glamorgan and Warden of Cardiff Castle. However, you must not mention Lovell, for he refuses to submit, and so he was not pardoned with the rest of us, and has been named in a bill of attainder. He will no doubt be executed if they catch him."

"He truly is alive now? We heard that he was dead."

"False reports," Wolveston said, "put about by the king himself to dissuade men from rallying to him. He has fled to sanctuary, but he ought to have submitted with the rest of us."

Alys was shocked. She had met Viscount Lovell often and liked him very much. "Surely, you do not reproach him for remaining loyal to his cause, sir."

Wolveston shrugged. "You are only a woman, my dear, so one cannot expect you to understand these things."

Alys struggled to hold her temper in check, for she had not yet learned what she most wanted to know. "I must suppose, sir," she said carefully, "that I am no longer the king's ward."

"Well, as to that," he replied casually, "it cannot signify for I have already agreed not to interfere with your betrothal."

Alys stared at him in astonishment. "My betrothal!"

He flushed, looking annoyed with himself. "I was to leave it to the king to tell you. We will say no more about it, if you please, for it is not right that I discuss it with you yet."

"But I understood that my betrothal to Sir Lionel—"

"You do not wed Everingham," Wolveston interjected hastily, "although as you have seen, he submitted to the Tudor when I did. But he could not hope, even then, to be allowed to claim you."

"Then who?"

He would not tell her, insisting he had already said too much, but she had not long to wait before one of the yeomen came to escort her to the dais. As she followed him, she saw standing beside Henry Tudor another, much older man, who watched her approach with interest, in much the same way, she thought, that a man would look over a mare he thought he might purchase.

"Lady Alys," the king said with regal bluntness when she had made her curtsy, "it is our pleasure that you shall accept the suit of Lord Briarly, who is connected to us through our good friends the Stanleys. Appropriate betrothal ceremonies will be arranged within the week. That is all. You may go."

Stunned, clearly dismissed, but not certain she ought to believe her own ears, Alys backed away from the royal presence. Lord Briarly stood where he was, still staring complacently at her but making no attempt to follow or even to speak to her.

She did not know him, but he was an enemy who filled her with loathing, and not at all the sort of man she had expected to marry. Even as the notion crossed her mind, she realized she had never thought really seriously about the man who would be chosen for her. She had accepted that such a thing would happen, that she would have no control over her own fate. At least, she thought she had accepted it. Now, turning away from Briarly in dismay, she knew she had not accepted it at all.

# 10

Blindly making her way through the crowd, Alys thought only of finding her brother, of making him say he would not stand for such a marriage, not to any member of the traitorous Stanley family, forcing herself to believe Roger would go to the king, would somehow right the world that had so precariously tilted beneath her feet. But before she could find him, her right arm was caught from behind, the gesture nearly oversetting her.

Madeline's eyes were twinkling. "Alys, you will never guess how much we have risen in the world! Her highness wishes to retire soon, and we are to attend her. Lady Emlyn tells me that it is a great honor to be admitted to the royal bedchamber."

"I must first find my brother," Alys said desperately, straightening the sleeve of her gown, which Madeline, in her excitement, had disarranged.

Madeline looked at her closely. "Are you well?" she demanded, adding before Alys could answer, "You must be well, for there is no time to be ill, and there is no time to be looking for brothers either. We must go." With that, she fairly dragged Alys along with her, chattering as she went. "Did you know we are to be paid forty pounds a year? 'Tis more than I have ever had of my very own before. Why, 'tis a fortune!"

"You are an heiress," Alys reminded her.

"True, but I have never had a cent to spend on myself."

"Well, forty pounds is hardly a fortune," Alys said, allowing herself to be pulled along while she looked anxiously about for her brother. "Anne spent as much on a single gown."

"Well, I am not Anne of Gloucester and it seems a fortune to me," Madeline said over her shoulder, adding as she turned again, "Look, Lady Emlyn is leaving. Make haste, or we shall be late."

Alys dug in her heels. "You go without me, Madeline. I must find Roger and speak to him."

"Not now, you goose," Madeline said, turning again to speak more urgently. "Did you know that as maids of honor we come third in priority after the great ladies and the ladies of the privy chamber? And do you know how lucky we are to have dined in company two nights running? They say that when the queen dowager dines alone with her ladies, everyone has to eat in the strictest silence and with great ceremony. Anyone who approaches her has to remain kneeling until she dismisses them, which she will frequently forget to do. One cannot suppose Elizabeth will act in a like manner, but we must not displease her now."

"Elizabeth has not the same need to prove her worth that her mother has," Alys said impatiently. On tiptoe, she twisted and turned, sure she had seen her brother pass by some distance away.

"I think Lady Beatrix has also gone," Madeline said. She, too, was stretching, trying to see over the heads of those in front of them. "For pity's sake, Alys, her highness will depart next! What do you mean, she has not the same need?"

"Only that Anne was used to say that Elizabeth Woodville assumed a greater haughtiness than any queen before her in an effort to make people forget her common beginnings. Elizabeth of York has not that same need. For all her faults, she is no mere commoner. To be sure, she is greedy, sly, and a prevari—" She broke off with a sharp cry of pain when her left arm was grabbed from behind and she was jerked sharply around to find herself confronting a glowering Sir Nicholas. "By the rood," she exclaimed angrily, "if people do not cease snatching at my arms, I shall soon be a mass of bruises! What do *you* want?"

Before he could reply, Madeline blurted, "Oh, thank heaven, Sir Nicholas, you must persuade her to make haste, for we dare not tarry. We are supposed to go to her highness's bedchamber to help prepare her for bed, only Alys insists upon dawdling!"

Nicholas, still gripping Alys's arm and visibly collecting himself, was silent for a moment before he said with forced calm, "I would have speech with Lady Alys, Mistress Fenlord, but you go on ahead. You need not both be unpunctual. I give you my word of honor that she will soon follow after you."

Madeline looked from one to the other but did not argue. Gathering her skirts, she turned and walked swiftly away.

Alys, ignoring the firm grip on her arm and continuing to search the hall for sight of her brother, said, "Thank you, sir, for sending her away. My brother is here somewhere, and I must speak to him, but Madeline does not understand, and she—"

"She is trying to protect you from your own foolishness," he said, "and though you may thank me for getting rid of her, you will not thank me for what I will say to you now. Nonetheless, you will hear it. Come with me."

"I cannot! I must find Roger!" She tried to free herself.

"Not now." He began to move toward the nearest doorway, still holding her arm, clearly expecting no more argument.

"No!" She stayed where she was, tugging against his grip. "You have no right to command me."

"Mistress," he said grimly, "if you do not come quietly, I will carry you. You seem to care not one whit what others may overhear, but what I have to say to you is best said in private, and must be said now. Then, like it or not, you must go to her highness's bedchamber if you have been commanded to do so."

She saw that several people were looking their way. Meeting his gaze again long enough to measure his willingness to carry out his threat to carry her, she found no softening in his expression, but in a last ditch effort, she said, "Sir Nicholas, you do not understand. Truly, I must speak to my brother."

"Then shortly I will send for Ian, whom I last saw flirting with one of the more comely players—or mayhap she was a rope dancer—and I will command him to find Lord Wolveston for you. In the meantime, I will see you safely to your duty."

She had not thought of Ian, but she knew he would be able to search the entire palace if necessary to find Roger, whereas she could not, and so, reluctantly, she allowed Nicholas to place her hand on his forearm and take her to that same doorway through which Madeline had disappeared moments before. Beyond it, in the corridor, he looked swiftly about before urging her toward an anteroom. Once inside, he shut the door behind them. The room was empty save for a pair of carved back stools against one wall.

Alys, feeling uncomfortably vulnerable, widened her eyes and said, "I ought not to be in here alone with you, sir."

"You ought not to do many things, mistress. 'Tis on that very subject that I mean to speak to you. I have had cause before to warn you about guarding your tongue, have I not?"

Moving a more prudent distance away from him and trying to sound casual, she replied, "You have said some such thing, I suppose, but I cannot think why you wish to talk with me now."

"Lady Alys, it is unwise to speak disparagingly of the Princess Elizabeth. She is safely wedded to the king now and will soon be the reigning Queen of England."

"There are many who doubt the Tudor's intention to allow her to reign beside him," Alys pointed out.

"Queen regnant or queen by marriage makes little difference to you, however. Stir her temper, and you will suffer for it."

Alys grimaced. "Soon enough, sir, what Elizabeth thinks of me will not signify, for I shall have gone beyond her reach."

"What she thinks of you must always signify so long as she

has the king's ear," he retorted, "but what makes you think your situation is about to change in any way?"

"I am to marry Lord Briarly." Suddenly, alone in that room with him, in the silence that followed her simple statement, she felt overwhelming despair. Roger would refuse to help her, and no one else could. Saying the words aloud brought the facts home to her more profoundly than before. She was to be married, and she would have absolutely no say in the matter. Though she had been aware since childhood that the day would come, it had seemed distant, unthreatening. But now, the king's blunt words, and her own, echoed again in her mind, haunting her, frightening her.

"So Briarly is to be the man," Sir Nicholas said slowly, his words carefully measured, his eyes narrowing speculatively, as though he would bring a portrait of Lord Briarly into his mind.

"Aye, and no doubt he will take me straight back to the north, for Elizabeth will certainly not bid me stay at court."

"One of the Stanley lot, is he not?"

"Aye, so the king did say." She wished she could read his thoughts in his expression, but she could not.

"Then I know of him. Old for you, I should have thought."

She made an impatient gesture. "That would not distress me, sir, for his age will undoubtedly be accompanied by both wealth and power, and thus would many account him an excellent match for me. 'Tis his politics I abhor. That his family betrayed their true king is a circumstance I can never forgive."

"*Duw bendigedig!*"

The fury in his voice made her wince, but she lifted her chin and said with tolerable calm, "I do wish you would not spit Welsh at me—and blasphemous Welsh at that, by your tone. I cannot think why my speaking the truth should make you angry in any event. You do not seem to be the sort of man who would commend another for betraying his king."

"I do not commend Briarly or his relations," Sir Nicholas said between his teeth. "As to the Welsh, I called only upon the blessings of God, which is no blasphemy but only a re-lieving of exasperation at the idiocy of some females. The plain fact is that what I think of Briarly's politics has no more to do with the matter at hand than what you think of them does, for the past is done, lass, and we must look to the future. If yours is to be with Briarly, you would do better to speak well of him than to condemn him, just as you would do well to speak of the king's bride only in such words as might be repeated to her pleasure."

"I am not such a hypocrite!"

"You are a fool!"

"You have no right to rebuke me."

"Your own father, were he here, would speak so. By heaven, even a more indulgent father would put you across his knee and smack some sense into you before he let you put your fool head on a block. Have a care lest I do more than just speak for him."

"Oh, how dare you!" she cried, turning angrily toward the door. "I will not stay here and listen to you. My father is dead, and you have absolutely no right—"

"You said that before," Sir Nicholas pointed out grimly, barring her way, "and I tell you now, mistress, to count yourself fortunate that I know I have no such right. I will find your brother for you. Perhaps he will attend to you as you deserve."

"You need not," she snapped. "I will send Ian myself to find him." There were tears in her eyes, and she dashed them away, angry that she should display so childish a reaction to his displeasure, and wishing she might simply draw a sword or dagger to defend herself against insults, as a man might have done.

"Do as you please," he said quietly. "I have only one more thing to say to you. Something I ought to have said long since."

That he was still angry was clear to her despite his even tone, and she struggled to keep him from seeing that his mood affected her. "Say it then," she muttered.

"When we met the king at Greenwich, I spoke to him

briefly of the reason for our delay in the north, and told him that all who had dwelt within Wolveston Castle had died. The sickness was already in London by then, and appeared to have spread throughout the kingdom, so we spoke at some length of that. Then I told him of your fostering, that you had been at Middleham and Sheriff Hutton, and were acquainted with the Princess Elizabeth."

"What of it?" She was curious now. The angry undertone was still present in his voice, but there was nothing in his words to explain it. "My acquaintance with her family is no secret, sir."

"The king recognized your family name," Sir Nicholas said. "He remembered your brother's name among those who had fought at Bosworth and he spoke of attainder, declaring that the Wolveston lands—a considerable property, he said—would be claimed by the crown if Wolveston did not submit. So certain was he that I did not debate the point, wanting to be certain of my facts first. Your brother did submit, but before he did I asked questions of men from the north who had no cause to speak falsely to me."

"What questions? I do not understand you."

He regarded her sternly. "It is possible, of course, that in England, just as the law gives land to only one brother, that if that brother is attainted, the others must be included in the bill, but . . . Ah, I see that that need not be the case."

Alys, comprehending at last the direction his thoughts had taken, felt warmth flood her cheeks and would have turned so that he could not see her guilt, but his hand flashed out to stop her.

"No, mistress. I have said nothing of this matter to anyone else, but I am loyal to my king—a point that ought to weigh favorably with you. I will have the solution to this puzzle. You have only one brother, have you not?"

He was looking straight into her eyes, and much though she would have liked to deny it, she could not. She nodded. "I had two others, Robert and Paul, but they died eight years ago."

"I thought as much. Those others at Wolveston?"

Squeezing her eyes shut so that he would not see the terror welling within her, she whispered, "I do not know."

"You saw the one."

"Aye, but I had never seen him before." That was true. She opened her eyes, fighting to hide her fear, pleading silently for him to believe her.

"You knew he was not your brother. Why did you not speak?"

Careful to keep her voice calm, she said, "I had no cause to trust you then, or any reason to speak." Remembering what her first thoughts on the point had been, she added, "I did suspect they might have been sons of some other, more prominent Yorkist family that my father's servants tried to protect by insisting they were part of ours, but I did not know. Then I became ill and forgot about them until now."

His gaze was a searching one, uncomfortably so, but she met it without flinching, and when after a long moment he still had said nothing, she said, "I . . . I must go now, sir. It will not do for my absence to be remarked."

"Aye, we have lingered here too long," he agreed, moving to open the door for her. Before he did so, he paused with his hand on the latch to add, "You mind that tongue of yours in future, lass. Say nothing that you would not wish to hear repeated."

She glanced up at him, her fears subsiding, replaced by curiosity. "Why does it matter to you what I do or what I say?"

The question seemed to take him aback, for his cheeks showed color, but he recovered swiftly and said with a shrug, "I suppose that, having taken responsibility for your safety before, I am finding it difficult to relinquish it now. I feel much the same way I would feel were one of my sisters to behave so foolishly."

"And I suppose that your sisters, poor creatures, would instantly obey you," she said sharply, having not the least idea why such a statement from him should instantly fire her temper again, but knowing that it did so, that she did not want him to treat her like his sisters. She glared, daring him to respond.

He was silent, but there was something in his expression when he returned her look that exasperated her. It was as though he were merely being patient with her, waiting for her to collect herself, to be sensible, to see that she was being foolish to taunt him. Instead of calming her, it had the opposite effect.

"Well, have you got nothing to say, Sir Nicholas?"

"There is no need to respond to such a statement."

"Such a *foolish* statement, I suppose you mean!"

He said nothing.

"Oh, you enrage me! You treat me like a child, warning me to hold my tongue, to keep my opinions hidden behind my teeth, as though Elizabeth did not already know what I think of her."

"There is a difference," he said severely, "between speaking your mind to one Elizabeth Plantagenet—"

"I did not merely speak my mind to her; I slapped her!"

"You *what*?"

"You heard me!" She had not told Madeline about the slap, but now that she had told him, her tongue seemed to rattle on of its own accord. "She arrived at Sheriff Hutton prating smugly of how Richard had sent her there to quiet stupid rumors that he had murdered Anne and wanted to marry her! 'Twas utter nonsense. I—I lost my temper, and I slapped her—hard!" Her palm tingled again at the memory, and she rubbed it hard against her skirt.

Sir Nicholas's lips pressed tightly together for a moment before he said, "There is a vast difference between that woman, bereft of her accustomed rank and forced to bend her knee to a usurper, and the king's bride. There are dangers you cannot—"

"What dangers? What possible danger can there be to me, the king's ward, here in the king's own palace? You speak nonsense, sir." Impatiently she moved again to pass him, to reach for the latch, since he showed no more inclination to open the door and let her out; but, as she brushed against him, he caught her arm, and before she knew his intent, he had pulled her hard against him with one hand and gripped her chin with the other, forcing it up so his lips could claim hers in a swift, bruising kiss.

She struggled in his grasp, but she was pinned against his powerful body, and her skirts entangled her legs when she tried to kick him. Her left hand was free but although she flailed at him, it had no more effect than a leaf battering a tree trunk.

She knew his intent was only to teach her the danger of thinking she was safe in a palace filled with men of every sort from rough yeomen guards to knights of the realm accustomed to having their most casual request obeyed instantly. But when his lips and hands touched her and she found her soft body clamped against his muscular one, a fire unlike any she had experienced before spread through her, flashing from lips to toes through every nerve and muscle of her anatomy. So hot was the flame that it took all the strength she had to keep from melting in its heat, melting against him, softening, yielding, surrendering.

Sir Nicholas did not prolong the moment but freed her within seconds, setting her back on her heels with a quickness that left her gasping. Recovering swiftly, her fury augmented—though she would rather have died than admit it—by the very speed with which he had released her, she raised her hand to strike him.

"Do not," he snapped.

The gesture froze in mid-air, stopped as much by the hard look in his eyes as by the tone of his voice. Knowing well that she could never trust him not to retaliate in kind if she did hit him, she stood unmoving, glaring back, holding his gaze with hers until suddenly, the glint of steel vanished from his eyes. His expression softened then, and for a moment she saw a look she had never seen before in any man's eyes, one she was not at all certain how to interpret. There was gentleness and something else, something that set the heat tingling within her veins again. But the look was quickly gone, followed by another she recognized only too well. He was amused.

With effort, she restrained her temper, letting her hand fall to her side again. In as offhand a manner as she could manage, she murmured, "Is that also the way you treat your sisters, Sir Nicholas?"

A muscle leapt high in his cheek, but whether she had annoyed him or only added to his amusement, she could not tell, for he turned away and yanked open the door, saying sardonically, "Go to your duty, *mi geneth*. If there be justice in this world, her highness will order you whipped for your tardiness."

She hurried away from him then, nearly running down the corridor toward the ladies' chamber, but at the turning, she stopped and looked back. When she saw him standing by the door to the anteroom, still watching her, satisfaction surged within her at the thought that, despite his callous final statement, he still concerned himself with her safety. Then, perversely, in the instant before the yeoman guard opened the doors to the princess's antechamber, she remembered that despite that intriguing look Sir Nicholas had given her no indication that he objected in the slightest to her impending betrothal.

Her disordered senses were recalled instantly when the yeoman opened the doors. At the same time, on the other side of the antechamber, the door into the princess's bedchamber opened, and Lady Emlyn appeared on the threshold, saying crisply, "There you are, Alys. Come in at once. Her highness will be here directly and all preparations must be completed before she arrives. You must go in and help the others make her bed."

Alys stared at her. "Surely there are proper servants to attend to that chore, Lady Emlyn."

Lady Emlyn's thin eyebrows lifted. "My dear Alys, surely you must have realized by now that her royal highness does not associate in any way with lowly servants. It is the honor and pleasure of her ladies to serve her in all such capacities.

Now, do you go at once, for the royal bedmaking has already begun."

Alys hurried into the bedchamber and discovered that making Elizabeth's bed was no small duty, for her ladies and gentlewomen observed a precise routine. The lavender bed curtains had been pulled wide and tucked out of the way. Next the covers were all removed and the mattress itself stripped from the bed and given a good shaking. And finally each cover, separate from the others, was replaced, great care being taken to ensure that no wrinkles remained anywhere. The pillows, a vast number of them, were plumped and replaced on the bed, and finally the counterpane, an elegant spread of lavender silk to match the bed curtains, was spread over the whole, and the curtains drawn again, but only enough to ensure that they hung properly and showed no creases.

"Mercy," Alys murmured to Madeline later in the anteroom when the ritual was done and they had been sent to procure hot water for the royal washstand reservoir, and cold for the royal ewer, "if this is only a part of the ritual that accompanies the princess to bed under ordinary circumstances, what she will expect when she is in childbed?"

They had reached the door to the corridor. "Hush," Madeline warned, but her eyes were twinkling. "Someone will hear you."

They had only to have the vessels filled by the yeomen servants already waiting outside the door, and return to the bedchamber, but before they entered the latter again, Alys said, "My bed is made in the morning, Madeline. Is not yours?"

"Aye," Madeline said, chuckling, "and so, too, is that of her royal highness, but feathers do not stay fluffed, you know, and it is not meet that the feathers surrounding a royal princess should be allowed to clump, Alys. Surely you must see that."

Alys shook her head but said no more, for Madeline had opened the door. One of Alys's daily tasks at Middleham had been to oversee the cleaning of several chambers, including, at times, the bedchamber of the Duke and Duchess of Gloucester. She had been there, after all, to learn about the proper running of a large household. But she could not recall that Anne or Anne's Dickon had ever expected a half-dozen or more people to attend their bedmaking or, indeed, the preparations for their retiring. She wondered if those customs had changed much when the Duke and Duchess of Gloucester had become King and Queen of England and removed to London, and decided that most likely they had not. It was much more likely that Elizabeth's notions of the ceremony due to her high estate had evolved from her mother's example.

Alys and Madeline were dismissed from the bedchamber as soon as Elizabeth entered, accompanied by both her mother and Lady Margaret. As Alys backed from the room, she thought the princess looked harassed. She was not at all sorry to leave.

In the corridor, Madeline said, sotto voce, "I should not care to be caught between those two. I doubt even Elizabeth, gentle as she tries to be, can manage to please them both."

Alys had no sympathy to waste on Elizabeth. "Madeline," she said, "I must tell you my news. I am to be betrothed and then married, I think, as soon as the formal annulment of my betrothal to Sir Lionel Everingham arrives from Rome."

Madeline stopped still in the corridor and stared at her. "You are just now telling me this! How long have you known?"

"Hush." Alys looked hastily around, then added in a low voice, "When the king commanded my presence tonight, 'twas to tell me of his decision to wed me to Lord Briarly."

"Who is Lord Briarly? I do not know him."

"He is one of the Stanleys. Come, do not stand like a post. We will be remarked." Alys feared that if they did not move, she would shriek. Just thinking of the possessive way Briarly had looked at her stirred waves of fresh desperation within her.

Madeline stood where she was. "You are to wed a Stanley!"

"Aye, but keep your voice down. You do not need to hear what I think about such a marriage, do you?"

"No, but my goodness, Alys, what will you do?"

"I do not know, but come," she said vehemently. "We cannot talk here. We must go to my room."

Madeline agreed, and they hurried along without talking, but when they turned into the corridor where Alys's bed-chamber was located, Ian MacDougal stepped out of the shadows to meet them.

"Ian," Alys cried, "I have an important commission for you!"

"Aye, mistress, and so Sir Nicholas ha' said when he told me tae await your return. I am tae find the Laird Wolveston, but what am I tae tell him? Master said it wouldna be richt for the mon tae set foot in your bedchamber, brother or no."

"Just tell him I must speak with him privately," Alys said, exerting herself to keep the impatience she felt from sound-ing in her voice. "Find him quickly, Ian, and then come back to me here and tell me where I am to meet him. Oh, and Ian," she added when another thought occurred to her as he turned away, "in case I should need you later, where do I send to find you?"

He grinned. "Best I coom here, mistress. There's a comely wee lassock dancin' her shoon off wi' the evening's players, and her troop leaves wi' the dawnin' for Oxford and Derby, then goes all the way north t' Doncaster and York till Easter. If the wee folk dinna interfere, I mean tae mak' m'self weel known tae the lass this verra night. I dinna ken where we might be."

Alys shook her head at him. "You are incorrigible, Ian, and you deserve to come to grief. Just see that you come back here if you cannot find Lord Wolveston, so that I do not spend the entire night wondering what to expect. And come to me first thing in the morning. I may have new or-

ders for you—that is, unless Sir Nicholas has commanded
you to attend to him."

"Nay, mistress. I be yours tae command, now as ever."

"But I cannot even pay you, Ian. I have no money."

"You need not, mistress. Sir Nicholas pays me."

"But that is not right," Alys protested.

Ian shrugged. " 'Tis wi' me," he said. "If that be all, mistress, I'll gae the noo and find his lairdship."

She let him go, not knowing what more to say and soothing her feelings by assuring herself that Roger would certainly pay for her servants once she pointed out the need to
him. And later perhaps, arrangements could be made with
Lord Briarly so that her own servants could attend her after
the wedding. That last thought depressed her again, however, and she turned with a sigh to follow Madeline into the
bedchamber. Molly was waiting to put Alys to bed, but she
dismissed her, telling her to come back in an hour. Then,
with the door shut, she turned to Madeline.

"I am only now beginning to take it all in," she said with
a sigh, "for besides being one of the enemy, Madeline,
Briarly is an old man. Though I told Sir Nicholas that would
not weigh with me, I do own that I should prefer a young
husband to an old one."

"Anyone would," Madeline agreed fervently. "But how is
this then? Does Sir Nicholas know the whole?"

"Aye, I told him. He was vexed with me for speaking as I
did about Elizabeth—"

"I still do not see any sign of wickedness in her," Madeline
interjected. "She smiles and nods, and scarcely ever speaks,
but when she does, 'tis always in a quiet, gentle manner."

"She has learned well to conceal her true feelings," Alys
said, but Madeline's opinion of Elizabeth no longer seemed
quite so important, so her tone was calm. "To understand
her, you must recall the world in which she lived. Everyone
around her was conspiring at one time or another, always
with an eye to his own benefit. In just such a way has Elizabeth learned to look after Elizabeth. But I do not wish to

discuss her, Madeline." She sat down upon the narrow bed and folded her hands around her knees, looking up bleakly. "My future appears to be set, does it not?"

Madeline agreed, but the two of them discussed it at length nonetheless. Since neither knew Briarly and could only speculate about his character, they were unable to agree on exactly what Alys's future might hold. They were still discussing it forty minutes later when, hearing a light scratching at the door, Alys opened it to find Ian on the other side.

Silently, he handed her a sheet of paper that had been folded in half but not sealed.

"Ah, good, you found him!"

"Aye, mistress, but it be as ye see there."

"You read this?" She eyed him disapprovingly, but Ian denied having done any such thing.

"He said flat out there be naught tae be done and he didna mean tae let hisself be plagued by your . . . appeals tae him."

"He did not say 'appeals.' What did he say?" She was scanning her brother's brief note as she asked the question, so Ian's hesitation was overlooked for a moment until she finished. Then, looking up at him, she said, "Well? Tell me."

"Sniveling's what he did say, mistress, but like as not, the laird didna mean—"

"The laird meant precisely what he said," Alys said grimly. "What a brother I have, Madeline! Only see what he has written."

She handed the note to Madeline, who read the brief scrawl in an instant, then looked up again with a grimace. " 'Obey, the matter has naught to do with me.' That is all?"

"As you see."

"Well, but in fairness, Alys, if the king commands it—"

"Aye, the king commands." She sighed again. "Go to your dancer, Ian. And you go to bed, Madeline. I shall see you both in the morning. Right now, I want to be alone."

When they had gone, she slumped down against the wall, ignoring the chill of the stones through her gown, trying to think of a way to avoid marriage to Briarly. To have one's husband selected by the king ought to have been an honor, even when the king was the Tudor, but the more she thought about Briarly, the more hateful the notion became. But if Roger was against her, there was no one else to whom she might turn. No one else cared what happened to her.

She wondered what settlement Roger would make, if he still had the power to provide her with a dowry. She had not thought about that before now. A dowry was of vast importance, for she was nothing without one, but who would provide it? Perhaps that was why Roger wanted no part of her. Perhaps he hoped to benefit from remaining silent. Before her father died, before Bosworth Field, she had had a respectable dowry, and her connection to the family of Anne of Gloucester had made her an excellent prospect for marriage. That connection was a defect now, and her dowry no doubt depended upon the king's whim. And no one cared. Not Sir Lionel Everingham or Roger. Not Nicholas Merion. Though why it should matter what Sir Nicholas thought, she could not imagine.

When Molly returned, Alys allowed herself to be prepared for bed, but many more hours passed before she slept. She told herself it did no good to bemoan her fate, since the only one who might possibly care was Jonet, and Jonet was dead. The tears came then, but she brushed them furiously away. Sir Nicholas had said that women frequently survived the sweating sickness—she had herself—so, if God had willed it so, Jonet was fully recovered and living happily with her sister Mary in Doncaster.

In any case she, Alys, was on her own. She began to wonder if there was any way to make the king change his mind. Nothing she could think of seemed likely to work, and she found herself thinking that it was a pity he was not as susceptible to feminine charms as Ian was. Then she remembered Ian's dancer, and an idea began to form. At last, gathering her courage and putting all thought of the king's wrath—and anyone else's—firmly from her mind, she decided what she would do.

# 11

Doncaster lay under a sugar-coating of new snow that frosted its rooftops, its cobbled streets, and the bare branches of its trees. The street known as the Kirkgate formed a tunnel for the morning's freezing north wind, and Alys felt as though she were being pushed by it up the hill. Drawing her thick wool shawl closer, she studied the houses, looking for the one she sought.

Towering above her on her right was the steeple of the gray stone church for which the street was named. Behind her, she could hear the chatter of Ian's teeth over the crunch of his boots through the thin crust of snow. And across the way, the upper stories of a row of ancient, adjoining cottages leaned out over the lower, giving them a top-heavy appearance. The way they had been angled to fit against the rising street made them look as though they were sinking. Crossing over and stopping before the last one, the sharp angles and crooked end-wall chimney of which made it appear even more tipsy than the others, Alys hesitated, glancing back at Ian.

"Art certain we shall find her here?"

The lad shrugged, hugging himself. " 'Tis what they ha' said at Wolveston, mistress, when I did ask."

"I wish I had gone with you."

"Aye, but the players might ha' left Bawtry wi'oot us, did we both gae, and we'd no ha' got here sae easily wi'oot them, or wi'oot takin' a far greater chance o' bein' recognized."

"No, but I do think that if anyone were searching for us, we ought to have learned of it by now."

He shrugged again, the gesture ending in a shiver. He nodded at the blue door of the end house. "Shall I rap?"

She nodded and found that she was holding her breath, but when the door opened she gasped out a cry of relief and flung herself, sobbing, into Jonet's arms.

"Lassie! Mistress Alys!" Hugging her and laughing, Jonet drew her into the tidy little front room, paying no heed to Ian until he followed and shut the door behind them. Her eyes widened then at the sight of the tall redheaded lad, and she drew away, striving to regain her dignity. She could not keep her eyes from her mistress, however, nor could she hide her delight at seeing her again.

Alys, too, was grinning broadly. "I had feared you dead, but at Wolveston they told Ian you were here with your sister."

" 'Twas that great gowk, Hugh Gower, who sent for Mary to fetch me," Jonet said. "He learned I had family hereabouts and commanded one of the monks helping the sick in the village to find them. Mary did think she would be fetching a corpse, but that herb woman looked after me, and I lived to spite the old witch. Come in and sit, the pair o' thee. Mary boasts a proper parlor with a hearth, she does, and two bedchambers above."

They followed her along a narrow passageway to the door of the cozy parlor, where, having realized that Ian's presence did not mean that Sir Nicholas or—clearly a more important factor to her—the giant Hugh had accompanied her darling, Jonet pressed Ian to take the second of the two stools in the room. Only when he had reluctantly done so did she busy herself stirring up the tiny fire that crackled beneath the plaster hood, and demand that Alys explain how it was that they came to be in Doncaster.

Alys began obediently, but she did not get far.

"You are to be married?" Jonet's eyes narrowed suspiciously when the news was broken, and she straightened, forgetting the fire. "And who would yon Tudor be a-choosing, if one might ask?"

" 'Tis Lord Briarly, a connection of the Stanleys."

"Och, nay!"

"That is what I thought myself," Alys told her with a mischievous twinkle, "and so did I decide to leave London."

"But why come to Doncaster? And who escorted you all this way, mistress? Surely, you never came with just him!" She gestured at Ian, who was perched on the edge of his stool as though he meant to bolt at the least hint of her displeasure.

Alys hesitated. She did not fear Jonet and was delighted beyond measure to find her alive and well, but she had had much experience with her temper and knew that if it were stirred Jonet could not be depended upon to remember her place. And since Ian's awe of Jonet was clear and his awe of his mistress had not survived the first of their three weeks with the players, during which he had frequently protested the foolishness of the venture, she knew he would not defend her if Jonet chose to scold.

Jonet glanced at Ian, saw that he was studiously regarding his boots, and looked back at Alys. "Mistress, surely you did not come all this way only to find old Jonet!"

"But we did," Alys assured her. "Not, in truth, that that was our first intention, for I was nearly certain that you had died of the sweat, but once Ian had visited Wolveston Hazard, from Bawtry, and discovered you were not only alive but here in Doncaster with your sister, it seemed best for us to remain with. . .that is, to travel on, to. . .to find you, after all." Alys glanced at Ian, but he avoided her eye, and Jonet's.

"Remain with whom?" Jonet demanded. "Art saying you *did* travel all this way with none but Ian to protect you!"

"No, but I fear you will not approve of my other companions, though I was as safe as could be in their company," Alys said ruefully. "The plain truth is we joined a band of players."

"Players? Do you mean common minstrels and jongleurs?" Jonet was shocked. "Dancers and actors? You never!"

"But we did," Alys said, grinning now. "Ian had met one of the dancers, and he convinced her—for he does have wondrous fine ways with the wenches—to smuggle us out of Westminster in their caravan. The chief jongleur of the troop, Master Bertrant, was as displeased as you are, so 'twas just as well he did not learn we had joined them until after we had passed through Uxbridge, or he might have taken us straightaway back to London."

"You never traveled all this way in such low company!"

"More than that, I learned to assist one of the jugglers, and Ian helped tend the animals, to earn our keep. 'Twas not what I am accustomed to, but in faith, it answered most excellent well. Had anyone chanced to search for us, they must have been confounded, for we did not take the Great North Road but went first to Oxford, then to Coventry, Leicester, and Derby, before crossing the Trent at Nottingham." Alys kept to herself the fact that she had enjoyed her time with the players. To be free of the restrictions that had surrounded her all her life, and to be with people who lived simply and enjoyed simple pleasures, had been blissful, but Jonet would not understand. "When the players stayed two days at Bawtry, Ian rode to Wolveston to see what the situation was there. That is when he learned you were here."

Jonet frowned. "So you have run from the Tudor, have you? God save us, that you do not bring his wrath down upon us all."

"In faith, how should I? It is true that since the players mean to go on to York till Easter, I had hoped we might stop here and stay with you. Ian says there are still soldiers at Wolveston, so we cannot go there, but I confess I should like to enjoy again some of those comforts to which I was born."

"I warrant you do." Jonet smiled. "You shall stay here, the pair of you, though the house be small. I can sleep with

Mary, and Ian can share the shed by the icehouse with our Davy."

"Davy is here?"

"Aye, you did not know?"

"No. In faith, if I gave any thought to him at all, I must have assumed he was dead, or with Roger in London."

"Davy said your brother was alive, but Wolveston had already left Nottinghamshire, or I would have sent a message with him to tell you I was well. You have seen him, though, I take it."

"Aye, for all the good it did me. He would not lift a finger to help me. But why is Davy not with him? He was not hurt at Bosworth or afterward, was he?"

"Nay, mistress, but Lord Wolveston could not be certain our Davy would be pardoned, and so it was that he did leave him behind when he rode to London to swear fealty to the Tudor."

Jonet's tone was neutral, but Alys read her disapproval nonetheless. She grimaced. "I cannot think why Roger submitted so tamely. To be sure, he did retain Wolveston thereby, and has kept his title. And many others have done the same, including Sir Lionel Everingham and Sir James Tyrell, who were said to be amongst the staunchest of Yorkists. But Lovell did not submit."

"Nay, not he." Jonet's expression was revealing.

"You have seen him!" Alys exclaimed. "I was told that he lived, but Roger said he had taken sanctuary. Where is he?"

Looking obliquely at Ian, Jonet frowned and said nothing.

Alys laughed and said confidently, "Ian will not betray him. He is loyal to me, and thus to my friends, art thou not, Ian?"

"Aye, mistress."

"His loyalty notwithstanding," Jonet said in the firm way she had often taken with the child Alys, "I can tell thee nowt. Mayhap when our Davy comes in, he will see fit to say more. Ah now, 'tis a plain day, the day, wi' the wind a-blowin' so thin. I shall send for ale to warm thee."

And though Alys tried several times to return to the subject of Lovell, no more would Jonet say about him, or about anything else of importance, except to bemoan Alys's intended wedding. And since that subject was not one which Alys wished to discuss, their conversation languished.

Davy Hawkins, when he arrived at last to seek his supper, was more forthcoming, for not only did he readily admit that Lovell was nearby in Yorkshire, but he agreed to carry word to him of Alys's desire to meet with him. Davy, a wiry man with much of the practical look of his sister about him, did not waste words arguing but said he would inform Lovell at once.

"Do you think he will agree to see me?" Alys asked. "The matter is most urgent."

"Dunno. Tha' mun bide here till I speak wi' the man."

"When?"

"When I do find him."

Alys had to be satisfied with that, for he would say no more. He finished his supper and departed. Alys and Ian spent the evening taking leave of their traveling companions, then carried their few belongings back to the house in the Kirkgate.

Two days later, when Alys, Jonet, and Ian returned from the church, where they had made their morning devotions, they found Davy and another man waiting for them in the tiny parlor, the latter dressed in a ragged shirt and breeches, a stained leather jerkin, and a large cap that had been pulled on in what looked to be an unsuccessful attempt to keep his shaggy hair out of his face. Dismissing Ian, Alys greeted Davy with tense anticipation.

"Did you find him?" she demanded. "Will he see me?"

To her surprise, it was the other man who answered her. "He will, mistress." With a glance at Davy, he added, "Privately."

Davy, taking Jonet by the arm, drew her unprotesting from the room, leaving Alys alone with the stranger. Not until the man removed his cap and pushed his hair out of his face, did she recognize him for Lovell himself and make a hasty curtsy. "My lord, I beg your pardon. I did not know you."

Lovell smiled, and she instantly recalled his charm. He was in his thirty-first year and not uncomely, even in peasant clothes. He motioned for her to sit, and when she had obeyed him he, too, sat down, saying, "Davy did say you have information for me, mistress. I thought it best to come to you, believing that my movements—in this guise, at any rate—would be less remarked upon than yours, coming to me."

Suddenly nervous, Alys glanced around, saw that the door to the passage was ajar, and got up to fasten it shut. Returning to her seat, she said quietly, "Sir, I do not know precisely how to begin, but I saw something rather startling when I returned to Wolveston Hazard ten days after the battle at Bosworth Field."

"Did you?"

His expression was blank. He would not help her. Taking a deep breath, she said, "You will think me crazed for saying this, but I believe I saw one of the sons of our late King Edward."

Lovell's expression did not change. His tone was calm. "Where did you see this person?" he asked.

"At Wolveston."

"And what were the circumstances?"

His calm had an effect, but her voice still trembled when she replied, "He was d-dead, sir, in a c-coffin."

"What?" The viscount sat up with a jerk. Eyeing her intently, he snapped, "Why do you think it was one of the princes, my lady, and which do you believe it to have been?"

She gave him back look for look. "You do not deny the possibility, sir, but pray, what can a prince of the blood royal have been doing at Wolveston Hazard?"

"There is naught in that to concern you now. Answer me."

She hesitated only a moment. "He looked like a Plantagenet, sir, all blond and. . . and. . . I do not know, in faith, but he did have a look of King Edward, not in size or shape but the Plantagenet look. You know what I mean. You must."

"Very fair? But frail withal? A thin face?"

"Aye."

"Was there . . ." He paused, looking at her again for a moment before he said, "Edward gave each of his sons a small, round medallion on a chain, engraved with his device, the sun—"

"The sun in splendor. I know. I saw no such thing, sir."

"He would have worn it round his neck."

"His collar was high. I saw nothing. But, sir, who else—"

Lovell sagged. "I do not know why I deny the truth. It must have been Edward. But what then of Richard?"

"They both were there then! 'Tis really true, sir?"

"Aye, for safety, Dickon did say. 'Twas better they were in the north, but not in Yorkshire, so Wolveston was chosen. Dickon did say the old lord was not one to stir enemies, that he would not be suspect, especially with the others at Sheriff Hutton. When it was learned that the Tudor had landed in Wales, Dickon decided to separate the lads—again for their safety—but he did not tell me the details. What has become of young Richard?"

"I do not know, sir. I was told only that he had gone away, to his fostering, they did say."

"Did not the old lord . . . ah, but I was forgetting. Davy did tell me he died of the sweat, but naught was said of the lads, and I assumed they were away safe. Was no name mentioned, no foster family?" he asked, looking at her now very keenly.

"No, for it was the soldiers who came to fetch me who told me what little I know. But. . ." She hesitated, frowning as she searched her memory. "My father did mention one name, but it cannot have had anything to do with Prince Richard, for the name he mentioned is that of a man who has submitted to the Tudor."

"Who? There is one more likely than all others."

"A man named Tyrell."

Lovell relaxed. "James is never the Tudor's man."

"But he is! Sir James did swear fealty to the Tudor, just

as Roger did. In faith, sir, he did retain his Welsh estates and his titles. The Tudor has even named him Sheriff of Glamorgan."

"James is a clever lad," Lovell said thoughtfully. His brow was furrowed, and after a moment's silence, he said, "The Tudor's own Wales would be the safest place to hide a Yorkist prince, and James owns vast estates there. If he has convinced the king of his loyalty, then all may yet be well with our Richard."

"But if he has changed coats, sir, as I fear he has, even if he does have the prince with him, Richard cannot be safe!"

Lovell smiled, and the expression lightened his countenance considerably. "A more loyal Yorkist never existed than James Tyrell. Whatever he has done, my lady, you may be certain it was done to secure the safety of his royal highness." A new thought struck him. "They cannot know that Edward is dead."

"They had gone before he died, sir, or so I was told."

"Are you certain that the soldiers who occupied the castle did not recognize the boy for a Plantagenet?"

"How could they? They were Welshmen and Scots, nearly all of them. Their leader is a Welshman who had never before been to the north of England or to London. He believed the boys to have been my brothers, and though he knows now that they were not, he does not suspect in the least that they might have been royal."

Lovell nodded. "Good, then I must think, for if Tyrell does not know the lad is the sole surviving heir—"

"But is he, sir? What about King Edward's prior betro—"

"Harry Tudor himself set aside their bastardy in order to marry Elizabeth," Lovell said grimly, "and even before that, York's claim was far stronger than Lancaster's."

"But if that is true," Alys said, "and if Richard of York is also dead, then Elizabeth would be the true heir, would she not?"

Lovell grinned but shook his head. "We shall never see a

wench on the throne, my dear. No army would support her. There was one once, to be sure—Matilda or some such, she was called—and mayhap others before her, unnatural though it seems to us today; but there will never be another. Ruling a country as important as England is no business for a lady. Neither Margaret of Anjou nor Margaret Beaufort attempted to claim the throne."

"Well, Elizabeth does expect to rule at his side," Alys said, "but as yet he has said naught of crowning her queen."

"Harry prefers to rule alone. He was willing to unite with the white rose, but he does not want people thinking he needs her to retain his position. We must think what is to be done."

"I'll do what I can, sir, but I know not what that may be."

"Do naught," he said firmly. "A gently bred lady can take no part in the sort of mischief I have in mind. 'Twould be safer by far to attend to your stitching."

"But I want to help!"

Lovell said soothingly, "Mayhap your help will be needed in future, Lady Alys, but just now, I must think of a safe way to get word to Sir James Tyrell that he holds in his keeping a life more precious than he can know."

"Could you not just send a trusted messenger to him?"

Lovell shook his head. "No man can be trusted with such a message, lest the information fall into the Tudor's hands. At present, Henry behaves as if those lads never existed."

"I know, and Elizabeth believes they are dead, though she did say her mother does not believe the same."

"You did not tell her what you knew?"

Alys shook her head.

"Good girl. 'Twas clear from the outset that Harry did not know where to find the princes, for had he known, he would have taken them into custody. And had he believed them dead, he would have accused Dickon publicly of having murdered them before Bosworth. He has done neither. Therefore, he knows nothing."

Alys said stubbornly, "If Sir James Tyrell gave up Prince

Richard when he submitted, would they not keep it quiet for fear Edward might then step forward? They cannot know he is dead."

Lovell shook his head. "Tyrell would no more have betrayed his king than I would. You cannot understand, I know, so you will do better simply to believe me. And accepting that and one other fact—that Harry Tudor would give his right eye to know where he might put his hands on the princes—there must be naught to connect any known Yorkist with Sir James. That means no messages from me. Of course, if you should simply chance to encounter him in London— How long before your return, my lady?"

Alys flushed. "I have no present intention to return."

"What?" He glanced around the tiny sitting room. "You cannot intend to reside here!"

She nodded. "At present I do."

"Davy did say something about your having traveled north with a company of players, but knowing you had fostered in the grandeur of Middleham, as I did myself, I could not credit his word on the matter. You are telling me he spoke the truth?"

"Aye. The Tudor did desire to wed me to a relative of Sir Thomas Stanley. I did not wish to obey, so I left London."

Lovell's deep-set eyes began to twinkle. "Did you now?"

Lifting her chin, Alys said, "I did, and I have no intention to return, sir."

He shook his head, his amusement clear now. "You cannot have thought the matter through, mistress. You cannot wish to live in the manner that would be required of you here."

She was silent. He was right. The cottage was not at all the sort of house to which she was accustomed, and already it had begun to seem small beyond reason, as though its inhabitants trod upon one another in going about their daily business. Mary Hawkins was not only older than Jonet, but more like Davy, and after the weeks on the road with the players, kind and amusing though Alys had found them, she longed for proper servants, proper surroundings, and most of all, an indoor privy. She had been avoiding Lovell's gaze, but she met it now directly.

"I have no wish to live here indefinitely, but I cannot return to Wolveston. Not only are there soldiers there still—"

"I know." He grinned at her.

"You know? Were you there?"

"Briefly, after Bosworth. We had gone before any soldiers arrived, but I keep my eye on Wolveston. Your brother may have bowed to Harry, but I warrant he would harbor me again even so."

"He will not harbor me, however, and I cannot return to London, for you must know that having displeased the king I should most likely find myself back in the Tower like Neddie. 'Tis a pleasant residence for royalty, but not so pleasant for those confined there against their will, as I was before."

"Tell me."

She obliged him with a recounting of her recent history, and though he laughed at some things, he was sympathetic toward the young Warwick, and understood Alys's desire to avoid the Tower.

"Still, I do not know what else you can do, mistress, for if your brother be content to leave you in the king's ward, you can have no recourse but to obey Harry's commands."

"But you cannot want me to wed a traitor!"

"No one will ask for my advice or my consent."

She sighed, and he rose a few moments later to leave her, pausing on the threshold to extract a promise that she would at least consider returning to the capital, where she might be of some use to those few remaining Yorkists who still had it in mind to annoy Henry Tudor. In his turn, Lovell promised that he would not abandon her but would visit her again one day if he could do so without endangering himself or her in the process. "I must think of things to do in the meantime to keep the royal mind occupied," he said, clapping his hat to his head and turning to leave. Sudden noise from the street stopped him in his tracks.

Davy hurried in from the passageway, and a heavy pounding at the door sounded as he hissed, "Soldiers in the street, master!"

"Let them in," Lovell said. Shooting Alys a mischievous grin, he jerked his cap lower over his eyes and pulled his long hair forward to cover more of his face. Then swiftly, he turned toward the parlor hearth, snatching a log from the basket, and kneeling to make himself busy with the little fire.

Alys waited tensely while Davy hastened to open the door. She never doubted for a moment who would be standing on the other side, though if anyone had asked how she knew, she would have been unable to tell them. First there were ringing footsteps on the stones of the passageway. Then several men entered the parlor, filling it, but the first one she recognized was Sir Nicholas, and despite an undeniable flash of relief in his eyes when he saw her, she knew instantly that he was furious.

Still helmeted, he pushed Davy aside as he came through the doorway, looking even taller than she remembered and saying grimly, "I am glad to have found you, Lady Alys. I had rather be serving my king with my sword, but for my pains in once having delivered you safely to him, I am commanded to repeat the trick. You may collect your belongings. We do not tarry." Glancing at Lovell, who was groveling at his feet by now, he added gruffly, "Begone, man! You may finish that task anon."

"Aye, master." And Lovell was gone on the words, backing obsequiously through the door and shutting it behind him.

Alys watched him go with mixed feelings of relief and abandonment. She had no wish to face Sir Nicholas alone. Not that they were alone. Not when Hugh and the three other men with him made the room seem as close as a sumpter pack. She glanced at them, then back at Sir Nicholas, raising her chin. "I have no wish to return to London, sir."

He glared at her. "You will do—" He broke off and said sharply to his men, "Leave us. Go into the street or the back garden, or perhaps you will find warmth in the kitchen."

Thinking Lovell would have gone to the kitchen rather

than out where he would meet more of Sir Nicholas's men, Alys said hastily, "The kitchen is small, sir, and will be smoky, for the cook fire is in the center and there is no proper chimney."

Sir Nicholas glanced at the hearth, where Lovell's efforts had produced less than admirable results. "The kitchen cannot be worse than this will be in three minutes' time, for that lout did not do his work properly. Here, Hugh, see what you can do with that fire before you go, or else we shall be suffocated in here."

"No doubt you frightened him," Alys said, paling when she realized that the others were going to the kitchen. That fact and the sight of Hugh made her wonder where Jonet was and why she had not come to the parlor the minute she knew they had visitors.

Sir Nicholas had been looking at her, and now he said in a gentler voice than he had used before, "What is it, *mi geneth*? Are you affrighted, too?"

"No," she said, too caught up in her own thoughts to wonder at the change in his tone, "but I am concerned that Jonet or her sister may be terrified when those men burst into their kitchen."

"Then Mistress Hawkins is here." He glanced at Hugh, still kneeling over the fire, and said, "I had heard so, and am glad that the Lord did spare her." When Alys said nothing, he added, "My men will not harm her or her sister, as you must know if you give the matter thought, and too, they will be gone the sooner for your quick obedience to my command."

Depression settled over her at the realization that he meant simply to return her to London like a stray lamb to the fold, and that she could not fight him. If she did, she knew he would just pick her up bodily and order one of his men to collect her things. Ian, no doubt. That thought brought a gasp of dismay.

"I pray you, sir, you must not punish Ian."

"He did only what I bade him do, mistress. He was com-

manded to serve you. I disagree with his interpretation of
my command, but I do not fault him for obeying it. You,
however . . ." He said no more, but his expression spoke
volumes.

Alys said through clenched teeth, "I won't marry a traitor."

"You will do as you are bid," he retorted, "and, pray, do
not trifle with me, lass, for I am not presently in possession
of my customary good humor. I had counted on service in
the field to prove myself to his noble grace, hoping to be
rewarded with English lands to go with my new title, but
your action deprived me of that opportunity. I have worn my
temper out, scouring the English countryside in search of
you, so do not vex me more, but go and prepare yourself to
travel, and that right swiftly."

"How did you find me?"

"I set Hugh to search London in the unlikely event that
you had got assistance from a Yorkist faction there, while I
traveled north in the greater certainty that you would make
for Wolveston. When there was no word of you there, I rode
on, thinking you might seek sanctuary at Middleham, not
realizing it is now in royal hands. I did even," he added with
a grimace, "journey to Drufield Manor. You are well out of
that place, mistress."

"Aye," she agreed. "What then?"

"Hugh and his men, not finding you in London, followed
us to Wolveston. Finding us gone north, Hugh thought to
inquire after the well-being of Mistress Hawkins and learned
that someone else had made a similar inquiry just before
him. He sent for me and met me on the road. But you dally,
lass. Collect your things."

The door opened, and Jonet entered behind him, curtsying and saying politely, "God give you a good day, Sir Nicholas. Will you stay to sup with us? 'Tis only Lenten fare, I
fear."

"Nay, mistress," he said, turning. "I have come to take her
ladyship back to London. We will depart within the hour."

Jonet folded her hands at her waist, looked directly at him

and said, "I will pack our things at once, sir." Then, before he could respond, she gasped, clapped a hand to her bosom, and stared beyond him at Hugh, who had finished his task at the hearth and rose now to his full height.

He regarded her with keen approval. "You look prickling pert again, lass. 'Tis glad we are to see you so."

Recovering herself, Jonet nodded brusquely at him, pressed her lips tightly together, and turned to leave.

"One moment, Mistress Hawkins," Sir Nicholas said.

"Yes, sir?"

Thinking he meant to forbid Jonet to accompany them, Alys said swiftly, "She goes with me, sir, or I will defy you every step of the way and complain of your treatment when we arrive."

"Almost you tempt me, *mi geneth,*" he said softly, adding in a louder tone to Jonet, "Prithee, tell Ian we depart very soon."

# 12

As soon as they were alone in the tiny bedchamber that had been allotted to her upstairs, Alys whispered to Jonet, "His lordship? Did he get safe away?"

"Aye," Jonet replied, "through the garden, with our Davy. The Welshman must not learn his lordship's identity. Nor that Hugh, neither."

"In faith, we must trust that they never do," Alys agreed fervently. She could not imagine how Sir Nicholas or Hugh might learn such a thing now that Lovell was well away, but halfway back down the stairs she realized she had forgotten to warn Ian to say nothing about the stranger he had seen when they returned from church, a stranger who had since mysteriously disappeared.

It was too late to do anything about that now, for Sir Nicholas was in the hall below, and he had seen them. He ordered two men to collect their baggage, then invited the women to come into the parlor again. When they had done so, he said casually, "The fire burns more briskly now, does it not, mistress?"

A note in his voice caused Alys to watch him warily. "In faith, it does so, sir."

"You must scold your servant for his carelessness when he returns," he said. "When will that be, by your reckoning?"

"I . . . I do not know, sir."

"I feared you might not," he said, nodding. Then with a

sharper look, he demanded, "What is his name, mistress?"

Alys went still with fear, feeling the blood drain from her face, and hoping he would not notice her pallor. He was a man who noticed such things. Speaking the first name that came to mind, she said, "I believe his name is Peter, Peter Fairbairn."

There was a moment's silence before he said softly, "It is never wise to lie to me, *mi geneth*."

She knew that, but she could not betray Lovell. Nor could she further endanger Jonet and her family, for merely by allowing Alys to meet with the viscount under their roof, they had put themselves at considerable risk. At last, unable to meet Sir Nicholas's penetrating gaze, she said gruffly, "I do confess, sir, that I did not speak the truth, but I cannot say more."

"The outlaw Lovell is known to be in Yorkshire," he said in that same soft, dangerous tone.

A stillness followed, and when the parlor door opened, Alys turned with profound relief to greet the newcomer. Hugh came in, looked slowly from one to another of them, then said in his deep voice, "The lads be ready, Nick."

When Sir Nicholas shifted his gaze from Alys at last, and nodded, she breathed a sigh of relief. He would not press for more information now. He knew she would not speak about Lovell.

Hugh said, "Will you take my arm, Mistress Hawkins?"

Jonet glared at him without moving, and Alys said, "I fear we have no palfreys to ride, Sir Nicholas."

"Just how did you come north, mistress?"

"With the players, sir, the ones who performed for the king and the Lady Elizabeth at Westminster."

"The Princess Elizabeth," he said reprovingly.

"Aye, sir."

"Are these players of yours Yorkist sympathizers?"

"No, merely players. Ian knew one of the women. We traveled with them, walking, or riding their mules or horses—even at times in their wagon, though 'twas most uncomfortable."

" 'Tis difficult for me to believe you would willingly choose such a method of travel, mistress, or such lowly companions. I must speak to Ian about his weakness for feminine wiles. 'Twas not suitable for you to travel in such a way."

She smiled. "Verily, sir, I can adapt myself to anything if I wish strongly enough to do so. And in truth, 'twas the players who were discomforted, for I am sadly lacking in the skills necessary to live as they do. They were kind and obliging, however, although they must often have wished that the devil who had brought me would fly away with me again."

Sir Nicholas turned quickly and moved past Hugh, through the open door, to the passageway, but Alys had seen the sudden gleam of humor in his eyes, and was grateful for it. Still, he had not said what they would do about getting a proper mount for her.

Hugh said to Jonet, "You are too silent, my little miskin. I would prefer to hear the tuneful clacking of thy pretty voice."

"If a din would suit you, Hugh Gower," Jonet snapped, turning from him toward the doorway, "then go put your great head into a kettle and beg the kitchen maid to beat it with a spoon."

Following Jonet into the hall, Alys called, "Sir Nicholas!"

He turned. Any look of amusement was gone. "What now?"

"Horses, sir. I told you, we have none."

"We have horses aplenty for you, mistress. I learned long since to leave naught to chance where you are concerned." He turned on his heel then, leaving them to follow with Hugh.

Their journey south was not a pleasant one, for neither the bad weather nor the poor condition of the roads improved Sir Nicholas's temper. They passed the nights at religious houses along the way, but although they received hospitality, there was little cheer to be found, and no meat, for it was Lent, and the meals were sparse. No more snow fell, but the temperature remained low, and the roads, when they were not slippery with ice, were rutted and slushy.

Jonet disliked traveling at any time, and Alys knew that only her loyalty to her mistress kept her from voicing her displeasure aloud. As it was, she resorted to her beads so often that Alys began to feel guilty every time she saw her reach for them. Hugh rode near them, keeping an eye out for difficulties, but Jonet continued to snub him, giving his impudent compliments short shrift, but more often than not, ignoring him.

Alys frequently found herself recalling her last trip with Sir Nicholas. By comparison, it had been pleasant. She recalled their conversations, things he had told her about himself and about Wales. He had seemed human then, not distant and irritable as he was now. From time to time, when she caught his gaze upon her, he looked pensive, and she would recall the brief flash of amusement she had seen in his eyes earlier. He was not amused now. Even the pensive look would vanish when he saw her watching him, and he would become gruff again. She reminded herself that he could be gentle, even kind, but it was more common now to hear him shouting orders and cursing those who were slow to obey them. He rarely rode anywhere near her, and since Jonet had made it clear that she did not want to ride near Hugh, they were limited to conversing with each other, and occasionally with Ian.

They found the court at Greenwich, and not much to Alys's surprise, she was directed at once to the ladies' side, where she and Jonet were greeted by Lady Emlyn Lacey.

With a brisk if not haughty air, that plump dame informed Alys that she was to remain in her bedchamber until such time as the king chose to send for her. "I will take you there, Lady Alys, and see that a maidservant is assigned to assist you. I am pleased to see that this time you have brought with you at least one of your personal servants."

"This is Jonet Hawkins, Lady Emlyn," Alys said. "Am I not to wait upon her noble highness?"

"Not until the king has spoken with you," Lady Emlyn said. There was a note in her voice that Alys could not decipher, one that made her wonder if she was in even more serious trouble than she had imagined. She had not enough courage left to demand an explanation; however, minutes after Lady Emlyn had left them alone, when the door opened and Madeline slipped into the tiny chamber without ceremony, Alys greeted her with rueful delight.

"Madeline, I am in such disgrace! Mayhap you ought not to be seen in my company."

"On the contrary, it will do me all manner of good," Madeline said, grinning. When Alys looked bewildered, her expression changed quickly to concern. "You do not know!"

"Know what? What has happened?"

" 'Tis your brother, Alys. He—" She broke off, peering into Alys's face as though she would read her feelings in her expression. "Did you care very deeply for Lord Wolveston?"

"I scarcely knew him," Alys replied. "In faith, when I left here, I had no liking for him at all. But you say 'did I,' as though he were . . . Mercy on us! Do you mean to say—"

"He is gone, Alys, dead. They know not how, but some do suspect foul play. He was hearty one hour and dead the next, as though he had the sweat, but no one has died of that in months now, and he did not display the proper symptoms."

"What symptoms had he?"

"Scarcely any. They say he collapsed where he stood, in the hall amongst the other men, his ale mug flung aside, and that he did groan and writhe upon the floor before he was gone."

Alys gasped. "Poison?"

"They say not, that the serpent's tongue was passed across his mug afterward and did not alter one whit."

Alys had more faith in a toadstone that would turn color and grow hot if it touched poison. A bit of unicorn's horn—

actually narwhal's tusk—was even better, for it was an antidote to all poison, but she knew that present fashion favored the serpent's tongue. One such, chased in silver, had been made part of the royal salt dish, which sat always on the king's table.

She was silent for a long moment, searching her emotions for the sorrow she thought she ought to feel at losing her brother. The suddenness of Roger's death stunned her, but she could not say she had cared for him. He had been much like her parents in temperament, cold and distant. She had never seen him clap a friend on the shoulder and laugh, as she had seen the Plantagenet men do often. Roger had not been merry or boisterous, nor had he been given to hugging or kissing the ladies in his family, or any other ladies for that matter. But he had been the last of her immediate family. She was alone in the world now, bereft.

"What is to become of me?" she wondered aloud. "Am I merely to dwindle into a pawn of the Stanleys now and nothing more?"

Madeline shook her head. "I know not what the king means to do," she said, "but I do know that the Stanleys are not pleased about this turn of events. You are an heiress now, Alys."

"An heiress?"

"Aye, to all of Wolveston Hazard and your father's wealth, as well. The king did return all to your brother, and you are his next of kin. The title falls into abeyance, but the wealth is yours, and they do say 'tis a surprisingly vast amount."

Alys stared at her. She had never given much thought to the material worth of her father or brother. If she had, she would have thought only of Wolveston Hazard, the rents owed to the castle by its tenants and those of its various estates. "Is Wolveston so profitable?" she asked.

Madeline shrugged. "It appears that our late king named your father Warden of the Eastern Ports, and that revenue pours straight into the Wolveston coffers. Did you not know? There are a number of villages, too, they say, that became part of the estate during King Richard's reign. The news of the worth of the place did surprise most people. Marry, the word had only begun to get about a day or so before Lord Wolveston's death."

"I did not know. There was always money, but I never thought about its source. Nor did I ever see much of it."

Madeline's eyes twinkled. "Sir Lionel Everingham, you will be interested to know, has renewed his suit for your hand."

"But I am to be betrothed to—"

Madeline shook her head. "I told you, the Stanleys are all muttering as if an imp had put ashes in their porridge. Talk is that the king means to prevent wealth from accumulating in only a few families as it did before. 'Tis his opinion—or so certain of the ladies do say their menfolk have said—that Richard made a grave error by allowing the Percys, Stanleys, and others of their ilk to grow so strong. Henry intends to scatter the wealth, to award it to his most loyal followers. Many are surprised that he did not merely seize Yorkist lands outright and gift them to his favorites; however, they do say he is a canny sort, that he does not want to alienate the northerners. Therefore"—she paused with an eloquent look—"he means to use the institute of marriage to introduce many of his favorite Welsh and southern lords to the north. They will thus get their rewards without stirring such outrage as there might otherwise be."

Alys was silent, thinking. She glanced at Jonet, but the woman said nothing, nor could anything be read in her expression. Remembering Madeline's comment about Sir Lionel, she said, "The Tudor will never betroth me to a Yorkist like Everingham."

"No," Madeline agreed, "but to hear Sir Lionel speak, one would never know he had had the least thing to do with Yorkists. He is now, he insists, the king's most loyal follower."

"He is naught but another turn-tippet then, and I shall refuse to have aught to do with him," Alys said firmly.

" 'Tis my belief you will be granted no choice in the matter," Madeline said. "The king seeks no assistance from others in political matters, but you need not fear marriage to Sir Lionel Everingham. *He* is not a royal favorite."

An image of one who was a favorite flashed through Alys's mind, stirring unfamiliar sensations in her midsection, which she had no wish to identify and which she promptly dismissed. Since the Tudor could command as he pleased, naught was to be gained by opposing him, and no one would support her. It was a pity, she thought, that as wealthy as Madeline believed her to be, she had no money at hand, nor any of the power that vast wealth would convey to anyone other than an unwed maiden. To have a say in one's future would be as intoxicating as heady wine, though she had not the slightest notion what she would choose to do.

The command for her to present herself to the king came late that afternoon, and by then her curiosity was well aroused, for Madeline, who had spent the intervening time imparting all the court gossip—including the interesting fact that there was cause to hope that Elizabeth might be carrying Henry Tudor's child—had likewise presented in turn, for consideration as bridegrooms, each of the Tudor's nearest followers. Her comments were pithy and amusing, but Alys knew none of the men personally, and what little she heard of them gave her no yearning to know more. It was, in any case, a matter of indifference to her what husband was chosen for her—or so she airily insisted to her companions. But when Lady Emlyn came to command her to prepare at once to attend the royal presence, she found it suddenly difficult to breathe or to speak.

"Do not stand gaping, child," her ladyship said sharply. "You have little enough time as it is. You there, woman, fetch out your mistress's best gown, and you, Mistress Fenlord, bestir yourself to assist us. I have been wondering these past two hours where you had hidden yourself."

Madeline ignored her, saying anxiously to Alys, "Shall I send for ale or wine? You are as white as newfallen snow."

"She requires not wine but rouge," Lady Emlyn snapped. "Fetch it out right swiftly, for she must not show that pale countenance to his noble grace, lest he think her ailing." She rejected as unsuitable the first gown Jonet brought forth, a pretty long-sleeved robe of rose velvet, bordered in gold braid. " 'Twould be best, Mistress Hawkins, in view of her recent transgression to remind his noble grace of her even more recent bereavement," she declared. "Has she nothing more somber in nature, yet nonetheless elegant, to wear?"

"Aye," Jonet said, returning to the wardrobe in which Alys's gowns had been placed and extracting a dress of brocaded dark gray damask edged in Naples lace. "Will this one do, my lady?"

Lady Emlyn nodded, then said, "Has she a silver belt to wear in place of that bejeweled, gold-link one she now wears?"

Jonet began to nod, but Alys, having had enough of being discussed as though she were air, said firmly, "I will wear the gold. 'Twas a gift from one I hold most dear, and I shall wear no other. Fetch out my pearl necklet, Jonet," she added quickly, fearing that Lady Emlyn would demand to know the belt's origin and then, learning that Anne had given it to her, categorically forbid her to wear it.

Lady Emlyn, however, folded her lips and disdained to continue the argument, saying nothing more until Alys was dressed. But when Jonet would have plaited her hair in order to confine it out of sight beneath her veil, Lady Emlyn interceded again. "Leave it free," she said then. "His grace prefers to see maidens with their tresses unbound. A black lace coif to match the trimming of her gown will suffice as her headdress."

When Alys was ready at last, she followed the plump dame to the presence chamber, her heart pounding harder the nearer they approached. What she had seen of the Tudor thus far did not lead her to suppose that he would greet her misdeeds with laughter. Even if he had changed his mind about betrothing her to Lord Briarly, he would certainly be displeased with her, and could, if he chose, arrange to make her life an endless misery.

To her dismay, when the yeoman guard opened the doors, the king's presence chamber was teeming with people, all gowned in rich clothing, chattering like squirrels, while a quartet of fiddlers played near the royal dais. The din thus produced was punctuated by an occasional tinkle of feminine laughter or a masculine bellow for more wine. Yeoman servants passed about, serving the hot mulled wine called hippocras in golden cups, and comfits from golden platters. It was the hour called voides, which by royal command now preceded the six-o'clock trumpet call of the heralds to announce that supper was about to be served. Alys had not realized the day was so far advanced.

A carpeted strip leading from door to dais, up the center of the long, rectangular room, was being kept clear, and Lady Emlyn, having paused upon the threshold, said to Alys, "Precede me, if you please. The king is waiting."

Taking a deep breath and wishing her heart would stop thumping, Alys obeyed, keeping her eyes downcast at first, until she realized that the sound level in the room was diminishing. Glancing from one side to the other, she saw that people nearby had broken off their conversations to watch her. And with each step she took, others fell silent. She raised her eyes then, to look directly at the king, determined that no one in the room should recognize her fear. Not until then did she become aware that Elizabeth was seated beside the Tudor, at his right.

As usual the princess's beautiful face was set serenely, but Alys looked into her eyes and saw smug triumph there. Whether the look was due to the fact that Elizabeth was thought to be carrying the king's child, or to the fact that she knew and approved of his decision regarding Alys's fate, Alys could not know. She did know, from experience, that Elizabeth's expression boded her no good. The room had fallen silent. She heard the clink of the gilded mirror at-

tached to Lady Emlyn's belt, against some other bauble she
wore, when the woman came up beside her.

Just then the king's fool, dressed in motley with a belled
cap perched atop his orange-dyed curls, and sitting on the
edge of the dais at his master's feet, leapt up, turned a hand-
spring, and pointing at Alys, burst into laughter and recited
tauntingly,

> "Pit pat, well-a-day,
>  Little Alys flew away.
>  Where did little Alys flee?
>  She fled into the north country."

Grinning in response to chuckles from the audience, he laid
a finger aside of his nose and went on in the same tone,

> "Pit pat, alas-alack,
>  Little Alys has come back.
>  Will she, nill she, ring-a-ling,
>  Bend Yorkist knee to Tudor king?"

Alys, feeling telltale warmth in her cheeks, did her best to
ignore both him and the chuckles she heard, and sank into
a deep curtsy. When the fool laughed again, she looked up
to meet the king's gaze. Not daring to appear to challenge
him by continuing to stare boldly into his eyes, she looked
down again.

The fool recited then, in his singsong voice,

> "Little Robin Redbreast
>  Sat upon a pole,
>  Niddle, noddle
>  Went his head,
>  And poop went his hole."

The shouts of laughter from the assemblage broke off as
if someone had slashed them with a knife, and Alys, blushing
deeply, looked up again to see that Henry had shifted his

gaze to the fool. The king said not one word, just looked at him, but with bells tinkling madly, the fool flung himself at the royal feet.

"Have mercy upon poor Tom Blakall, my master! His tongue hath run away with his brains!"

"Begone from our sight, Tom Blakall; thy words displease us," the king said quietly. When the fool, not daring to speak again, had fled, Henry said, "Rise, Lady Alys. The antics of Tom Blakall do frequently amuse us, but he has offended our taste by failing to heed your recent loss. We have beseeched our Lord to look mercifully upon you in your bereavement."

"You have my thanks, your noble highness," Alys murmured, rising obediently. She was grateful that he had sent the fool away, but her gratitude was overridden by an undutiful wish that Henry might look as mercifully upon her as he had beseeched the Lord to do, and an even stronger wish that he had chosen to say whatever it was he meant to say to her in a more private moment.

He looked at her thoughtfully for a long moment before he said, "You did not choose to wed our cousin Stanley?"

Alys flushed. "I crave your pardon, sir. I behaved badly."

"In good sooth, 'tis true. But circumstances having altered, it is no longer our wish to see you wedded to him. To see the Wolveston estates added to the Stanley coffers would not suit us. Your future lies otherwise, Lady Alys, and we trust you will not see fit this time to defy our command."

"N-no, sir," she replied, wondering why it was that her skin was prickling when the man had made her no threat, had not even seemed especially displeased with her. His very calm was disturbing to one who had known the Plantagenet rages of King Edward, the generally milder but no less ominous displeasure of his brother Richard, and the equally disturbing tempers of Sir Nicholas Merion. There seemed to be no passion in Henry, only a subtle intensity of manner that baffled Alys, and frightened her. She believed him to be a ruthless man who permitted himself neither emotion nor illusions.

He stood up, and Alys stepped involuntarily backward, treading upon her own skirt, but she managed not to fall.

The king smiled. His smile was singularly attractive, bringing animation to his aquiline features, and lighting his face. A twinkle began to dance in his eyes. For the first time he looked amiable, even cheerful, and Alys began to understand how it was that men had chosen to follow him. He looked past her for a brief moment before his gaze came to rest upon her again.

Elizabeth stood now, too, smiling at someone behind Alys, and Alys wished she had the nerve to turn and look.

"Lady Alys," Henry said, "there is one not unknown to you who deserves our grace and favor."

Alys's heart skipped a thump. Her breath caught somewhere between her breast and her throat. Though she was aware of movement and speculative murmuring from the company around her, she dared look only at the royal feet on the carpeted dais. She strove to breathe slowly, evenly, as Anne had taught her to do.

The king's voice came again, this time as though he spoke through a long tunnel, from far away. "Sir Nicholas of the Welsh house of Merion, step forward."

Alys swayed and would have fallen, were it not for a firm hand clapped beneath her elbow. For a moment, she thought the hand belonged to Sir Nicholas, until Lady Emlyn's sharp voice sounded in her right ear.

"Collect yourself, girl! Would you disgrace yourself before the entire court?"

Alys drew herself up but refused to turn to see if Sir Nicholas had obeyed the royal command. Looking instead at the king, she saw that he was remarkably pleased with himself.

Sir Nicholas made his bow beside her.

Henry grinned at him. "We are pleased to commend our ward to you as a suitable bride, sir. What say you?"

Sir Nicholas was silent for so long that Alys, suddenly indignant, turned to glare at him. He ignored her, but she recognized the glint of humor in his eyes when he replied to the king, "I suspect you do me no great favor, my liege. She has already led me a dance the length and breadth of all England."

Alys heard a gasp from somewhere behind her and feared that Sir Nicholas had overstepped himself, but a deepening of the royal twinkle proved that he knew his master well.

Henry said, " 'Tis good she has given you opportunity to see the English countryside, sir, and marriage to her will benefit you in other ways as well. 'Tis a sadness now that we sent Tom Blakall from our presence, else he might enumerate them for us."

Chuckles could be heard from the company, and Alys felt as if her cheeks were on fire. She dared not look at anyone.

Sir Nicholas said evenly, " 'Tis to be hoped those benefits will outweigh the heavy penalties, my liege."

"I warrant you will know how to master the wench," Henry said bluntly, adding in a louder, more formal tone, "There being no concern in this instance with consanguinity, but dispensation being required to allow you both to marry outside your parish, it is our decision that you shall be wed by special license. Our royal chaplain will therefore perform the betrothal service before we sup, and the marriage can take place on Simnel Sunday."

Less than a fortnight, Alys realized, her thoughts whirling and her knees feeling suddenly too weak to support her. Mid-Lent or Simnel Sunday—named for the little cakes of light grain, or simnel, that were customarily eaten that day—was usually a welcome date in the midst of the long, harsh Lenten fast; but now she doubted she would look forward to the feasting as much as she usually did. Under cover of the surge of conversation that arose while the chaplain was being hastened forward, she turned to Sir Nicholas and muttered, "You will rue this day, sir."

Leaning close to her, he retorted, "I had better not, *mi geneth*. You have this betrothal and little else to thank for the fact that I have not yet apprised his sovereign grace of your secret parley in the north with the outlaw Lovell."

Alys stared at him in shock. It had never occurred to her that, even if he had guessed the truth, he might contemplate such a thing. He smiled sweetly back at her and took her hand in his.

The chaplain took his place before them.

# 13

The evening that followed Alys's betrothal to Sir Nicholas passed swiftly amid a din of comments and plaudits from people she knew and others she did not know. Her senses were reeling one moment, numb the next. She was so dazed by it all that had she been asked when she left the table what she had eaten, she would have been unable to reply with certainty. It all had happened too swiftly. If she spoke to Sir Nicholas, she did not recall it later; and their parting came, as everything else that night had come, with bewildering abruptness. Sir Nicholas simply announced that it was time she was in bed, and signed to a servant to see her to her room. Briefly she considered sending the man to find Madeline, but even as the thought entered her mind, she knew she did not want to talk to anyone until she had sorted out her feelings.

Jonet was waiting for her, and after one look at her, began preparing her for bed, chattering the whole while in a manner that showed she had no expectation of a reply, speaking thoughts aloud as they came to her. Alys made only token replies, letting the words flow past her, taking comfort from Jonet's presence, but grateful nonetheless when she went away to her own pallet at last. Alone in her bed with the protective darkness close about her, Alys tried to remember precisely what Sir Nicholas had said or done that night to indicate how he felt about their betrothal, but the only com-

ment she could actually recall his having made to her was
his remark about Lovell.

That in itself was frightening. If their betrothal was all that
had kept Sir Nicholas from betraying his suspicions of her,
she had grievously misread him. There had been a single
moment, the first moment that she had recognized the Tudor intent, when her heart had sung with joy. The sensation
had been unlike any other in her memory. She tried to tell
herself that it had been no more than a surge of relief at
realizing that she would not have to marry Briarly, but overriding that thought came the memory of Sir Nicholas's lute,
and his deep melodic voice when he had sung to her. She
remembered that he had paid Ian to look after her in the
Tower, but there were less pleasant memories, too. He had
been quick to anger, and quick to scold. He had flogged Ian
and made her watch. He had forced her to eat when she
hadn't wanted to eat, but he had brushed her hair for her
when she had been too weak to do it herself. There was
much in the man that stirred her to rebellion, but there was
something else that stirred other, stranger reactions deep
within her. One moment she wanted to trust him, the next
to slap him. Until she knew him better, she did not dare to
do either.

She was hot under the coverlet and pushed it off her,
wondering where Sir Nicholas was at that moment, and if
he was thinking of her. What did he think? More than once
she had thought he cared about her. That first moment in
Doncaster, before she saw anger, she had seen relief and
knew he had been worried about her. But tonight there had
been no sign of pleasure in him, only half-grateful accep-
tance of his reward.

She remembered his remark about her meeting with Lovell. Since she had never admitted that Lovell was the man
in the Hawkinses' parlor, she wondered what had made him
so certain, but it was not until two days later, when the entire
court went hunting with the king, that she found an opportunity to ask him.

Henry Tudor liked to hunt, and when he did, his male courtiers all accompanied him. They were frequently accompanied, partway at least, by the more adventurous ladies; however, since the elaborate costumes suitable for court required them to ride aside rather than astride, on velvet-covered saddles wholly unsuited to the chase, the ladies were generally left behind once the quarry was sighted. That particular morning, when they rode out early to the forest south of Greenwich Palace, a number of women rode with them, including Alys and Madeline.

Alys wore a skirt and bodice of tawny wool beneath a dark green jerkin, with a straw hat pinned on over her veil. She rode between Madeline and Sir Nicholas, just behind the king and the Earl of Lincoln. The latter had greeted Alys with a kindly, indulgent manner, as though he had never been displeased with her. He did not even mention Sheriff Hutton, which did not surprise her, for she knew him to be a man who avoided offending, preferring harmony at almost any cost.

Elizabeth, due to her supposed delicate condition, did not ride with them, and Alys felt carefree, and was able to delight even more than usual in the herbal scents of the royal forest and the crisp, cold air of the sunny morning.

The king hunted with hounds, spaniels, mastiffs, and greyhounds, and since it was the fashion to hunt nearly anything that moved, it was not long before the first quarry, a young roe deer, was sighted. Henry, his bow held high, gave spur to his mount, and the other men followed at a gallop. Alys, finding the excitement of the chase rising swiftly within her, urged her palfrey to a more rapid pace, hoping they would not be left too far behind. But even as the thought flitted through her mind, a gloved hand shot out and grabbed her bridle, and her palfrey was drawn away from the others, into a small leafy glen.

Nearly as indignant with Madeline and the other women for riding merrily on without her as she was with Sir Nicholas for interfering with her, she glared at him and demanded angrily, "By what right do you dare to stop me like this, sir?"

He said quietly, "I have every right, *mi geneth*, by royal command, and I want to speak with you."

She bit her lip, remembering that the betrothal ceremony bound her to him almost as solidly as marriage itself, for even if the marriage did not take place, she was now ineligible to wed anyone else without the consent of the Church to set aside the betrothal. If she did, her children would be bastards like those of Edward the Fourth, unable to inherit her husband's goods and titles, or her own. Her property—in law, a mere extension of herself—was already Sir Nicholas's to control. Finding this knowledge rather disheartening, she resorted to another argument. "We are being left behind, sir. We shall find ourselves subject to criticism, if not to censure, for such behavior."

Sir Nicholas cocked his head to listen, then said, "I hear their shouts, so they have brought down the deer, or some animal. We'll hope for their sake 'tis not a polecat or a stoat." When she continued to glare, he added, "There is too little privacy at the palace. One can never be sure of having more than a moment or two alone, and I did not know when another opportunity might present itself to say what I wish to say to you."

Warned by the gravity of his tone, she braced herself. "What is it?"

"Only that I hope you are not too displeased by the king's decision to betroth us. I know you dislike me—"

"No! That is . . ." She searched for words to explain her feelings without betraying how vulnerable she felt. "I do not dislike you, sir. 'Tis only that at present I am bewildered by the very notion of marriage. My world has so recently come down around my ears that I scarcely know if I am on my head or on my feet. Nor do I know you, after all, except as one of the enemy."

"I am not your enemy, *mi geneth*."

"Mayhap." She looked into his eyes, wishing she could believe that the gentleness in his tone meant she might confide openly in him. "Why did you not. . . That is, last evening, before the ceremony, you told me . . . You . . . you said . . ." Giving up, she fell silent, unable to find words to challenge him without confirming what she hoped were no more than suspicions of his regarding Lovell.

Apparently finding nothing odd in her faltering speech, and reading her thoughts as he so often seemed to do, he nodded and said, "I ought to report your meeting with Lovell, but I will not do so. I did not do it before because I was not yet certain. Now that I am certain, you are to be my wife, and thus am I bound to protect you. But hear me, *mi geneth*," he added in a much sterner voice. "There must be no more such meetings. You will obey me in this, or I will make you very sorry afterward."

Discounting the threat, she said curiously, "Why are you so certain now that I met with him? You cannot know it."

"You told me."

"I did not!"

"Aye, you did. In Doncaster, when I mentioned his name, your expression revealed the likelihood, but I was not certain until yestereve. 'Twas but a gambit when I said I had not spoken of it to Harry, but your look of guilt then was as good as a confession. Nay, do not look daggers at me. You did wrong, and 'tis my duty to forbid you to behave so in future. Henry Tudor is king now, and to consort with his enemies, utter foolishness."

Alys stiffened angrily. "So now I am a fool, am I?"

"Aye," he said, smiling, "but no more than most females."

"Oh!" Forgetting that he still held her bridle, she lifted her reins and kicked her horse, intending to ride off and leave him where he was. The palfrey stirred helplessly, held firmly in place by a tightened fist. "Let me go!"

"Presently. I mean to be certain you understand me, my lady." There was an unmistakably possessive note in his voice now. "You are to have nothing further to do with any Yorkist sympathizer unless you want to incur my gravest displeasure."

Alys glared into space, refusing to respond, waiting with increasing apprehension to see what he would do next.

He did nothing. Neither did he speak. He waited patiently until she could bear the silence no longer, glared at him again, and said in a sharp voice, "What would you do?"

"That," he said calmly, "would depend upon the circumstance, but you would be wise to have naught to do with any Yorkist plot now in the making. That is to say," he added with a gentle note that was somehow more ominous than if he had spoken angrily, "if the outlaw Lovell expects aught of you, you must disappoint him."

Looking directly at him now, forcing what she hoped was the same calm note as his own into her voice, she said, "If there is a plot, sir, I am not party to it. For that you have my word."

He nodded, releasing her bridle. "It is enough, *mi geneth*. We will find the others now."

She had not expected him to accept her word so readily. In truth, she was disappointed that he had ended the conversation so abruptly. And in the days that passed before their wedding, though she had hoped to spend time with him, to get to know him better, she was disappointed in that as well, for Sir Nicholas was scarcely ever to be seen for longer than a moment or two.

The court moved by barge to Westminster the following week, and when Sir Nicholas was not in attendance upon the king, he was riding off with a troop of his men to look into some small matter or another for him. None of these sorties took him far from Westminster, but even when Alys knew him to be in the palace he made no effort to seek her out.

She assumed that his behavior was due to concern for her reputation, for although they were betrothed, she knew they must not seem to anticipate the marriage ceremony. The fact that he had accompanied her, not once but twice, on a journey of more than a hundred miles without anyone else present who might be thought a proper chaperon—Jonet, being only a servant, did not count—would not distress anyone, for he had been acting as her protector, commanded to do so first by Sir Robert Willoughby on behalf of the king, and then by the king himself. And even to the most determined rumormonger, she decided, his troops must be accounted to have been some protection to her honor.

Once, to her shock, she found herself wishing it had been otherwise, and that she knew him far better than she did. She wondered what it would be like to be possessed by a man who could make her fear his anger one moment and watch for his smile the next. She knew little of coupling. That was one disadvantage to the way she had been raised. In less private establishments, she knew that men and women coupled where and when they would, but she had never seen such things. She had seen animals mate, but whenever she tried to imagine herself and Sir Nicholas in such positions, her imagination boggled. It would be better, she thought, had they had the opportunity at least to sit and talk about themselves, but of course men and women rarely talked in such a fashion. Men dictated and women submitted, and that was that. The thought that Sir Nicholas would dictate to her and expect her to submit to his every wish had much the same effect upon her imagination as thinking of the mating animals had had.

He might have made more of an effort to seek her out, she knew, had opportunity arisen to do so, but the male and female courtiers might have been residing in two separate palaces for all that they saw of one another. Elizabeth was feeling sickly, and it had been agreed that she ought not to tax herself. There was still no official declaration of her condition, and when Alys asked, she was told the subject was not suitable for discussion. Nonetheless, with the king's full consent, Elizabeth was pampered and coddled. Her ladies read to her, waited upon her, and tended her as though, Alys thought wryly, she were made of glass, as though women through the ages—Elizabeth's own mother, for one—had not birthed child after child without much difficulty at all.

Lady Margaret, however, had not had such an easy time

of it, having produced only Henry Tudor. She was resolved that nothing would threaten one whose womb most likely carried the first seed of his dynasty, and in this, Elizabeth Woodville agreed. The queen dowager had not worked to see her daughter on the throne, only to have that position endangered through loss of the babe.

Elizabeth accepted the attention as her due, but Alys spent only a small portion of her days waiting on her, for the king, despite a growing reputation for being close with a shilling, had commanded that she be gowned as befitted his ward and the heiress to Wolveston. Alys had no objection to make to that plan and willingly stood for hours while elegant fabrics were draped about her and suitable colors and styles discussed. Not only did Madeline and Jonet offer advice but also the Lady Margaret, who, once her son had been generous enough to give the command, was determined to see it carried out in style. The result was hours of meetings with seamstresses, cobblers, milliners, and their ilk, hours more of embroidering such items as Lady Margaret deemed it necessary for Alys to do herself, and then yet more hours of fittings. The result was a wardrobe filled with more gowns, capes, surcoats, chemises, smocks, hats, shoes, and other such apparel than Alys had ever owned in her life.

The high-waisted wedding gown was fashioned of pale blue velvet, its low-cut bodice, hemline, and cuff edges trimmed with the expensive gray-and-white fur of tiny Siberian squirrels known as vairs (their fur reserved by sumptuary law to the nobility). It was worn over a white silk, lace-edged smock, the edges and trim of which could be seen both at the neckline and where the overskirt parted in front. Alys thought it truly lovely, but on the morning of her wedding day, as Madeline, Jonet, Elva, Lady Emlyn, and Lady Beatrix fluttered around her, fussing, fixing, and adjusting, she felt numb and distant, as if it were all happening to someone else. The morning swirled by in a daze of color, noise, and ritual, while she moved where others told her to move and performed as others commanded her to perform.

"You look as fine as a princess," Madeline said when she knelt to fasten Alys's jeweled girdle around her hips. She touched in turn each of the three pretty objects appended to it—a mirror set in gold, a pair of jeweled scissors, and a jeweled eating knife. "Splendid baubles," she said. "Was this a gift?"

"From Sir Nicholas," Alys said, feeling warmth rise to her cheeks as she said his name.

Madeline's eyebrows rose comically. "Mayhap there is something to be said for marriage, after all. Pray, hand me some of those bride laces, Lady Emlyn," she added, standing up again. Taking a handful of the colorful ribbons, she proceeded to attach them to various parts of Alys's gown. They would be pulled off after the ceremony by guests wanting a keepsake of the occasion.

While Madeline and Lady Emlyn attached the laces, and Jonet and Elva smoothed Alys's long hair and put the finishing touches on the lace-flower wreath that served as her only headdress, Alys took the pair of elegantly embroidered gloves Lady Beatrix held for her, and drew them on. She saw that her hands were shaking.

"Collect yourself, Alys," Lady Emlyn said sternly, standing back to survey the finished product. " 'Tis a measure of Sir Nicholas's favor with the king that the Archbishop of Canterbury himself is to preside over the ceremony at Westminster Abbey with the full court in attendance. You must not tremble or falter in your responses. You must do him honor."

Alys nodded, but her hands continued to shake and her knees felt weak. She was grateful that there were others to tell her what to do and show her where to go.

In the procession from the palace to the abbey, led by the groom and his attendants, with the bride and hers following after them, Alys felt as though she were in the sort of dream that would end with a whirling, falling sensation, a dream from which it was beyond her power to awaken. When the procession stopped at the abbey steps, those who had attended them along the way fell silent behind them, and those who had not taken part in the procession could be heard inside, rising to their feet.

Standing beside Sir Nicholas, before the archbishop, at the open doors of the abbey, Alys knew that not even the great pomp and circumstance she had known at Middleham, or at court before this moment, had prepared her for the triumphal blare of trumpets announcing her arrival at the church door or, indeed, any of the magnificence of her wedding day. Even the archbishop's grave intonations failed to make it real, though the ritual had been carefully explained to her by none other than the Lady Margaret, whose practice it was to leave nothing to chance. And thus, when Sir Nicholas's deep voice sounded beside her, Alys started and looked at him much as though she were surprised to see him there.

"I, Nicholas ap Dafydd ab Evan of the Welsh house of Merion," he said in a loud, clear voice, turning to face her and taking her right hand in his, "do take the Lady Alys Anne Wolveston to my wedded wife, to have and to hold, for fair for foul, for better for worse, for richer for poorer, in sickness and in health, for this time forward till death us depart, if the holy church will it ordain, and thereto I plight thee my troth."

Alys's small hand felt lost in his, though she was aware of the warmth of him. She stared at his elegant, heavily embroidered doublet and found herself wondering suddenly who had done the flawless work.

He reached for her left hand and slipped a ring on the third finger, saying, "With this ring I thee wed, and this gold and silver I thee give, and with my body I thee worship, and with all my worldly chattel I thee honor."

She looked at the ring, surprised to see that it was a miniature replica of his own, different only in that the golden wyvern was quartered with the arms of Wolveston, emblazoned in their proper colors by enamel applied to the base of the setting, then carved into the white sapphire above. The colors showed through the transparent stone, their effect heightened by its brilliance. Delight surged through her, and she looked up at him, her pleasure in his gift evident to everyone.

The archbishop cleared his throat, and becoming aware of the silence filling the abbey beyond him, Alys realized that he had already prompted her to speak her lines. Dread filled her that she had forgotten them, but the phrases came to her, and she looked directly into Sir Nicholas's eyes when she spoke them.

"I, Alys Anne Wolveston, do take thee, Sir Nicholas Merion, to my wedded husband, to have and to hold, for fair for foul, for better for worse, for richer for poorer, in sickness and in health, to be meek and obedient in bed and at board, till death us depart, for this time forward, and if holy church it will ordain, and thereto I plight thee my troth."

The trumpets rang out again, and the whole procession moved inside the abbey, bride and groom to kneel on satin cushions before the archbishop at the altar rail, all others to take their places in the pews behind them for the nuptial mass. When the mass was done, the procession reversed itself to return to the palace for the wedding feast.

The great hall rang with music and the roar of four hundred voices laughing and talking while they found their places at the tables that had been set out below the dais. The scene reminded Alys of the feast that followed the Tudor's wedding to Elizabeth, but this time she and Sir Nicholas sat at the high table with the royal couple. Not until she was actually sitting beside him did Alys attempt to think calmly about what was happening around her, and to search for familiar faces in the crowd.

She saw Sir Lionel Everingham, who looked disdainful, and Lord Briarly, who looked more as if he were at a funeral than a wedding feast. Hugh Gower towered above the other men, and there was Lincoln, smiling and elegant. She saw Lady Emlyn and one or two others she knew, but not Madeline. She wished Madeline might have sat with them on the dais, but she was somewhere below, no doubt flirting with one gentleman or another, or laughing and chatting with other ladies in waiting.

Alys reached for the gold goblet on the table before her, but Sir Nicholas's hand caught hers and squeezed it.

"Not yet, *mi geneth*," he murmured close to her ear. "Wait until the king drinks his toast to us."

Flushing, she realized she had not thought about what she was doing, that she had nearly committed a grave error. There was a swish of silken skirts behind her, and she turned to see that Elizabeth had risen from her place beside the king and now stood directly behind her. Awkwardly, Alys also rose, well aware that it would not do to push her chair into Elizabeth, and aware too that Elizabeth had meant the situation to be awkward.

"Madam?" she said, curtsying as best she might under the circumstances and rising without awaiting permission to do so. "Did you desire to speak to me?"

"Yes, I did," Elizabeth said in her soft voice. "I requested permission of his noble grace to sit beside you for a time, whilst we eat, since you will no doubt prefer the company of a woman at such a time as this. 'Tis a pity that your mother and father did not live to enjoy this day with you."

Sir Nicholas having also risen, overheard, and said with a smile, "Your kindness, madam, is a byword, and I have no doubt that my wife is particularly grateful for it on this occasion. The day has been a full one, and she has had few to support her."

"But you, sir, also have had to celebrate this day of days unsupported by your family," Elizabeth said.

" 'Tis kind of you to express such sentiment, madam," Sir Nicholas said, smiling again at her, "but 'twould have taken more than a fortnight at this season for my father and brothers to learn of the occasion and ride to London."

"Perchance," Elizabeth said, shooting a glance at Alys, "you will desire to take your bride from us, sir, to introduce her to your family and the wilderness of Wales."

Unable to remain silent longer, Alys said, "I am told that

Wales is not so wild as we have thought, madam. Sir Nicholas has told me that many things there are much the same as in England."

"Nevertheless," Elizabeth said, "you must long to see your future home, Alys dear."

"Wolveston Hazard is my home, madam," Alys said firmly. "No one will ever—"

"Will you not sit down, madam," Sir Nicholas cut in swiftly, drawing Alys aside and turning her chair so that Elizabeth might sit. Glancing at the king to see that he was conversing at that moment with a black-robed nobleman who had stepped onto the dais, he went on smoothly, "Alys may have my chair, and I shall sit in his grace's place for the present. That way I can sit by my bride as I am expected to do, and we may all be comfortable."

When Elizabeth and Alys had sat down again, he said, "My duties with the king will keep me from presenting Alys to my family for some time yet, madam, but I should be pleased to tell you about Wales if you like. Many of our laws will seem unusual to you. For example, my father's home will one day come to me as the eldest son, but by our laws, only a third of his land will be mine, for I have two brothers and we must share the wealth."

Elizabeth, arranging her skirts more to her liking, said to him across Alys, "I have heard about these strange laws, sir. How odd it would be if royal lands were to be thus divided."

"Odd!" Alys exclaimed. "Why, considering the battles that have been fought these thirty years past, I should say—"

Elizabeth's arched brows rose; however, it was not that sign of disapproval which silenced Alys but Sir Nicholas's foot treading hard upon her own. Stifling a squeal of pain and indignation, she said through clenched teeth, "I do apologize, madam. War is not a fit subject for such a day."

"No," Elizabeth said, "and we must not speak at all just now, for my husband is about to make his toast."

The king's toast was but the first of many, and when those proposed by members of the court had ended, the entertainment began. Minstrels, jugglers, a rope dancer, and a play were all interrupted by more toasts, each of which had to be returned by the bridal couple. By the time the king and Elizabeth retired, and Madeline and several other ladies came to accompany Alys to the bridal chamber, she had drunk much more than her fill. She rose tipsily from her chair, put her hand upon Sir Nicholas's arm to draw his attention away from the gentleman with whom he was speaking, and attempted to curtsy to him.

He caught her before she fell, and steadied her, saying with a chuckle to Madeline, "Get her ladyship to bed, lass, and do what you may to keep her awake until I get there. I've no wish to find my new wife snoring and dead to the world."

Laughing, Madeline said, "I shall attend to her, sir, never fear. Take my arm, Alys. It will not do for you to appear ape drunk before this company. Not," she added with a sapient look around the hall, "that any of them are much the better for drink than you are. It is to be hoped they will be satisfied to snatch a few bride laces and leave your virtue intact."

"How now!" Sir Nicholas said with a frown. "She must not be troubled on her way by any drunken louts. You there!" he called to one of the yeoman servants. "Find several other stout lads, and attend the Lady Merion and her attendants to my chamber. I will give you half an hour, Mistress Fenlord, to prepare her."

Finally, accompanied by a chorus of ribald comments from the company, most members of whom would not have dared, even in their besotted condition to shout such things had his noble grace still been present, Alys and her ladies took their leave. Having passed most of the day in a state of confusion and a sense of unreality, Alys felt numb again and was having all she could do to keep from disgracing herself before she escaped.

The bridal chamber, on the other side of the palace, was one of the apartments set aside for those of the king's favorites who merited rooms in whatever royal residence he chose to occupy. There were two rooms, an anteroom that served as a sitting room or parlor, and the large bedroom behind, where a fire crackled merrily in the hooded fireplace between two tall windows, and where Jonet awaited her charge. Since it was Sir Nicholas's chamber, Alys had not seen it before, but her belongings had been transferred there during the day, and her brushes and bottles graced the elegant dressing table with its Venetian mirror and velvet-covered stool. Never had she owned such a piece of furniture, and she stared at it now in amazement.

"How beautiful," she said.

Madeline, beside her, peering into the glass, was likewise impressed. "Any woman with that mirror cannot help but look her best every day. But here is the hot bath I commanded!"

"Not so hot, my lady," Jonet said quietly, looking with open disapproval at the giggling, laughing group of women who had accompanied them from the corridor and were trying now to follow them into the bedchamber. "Must they all be here?" she asked.

Madeline turned to look, called out the names of three, and said, "You may stay to help, but the rest of you must wait in the outer room to bar the way to any gentleman who attempts to offer assistance. Go now. Shoo!"

Laughing even more, the others left, and she shut the door behind them, muffling their chatter. Madeline turned briskly. "Isabel," she said to the first helper, a tall brunette, "turn down the bed and fluff the pillows; Marjory"—to a small, plump blond—"fetch out Lady Alys's green silk robe from that leathern coffer; and Sarah," she said to the third, a meek-looking girl, "you attend to the candles and stand guard over that door. I do not want an invasion of this room. Jonet, I will help you."

Alys, feeling as if the room were closing in on her, had moved toward the nearest window embrasure, hoping to find, behind the heavy blue curtain that matched the bed hangings, that the window was open. She desperately wanted a breath of fresh air.

"Oh no, you don't," Madeline said, laughing when she caught her. " 'Tis a bath for you, my lady bride, to waken you, and to freshen you after your long day in that heavy gown. Your husband will not want to cuddle a lady who reeks of smoke from the hall fires and the stench of grease from too many trenchers and too many unwashed bodies. Moreover, it will help you stay awake until he arrives. I, for one, would not wish to face him had I failed to obey his command, for I do not think Sir Nicholas a man with whose orders one might safely trifle."

"Sir Nicholas . . ." Alys began in a grim tone, but Madeline interrupted before she could say more.

"No time for chatter," she said. "Jonet, is that tub ready for her ladyship?"

"Aye," Jonet replied, "though it is no longer hot, mistress, as I tried to tell you. The men brought the water an hour ago."

"That will not signify. Marry, 'tis no doubt better thus." While she talked, she rapidly divested Alys of her clothing, and as soon as that was done, urged her toward the bath. The world had steadied a bit during the walk from hall to bed-chamber, but Alys was by no means recovered, and the room was filled now with the scents of burning logs, bath herbs and perfume, scents that generally delighted her but which she now found cloying and distressing to her senses.

Her stomach churned when she drew near the tub, and she said, "Where are the bath curtains? This is unseemly."

"Do not be difficult," Madeline said crisply. "You are to go naked to the marriage bed, my girl, so let us have no untimely modesty now. Make haste lest the gentlemen arrive."

"Gentlemen!"

"Aye, for although the king has proclaimed that there shall be no unseemliness about these celebrations, one cannot count upon the gentlemen to remember that now that their noble graces have retired. Better you should be safe in your bed."

Shocked by the thought that she might have to face a roomful of drunken men, Alys stepped more quickly than she might have done into the tub, only to find that Jonet's prediction was correct; the bath could make no claim whatever to warmth. When she cried out, however, her assistants forced her down into the tub, sponging her thoroughly despite her protests, but being mercifully brief in their ministrations. A few moments later, she stood up again, shivering despite the fire, and accepted with profound gratitude the huge towel Jonet wrapped around her.

They dried her and perfumed her, but there was no need for her green robe, for it was with only scant moments to spare that they urged her into the bed before the door opened without any ceremony whatever. If there had been any increase or decrease in the noise level from the anteroom, no one, including the meek damsel standing guard at the door, had noticed the fact.

Sir Nicholas stood on the threshold, a bevy of feminine faces leering over his shoulder at the bedchamber but without any sign of accompanying gentlemen. Alys sighed in relief but huddled under the quilts, her clenched fists gripping the covers tight against her naked body.

Sir Nicholas grinned at Madeline. "Many thanks, lass. I see she is awake and ready to receive her husband. You may go."

Jonet, curtsying, said, "I shall send for lads at once to remove the bath, sir."

"No need," he said brusquely, his ardent gaze fixed upon the figure in the bed. "Get thee gone now, every last one of you."

The ladies fled, leaving him alone with his bride.

# 14

Alys listened intently till the last noises faded from the anteroom. Not until the thud of a door closing in the distance put an end to all sound but that of the crackling fire did she dare to peep round the bed curtains at her husband.

He stood with his back to the hearth, surveying the room, and she wondered what he was thinking. Since he had married her by royal command for the purpose of controlling her estate, she could not believe he had any strong feelings beyond, perhaps, thinking her a nuisance. She hoped he would be kind to her, and she wished she could discern his thoughts from his expression.

He moved at last toward the dressing table, stepping around the tub, pulling off his hat with one hand while he removed the heavy gold-link chain he wore with the other. Large as the room was after Alys's small, stark chamber, he seemed to fill it as she, the splendid furniture, and five other women had not.

She swallowed, gripping the covers closer than ever, her knuckles aching, her heart pounding so hard she could hear it.

He turned his head to look at her over his shoulder. "Art still awake, madam wife? Do not fall asleep just yet. 'Twould be no good way to begin our marriage."

She swallowed again, managed to mutter, "No, sir," and continued to watch him through wide, wary eyes. She had not paid particular heed earlier to his attire, for it was much like that of the other men, but now she was fascinated by every thread.

He shrugged off his black velvet gown and laid it with his hat on a coffer near the wardrobe, then straightened, his hands going to the gold fastenings of his satin doublet. She watched silently while he undid them, one by one, with deft twists of his fingers, and removed his doublet to set it aside on the stool. His shirt was snow-white and of the finest linen, its sleeves softly draped, its body molding his broad chest and shoulders. Standing in only his hose and shirt, his back view reflected in the glass behind him, he was magnificent.

He smiled at her, and her heart leapt, stopping her breath and setting her every nerve atingle. "I brought no servant with me," he said. "Will you make me continue my disrobing unaided?"

She stared at him, dismayed. "I . . . I am un—unclothed, sir," she stammered.

"I had not believed otherwise, but 'tis a natural state, is it not? And I am now your husband."

She had promised to obey him. In fact, as she recalled the words, she had promised to be meek and obedient in bed and at board. And here she was in bed, but meekly obedient was the last thing she wanted to be. Were it possible to vanish from his sight, to pull the covers over her head one moment and put them down the next to find herself safely back at Middleham with Anne of Gloucester, she would not hesitate for an instant.

But Sir Nicholas was waiting.

Alys said between her teeth, "Sir, I cannot. I am not accustomed to walking about before a man without my clothing. I am sorry to displease you, but I cannot do it."

"Walk about?" His brow creased in puzzlement, and then he grinned at her. "By the bones of St. David, wife, you have a robe there on the bed, do you not? I did not mean you to serve me naked—not just at present," he added, his grin becoming more roguish. "Later, we will consider the matter."

To her surprise, instead of shocking her, his words sent a river of warm blood coursing through her veins, and while her pulses raced, in the pit of her stomach a new sensation stirred, one she could not identify but had no desire to suppress. It radiated downward, making her aware of a part of her anatomy to which she rarely gave much thought, but a part from which every nerve now seemed to emanate. Nervously she licked her lips.

When he chuckled she realized that he had been watching for her reaction, and she saw at once that it had stimulated him. She could feel a crackling in the air between them now that had not been there before. "Put your robe on, madam," he said, "and I will show you how a proper wife ought to behave."

"And how," she demanded with spirit as she leaned forward, still clutching the bedclothes about her, to reach for the green silk robe, "do you know aught about proper wives?"

His eyes opened wide with innocence. "Why, my mother taught me, of course. She has long insisted upon serving my father in just such a way, preferring to attend to his personal wants in the place of our servants. Do you disapprove?"

She drew the robe around her shoulders, hoping he would not offer to help her, and grateful when he remained where he was, though he did continue to watch her. There was an awkward moment when she had to let go of the bedclothes to clutch the robe close across her breasts, but she managed it at last, and arranged the material around her as best she could before pushing back the covers and sliding barefoot to the floor.

There was a sash to the robe, and she tied it tight, feeling nonetheless vulnerable in the thin garment with her hair tumbling down her back. Her toes wiggled in the soft dark fur of the rug near the bed, and she waited for his next command.

Nicholas had been watching her, and she saw that the warmth in his eyes had deepened to a more sensual, more carnal look that made her heart beat faster. As if he sensed her alarm, he turned away just then to the dressing table, and hearing a popping sound and a clink, she realized that among the other things on the table there must have been a bottle and goblets. He turned back, a gold-edged silver goblet in each hand. "Gifts from his noble grace," he said quietly. "He thought solid gold too heavy for you, and had these made. Each bears our name and device."

Reminded that she now had her own device, she looked down at the ring on her finger, then up at him, saying shyly, "Thank you for my ring, sir, and for my jeweled girdle. Both are wonderful gifts. I only wish I had a proper gift for you."

"You do, *mi geneth*," he said, his voice low in his throat, "you do." When her only response was a deep flush, he handed her one of the goblets, watching her turn it in her hand to examine the engravings. He frowned when she did not drink. "The wine will relax you, you know."

She gave him a twinkling look and said, "Verily, sir, 'tis not relaxation I fear but interior strife. My stomach has accepted a great deal of wine tonight, and only since my bath has it ceased its protesting. I'd as lief not test its patience."

He shook his head in amusement but said, "You cannot disappoint our Harry. He was vastly pleased with his goblets, intending them to be used for this purpose, and he will ask me if 'twas successful. Would you have me banished from court for disdaining their use or, worse, for disobeying my king?"

"You need not tell him."

His eyebrows flew upward in pretended shock. "You think it better that I lie to my sovereign liege lord? You surprise me."

Alys, her judgment dimmed by wine, and her sense of humor stirred by his teasing, managed a casual shrug and said, "He is only a Lancastrian, after all. What can he care about truth?"

Sir Nicholas's amusement vanished on the instant, and he snapped, "You must not talk so. I forbid it."

She opened her mouth to offer a saucy suggestion as to what he could do with such undesirable orders but remembered in time, and with a jolt of shock, that since he was now her husband there could well be unpleasant consequences to such a speech. Warmth flooded her countenance, and she lowered her eyelids, still watching him through her lashes, weighing courage born of too much wine against the likelihood of arousing his temper.

He nodded with satisfaction. "You do well to think before you speak," he said. "Continue the practice. And now, I pray you, madam, take one small sip of that wine, so that I may in good conscience tell our king how much we enjoyed his gift."

She obeyed, feeling the warmth of the wine soothe her all the way to her stomach. It was heady stuff, and the languor that had begun to abate came back in full force. She drank more deeply and felt herself begin to sway where she stood. When his hands came to her elbows to steady her, she leaned toward him, sighing when his arms went around her and he drew her close.

He murmured softly against her curls, and not understanding his words, she looked up at him curiously. "What did you say?"

He chuckled, the sound low, caressing. "Madam wife, I must teach you Welsh. 'Twill make matters far easier. I said that you are like the wine itself, deep, intoxicating, and delicious. But I suppose you have heard such compliments all your life."

"Not like those," she said in surprise. "Why should I?"

"As beautiful as you are, you need to ask? I have had to avoid you of late to keep my lust from overcoming my good sense."

"Am I so beautiful?" she said, glad to hear he had reason for his apparent neglect, but fearing to put too much faith in his words. He was ambitious. He had said so, and she was as certain now as before that he had accepted their betrothal and marriage with grace because of the wealth she had brought him. Now it appeared that he had also been prompted by lust. She could see it in his silent response to her question, and she knew that men could be motivated by their desires. Had not two women stirred the powerful King Edward to promises of wedlock with only their wiles and the alluring curves and cushions of their bodies? Women had very few weapons with which to sway men or to protect themselves, so it was gratifying to learn that she could arouse Sir Nicholas. However, recalling earlier attempts to influence him with her feminine wiles, she said, "I remember that you did once avow a preference for dark-haired, coal-eyed women."

"Such women are well enough," he murmured outrageously, his lips brushing her curls lightly before he set down his goblet and brought his hand to her chin, tilting her face up so that he might kiss her properly.

She had kissed many men, for kissing was not an uncommon greeting in the area where she had grown up, but she had never been kissed as he kissed her. His lips were warm and possessive, taking hers, tasting them, caressing and exploring them; and she found herself responding as though she had been doing such things all her life. She still held her goblet in her hand, and when he took it from her, she scarcely noticed. He put it behind him, meaning to set it on the table beside his own but misjudging the distance. When it fell to the floor neither of them noticed. His other hand had begun to explore her body, and now both hands began to move slowly, tantalizingly, over the smooth silk robe. Before long, he found the sash and loosed it, slipping his hands beneath the silk to her bare skin. She trembled.

"Your skin is as smooth as the silk, and my hands are rough," he murmured. "Tell me if I hurt you."

"You don't," she said quickly, afraid he would stop. She had never imagined feelings like those filling her body now. Her senses soared, and when his palms moved across the tips of her breasts, first one then the other, her eyes closed and she stopped breathing altogether, tensing, her mind focused totally on the sensations his touch created within her.

He caressed her gently for a long moment, while her breasts strained toward his touch, before his hands moved to her shoulders, to slip the silk from her skin. With a light, swishing sound, the robe slithered to the floor, a green puddle at her feet, but Alys paid it no heed, waiting blind and breathless until the magic hands returned to work their wonder.

Suddenly, Nicholas pulled her close, one hand again stroking her breasts, while the other moved behind, over her slim back to her narrow waist. He kissed her mouth again and then her cheeks, her eyes; and Alys stood, a supple statue now, letting him work his will with her, delighting in her body's response.

"Kiss me, little wife. Do to me as I do to you."

Her eyes opened in shock at the thought of fondling him as he fondled her, but then curiosity crept in, touching her mind, stirring her body to movement. He straightened, easing the strain of his position, so he did not seem quite so close, so intimidating. Her hands moved to his face, feeling the light stubble of his beard, for he had not been shaved since morning. Next she touched his lips, his nose, his eyes, and when he smiled, she stood on tiptoe to kiss him lightly on the lips.

"Don't stop," he said when she leaned back to see how he was reacting, "unless you've a wish to uncase me from the rest of my clothing. 'Tis most difficult for me to undo my shirt laces and hose points all by myself."

Her lips twitched, but she discovered that the thought of uncasing him was not a disturbing one. At least, not disturbing in the usual sense of the word. His nearness did disturb her, but her curiosity by now was overwhelming. Her fingers moved to the lacing on his shirt. A moment later, the shirt had joined her robe on the floor and her hands were exploring his chest, fingers moving through a forest of dark hair, while her eyes fixed with interest upon the movements of his breathing. To her amazement, she could tell from the change in the way he inhaled that she was arousing him more, and the knowledge delighted her. She looked up, smiling, seeing in his eyes the pleasure he felt.

Instinctively, she wanted to tease him. She began to touch his chest lightly all over, exploring its contours, spreading her palms across the forest of hair so lightly that the hairs tickled her hands, then pressing harder as though she would push him away. He resisted automatically, watching her, and she pushed harder to see what would happen.

He shook his head. "You'd never win a match of strength, lass. Continue with your task."

"I warrant you'd like to have a bath, sir," she said daringly. "The tub yonder has been used but once this night, so the water is nearly fresh."

"Wouldst bathe me, madam wife?" he murmured. "Wouldst rub me all over with thy perfumed sponge? Everywhere?"

She blushed. " 'Tis, as you once pointed out to me, sir, but common practice in most households." Suddenly, she realized she would like nothing better than to have the opportunity to see his body, to be able to run a sponge over every inch of it. The thought was nerve-tingling. Her senses threatened to overcome her, and the warmth in her cheeks now was like fire. She wondered if the task of bathing a man always filled the bather with such feelings. She looked at the wooden tub, which was behind him, to the left of the hearth, then back at him.

Nicholas laughed. "The water in that tub must be like ice, so you must wait for another opportunity, wife. I have no intention either of subjecting myself to torture or of waiting until hot water can be produced."

She sighed, making him laugh again, and he said, "You delay matters, madam. I would have my lower half uncased as well. You may begin with my shoes."

Conscious as she had not been before of her own state of

nakedness, Alys bent quickly to retrieve her robe. Nicholas's eyes glinted with laughter, and for a moment, holding the robe before her while she removed his shoes, she feared he would forbid her to put it back on when she stood up, but he did not. He assisted her, smoothing the silk into place over her breasts in such a way as to make her gasp at the sensations he caused.

"I like a responsive wench," he said, grinning.

Flames of jealousy leapt within her. Just as she had never before experienced the physical feelings he stirred, she had not known she could feel such fiery hostility. "I warrant," she said grimly, "that you have known a vast number of such women."

"Oh, not so many," he said, catching her hands when she would have tied her sash, drawing them instead to the ties of his codpiece. When she would have pulled them away again, he held them tightly, looking down into her eyes. "Unlace me, lass. I want you, and I am not a patient man."

She had noticed before that the codpiece, that flap of cloth forming a pocket at the fork of his knitted silk hose, bulged to contain his private parts; but now, as he spoke, the cloth strained all the more. He grew larger before her very eyes. He released her, and reluctantly, tentatively, she reached to apply her fingers to the lacing.

"Ah, yes, madam, you will learn," he murmured, slipping his hands again beneath the silk of her robe to tease her breasts.

Startled, she stepped away from him, protesting, "But I thought— You let me put it back on!"

"Only so that I might have the pleasure of removing it again," he said. "Come here to me." When she did so, licking her lips and then, when he merely stood waiting, raising her hands to his laces again, he said, "Perchance you will become an obedient wench in time if you are but properly guided."

Alys gritted her teeth, looking up from her task to say, "I will do as I must, sir, but I pray you, do not taunt me."

"But, *mi geneth*," he said softly, reaching out now to caress

her again where the robe fell open, "you must heed whatever
I say to you, must you not, now that we are wed? 'Tis the
law of God, and of man, as well. You must obey my commands and serve me as a proper wife serves her husband,
or suffer the penalties. Just as, for similar good reason," he
added with another, less easily decipherable note in his voice,
"you will learn in time to alter your political opinions in order
to accord them with mine."

Alys went still, her hands loosing their hold on his laces,
so that the flap slipped and her fingers suddenly encountered
bare skin. Snatching her hand away, she said fiercely, "I
doubt that I shall ever do any such thing, sir."

"Oh, I think you will do just as you are told, my little
Yorkist," he said, capturing her hand again and putting it
back where it had been, pressing it against his flesh, watching
her, his expression challenging her to defy him. "You are my
wife now and thus will soon become a good Lancastrian."
He released her hand, watching to see if she would dare take
it away.

She drew a long breath, measuring his mood, considering
her options. They were near the fire, and the tub was just
behind him to his left. She moved slightly, feeling that sense
of power again when he turned with her, his ardent gaze
fixed now upon the rise and fall of her breasts. "Women,"
she said quietly, "have from time to time been known to
exert strong influence over their husbands, sir. I might
change you into a good Yorkist instead."

"Never," he said firmly. "I am not such a fool."

"Fool, sir?" She turned a little more. "That makes twice
tonight that you have named me fool. Do you truly think me
one?"

"Nay, *mi geneth,* for you will change," he said, grinning at
her and confidently putting his fists on his hips as he pressed
himself more firmly against her hand.

"I think you must be taught that we Yorkists are not so
easily commanded, Welshman!" As she snapped the words,
she smacked both her hands flat against his chest and, her

strength increased by her anger, gave him a powerful shove.

Had the tub not been so close behind him, he might have saved himself, but when he stepped backward to regain his balance, his leg hit the side of the tub, and down he went. Even so, his coordination and strength after years of training to be a soldier were such that he only sat down hard, catching the sides of the tub as he did, and sending a flood of the chilly water over the stone floor. His legs bent absurdly over the rim.

When he fell, he reached out reflexively for Alys. Only the fact that she leapt backward, appalled by her temerity and stunned by its result, kept him from taking her down with him. When she saw him about to heave himself out again, she spun toward the door, her robe billowing behind her, her primary impulse being to seek safety as far from him as she could run.

"Don't touch that door!"

She had nearly reached it, but his tone, if not the words, stopped her in her tracks. She turned back slowly, drawing her robe protectively around her, to see that he had hauled himself out and was standing, dripping, by the tub.

"Come here."

She swallowed hard. By rights, with wet silk clinging to his powerful legs and his codpiece hanging open, its contents exposed and considerably diminished in size, Nicholas ought to have looked ridiculous, but Alys felt no inclination to laugh. His fury was tangible. She felt its waves from across the chamber. She saw it in his eyes, in his countenance, in the very way he stood. What little courage she had left evaporated at the sight. She remained where she was.

"I said, come here."

"What will you do?"

His eyes narrowed. He said, "I have been told of an English tradition called the rule of thumb. Do you know of it?"

She nodded, biting her lower lip. A man was not supposed to beat his wife with a stick thicker than his thumb.

"In Wales," Nicholas went on, "one law fixes the proper

penalty for a wife's insolence at three blows of a broomstick on any part of her except her head, or a more thorough thrashing with a switch the length of her husband's arm and the thickness of his middle finger." He held out his right hand as though to examine it. "Which shall it be, *mi geneth*, England or Wales?"

She had never before thought his hand could look so large. And although he had no stick, and she doubted that he would send for one, she was well aware that in England—and no doubt in Wales, as well—a man might legally, and at any time, use his hand alone to correct an erring wife.

"Well?" His hands were on his hips again, his feet slightly apart. Indeed, he stood precisely as he would have stood fully clothed, as though he had no awareness of his seminaked state or of the fact that he still dripped rivers of water on the floor.

Challenged, Alys drew a steadying breath, straightened her shoulders, and looked him in the eye. "You ought not to have provoked me, sir. You taunted me. I asked you not to do so."

His jaw tightened visibly in response to her words, and a thrill of fear shot through her, but there was an arrested look in his eyes. He said thoughtfully, "You have courage, little wife, but I am not convinced that you have wisdom. Come here."

His tone was gentler now than it had been before, less threatening. Bracing herself, she took several steps toward him, and when his demeanor did not alter, she went on until she stood before him, her gaze locked with his. The stone floor was wet beneath her feet, but she did not look down.

"Take off your robe," he said.

Still watching him, she raised her hands and slid the silk back over her shoulders, then lowered her arms and let the robe slip down them and fall to the floor. His breath caught audibly in his throat, and in that moment she thought he might begin to caress her again, and hoped that perhaps the danger was past.

"Continue with your task," he murmured huskily.

Her gaze flitted briefly, involuntarily, downward, and to her amazement, she saw that he had grown again. The sight was an unnerving one, and she glanced back at his face uncertainly.

"Do you wish to defy me further?" he asked in a tone that made it clear the danger had not passed after all. But when she shook her head, a twinkle crept into his eyes, and he said, "I did not think to spend my wedding night conversing in sodden hose, madam. Make haste, lest despite the fire on that hearth and the one that burns within me, I fall victim to an ague."

Reaching out to touch the wet silk with one hand, then with both, she tugged, tentatively at first and then when the material did not submit, more forcefully; but the task was not an easy one, and Nicholas did not help her. He stood as he had been standing, feet still apart, doing nothing to assist her, and before she finally succeeded, Alys felt as if she had indulged in a tug of war. The wet silk clung as though it had been glued to him, making it necessary for her to peel first one side a bit and then the other until at last she had them all the way down.

She looked up at him then. "You must lift your feet, sir. I cannot do that for you."

He complied and, free of his wet things, bent down without warning, scooped her up in his arms, and carried her to the bed.

"You must dry yourself," she protested, enjoying nonetheless the sense of being carried like a child in his arms. His skin felt warm, not chilled at all.

"Be quiet," he said gruffly, placing her on the bed, turning back to snuff the candles, then climbing in beside her. As he leaned over her, his lips close to hers, he murmured, "We have waited overlong, *mi geneth*. We've a duty to be done, a holy obligation to consummate our marriage."

"I am afraid, sir," she murmured back, speaking the first words that came to her mind but thinking at the same moment that though he was so large, so powerful a man, and now her husband, the words were not true. She had defied him, made him angry, even physically assaulted him; yet, he had not retaliated as he might have done. He had frightened her, to be sure, but he had controlled his anger, and now she was not so much frightened of him as apprehensive of what lay ahead.

She said none of these things to him in the silence that followed, and she realized suddenly from his expression, lit by the glow of the dying fire, that he had been taken aback by her confession of fear.

"I will not hurt you if I can avoid it," he said softly. "I will go slowly."

And he did, kissing, stroking, caressing, and teasing her, preparing her so thoroughly, in fact, that by the time he claimed her she was moaning, burning for him, her body alive and yearning for his. And if the claiming itself was not so pleasant, the ache that followed became a small part of the memories that lingered. Before she slept, she lay beside him, looking into the darkness overhead, distantly aware of a few last cracks from the dying embers on the hearth, and filled with wonder that a mere man could make a woman experience such marvelous feelings. She wondered, too, if she had stirred similar feelings in him.

# 15

The next morning Alys awakened early to the sound of voices in the room. The bed curtains were drawn, but she peeped out between them to see, in the gray dawn light from the two windows flanking the hearth, that Tom was helping his master to dress. Embarrassed by the squire's presence and by a sudden flood of memories from the night before, she ducked back before he might see her. Lying back against her pillows, listening to the soft murmur of their voices, she soon drifted back to sleep, and when she awoke again, the room was empty. She realized then what she had not really noted before, that Sir Nicholas had been dressing not in courtly attire but in his mail chausses and brigandine.

Jumping out of bed, she found her green silk robe, put it on, and padded swiftly, barefoot, to the door. Pulling it open as carefully as she could, she peeped into the sitting room. To her relief Jonet was there, with a basket of her mending.

Looking up, Jonet smiled and greeted her, putting away her work and getting to her feet as she talked. "I thought you would sleep all day, Lady Alys. Her grace, the queen, has twice sent to ask of you, but she most kindly forbade me to waken you."

Alys had meant to ask at once where Sir Nicholas had gone, but her attention was caught by one phrase among the tumble of words. "The queen? Elizabeth has not yet been crowned queen."

"Nay, but she is wife to the king, madam, and we have been commanded to style her so henceforth."

Alys sighed. "And now you choose to call me madam? I vow, Jonet, when Sir Nicholas spoke of the changing world, I did not understand how rightly he spoke. I do not like it so."

"Then, when we are alone, mistress, I will continue to call you as I have before. I, too, prefer it, I confess." She moved swiftly past Alys into the bedchamber, and went to open the wardrobe. "What will you wear?"

"Anything," Alys said. "Where is Sir Nicholas?"

"Gone into the city, Miss Alys. A matter of duty, he said; and, God be thanked, he has taken that pestrous fool Hugh Gower with him. The man is addled. Blurting his so-called compliments where all and sundry can hear them, then looking hurt when I tell him to stop, as if he has done me a kindness and been slapped for it." Jonet began to riffle through the clothing in the wardrobe.

"He means well, I suppose," Alys said. She sighed. Clearly her husband's feelings about the previous night were different from hers. She had wanted to talk with him, to watch his face when he responded, to touch him again. Waking to find him gone from her bed had been bad enough, waking to find him gone away altogether was worse, and discovering that he had been able to go without even waking her to say farewell was the worst of all.

She soon discovered that there was more unpleasantness in store for her, for once she had dressed and broken her fast, she had no further excuse to avoid the ladies' solar. Elizabeth was absent, but many of her ladies were present, including Madeline Fenlord, for it was nearly eleven o'clock, and dinner would soon be served. Alys's entrance was greeted with gaiety and laughter. Some wished her well; others made bawdy references to the duties of marriage, which made her blush and wish herself elsewhere. She was grateful when Madeline turned the conversation to some matter of gossip and the others finally left her in peace.

When everyone began to adjourn to a nearby room for the midday meal, Madeline moved close to Alys and said, "They are like starving children when it comes to snatching up the crumbs of other people's lives, are they not?"

"More like ravenous birds," Alys said, listening to the rattle of chatter around them, "unable to remain still for long before they must feed again. But unlike the hungry children with whom you compare them, one does not pity them overmuch."

"I do," Madeline said firmly. "Only look at them as they truly are—at us all, for that matter—confined to these rooms, to the court, with only one another for company. There are very few who are true friends, for experience in past years has taught us all that a friend today might prove our enemy tomorrow, only for his or her own advancement, or that of a father or husband."

"Or brother," Alys agreed, her eyes upon Sir Lionel Everingham's youngest sister, Sarah, a pretty, dark-eyed child, but newly come to court, and looking daggers now at Alys.

Madeline made a face at Sarah, who flushed red and turned quickly away to speak to someone else. "That little bitch deserves thrashing," Madeline said grimly. "She has been going about this past sennight preaching idiocy, if not treason."

"Treason!" Alys's eyes widened.

"Aye, if you believe that to disagree with the king is such, as we—may God preserve us—have been warned it can be." She swiftly crossed herself, then bent nearer. "Sarah declares that her brother was promised your hand in marriage and that the promise ought to have been honored by the king, since Sir Lionel did swear allegiance to him. I tell you, the girl is mad. She does not even hold her tongue in Elizabeth's hearing."

"Elizabeth will not punish her for speaking ill of me."

"Marry, that may be so, but when Sarah says such things, she speaks ill of Elizabeth's dearest Harry, not just of you."

"Madeline!" Alys glanced swiftly around, then sighed with

relief when she realized no one was near enough to overhear them.

Madeline shrugged. "I have already displeased her noble grace, I fear, for she asked me yestereve if I did not likewise desire a handsome husband—like your Sir Nicholas, she said. I said I did not think so highly of such men—too full of purpose, I said. Not that he is not handsome, for he is, in his way. And to think of him possessing one, why it must be most exhilarating, and mayhap even pleasant. Well, is it not?" she demanded.

Knowing she must be as red as fire, and not having any wish to reply to such a question, Alys moved to follow the others. Madeline was at her heels and sat down beside her after the blessing, but there was no more opportunity for private conversation. The ladies dined alone that day, so the meal was silent, and instead of minstrels afterward, they had more prayers. It was still Lent and Lady Margaret was present.

Lady Margaret did not accompany Elizabeth and the others back to the solar, however, and the early afternoon passed with unusual lightheartedness, the ladies being entertained while they worked at their tasks by Patch, Elizabeth's fool, who had been a gift to her from the king. Patch was not as sharp-witted as Tom Blakall, but he had a talent for storytelling, and for making his mistress laugh, and his voice was pleasant to the ear. On this day, seated on the dais at Elizabeth's feet, he recited a lengthy, sweetly romantic poem.

When he had finished, Elizabeth set aside her work to thank him, then dismissing him, said idly, "We will have music now. No, Lady Emlyn," she said when that dame instantly picked up her lute, "you would prefer to finish your sewing, as we know, so our new Lady Merion shall entertain us. As we recall, she played passably well for us when we were in residence in the north."

Alys, having noted Elizabeth's thoughtful gaze upon her from time to time during dinner and afterward, while the fool recited his poem, had wondered if she had somehow offended her, but she had not expected this. Reluctantly she got to her feet.

"Madam, I regret I have no instrument."

"Lady Emlyn will lend you hers," Elizabeth replied, taking up her needlework in a manner precluding further discussion.

Gulping nervously—her skill on the lute being less than laudable, as Elizabeth well knew—Alys stepped forward to take the proffered instrument.

"Sit here on the dais," Elizabeth said, "where Patch did sit to recite to us. 'Twill make it easier for all of us to hear you. Perchance you will choose to entertain us with a ballad."

Alys glanced at Madeline, who clearly had realized something was amiss, but all she got in response was a sympathetic smile. By now, the other ladies in the room were staring at her, waiting for her to obey the royal command, so she could not even indulge herself by glaring at Elizabeth. She could only obey.

It occurred to her then that perhaps she was making too much of a small thing. She would sit down, take up the lute, and show that she had too little skill to be asked often to repeat the task. Elizabeth would have the satisfaction of having shown her in a poor light to the others, and life would go on as before. The experience would be humiliating, to be sure, but it was not as though she were being thrown to lions or hanged, drawn, and quartered before a mass of gawkers at Tyburn hill.

Her courage bolstered by these thoughts, she stepped to the dais and took her seat, telling herself as she arranged her skirts that it was not so much that she was at Elizabeth's feet as that she was at the head of the room. Taking up the lute, she plucked the strings to be certain they were not disastrously out of tune, tried desperately to remember the words to the simplest ballad she knew how to play, and began.

She had a pleasant singing voice and hoped it would cover

her lapses on the instrument, but no sooner had she finished the song than Elizabeth, shaking her head sadly, said, "You do not seem to have practiced as you ought, Lady Merion. Your voice is well enough, we suppose, but your playing displeases us."

Flushing as much with anger as with embarrassment, Alys said, "I do apologize, madam. I am not so skilled upon the lute as I should like to be."

"Perhaps there is another instrument you would prefer to play for us instead," Elizabeth said sweetly.

"No, madam, I fear not." Alys hated her then as she had not hated her since leaving Sheriff Hutton.

"But this state of affairs is unacceptable, Lady Merion. It is our . . . our desire that you will inform your new husband at once of this dismal lack, and beg him to hire a tutor for you. Since you will need leisure for your lessons, until such time as you believe your skill sufficiently improved to warrant a request that we permit you to play for us again, you may be excused from such duties in our bedchamber as you have hitherto performed."

"May I have leave to retire now, madam?" Alys asked grimly. Desire or command, it made no difference, for they were equal when spoken by the king's wife, and it was no minor matter to have been denied entrance to Elizabeth's bedchamber. There was small hope that Sir Nicholas, as ambitious as she knew him to be, would not be displeased with the situation. Elizabeth was taking full revenge for Sheriff Hutton, and Alys wanted time to think.

But Elizabeth said, "There is no cause for haste, Lady Merion. Lady Emlyn, do you take the lute now and show her the level of skill to which she must aspire." When Alys had returned the lute, she added, "Prithee, return to your place on the dais, Lady Merion, until such time as we choose to dismiss you."

Redder than ever, and seething inside, but knowing she dared not reveal her fury, Alys sat down again on the edge of the dais, aware that every eye in the room must be upon her and wishing she knew such an effective way to make Elizabeth squirm. She sat stiffly erect until Lady Emlyn had plucked her last note, but when Elizabeth said serenely that she thought it time they all retired to their chambers to prepare for the evening meal, which she would take that evening in the great hall with the king, Alys leapt to her feet, her countenance betraying her relief.

"Lady Merion," Elizabeth said gently, "we did not know you were so eager to depart, but you have surprised us in other ways before now, have you not? In truth, we confess we had not known you were so well resigned to this marriage of yours as it appears you must be. Knowing, after all, that you had hoped to wed Sir Lionel Everingham, so handsome, so . . ." Breaking off with a dismissive gesture, she said, "But 'twould be ungracious of us to suggest that your new husband is in any way the lesser knight."

"By my faith, madam," Alys said, turning to look her right in the eye and speaking with unfortunate clarity, "since we are both wedded to Welshmen, I had expected you to rejoice with me."

A hushed silence filled the room, and for a moment Alys thought the royal serenity would falter, but it was only a moment. Then Elizabeth said, "Indeed, madam, we do rejoice." Handing her needlework to Lady Emlyn, she arose with her dignity apparently unimpaired and left the room.

In the corridor, moving swiftly toward the stairs with the other ladies, Madeline grabbed Alys's arm with enough force to leave bruises and hissed into her ear, "Are you mad? How did you dare to speak to her so?"

"Shhh," Alys hissed back. "Come with me to my chamber."

"But what if Sir Nicholas is there?"

"I do not care if he is, but he will not be. He rode out this morning on some stupid duty or other, and was in such haste that he did not even pause to bid me farewell."

"Well, I told you husbands were not assets to one's life,"

Madeline retorted in her normal tone, causing more than one nearby head to turn toward them.

They spoke no more until they reached Alys's chambers, but finding that neither Jonet nor the maidservant who helped her had arrived yet, Alys said without hesitation, "I should like to kill Elizabeth! There now, it is said. What am I to do now?"

"She does not like you," Madeline said, hoisting herself to sit upon the bed and nearly tumbling off again when she tried to free the elegant feathered fan, dangling by a gold chain from her girdle, which she had somehow managed to sit upon.

"She knew I could not play well," Alys said. "She did the whole business on purpose to pay me back for . . ."

"For what? Here now, what is this?" Madeline demanded.

" 'Tis nothing."

"Oh no, my friend. This is Madeline. You will tell me or I do not leave this room." She leaned forward expectantly.

Alys grimaced, but short of putting Madeline bodily out of the room, there was not much else to be done but to tell her. She made the tale as brief as she could, but Madeline's mouth hung agape when Alys finished.

"You slapped Elizabeth of York! Marry, were you crazed?"

"She lied through her teeth about Richard. She infuriated me. Oh, I do not want to talk about it anymore. Where is Jonet? By my faith, that woman ought to know when she is wanted."

"That woman is here," Jonet said with chilly calm from the doorway. "It is bad luck to sit upon a bed, Mistress Fenlord."

"So it is," Madeline agreed, sliding to her feet and looking at her fan. "I have lost two feathers from this pretty bauble. I leave you now, Alys, for I must dress for supper if we are to attend her grace in the great hall. But we will talk again later," she added with a look that made it clear she meant to have the long tale before she was done with the matter.

No sooner had Madeline gone than the maidservant ar-

rived, so Alys had to endure Jonet's near-silence until the
wench had been dismissed. But as soon as the door had shut,
before Jonet might speak her mind, Alys said, "I should not
have spoken as I did. I was unkind, but I was angry and did
not think." It occurred to her that she could not explain the
matter in greater detail without speaking improperly about
Elizabeth; and although she had certainly discussed her with
Jonet in the past, she decided that Sir Nicholas was right.
Now that Elizabeth was the king's wife, it was unwise, perhaps even unsafe, to criticize her to anyone. Thinking of Sir
Nicholas brought his image into the room, however, and she
silently cursed Elizabeth again for making it necessary for
her to tell him about the incident of the lute, if not about
the exchange she had had with Elizabeth afterward.

She did not encounter him until that evening after the
tables had been cleared. By then the room was buzzing with
talk of the king's intent to begin a progress to the north in
the near future. Elizabeth would not go with him since it
was still hoped that her condition was too delicate to sustain
a journey, and Alys heard more than one person suggest that
Viscount Lovell, if he had not already broken sanctuary,
might choose to do so to lead an assault on the royal party.
It was not the first time she had heard such talk, for there
had been rumors before she fled north, but now she had all
she could do not to reveal, by expression or word, her own
knowledge of Lovell's whereabouts.

No sooner had she turned from one such conversation
than she was accosted by Sir Lionel Everingham, and she
realized at once that his sister Sarah was not alone in believing that he had been cheated. His polite, inconsequent
discourse did not conceal his hunger for her, and Alys knew
not whether to be complimented or dismayed by it. So determined was she to parry his bold looks and the tendency
he had to stand closer to her than was comfortable, that she
did not attend as she might have to his actual words, until
he mentioned his lute.

"I am proficient with the instrument, my lady—indeed

with many instruments," he added, leering and shifting his weight in a lewdly suggestive manner. "I should find it an extremely great pleasure to provide you with the lessons you require."

She stared back, at a loss for what to say to him.

"My wife requires lessons from no one but me," Sir Nicholas snapped, startling Alys nearly out of her wits when he spoke from right beside her. Possessively, he put his arm around her.

Sir Lionel bowed. "Your servant, sir."

Sir Nicholas nodded, saying, "You will excuse us, I know. 'Tis but the second day of our marriage, and I have been denied my wife's companionship for the entire day."

"To be sure," Sir Lionel said, but his expression was not particularly amiable when he walked away.

Alys turned to Nicholas, words of gratitude upon her lips, but one look at his set expression warned her that she had not been rescued after all but had only fallen from the pot into the cook fire. She made no protest when he led her from the room, nor did either of them speak before they reached his chambers.

Then, shutting the outer door with a snap, Nicholas turned and gave her a shake, demanding, "What devilment has got into you, madam? Whatever did you think you were about?"

"He accosted me! I did not invite him."

"I do not speak of Everingham; I speak of Elizabeth."

"That was not my fault!" she cried, pulling away from him. "It **was** Elizabeth. That chitty-faced bitch knew I could not—" When his hand flashed up to strike, she broke off, jumping back out of his reach and saying hastily, "I cry pardon, sir! I should not have spoken so, but she made me angry and you are blaming me for a scene that she created. She said I had married beneath my station. She...she compared you to Sir Lionel!"

His hand fell. "I know."

"All that, as well? What prating-Jenny dared to tell you?"

"The king."

"Oh." She bit her lip. "Was he angry?"

"No, our Harry has a sense of humor, fortunately, and he enjoyed the bit about our both being Welshmen. But you said 'as well,' madam. What more is there for me to know?"

Alys was too indignant to reply to that question. "I do not think it at all funny that she compared you to Sir Lionel, but who has dared to carry tales of Elizabeth to the Tudor?"

"Elizabeth herself," he said flatly.

"Elizabeth! But why, when the tale discredits her?"

"Mayhap you had better tell me the whole," he said, reaching toward her. When she evaded his hand, he frowned. "I won't harm you. I just want to know what happened. No more *baldarddws*, either, lass. I want the whole truth."

"What is b-balderdoosh?" she asked curiously, trying to say the word as he had said it, at the same time letting him urge her from the parlor into the bedchamber.

"Foolishness, nonsense, female prating," he said impatiently, shutting the door. "Now, tell me."

"Aye," she said. Standing before the fire, she told him what Elizabeth had done. She was precise, and she made no effort to spare herself in the tale. When she finished, he shook his head.

"Women!"

"Art angry, sir?"

"Nay, lass. You ought not to have spoken, but I grant the provocation. And I doubt the deviceful wench told our Harry about the lute-playing bit, for he did not mention it to me. By the rood, I warrant she said only what she had to say to protect herself against any gossip there might be, but he is like to hear the whole soon enough if Everingham has heard it. 'Tis why the fellow was offering to give you lessons, is it not?"

She nodded, still uncertain of his temper.

"Elizabeth won't like it if Harry does hear the tale, for it will not amuse him." He sighed. "There must be no more of this, lass. 'Tis plain now that I cannot leave you here."

"Leave me? But—"

"Didst think you would accompany our king on his progress to the north, *mi geneth*, when his lady stays behind?"

"No, but I did think that you might . . ." She hesitated.

"I follow my liege lord," he said, "or such was my plan, and what he does expect. I must disappoint him, I think, but it will not serve for me simply to take you to Wolveston Hazard."

"Why not?"

"Your leaving will make an odd enough appearance when the queen stays, and I cannot tell Harry I want to take you to Wolveston to see my new estate. His route takes him through Bawtry and Doncaster, so I would be close enough to look it over, in any case. There is no need to take you."

" 'Tis my home," she protested.

He shrugged. "You serve the queen, madam. Your place is with her, not in Nottinghamshire. Be still now," he commanded when she opened her mouth to say more. "Let me think."

She stared into the fireplace, angry that he thought she could not protect herself against Elizabeth, and angrier that he would not take her with him to Wolveston. Surely they could travel apart from the king's procession of knights and gentlemen.

Almost as though he were thinking aloud, he murmured, "I could take you to Wales. Not only did Elizabeth herself suggest such a trip but Harry will understand that my family must want to meet my bride. And from Wales we can go on to Wolveston. If we travel swiftly enough, I can join him at Doncaster."

"How soon will he be there?"

"He has said he wants to make haste, but 'twill take time nonetheless, for he is to spend Easter in Lincoln, then go to Nottingham Castle, and from there through Sherwood Forest to Doncaster and York." He smiled at her. "Should you like to see my home, madam? 'Tis in Brecknockshire in the valley of the river Honddhu. Our market town is Brecon, fifteen miles away."

"Is Brecknockshire not near Glamorgan?" she asked, re-calling that he had once said something to that effect, and that Sir James Tyrell was Sheriff of Glamorgan. She had not yet been able to help Lovell, but perhaps her chance might yet come to do so.

"Glamorgan is the next county to the south, beyond mountains called the Brecon Beacons. Why do you ask, *mi geneth*?"

She smiled. " 'Tis the only Welsh county whose name I have heard before. I heard it first when you explained the name your men call Hugh Gower, and told me of the legends about the giant. I look forward to meeting your family, sir, and seeing your home. But I do confess," she added with a sigh, "I have had my fill of traveling with only soldiers and servants to bear me company. Might I have leave to invite Mistress Fenlord to accompany us?"

He hesitated, but a thoughtful look came into his eyes, and he said, "She is an heiress, is she not, and as yet unpromised?"

"Aye," Alys said, "but she does not want to be married."

He paid no heed to the last, saying in a musing tone, "She's a pretty lass, too. I'll warrant she'd suit my brother Gwilym."

"She would not," Alys said. "She has no wish to marry, sir, and she is accustomed to having her wishes indulged."

He laughed. "Is she? Well, if you promise to behave, lass, I'll ask Harry to let her go with us. First, however, I must gain his permission for myself and my men. The rumors flying about just now are making him a bit nervous." He gave her a straight look. "Some say that the outlaw Lovell has fled to the north, where he is plotting against the king."

"And what do you say, sir?"

"Only that Harry ought not to be too quick to discount what he hears. He still hopes Lovell will submit, and has said he is certain the bearers of the rumors want only to advance their own positions at court by condemning York's last ca-pable leader."

"When must we leave, sir?" she asked, having no wish to encourage further discussion of the matter.

"The king leaves Wednesday morning. Can you and Mistress Fenlord be ready to leave so soon?"

She grinned at him saucily. " 'Tis a vast amount of time, sir. You do not usually give me so much. But what if the king denies us his permission?"

"He will not. His lass will see to that, and I shall see that you have your lute lessons, *mi geneth;* but I'll hire you no tutor. I will teach you myself." He smiled. "I enjoy teaching you. Indeed, I believe there is time right now for a lesson. 'Tis a pity we have no lute at hand." His expression warmed provocatively, and he reached for the laces of her gown.

She responded at once, and with pleasure. Some lessons, she thought, were much more pleasant than others.

Whether by virtue of Sir Nicholas's persuasiveness or that of the queen, on Wednesday morning a cavalcade comprised of Sir Nicholas, Alys, Madeline, Jonet, Elva Dean, and forty men at arms left Westminster Palace shortly after dawn.

They enjoyed beautiful weather along the way, and made excellent time, riding west along the Thames to Uxbridge, then to Oxford, crossing the Severn at Gloucester. They spent that night and the following day, which was Sunday, at an abbey south of the town, and the following day, they crossed into Wales at Monmouth.

Early the next morning they were off again, traveling alongside the river Usk to Abergavenny. When Sir Nicholas identified the massive tower of Raglan Castle in the distance, Alys was impressed. She knew Raglan by reputation.

" 'Twas a good Yorkist stronghold," she said.

Madeline, riding beside her, said, "Yorkists in Wales? I thought all here would be Tudor people. But then," she added with a laugh, "I know little history. 'Tis boring stuff."

Sir Nicholas said, "There was much Yorkist influence in this part of the world, but at least one rebellion against the late king—that of Buckingham—began in Brecon, and the Welsh are well pleased with Harry. He may not be as Welsh

as some would like, but folk hereabouts are pleased that he
traces his heritage to Cadwaladr and thus fulfills that great
leader's prophecy that a Welshman would one day rule over
England."

The landscape changed beyond Abergavenny. The gentle
slope they had followed up the valley was steeper now that
they were climbing into the mountains known as the Brecon
Beacons. The air was filled with birdsong and the scent of
sun and flowers, for the Welsh countryside was lush, the
hillsides around them thick with green grass, shrubbery, and
gaily colored wildflowers. But the lush foliage lasted only
until they reached the summit, where they were greeted by
a stiff breeze and wind gusts strong enough to blow the hat
off one's head, if it was not firmly secured. The view at the
top made Madeline and Alys stare in amazement.

"It is so barren here," Alys murmured when they had
drawn up to rest the horses. "There is naught to see among
these high peaks but tiny pink windflowers hugging brown
dirt and those tall, pillarlike stones in the distance. What are
they?"

"They are called longstones," Nicholas said, "or standing
stones. Some say the Romans brought them, others that they
were thrown here by giants." He grinned at Hugh. " 'Tis
most likely the Romans used them to mark ancient track-
ways, or as monuments to persons of importance. But the
Beacons are not always as bare as they look now, lass, and
although they seem gentle and mild today, they can be ex-
ceedingly dangerous. The fog rolling up from the sea is
sometimes so thick that a man cannot see his hand before
his face, and there are treacherous cliffs and rush bogs where
anyone putting a foot wrong can disappear forever."

They did not linger, and the stunning change in landscape
was reversed when they left the heights to descend into the
lush green valley where the rivers Usk, Tarell, and Honddhu
met in the town of Brecon. It was a busy town, the center
of the Welsh cloth trade, and the women were amused to
see, lining the two main streets, row upon row of flannel

cloth hung on tenterhooks to dry after processing. Nicholas pointed out the Blackfriars' school when they passed it, and they spent the night at the Benedictine priory crowning the hill north of town. While Nicholas saw to his men's needs that evening, the women walked in the peaceful priory garden. But the journey was nearly over, and the next day when they entered the lovely green valley of the Honddhu, Alys saw a dramatic change in her husband's demeanor.

He had been cheerful enough before, but distant, spending no more time with her than with the other women. Each time they had stopped for a night, even when they accepted the hospitality of a religious order, the women stayed together, and Nicholas slept on the men's side of the guest house. He was polite, and even found time most evenings for Alys's lute lessons, but she had hoped for more intimacy. She seemed to have no power to stir him while his men were near, for he maintained strict control over himself.

Hugh frequently rode near them, and he was always willing to chat, but his reception from Jonet was no warmer than before, even when he and Nicholas began pointing out scenes from their respective childhoods, revealing their excitement at being home again. Alys began to commiserate a little with Hugh.

The valley was beautiful. The hawthorns by the river were not yet in bud, but silvery catkins decked red willow branches, and snowdrops and marsh marigolds grew everywhere. There were long-horned, short-legged black cattle on the hillsides, and lots of sheep. Sir Nicholas, grinning now, his eyes sparkling with pleasure, increased the pace, and shortly before noon, when a man came out of a cottage and waved, he waved back and shouted a greeting. The man peered more closely at them, then shouted back and waved both hands with wild abandon. Nicholas ap Dafydd ab Evan had come home.

# 16

The first sight Alys had of Merion Court, situated near the top of a hill overlooking the west bank of the river, was the great round stone tower near the crest of the hill. Astonished, she cried to Sir Nicholas, "You never said it was a castle!"

"It is only a fortified manor house," he replied. "There once was a castle, built by a Norman knight, but the keep is all that remains. The house was built early in the last century."

She could see it now, two stories high and very broad, built of pale gray stone. A narrow roadway led up the hill to a gatehouse, standing sentry near tall iron gates in the high stone wall at the front. The gates were open. Nicholas had sent a small party of men ahead, and they were expected.

The cavalcade passed through the gateway into a cobbled courtyard, where wide, shallow stone steps swept up to a pair of double doors, standing open. Three men hurried down the steps, and Sir Nicholas dismounted and strode to meet them, holding his arms wide. The oldest of the three, a graying man in a knee-length, belted black robe that had been fashionable some years before, was the first to embrace him, and Alys decided he must be Dafydd ab Evan, Nicholas's father.

She sat patiently, exchanging a look with Madeline when the four men began to talk excitedly to one another in Welsh. But Sir Nicholas soon recalled that he had not come alone, and turned back, laughing, to say in English, "But, by the bones of St. David, I have left her sitting! 'Tis lucky I'll be if she does not comb my hair with a joint stool. Come you down from there, lass," he said, reaching to help her, "and meet my father, and my brothers, Rhys and Gwilym." To the elder of the two other men, he added, "Gwilym, do you go and assist Mistress Fenlord."

Hugh dismounted to help Jonet, who accepted his aid with haughty disdain while a second man helped Elva. There was little conversation before they were taken inside and across a paneled, rush-strewn hall that rose two stories to the high, beamed roof overhead. They went up more stone stairs, along a timber gallery to the family's private chambers, where they found Nicholas's mother, Gwenyth, and his sisters, Bronwyn and Alvyna, two lively damsels of twelve and ten. The welcome from all three was enthusiastic, and Alys took an instant liking to them. The men, however, Alys thought taciturn and distant, for despite their voluble warmth toward Nicholas in the courtyard, they seemed to have little to say to her or to Madeline.

Madeline agreed with her assessment. " 'Tis plain to see they are not courtiers," she said in a low tone to Alys. "That Gwilym is handsome enough but more like one of the tall stones we saw whilst riding through the Beacons. Only look at him standing there by the fire as if he had granite in his veins instead of good warm blood. At least young Master Rhys knows how to smile."

Having already observed that Master Gwilym, despite having politely helped Madeline to dismount, had seemed to take no other interest in her, Alys decided Nicholas must have thought better of the notion of Madeline as a prospective wife for his brother.

Nicholas's mother expressed dismay just then at the intended brevity of their visit. "A sennight only!" she exclaimed. " 'Tis not to be! You must stay a month, or at least through Easter."

"We cannot," Nicholas said with regret. "I am pledged to

meet the king at Doncaster, to travel with him to Pontefract and York. There are rumors of unrest in the north, and my men may be needed. We will spend Easter at Burton Abbey if the weather permits, or at Worcester if it does not."

"But there are always rumors of unrest nowadays," Gwenyth said, "and certes, you will not take Alys and the other women with you in such a case. You must leave them all here with us until you can return from your duties to fetch them."

His sisters instantly added their pleas to hers, and for a moment Alys feared he would agree. Determined to stay with him, she opened her mouth to protest but shut it again at once when Nicholas turned his stern gaze upon her.

He said, "I know Alys would like to visit longer, but her home—ours now—is near Doncaster, and in a dismal state when last she saw it. She longs to set it to rights. Moreover," he added glibly, "I will need her there to show me how to go on."

Since his family did not know that Alys had spent most of her life in residences other than her own home, and since his sisters' presence made it plain that fostering daughters was less common in Wales than in England, she had no doubt his explanation would be accepted, and breathed a sigh of relief.

She enjoyed her visit and soon came to agree with Gwenyth that a sennight was too short a time. The days passed swiftly, giving her little time alone with her thoughts; but the hope she had harbored before leaving London, that with Brecknockshire so near Glamorgan she might somehow manage to make contact with Sir James Tyrell, and perhaps even with Richard of York, had already died. The heroic vision of herself as the savior of the Yorkist cause, who would put a more deserving candidate on the throne of England than the man who sat there, had vanished amidst the treacherous Brecon Beacons with her realization that Glamorgan lay beyond them. Even had her imagination amazed her by devising a plan to see her safely deposited in Glamorgan, and able to find Cardiff—let alone Tyrell and the prince—once she arrived there, there was no time to put such a plan into action.

She had become aware soon after their arrival that Nicholas, though delighted to be with his family again, and more properly attentive to his wife than he had been on their journey, was growing restless. He did his best to hide his fidgets from the family, visiting cheerfully with his mother, riding out hunting with his father and brothers, and playing with his little sisters. He found time, too, to continue Alys's lute lessons. But on Palm Sunday he spent as much time preparing for the next day's departure as he did in prayers and pleasure with his family, relaxing only at supper, when fig pies and fish graced the menu. In Wales, as in other places far from Rome, the rules of Lenten fare were relaxed, though not so much that mutton was offered, a fact that Nicholas was quick to bemoan.

"Mutton?" Alys said in surprise. " 'Tis generally stringy, coarse stuff. If you crave meat, sir, why not beef or chicken?"

"Welsh mutton, *mi geneth,* is tender and tastes of the wild thyme of the Welsh hills. A true son of St. David misses nothing else so much when he is away."

"In fact," Bronwyn said, her grin showing a missing front tooth, "we often have chicken and fish. 'Tis only four-legged animals that do not get eaten on fast days or during Lent."

Once the children had been sent to bed that night, Nicholas insisted that the members of his party must likewise retire, so as to be ready to leave as soon after dawn as possible. His mother repeated her wish that he would linger one or two more days, but he said, "This good weather cannot last, madam, and 'tis two hundred miles to Wolveston, a journey that will take us at least ten days, for we must rest the horses now and again, and we ought not to travel on Easter Sunday."

"In good faith, sir," Gwenyth said with a frown, "you ought not to travel at all during Holy Week. Maundy Thursday and

Good Friday are just as holy as Easter is. Do you not agree, sir?" she demanded of her husband.

"Let the man be, madam," Dafydd ab Evan replied. "He serves his king well, and that is as it should be now we've got a proper Welshman on the throne at last."

Nicholas shot a look of warning at his wife, and she smiled sweetly back at him. Did he really think, she wondered, that she would join battle with his father? Her sympathies had not changed, but she was no fool. When Dafydd ab Evan continued to expound on the subject, she glanced at Madeline, but that young woman was sitting with her attention fixed upon her stitchery, the very picture of a proper lady of the manor. The pose was not one in which she was often caught, so Alys looked about for the cause but saw only Gwilym, motioning to a servant to stir up the fire. Since he appeared to be paying no heed to Madeline, and since Madeline had continued to assert her indifference to all members of the male sex, Alys told herself she was imagining things and returned her thoughts to her husband.

They had been married more than a fortnight, but she knew him no better than before. She enjoyed her lute lessons, and he shared her bed at Merion, but his attentions seemed more dutiful than passionate, and he did not take the same care that he had taken on their wedding night to fulfill her. Deciding that his attention that night had been unusual and that his thoughts had been with the Tudor since, she had not complained. It was enough to reassure herself that her body still had the power to stir his. With delight she remembered one particular night when she knew she had inspired him to retire early simply by adjusting her jeweled belt beneath her breasts while his eye was upon her.

But even that night, although he had laughed when she teased him about having had to entice him to do his duty, and had kissed and caressed her until she moaned aloud, he had finished more quickly than she had hoped. She recalled now, perversely, that he preferred dark-haired women and, with a twinge of jealousy, wondered if any he knew—and perhaps had been thinking about when he mentioned his preference—lived near Merion Court. But then, remembering that she had heard him tease Ian about his "weakness for women," she wondered suddenly if Nicholas viewed his interest in her as a weakness, a fault that he must overcome if he was to stand well in the eyes of his men. Or perhaps, she told herself, it was only that the men of Merion were tiresomely dispassionate.

Just then, Alys saw Hugh stoop to pick up a ball of thread Jonet had dropped, and saw, too, how he caught and held her gaze when she looked up from her work. But when Hugh smiled, Jonet turned away abruptly, putting her nose in the air. He grinned.

"Such mild behavior does encourage me, my peevish wee mouse, but 'tis common courtesy to thank a man who does you a kindness."

Jonet did not deign to reply.

Shaking his head, Hugh went back to the fire. Young Rhys had seen the exchange and, looking up, caught Alys's eye. When he grinned, dark eyes atwinkle, inviting her to share his amusement, she found her opinion of him shifting and wondered if there might be more to the men of Merion than she had thought.

When she reached the courtyard early the following morning, she discovered that she would get the opportunity to learn a good deal more about one of them, but it was not Rhys. Nicholas's men had already gathered for the journey, and when they had mounted, Alys saw that Gwilym was with them, riding a glossy black almost as magnificent and well mannered as Black Wyvern—not surprising, since, as Nicholas soon informed her, the two destriers were offspring of the same sire, and Gwilym had trained them both.

"Why is *he* coming with us?" Madeline muttered to Alys, her words barely audible above the din of harness, iron shoes on cobbles, and shouted masculine orders. "Who asked him?"

Before Alys might have responded, Gwilym rode nearer,

looked them over briefly, then shouted for a man to come and adjust Madeline's leathers.

She said, " 'Tis kind of you, sir, but I need no adjustment."

"You will allow me to be the better judge of that, mistress," Gwilym said calmly, nodding at a man who approached on foot. The man glanced from one to the other but obeyed Gwilym.

Madeline sat rigidly, staring straight ahead until the adjustment had been made and the man had gone away again, before saying evenly to Gwilym, "You take too much upon yourself, sir."

He bowed from his saddle and rode away. Less than a quarter hour later the cavalcade passed through the iron gates, but instead of riding down the valley the way they had come, they forded the river to follow a track through the hills to the valley of the river Wye. Looking back from the crest of the first hill, Alys could see the dark shadow of the house in the distance, beside the tall stone keep, with fluffy white clouds floating above it. Two hours later the sky was black, and long before they reached Hay, rain was pouring down upon them.

By the next day the downpour had diminished to a drizzle, but when they entered Worcester, two days later, the women were miserable, and the river Wye was running red with clay washed down from the hills. Nicholas, his impatience increasing by the hour, insisted upon pushing ahead the next day, though both Gwilym and Hugh urged him to stay in Worcester one full day to rest both horses and riders. Alys had been disappointed to discover that the sleeping arrangements were the same as they had been on the journey from London, but once she had been reminded of how brusque Nicholas could be, particularly while traveling, she decided it was better to share her rooms at the various religious houses with Madeline, Jonet, and Elva, than with him.

Their pace was slower than he would have liked, but they made Birmingham by early afternoon on Maundy Thursday. Thus he was encouraged to press on the following day to

Burton Abbey, where the women, Sir Nicholas, Gwilym, and their body servants were directed to the guesthouse, a building of considerable size and elegance set at a distance from the cloister, so that guests would not disturb the monks by their untimely comings and goings.

The rest of the men were to be housed in the cellarer's hospice, and before following the rotund little guestmaster into the house, Sir Nicholas called to Hugh to see that both the men and their horses were ready to depart by daybreak.

"Your husband is an ogre," Madeline declared when the women were installed a short time later in the ladies' hall, where although they would sup together with the gentlemen, they would spend the night separated from them. "It is not enough that we have had to subsist upon Lenten fare—and at religious houses at that, where the rules are formidable—but he pushes us and pushes us to ride through muck and mire until we resemble naught so much as mud hens. Speak to him, Alys. Mayhap he will listen to you."

Alys grimaced, for when she had dared to protest earlier, she had received short shrift from her husband. "He does not heed what anyone says," she told Madeline. "He is obsessed with reaching the king. I think he frets over what might happen if he is not there with him to protect his royal backside."

Madeline sighed. "His lunatic brother is obsessed, too, I think. The man is forever watching over me, as if I were a want-wit unable to look after myself. 'Pull your cloak tighter about you, mistress,' he says. 'Do you not have a hat with a wider brim, mistress?' 'Do not tread in that puddle, mistress.' And when I dropped my whip and he picked it up for me, he told me not to be so careless. As if I had not always been a trifle clumsy—marry, you know I have, Alys! But *he* says I am merely careless! I have never known any man like him. He cannot converse in a courtly manner, and when I asked him most politely to point out to his elder brother that the horrid clouds overhead were dripping on us, he said only, .

'The Lord controls the weather, mistress; Nicholas does not.'
I tell you, he is daft!"

Alys smiled then, but Jonet, who was busily ordering two
lay brothers to see to the cloaks and coffers, turned at hearing Madeline's words and said wryly, "I believe it is a general
condition of Welshmen to push themselves in where they
are not wanted, Mistress Fenlord. In Worcester this morning, that elephant, Hugh Gower, actually lifted me right off
my feet and carried me across that wet courtyard to put me
on my palfrey. The audacity of the knave!"

Alys and Madeline, having both enjoyed the sight of an
indignant Jonet being carried as though she were a child in
arms and not the woman of generous proportion that she
was, exchanged grins but did not so lose their senses as to
tease her. Instead, Madeline said, "Just so. There can be no
doubt about it; all Welshmen are mad. But, Alys, surely you
can do something about this wicked pace Sir Nicholas is setting! We shall all catch our death of cold and damp. In point
of fact, I heard two of the men muttering something about
an outbreak of the sweating sickness. I did not hear the town
they mentioned, nor did I want to ask, but it just goes to
show what we can expect." She shivered.

It was not sickness that slowed them, however, but the
round little guestmaster, who expressed profound dismay at
the notion of traveling on the very eve of Easter. Being excused by virtue of his position from the rule of silence at
Burton, he did not hesitate to expound at length upon the
subject to Nicholas himself. The exchange took place after
vespers when they returned to the hall of the guesthouse for
their supper, the only meal served at Burton on fast days.

Alys fully expected Sir Nicholas to snub the kind little man
and was pleasantly surprised when he said only, "I am but
heeding my duty in going to meet my king, Father."

The master, looking like an plump indignant gnome in his
black cowl and cassock, was unimpressed. "His grace, as all
here know well, my son, is secure at Lincoln for the holy
festival. Being a good man of pious habits who knows his

duty to God, he has been there since Wednesday. Therefore, if you insist upon departing at daybreak, I shall have no choice but to summon the lord abbot himself to dissuade you. And his commands," he added darkly, "must be obeyed as if they came from God. Do not doubt that he will order the stable doors locked and barred, if he believes it necessary, to keep you here at Burton."

Routed, Sir Nicholas gave in with what little grace he could muster, but his mood when he observed the plate of porridge set before him was not pleasant. Alys, watching him, forbore to speak her own thoughts about the paucity of the meal. It was, after all, nearly the last day of Lent.

She felt clammy and filthy, and would have traded her best velvet gown, if not her pearl necklet, for a bath. But after supper when she suggested to the guestmaster that one might be provided for her, he stared at her in dismay.

"Baths are available only for the sick, my lady. Being an indulgence of the flesh, they are discouraged at Burton. Oh, but wait," he added, brightening. "Tomorrow eve, being the night before Easter, is one of the two days of the year when one might indulge oneself. I shall approach the abbot on your behalf."

He made Alys feel as if he were doing her a great favor, and she was not optimistic about his efforts, but he surprised her. Although the following day passed uneventfully, that evening, just before the bells began to ring compline, two lay brothers carried a tub into the ladies' hall, and brought water to heat over the fire. With alacrity, Jonet fetched Alys's French soaps and herbs, and although Nicholas, Gwilym, and their servants retired to their chambers after supper, the evening was spent much more pleasurably than those that had gone before it.

Despite her bath, Alys did not sleep well, for it seemed to her that the bells rang all night long, and after lauds she did not sleep again. Since Easter was one of the five great feasts of the church calendar, there was great ceremony attending it, and the whole house at Burton strove to do honor to the occasion. The guests, attending early services as well as a high mass at noon, found the entire church decorated. The finest furnishings had been placed on the altar for the occasion, the best vestments were worn, and all the seats were draped in costly fabrics. The floor coverings had been renewed, so that each step released the tansy scent of costmary or the minty aroma of fresh balm. There was elaborate music, constant ringing of the bells, a splendor of lights and incense, and the services were long.

After mass the guests dined in the refectory with the monks. Festal tablecloths covered the tables, which were decorated with spring flowers, candles, and gold plate. There were soft towels to dry their hands after washing, and the cutlery gleamed. Sir Nicholas, Gwilym, Hugh, and the women sat at the high table with the abbot and guestmaster; and, giving heed to the splendor of the occasion, Jonet, seated beside Hugh, allowed him to serve her without snubbing him. The general mood was festive, and when the Paschal lamb was brought to the abbot's board to be carved, and Madeline sighed her pleasure aloud, twinkles of delight could be seen in more than one otherwise stoic face at the lower tables.

When the huge meal was over, the guests retired to the guesthouse again to rest. As Alys was moving to join the other women, a hand on her arm brought her around to face her husband.

He smiled ruefully. "I have neglected you sadly these past days, wife. Do you fetch your lute and bring it down to the hall. We can have a lesson while the others rest."

She went gladly, delighted to have an opportunity to spend some time with him and hoping that the warmth she had seen in his eyes might later be kindled to something stronger. When she returned, however, she discovered that they would not be alone in the hall, for the roaring fire had drawn the others. Madeline had found a book to read, and Jonet and Elva had their baskets of mending. Even the two lay brothers had unearthed a board upon which to play Fox and Geese, and had sat down upon the floor at a distance from the others to enjoy themselves.

Gwilym, coming into the hall a few moments later, looked speculatively at Madeline and then at the fire before he settled himself in the inglenook to doze.

Alys made herself comfortable on a cushion near the hearth, and Nicholas sat down cross-legged beside her, his lute in hand. She began to pluck a simple tune on hers, to limber her fingers, and after listening critically for a few moments, he matched his playing to hers. They had been playing for only a few moments when Gwilym murmured to no one in particular, "The music is well enough, but 'twould be more pleasant, withal, if someone would read aloud to us for a spell."

One of the lay brothers offered to fetch a Bible or a book of psalms from which to read, but Madeline, looking at Gwilym over her book, said sweetly, "You might well benefit from more prayers, sir, but I have had a surfeit of them, and 'tis but an hour before vespers when Master Guestmaster will no doubt insist once again that we join the holy brothers at their worship."

Alys saw muscles tighten in Gwilym's jaw, but he replied evenly, "You would not wish to miss the reading of psalms for your relatives, mistress, nor the singing of the Easter anthems. Such flightiness on such a holy day becomes you not. You must know that I meant it would please me, and the others, if you would read aloud to us from your tale."

Flushing visibly and giving an angry toss of her head, Madeline snapped, "When I want a sermon, Master Pope-Holy, I shall send for a priest to speak it. No one wants to hear my voice drown out the pretty music of the lutes."

Nicholas, with a glance at his brother's rigid countenance, said quietly, "Your voice is most pleasant, mistress. I warrant that we all should enjoy your reading."

"Certainly, sir," Madeline said, according him a regal nod. "I would be happy to do so when *you* ask me so courteously."

The emphasis in her friend's tone made Alys look quickly

down at the strings of her lute, so that her amusement would
not be visible to her husband or his brother. She was beginning to think that Madeline's vanity, so long indulged by the
men in her family, and others at court, had been pricked by
Gwilym's failure to treat her as she was accustomed to be
treated. He seemed both impervious to her charms and unimpressed by her beauty or temper. Alys still could not imagine he had any desire to marry her friend, but she found
their exchanges amusing and wanted to watch for further
developments; however, when Madeline began to read
aloud, Nicholas drew his wife aside to continue their lesson.

Madeline had just closed her book, declaring that her
voice was failing her, when the bells began to ring for vespers. The lutes were put away, and everyone adjourned again
to the church. Alys, walking to her place beside her husband,
peeped up at him from beneath her veil, wondering if he
would desire to continue her instruction later, in bed. Then,
crossing herself for such unholy thoughts, she bowed her
head and knelt beside him.

The service, like the others before it that day, was longer
than usual, but they emerged at last and headed with relief
toward the guesthouse. The guestmaster had told them there
would be a small supper served in the hall when they returned, and although no one had believed they would be
hungry again, Alys was looking forward to it, and thought the
others must be, too.

She saw the black-clad monks moving like shadows to their
dormitory for the night, each being sprinkled with holy water
as he passed the abbot, and as she turned with the others to
cross the cobbled court, there came a clatter of hooves on
the stones.

A horse and rider careered into the yard and came to a
plunging halt not far from the little group. The monks
paused in their procession, and Sir Nicholas's men on their
way to the cellarer's hospice paused too, to see what news
had come.

"Sir Nick Merion?" the courier shouted.

"Aye!" Nicholas shouted back.

"You're to ride to meet his sovereign grace, the king, at Barnsdale in Sherwood Forest by midweek, sir, with all your men, or to join him on the Nottingham road before then. His grace departs Lincoln at dawn for Nottingham Castle, and goes straight on to Pontefract from there. There be wickedness afoot!"

"I knew it," Nicholas exclaimed, glancing at Alys, who stared silently back at him. " 'Tis that outlaw, Lovell!"

"Aye, sir, 'tis himself. There was rumors afore we left Lunnon, and they did be confirmed at Lincoln. His noble highness has sent for Northumberland and dunamany knights of Yorkshire. He does regret the fact that my Lord Derby, his uncle, has gone into Wales to attend to his lands there."

Or, Alys thought to herself, to visit Sir James Tyrell. She had no liking for Jasper Tudor, an earl now and the king's chief supporter, and was glad he was not near enough to harass Lovell.

"Get some food and find a bed, man," Sir Nicholas said. "I will go at once. Hugh," he shouted, "get the men mounted!"

Without thinking, Alys snapped, "And just what about us, sir? Do you leave us here at Burton, to the care of the monks?"

He replied crisply, "I did not forget. Gwilym!"

"Aye," Gwilym said quietly, behind him.

Nicholas turned. "Take the women on to Wolveston. Ian MacDougal knows the way, and you may have two others, but they are all I can spare."

"We do not require Gwilym," Alys said stiffly. "Ian and the others will be sufficient, or the abbot can provide more men for a proper escort. You will want your brother with you."

"Gwilym will escort you," Nicholas said. "He was never meant to accompany me but came with us only because I do require someone to manage Wolveston in my absence." He stepped away toward his men, dismissing her in his hurry to issue more orders.

Alys stood, stunned, staring after him for a long moment before her rising fury spilled over in words. "Hold there, Sir Nicholas Merion," she cried. "You overstep yourself."

He stopped, stiffening, but he did not turn. The silence in the yard suddenly matched that in the cloister.

Recklessly Alys shouted, "Wolveston Hazard is *my* home, sir, *my* inheritance, and I have been raised to be its mistress. I require no manager, Nick Merion, and you do wrong to set one over me. I do not need your brother, nor do I want him, so you just take him yourself! You will need every man you can get, believe me, because you much mistake the matter if you think any great host of Yorkshire knights will answer the Tudor's call. They will not! They will support my Lord Lovell, to a man!"

The silence that greeted her words lasted a full thirty seconds before Nicholas turned slowly to face her and said loudly enough for all to hear, "Ian, fetch me a good stout strap from the stable."

Silenced, and flushed with mortification, Alys looked around, her gaze taking in the monks, their abbot, the guestmaster, Hugh Gower, all the rest of Sir Nicholas's men, Madeline, Jonet, Elva, the lay brothers, and the courier. Every single one was staring at her as though he could not believe what he had heard. She had not forgotten they were there, not entirely; she had just failed to consider her words before she shouted them, or the effect they would have on her husband, particularly before such an audience. Overwhelmed by the enormity of what she had done, she looked again at Nicholas and panic seized her, rooting her to that spot on the cobblestones, and filling her with dread.

Ian had not leapt to obey the command. He said now, bravely, "I'm thinking a tawse be a fearsome weapon wi' which tae tame a lassie, master. Will ye no consider takin' a sturdy switch tae her backside instead?"

Alys bit her lip, not taking her eyes from Sir Nicholas.

Nor did he take his from her. He gestured impatiently at Ian. "Go, now, at once." To Alys he said, "Seek your chamber and wait for me to come to you."

She stood where she was, unable to obey. Her skin felt too tight for her body. Her nerve had deserted her, and she wanted nothing so much as to run from him, to run and run until she was safe. But she could not run. She could not seem to move. Never had she seen a man so angry as the one who stood before her now.

He said, "Go now, madam, or as God is my witness, you will take your punishment here before them all."

She went then, walking with as much dignity as she could manage until she was inside, then running up the stairs to the ladies' chamber, her mind racing as fast as her feet. When she heard running footsteps behind her, she whirled on the step, nearly losing her balance in her panic. But it was not Nicholas. "Madeline! No, you mustn't come!"

"Elva and Jonet are right behind me," Madeline said calmly. "He sent us inside. He did tell us to go into the hall, but—"

"You will only make him angrier than he is already if you try to defend me," Alys interjected with a grimace.

"That we shall see," Madeline said. "When we left, there were any number of persons doing their best to talk him out of what he means to do, and I saw the abbot making his way toward him from the cloister. Mayhap if Sir Nicholas finds us with you when he comes, he will calm down a bit, if nothing more."

Jonet and Elva were behind her now, but Jonet offered no advice for once, and Alys knew she would express no sympathy. Jonet had warned her often over the years about minding her impulsive tongue, but never had it led her into such a mess as this one. Knowing that nothing they could do would help her, she forced herself to think, and by the time they reached the ladies' chamber, to find a fire burning warmly on the hearth, evidently tended in their absence by one of the ubiquitous lay brothers, she had calmed a little,

and her brain began to function again with its customary ease
and rapidity.

She had gone too far, and she knew Nicholas meant to
punish her as he never had before. That she had defied him
before his men he would view as a fundamental challenge
to his authority, a challenge she knew he would never tolerate, for if he could not master his own wife, what respect
would his men have for him? He would believe he had no
choice but to punish her. Indeed, he had promised to do so,
in front of them all, and she had no way to protect herself
against him, not the smallest weapon of which he would take
notice. Or had she? Memories teased at her mind, planting
the seeds of a plan, which began to take root at once and
blossom. Offering a brief prayer—and an apology—to God,
she turned quickly to the others to request their help.

# 17

Alys ordered Jonet to light more cressets and candles, and to fetch her brush. Then, yanking her veil from her hair, she pulled out pins until the thick, golden tresses spilled over her shoulders to her waist. There was too little time. In her frantic haste to pull off her gown, she tore the bodice lace.

"Miss Alys!" Jonet exclaimed, scandalized. "Where have your wits gone begging?"

"Never mind my wits," Alys snapped. "Help me! Elva, fetch my perfume, and Madeline, fetch out my green silk dressing gown from the coffer there by the hearth. Make haste!"

Madeline's eyes lit with sudden, irrepressible amusement, but she held her peace and hurried to obey, bringing Alys a pair of narrow green silk ribbons, which matched the robe, as well.

"Here," she said, handing them to her. "Tie one round your throat whilst I thread the other through your curls. 'Twill make you look more feminine, more fragile to his eye."

" 'Tis more like to provide him with a line along which to slit my throat," Alys muttered, but she obeyed.

Madeline chuckled. "Why not leave off the robe and greet him in your smock, or better yet—"

"Good God, I don't want him to ravish me," Alys exclaimed. "I want only to remind him that he has reason not to murder me. Hurry with that ribbon, won't you?"

When the second ribbon was tied, and Jonet had loosened her bodice, she stepped out of her overdress and snatched up the robe, flinging it on over her low-cut smock and petticoats. Taking the perfume vial from Elva, she began to dab lilac scent behind her ears and on her wrists, but her head came up sharply when she heard the thud of leather boots on the flagstones of the gallery. "Hush," she warned. "He comes! How do I look?"

"Like a sacrificial virgin," Madeline said with a wry grin.

Jonet shook her head in disapproval, saying nothing.

The door banged back on its hinges, and Alys straightened, letting the robe fall open when she turned to face Sir Nicholas, but her courage nearly failed her at the outset.

He stood on the threshold, the strap dangling from his right hand. His eyes blazed, and his face was rigid with fury.

"Begone, the lot of you!" he snapped at the other women.

Elva fled, sidling past him, and Jonet tugged at Madeline's arm, but the younger woman resisted. Her grin had vanished at the sight of Nicholas, and she clearly meant to stand her ground.

Striving to sound calmer than she felt, Alys said, "Prithee, leave us now. My husband would be private with me."

With another wry twist of her lips and one last look over her shoulder as she turned away, Madeline responded at last to Jonet's silent urging and went.

The instant they had crossed the threshold, Nicholas kicked the door shut behind them and strode purposefully toward Alys.

Swiftly she curtsied before him, her petticoats billowing around her, her head bowed, albeit not low enough to impede his view of her plunging décolletage. "You are right to be angry with me, sir," she said. "I behaved badly, and though I am very sorry, I have no right to expect you to remember that my body bruises easily." Taking a deep breath, she raised one delicate, shaking, pink-nailed hand to the line between her breasts, hoping the gesture looked properly submissive, knowing it must draw his attention to that portion of her anatomy she knew he admired most. "I cry mercy, Nicholas, but you must do as you will."

"*Esgyrn Dafydd!*" he swore, looming over her. "You are acting like a little whore, madam! Do you seek to disarm my temper with naught but soft words and a winsome body?"

"Aye," she said honestly, looking up at him at last. "I know I am not behaving like a lady, Nicholas, but I have no wish to be beaten. I deserve to be for speaking to you before your men as I did, but I dared hope that since you have not claimed a husband's right for days, and since my body can give you small comfort before your journey if it be bruised and painful, you might find enough mercy in your heart to spare me this one time. It has been made plain to me," she added, blushing rosily, "that you do enjoy my moans of pleasure, sir, but I doubt you are a man who can be aroused by feminine cries of pain."

"Husband's right?" he murmured, ignoring the rest. His posture had not changed, but his voice was pitched lower now, deeper in his throat; and, noting the change, and the promising gleam in his eyes, she lowered her lashes, hiding her relief when he went on in the same tone, " 'Tis not your general habit so to describe our fleshly encounters, wench. In sooth, I do recall at least one somewhat impudent reference to a husband's *duty*."

Suddenly shy, not looking up, she whispered, "I care not if it be duty or right, sir. I do enjoy such attention from you and have missed your caresses, for you have not lingered properly over our lovemaking since our wedding night, which I do recall with great delight."

"Stand up."

The deep, throbbing tone was gone, and the two words were spoken crisply enough to send icicles of fear lancing through her, but she did not dare disobey him. Slowly, reluctantly, she got to her feet.

"Look at me."

She did, and the expression she saw on his face was not an auspicious one. She sighed. Though she had done her best, she feared that what little power she had to sway him had not been enough to counter his determination to prove, to himself if not to his men, that he was master of his own wife.

"Do you know that the abbot himself recommended that I teach you better manners?" he demanded, holding the strap with both hands now, looking down as though to examine it more closely.

"Did he?" She, too, fixed her gaze upon the strap.

"Aye, he did, and so did Gwilym."

"I believe it about your brother," she said with a grimace, "but I had hoped the abbot might stand my friend."

"He cannot condone defiance of proper authority." He shot her a look from under his brows. "He forbade me to depart before this Easter day is done, since I go for no good purpose, he said, but to kill in the name of the king—the same excuse, he reminded me, as they did employ who crucified our Lord. He said, too, that since my wife's undutiful behavior was as much an offense against God as against man, I must, by his command, remain here till morning in order to have adequate time to attend to her."

She swallowed hard. "He said that?"

"Aye, and his commands are said to come straight from God." A silence fell before he said, "Art truly contrite, *mi geneth*?"

Tears welled in her eyes. "Aye, sir," she said.

"Wouldst comfort me?"

"Aye."

"And dost truly delight in my touch?"

"Aye." The tears spilled down her cheeks. "Oh, Nicholas, I have yearned for your touch. You cannot know how often I have wanted you to do all the things you did that first night, the things you have not lingered long enough to do since. I know it is not my place to tell you what to do—"

"Come here," he muttered hoarsely, flinging away the strap and opening his arms to her. With a sob she threw herself into them. He murmured against her curls, "I did not know you felt so about our couplings, lass. I had believed you suffered marriage only because you had been commanded to do so, and I thought to spare you when I could. I would spare you now, but I cannot have my men think me weak, softened by a wench's wiles."

"There is no weakness in mercy, sir. Only the strongest of men may be merciful."

Still holding her, he made a sound of protest. "Anyone may be merciful. By nature, mercy is naught but caprice."

She looked up at him. "Men did say Richard was capricious in his mercy, that it was a fault. But if you are right, 'twas no fault at all but only the nature of—"

"We do not talk of Richard," he cut in impatiently, sweeping her up into his arms. "Which is your cot?"

"The first," she told him, pointing to the one nearest the fire, "but we cannot stay here the whole night long, sir. Where will Jonet, Madeline, and Elva sleep?"

"Do they all sleep here with you?"

"Aye." She smiled at him, relaxing completely, her head against his shoulder. The danger appeared to be over.

He moved toward her cot. "I care not where they sleep."

"But they will come up, thinking you have gone to bed and left me to weep the night away in abject misery."

"Would you have wept?" he demanded, a glint of irony in his eyes. "Methinks you do not know the meaning of abject misery, wife, but have always beguiled your way out of punishment."

She opened her eyes wide at that. "But I told you what it was like at Drufield," she said. Wrinkling her nose at him, she added, "I spent many a night in misery there, sir, but I warrant that you approve of Lady Drufield's methods."

He did not smile as she had expected, or disclaim. Instead, seriously, he said, "Do you truly know what you deserved tonight, madam, or were all your words rehearsed merely to unman me?"

She touched his face. "I do know, Nicholas, and I am

sorry. I was wickedly undutiful, just as the lord abbot said I was."

" 'Twas more than lack of duty," he said, turning toward the door. "Those last words you shouted were downright treasonous. Should I allow them to go unpunished, not only would it be wrong, but such leniency would seriously undermine my authority over my men. They are not all law-abiding fellows, *mi calon*. We breed as many rascals in Wales as you do in England, and some of mine, you will recall, are Scots. It would not do for them to think me too weak to control a mere female, and my own wife, at that."

"Aye, sir, I know that."

He was silent, concerned for the moment with the task of opening the door without having to put her down.

"Where are you taking me?"

"To my chamber. Tom will be comfortable enough down in the hall on a bed of rushes. I'll not need him this night."

"But my clothes!" she cried, recalling that it was necessary to go to the ground floor and up a second stairway to reach the gentlemen's side of the house. She clutched her robe tightly across her breasts. "You cannot mean to carry me through this house in naught but my robe and petticoats, sir!"

"Certainly I can. By rights, I ought to strip you bare and carry you over my shoulder for all to see, with your backside as red as fire." He paused significantly, then added in a gently provocative tone, "Do you wish to discuss my husbandly rights any further this night?"

She held her tongue until he began to descend the stairway to the hall, when she gathered her dignity and said, as though she were merely conversing to pass the time, "What was that you said? It was a new phrase, *mi . . . mi calon*?"

To her surprise, he did not answer as readily as he usually did, and when he did there was new color in his cheeks. He said only, "Is that what I said?"

"Aye. What is it?"

He shrugged. " 'Tis merely a term for one's wife. In Welsh

the word for 'wife' means prudence and discretion, but it also means cunning, and that suits you well enough, does it not?"

She was learning to hear more in his voice than the words he spoke, and she knew he was not being entirely truthful. He had never, to her knowledge, lied to her, but she thought he might be capable of shading truth if truth made him uncomfortable, or if he thought he might betray vulnerability of a sort he thought unmanly. She did not tax him with her knowledge, however, for she was too grateful to be spared the full force of his temper that night to ponder at any length over his possible deception.

If she had hoped he would carry her quietly down one stair and up the other, she was disappointed, for when they reached the hall, they discovered that not only were Gwilym, Madeline, Jonet, and the lay brothers present, but also Hugh Gower and several other men, including Tom and Ian. The men were sprawled before the fire, casting dice and drinking spiced ale that had been heated with a poker, now lying with its tip in the embers to stay hot. The women sat talking as they plied their needles. No one looked up when Nicholas reached the foot of the stair.

"You there, Tom!" he bellowed to his squire. "You sleep down here tonight, lad, but see that you wake me when the brothers have begun to sing matins. And, Hugh, you have the men ready to ride as soon as they have broken their fast."

Everyone was staring now, just as he had wanted them to do.

"Ladies," he said, "you may have your chamber to yourselves. My wife will bear me company in mine own. But first," he added sternly, setting Alys on her feet, "she wishes to apologize to you all for her unseemly behavior in the courtyard earlier."

Caught off guard, Alys clutched her robe tightly across her breasts, glanced uncertainly up at him and then back at the others. "I . . . I do apologize for my . . . my unseemly behavior," she stammered. "I ought not to have spoken so."

Nicholas hooked his thumbs in his belt and said, "Do not be shy, wench. Get it all said. You ought not to have shouted in a manner so unladylike as to embarrass the holy brethren. Go on, now," he added, removing one hand from his belt to gesture impatiently, "say all of it."

"I ought not to have shouted," she said obediently. " 'Twas most unmannerly."

"And undutiful," Nicholas murmured behind her, "to speak so disrespectfully to your lord and master."

"And undutiful," she repeated.

"Continue with the rest," he said gently, "as I bade you."

She glared at him, and then at the others when she saw laughter in Madeline's eyes and approval in Gwilym's. Although she was certain they could not hear Nicholas's words, they could tell he was pressing her to say more than she wanted to say. She muttered, "I was undutiful to speak so rudely to my husband."

Nicholas shook his head and said in a normal tone, "Your attempt to show proper humility bespeaks a lack of practice, madam. You have not yet mentioned your sincere regret at having uttered words that, to those who do not know your mischievous tongue, might have sounded a trifle treasonous. What say you?"

She looked at him again, her emotions a mixture of anger and uncertainty. She would have liked very much just then to snatch up one of the bone goblets and dash hot spiced ale in his smug face, but she did not dare, knowing he might well retaliate by baring her backside before them all. The worst of it, she acknowledged grimly to herself, if not to him, was that he was in the right. If the things she had shouted were ever repeated to the king or to Elizabeth, she could well be accused of treason.

Straightening her shoulders and raising her chin, she said clearly, "My husband is right to remind me that foolish words shouted in a fit of temper might be misunderstood, might even be given more weight than they deserve."

"I wish the king no ill," Nicholas prompted for her ears

alone. When she did not respond at once, his hands gripped her shoulders from behind, and he said insistently, "Say it."

"I wish the king no harm," Alys said.

"I pray he will defeat his enemies," murmured her prompter.

Instead, she said, "And now, having made my apologies to you all, and having made it clear that I am no enemy to the king, I do beg you all to forgive us if we leave you now. My husband has expressed a wish to retire. Have you not, sir?" she inquired sweetly, turning toward him.

"I have," he agreed, his undertone grim. "We bid you all good night." And with that, taking her by the arm, he hastened her toward the second stairway, adding, again for her ears alone, "You would be well served if I did put you over my knee, madam."

"I am no puppet, sir," she snapped, hoping the minute the words were out that she had not spoken too loudly, but determined nonetheless to make him understand. "I do not speak words others put in my mouth if those words do not express my feelings. 'Twas bad enough, in faith, to have said I wished no ill to the king. He has not business to be king, and while I do not wish him harm, precisely, I do want him off the throne of England, and therefore will I cry victory when my Lord Lovell's men defeat him!"

"And me, madam? Will you cheer if I am killed by that damned outlaw, while I attempt to defend my king? Or if Hugh is killed, or Ian, or Tom? Will you cry victory over our graves?"

His words halted her on the stair, her hands clutched at her breast, for it seemed that her heart had ceased to beat, that her breath had died in her throat. Her knees quaked with the dread of the images he had forced into her mind, and for a moment she was afraid she would faint where she stood.

"I never meant such a thing," she whispered, her gaze begging him to believe her. "I would never cheer your death, or any of theirs. And in faith, sir, you did promise that Ian should go with me to Wolveston Hazard."

"Oh, aye, the lad will thus be spared, will he not? And perchance, wench, if you should write him a safe passage in your own hand, your hero Lovell will spare you Ian even if he should chance to be caught with me."

Reaching a hand toward him, she said, "Prithee, try not to be angry with me, sir. Once again I spoke hastily and without thought. I never meant harm to you or them. In truth, had I my own way of things, I should ordain an end to war and violence altogether. No good ever comes of such."

Taking her outstretched arm in a bruising grasp, he turned her abruptly on the stair and urged her upward, saying curtly, "Have done with your pleadings, madam, and get yourself up those stairs. I have had my fill of female blandishments for one night and would see you serve me in your proper place. I have been patient and most merciful, I believe, and my thanks is that you would wish my king dead on a field of battle. Nay, say no more," he added angrily when she stopped again, "You have said enough."

She knew she had pushed him too far again, that to argue more would only put her in danger of what she had so recently averted. Knowing no way to make him understand her feelings, she gave it up for the moment and hurried up the stairs.

His chamber was much the same as the ladies' chamber on the opposite side of the house. A fire burned brightly on the hearth, and the hangings at the windows were of the same velvet cloth. Only one detail was very different. There was but one bed, a huge one, with a small truckle bed pulled out at one side, where Tom clearly had thought he would be sleeping. Nicholas, seeing it, shoved it back under the big bed with his foot.

"I would retire at once," he said. "It will be a long, wearisome day tomorrow if we are to make the forest by dark."

The mood she had created earlier was broken, and for that she was sorrier than for all the rest. She did not think he would be killed defending the Tudor. Nicholas was too big, too competent to fall. And he would have Hugh at his side, and all his other men besides. Still, the images he had drawn in her mind lingered there, and when he got into the big bed beside her, she wanted him to hold her close, to make the visions go away. Instead, without even drawing the bed curtains he moved swiftly to take her, apparently without concern that he might hurt her.

When she stiffened beneath him and cried out in alarm, however, he paused, looking down at her, his face in the fire's glow radiating first his annoyance, then dawning guilt. "By the holy rood, I ought to have beaten you," he muttered gruffly.

"I am glad you did not," she whispered. "You are so big, sir, that when you are angry, you frighten me witless. I have tried to be a good wife to you, but I have never learned to control my temper as I should, and when I lose it, I seem to lose my senses altogether. I did not mean to be a bad wife."

He shifted his weight to lie on his side with one hand propping up his head, the other resting idly on her hip. "You are not such a bad wife," he said, "but you do arouse all the furies of hell in a man when you behave as you did tonight. Methinks your foster parents would have done us both good service had they thrashed you soundly once a sennight."

"At Drufield they nearly did so, but my Lady Anne did train me to manage a large household," she said quietly. "You gave my home into your brother's charge, sir, ignoring the fact that I am better trained to manage it than he can be. That made me angry."

His expression hardened, and for a moment she feared she had stirred the coals of his anger again. He said, "It is enough that I decided to put Gwilym in charge at Wolveston. I need not explain my actions to you or to anyone. Do you understand that?"

"Aye," she muttered, "but 'tis most unfair."

"Mayhap." He was silent, but the hand on her hip began

to move slowly down her thigh and back again, almost as though he did it unknowingly while his thoughts were elsewhere. Then, just as she had begun to give herself up to the sensations he was stirring, he said, " 'Tis one thing to have training, *mi calon,* another to have experience. And just now, with the world in turmoil around us, and rebellions sprouting up hither and yon, while the country adjusts itself to Henry's rule, Wolveston is not safe under a woman's command. The place was ravaged by the sweat. I have no knowledge even of how many men are left there, how many tenants. I have seen only one village, the one time, and it was no concern of mine when I did so. The villages may have been overrun, or they may be deserted. It is also possible, in view of the fact that your father's sympathies were with the Yorkists, that his people now support Lovell and the Staffords."

"The Staffords?"

"Aye, we have heard rumors since we passed through Worcester that Sir Thomas Stafford and his brother Humphrey are trying to raise the Midlands against Harry, just as Lovell is raising the North. I forbade the men to say anything in your hearing because I did not want you or the other women made uneasy. 'Tis safe enough, I think, for you to travel betwixt here and Wolveston, but with the whole of England unsettled, it is no time to leave an estate the size of Wolveston Hazard in the hands of a woman."

She was silent. His hand trailed now to her waist and upward to her breasts, toying with her, still idly but with tenderness, and the feelings coursing through her body were impossible to ignore. Turning more toward him and putting a hand to his cheek, she said, "Perhaps you are right, sir, I had not thought of that. Our people will accept a man's hand on the reins more easily than mine at such a time as this, but I should prefer that the hand be yours, Nicholas, not Gwilym's."

"I, too, but that is not possible." Catching hold of her hand, he silenced her with kisses, forgetting their arguments as his need to quench his passions grew. But when he slept,

she lay beside him, sated but wide awake, thinking for a long
while.

She thought she was beginning to understand him better.
Men were difficult to know. Women were easier. She knew
she had enraged him and was surprised that her tactics to
mollify him had worked so well. At best, she had hoped only
that her woman's weapons would get her off with a whole
skin. But then, having spared her, Nicholas had grown distant again, almost angrier than before. She began to suspect
that his pride had been touched, that his anger had turned
inward, toward himself. She was nearly certain that he still
thought he had been weak not to punish her.

He awakened her early with kisses, and when she responded with a passion to match his own, he seemed to
forget he had meant to be gone before lauds, and lingered
with her, teasing and stimulating her until she feared her
moans of pleasure would be heard in the cloister. When he
entered her at last, her body leapt to meet his, and when it
was over, she lay trembling in his arms, waiting for the last
tremors to pass.

She sighed. "I am limp, sir. I shall never stir again."

He chuckled. "I will miss you, lass."

"Meistr?" It was Tom, and Alys was profoundly grateful
that Nicholas's body prevented her from seeing the squire's
face. "Will ye dress now, sir?"

She murmured, "Send him away," but Nicholas had already begun to sit up, and a moment later he was out of the
bed, the bed curtains had been drawn for her privacy, and
she heard the familiar sounds of his morning ritual with Tom.

An hour later in the courtyard, her husband's disposition
had changed yet again, and he made it a point to command
her in full hearing of his men and the abbot to obey Gwilym's
orders as though they had been his own. His attitude was
stern, his demeanor inflexible, just as though he had not
been kissing and caressing her from the moment he awoke.

His command aroused instant resentment in her, but she
hid it, gritting her teeth and behaving so well that the abbot

nodded his head in approval. At last, with a final command
to Gwilym to follow side roads and byways rather than the
Great North Road to Doncaster, Nicholas signed to his men
to proceed. When Alys saw him pass through the gates, looking magnificent on Black Wyvern, she felt suddenly bereft.
He had said he would miss her, and she had not even had
a chance to respond. But she knew she would miss him, too,
dreadfully. It took every ounce of control she could exert to
keep from calling him back to her.

Beside her, Jonet sighed, and Alys looked at her. Her per-
ception sharpened by her own feelings, she said quietly, "You
ought to be kinder to Hugh Gower. He cares for you."

"That whimling?" Jonet snorted. "Talks with a silver
tongue, but the niggish dogbolt's not got an ounce of spirit."

She would say no more, and their own little company departed soon afterward, their way proving to be so roundabout
that it was a full four days before they neared Wolveston.
Tempers were taut by then, or at least Alys's and Madeline's
were; the other women merely did as they were told, and
the men were as stoic as their leader. But neither young lady
appreciated Gwilym's high hand.

When it came to his telling them brusquely not to chatter
as they rode, for fear their voices would draw unwanted attention, it was Madeline who said sharply to him, "I warrant,
you think the woods are crawling with enemies, sir. Let me
remind you that no Yorkist knight will harm either of us, or
our people."

"Perchance you are right, mistress," he growled, "but I
have no right to take that chance. And you might recall that
men, being men first and Yorkists second, might not pause
to consider your politics before taking your purse or your
maidenhead."

"Fine talk," she said scornfully. "To try to frighten us is
behavior one has come to expect of you, Master Merion, but
we do not frighten so easily, as you ought to know by now."

" 'Twould be better for us all if you did, mistress. Now
hush before I lose my temper."

Tossing her head, Madeline said sweetly, "I am sure 'tis an awesome sight, sir, fit to set the leaves on the trees trembling with dread, but we cannot fear what we have never seen."

Alys, hiding a smile at the flush on Gwilym's cheeks, said quickly, "Look, Madeline, there is the castle yonder on the hill. Is it not a beautiful sight?"

Wolveston Hazard, crowning the hilltop with sunlight shining down on its gray bulk, looked clean and inviting after the rains. The hillside was green with new grass, and patches of spring wildflowers made splashes of vivid color. From their present vantage point they could see the river Trent winding at the foot of the hill, with green fields, marshland, and fens beyond. It was a peaceful scene, and one that caused Alys to draw a breath of pleasure. Certainly, the castle looked a good deal more inviting now than when she last had seen it.

The sight stirred them to haste, assured of warm fires and a proper meal, and the safety of solid stone walls and sturdy iron gates. Less than half an hour later, they rode in through the main gates, which had been, rather surprisingly, left open.

Alys said to Ian, "I thought you told me there were people here. Were these gates open like this when you came before?"

He shook his head, glancing at Gwilym, then around the open, deserted courtyard. His attitude was curious, nothing more. But Gwilym, overhearing Alys's question and Ian's response, laid his hand on his sword hilt and held up a hand for silence. Not a sound could be heard but the whistling of the breeze across the ramparts until finally, in the distance, a bird chirped and was answered by another.

"I did think someone would be here to welcome us," Gwilym said in a low tone. "Nick said the sweat ravaged this place but that a few soldiers were here, so unless the king sent for them to come to his aid, this is not right. Even in such a case as that, some men ought to have remained to look after the place."

Ian nodded. "There was men aplenty here afore, master, when I coom from Bawtry tae learn the fate o' Mistress Hawkins for m'lady. The gates did be closed then, wi' men tae guard them."

Madeline said impatiently, "What matter where they are? We are here, and I for one am nigh to dropping with fatigue and hunger. Do let us go inside and light the fires so that a proper meal may be prepared. After that, at our leisure, we can discuss finding more men to guard the place and set it to rights."

Alys agreed. "Once it is known that I am come home, men will come to pledge their fealty, sir. I have been told that my father's estates are vast, so even if many have died hereabouts, there will be a sufficient number to serve us. Let us go in."

Gwilym hesitated only for a moment. Then, dismounting, he drew his sword and motioned to the other two soldiers to do likewise. "Ian, can you close the gates alone, lad?"

"Aye." Ian turned his horse toward the gatehouse, and a few moments later the great gates, controlled by counterweights, began to swing shut.

Once they were closed, Gwilym seemed to breathe easier. "Now, lads," he said, "follow me and keep your eyes skinned. Stay behind us, you women. I do not like this, but 'twould be the gravest folly to leave you here in this courtyard."

The little party crossed the cobblestone court and, avoiding the main entrance with its tall iron-barred doors, made their way to the postern door, the same by which Alys had made her previous visit to the castle. When it opened to Gwilym's touch on the latch, he hesitated again, but only for a moment. Taking the spiral stair to the main floor, then checking side chambers as they went, they passed without incident along the stone gallery to the arched entrance into the two-story great hall. Pausing on the threshold to assure himself that the chamber was empty, Gwilym strode inside, followed by the others.

At that moment, in a sudden flash of premonition, Alys

remembered there was a musicians' gallery and another, similar alcove, opposite it, but it was too late for warning.

Soldiers appeared, swords drawn and poleaxes at the ready, as if the very walls had spewed them forth. There were a dozen or more of them, and the sight of them froze Gwilym, Ian, and the other two men in their tracks. Before they could react, a loud voice commanded them to hold where they were.

"You are outnumbered two to one, and there are more of my men outside the castle, so if you have no yearning to be spitted where you stand, put down your arms and surrender."

Alys, recognizing the voice with astonishment, turned toward it and exclaimed, "Sir Lionel Everingham! What on earth, sir, do you think to accomplish here?"

"Why, mistress, I have come to claim you and yours for mine own, as by rights you should have been from the outset! Now, man," he added, his sword at rest, his fists on his hips as he glared at Gwilym, "do you yield or do you die where you stand?"

"We yield, sir."

Beside Alys, Madeline sighed with relief.

# 18

"Take the men below with those others," Sir Lionel ordered, adding to Gwilym, "We have a number of the Tudor's men in the dungeons already. You can bear them company for a time until it has been made clear who is the master here."

"Wait!" Alys cried. The men were being disarmed.

"What is it?" Sir Lionel said impatiently. "You do yourself no good by attempting to set your will against mine, Lady Alys."

"I do no such thing, Sir Lionel," she replied, thinking quickly. "In faith, to set my will against a man so brave as to take on both the Tudor and his strongest knight in arms would be most foolhardy. But you are about to send my manservant with the others. Ian is only a lad, sir, and is loyal to none save myself. He serves me right well, however, for he has learned my ways. I pray you, allow him to remain with me."

"He looks stout enough," Sir Lionel said doubtfully, "and he bears a sword and dagger like any other soldier."

"Only because our party was so small," Alys insisted. "He does not wear proper armor, sir, as you see, but only a leather brigandine and chausses." She hoped he had not been privileged to see the rest of Sir Nicholas's men, for most wore no more than that, trusting to speed rather than to heavy armor to protect them. Gwilym and one other who had accompanied them wore metal breastplates, and it was to that fact that she pinned her hopes.

Sir Lionel was in a mood to be generous. "Very well," he said at last, "the lad may stay. He can stir these hall fires to life, so that when the servants return they can get on with preparing a meal. But mind that you do not displease me, lad," he added, looking grimly at Ian. "At the slightest offense I shall order you sliced to ribbons and fed to my dogs."

Without so much as a glance at Alys, Ian nodded, pulling his fiery forelock and somehow looking even younger and more harmless than he had looked a moment before. He moved swiftly to kneel by the fire, taking up a few chunks of wood and casting them onto the bed of banked embers, then stirring and poking industriously until the coals glowed bright and burst into flame beneath them.

Sir Lionel watched him, then, realizing that his men were also looking on, said sharply, "Go, take those others below."

Gwilym, his voice sounding as though he controlled it only with strong effort, said, "I give my parole, sir, not to attempt to escape or to overpower you if you will allow me to remain here. I have promised my brother to look after his wife and the other women, and am loath to leave them to face you alone."

"Are you now? Well, you've little choice in the matter, sirrah, and I tell you man to man, you're a sight more likely to keep your head attached an you go with the others now. I've a short temper, and the Lady Alys will be your brother's wife only long enough for me to make her a widow, so you need not bother your head about any promises you've made to the man. As to the others, they'll be safe enough till we have use for them."

Madeline and Elva gasped, and Jonet reached out to grasp Alys's arm, but Alys needed no such warning to keep her wits about her. A chill had knotted the pit of her stomach at Sir Lionel's casual mention of killing Nicholas, and she saw that Gwilym had stiffened his resistance against his captors' efforts to push him from the hall. Hoping that he and the other two still might manage to get the upper hand if she could divert Sir Lionel, she turned a calm face toward him and said, "What can you hope to gain by making me a widow, sir? You cannot believe the king will give me or my inheritance to a former Yorkist."

He laughed. " 'Tis no longer expedient to be a Yorkist of any sort, my lady. You see before you a staunch Lancastrian."

"But you have imprisoned some of the king's men below!"

"Aye, that too was expedient. But Harry Tudor understands these matters if you do not. These thirty years past, and more, men have won both women and property through just such tactics as these, and he will know how to reward my efforts on his behalf."

"On his behalf!"

"Aye, for 'twill be easy enough in such uncertain times to assure him that the castle had been taken by that rascal Lovell—fool that he is in not knowing when a cause is lost—and that I have but rescued castle and lady, albeit not in sufficient time to save poor Sir Nick Merion. The king, having accepted my oath of fealty, will admire my daring and allow me to keep the spoils of my victory. Harry Tudor has said he cares only for spreading the wealth so that it does not accrue in one family. He will have no objection to my taking you and yours unto myself."

"But why?" Alys asked. "You did not want me before. When I arrived in London you did not look at me; and, to my knowledge, you made no objection when our betrothal was set aside."

"You were not then such an heiress," he said, "and I was taken up with establishing myself at court. Not until I discovered the vast worth of your father's estate did I realize my error in not pressing my claim from the outset. I soon set about putting the matter to rights, however."

A certain intensity in his expression sent a shiver up her spine. She fought the thought forcing itself upon her, but it would not die. "Roger," she said, her voice breaking on the name. Emotions that had not touched her at all when she had learned of his death touched her now, and there were tears in her eyes at the thought that, without knowing it, she might have provided motive for murder. "They called his death mysterious."

"Not so mysterious," he said casually, "if you but knew it."

"You killed him."

He did not deny it, nor did he say more about it. "Enough of this claptrap," he said. "Get those men below, lads. And you send your women above, mistress. You will remain here with me."

"No!" Madeline cried, stepping up beside Alys. "We will all remain together, Sir Lionel, or— Take your hands from me!" she shrieked when a soldier grabbed her by her arms from behind.

Gwilym bellowed a protest, struggled vehemently with his captors, and was knocked to the floor for his trouble.

Madeline turned white and went very still.

Alys said sharply, "Order that man to unhand her, Sir Lionel. I will not send my women away, for I do not trust your men to leave them in peace. Moreover, if you want to see supper on the table, you would do well to let my women attend to it. I see no sign of those servants you mentioned earlier."

"They are below," he said, "and will come when the others have been locked up. They are harmless enough, for they are more frightened of me than of a master they have never seen, so do not think they will aid you. But the women can stay and help. You are no doubt right about my men. Most have not had a woman in days, for we have been watching the roads for your party. I confess, I had hoped Sir Nick himself would bring you to me; but once I learned that Lovell has been making mischief hereabouts, I was not surprised to see your party limping in alone."

Not long after the prisoners were led away, a few servants did appear, and with Ian's help and that of Jonet and Elva, they began to prepare the evening meal. Alys watched with increasing appreciation the way in which Ian avoided draw-

ing the attention of Sir Lionel or his men. He blended in
with the other servants so well that were it not for his red
hair, Alys herself would have been hard-pressed to pick him
out.

The meal, when it was ready, was a trial, because Sir Lionel was by turns charming and surly, his clear intent to ingratiate himself with her foiled both by her own lack of
response and by Madeline's caustic comments. Afterward,
when Alys would have liked to withdraw to another room
with the other women, he prevented her, saying abruptly
that he would like some music.

"I am certain," he said, attempting to speak more politely,
"that you have been improving your skill upon the lute, mistress. I would hear the result of your efforts, if you please."

The reminder of her humiliation at Elizabeth's hands annoyed Alys and tempted her to say she did not have a lute
with her, but she decided against it. The lie was too easy to
disprove, and the time might come when she would want
him to believe a far more important one. The less experience
he had then of what little skill she possessed for deception,
the better it would be for all of them. She asked Ian to fetch
her lute, and sat with it on a stool near the fire, plucking idly
for a time. The other women occupied themselves as they
usually did after supper, except for Madeline, who sat with
her hands folded in her lap, glaring by turn at Sir Lionel and
his men.

"Madeline," Alys said, after she had been idly playing for
some time, "pray, fetch me that bit of parchment on which
Sir Nicholas wrote musical notes for me to practice. 'Tis in
the pack yonder by the fire, the one from which Ian took
the lute."

If Madeline thought the request an odd one, especially
since Ian was nearer the pack than she was, she did not say
so, and Alys was grateful for her silence. Taking the parchment from her, Alys said in an undertone, "Do not be constantly challenging them with your eyes. 'Twill only make
them the more alert. We shall do ourselves more good by

submitting wherever possible, so as to make them think us harmless."

"Speak louder, Lady Alys," Sir Lionel commanded. "Your voice does please mine ear, and I would hear what you say to Mistress Fenlord."

Alys, feeling warmth surge into her cheeks at having drawn his notice, hoped he would take the added color for maidenly blushes and said diffidently, "Please, sir, 'twas but female's talk, not meant for masculine ears."

"Nevertheless, madam, I would hear it. I will allow no secrets betwixt you here."

"Forsooth, sir," Madeline snapped, "if you must know, she was but saying she wanted me to accompany her to the garderobe. We trust not your men, nor you, but I do not doubt you will all insist upon bearing us company whilst we do relieve ourselves."

"Madeline!" Alys fought down her amusement at the appalled look on Sir Lionel's face, and struggled to appear as though Madeline's forthrightness had shocked her.

Sir Lionel grimaced. "You may leave, the pair of you, but do not be gone long, else I will come searching for you, and you will be right sorry then to have put me to the trouble."

Thinking swiftly as she arose to her feet, Alys glanced at Ian to see that the lad was surreptitiously watching her while he helped clear away the tables that had been set up for their supper. Shifting her glance pointedly toward the door leading onto the gallery, she looked back at him to see if he had understood her. His nod would have been unnoticeable to anyone not looking for it.

Sir Lionel said, "Shall I send one of my men to escort you?"

"I thank you, but no," Alys said before Madeline could refuse the offer more rudely. "We shall not be gone long, sir."

"See that you are not. And remember, your other women remain here with me. They will suffer if you play games with me, girl."

Taking time only to set her lute aside and to shake out her skirts before hurrying to the gallery with Madeline close upon her heels, Alys went toward the northwest tower and nearly jumped out of her skin when a shape loomed up before her as she neared the spiral stair. "Ian! You nearly frightened the liver and lights out of me! I did not see you leave."

"Sorry, mistress. They didna heed me. They be like most o' their ilk, taking servants for naught but bits o' furniture. I did ha' a great pot o' water in hand, and they didna think tae ask whither I were bound wi' it."

"Good. We dare not be long, Ian, but I want to show you the trick of the postern gate."

"The gate, mistress?" He glanced around nervously.

"Aye, come below."

"But the ladies' garderobe lies abovestairs!"

Madeline said, "The gate is below, lack-wit!"

"Hush, Madeline," Alys said softly. "That we are prisoners is not Ian's fault, so do not berate him." She was hurrying down the steps as she murmured the words, but she did not fear to be overheard. Sir Lionel's men were not so many that he would have one posted at every turn. At the bottom, she peered out the tower door, then slipped through the darkness to the little gate set into the wall. "Here, Ian, look," she said, silently opening it. Taking his hand, she placed it on the secret knob. "This knob controls the bolt from without. You can slip the bolt, go out, and then slip it back again from outside. The knob cannot be seen from either side if one does not know it exists."

"Do I go at once then, mistress?"

The temptation to send him was nearly overwhelming, but she resisted it. "Not until the castle is asleep. You would be missed. We must hope he does not lock you in the dungeon with the others, but I think he has dismissed you as a danger. You have done well, Ian. Continue to be invisible amongst the other servants, and later, when all are asleep, you can slip out. This gate is not guarded now. It should not be later,

either. Once you are safely away, you must find Sir Nicholas
as quickly as you can and tell him what goes forth here."

"I will do what I can, mistress, but it will take time tae
find him, afoot as I'll be."

"You will not be afoot for long if you go downhill to the
river—you can hear it now below us—then bear left to the
nearest village. The villagers are loyal, and someone will have
a horse. Then ride to Bawtry, for 'tis closer than Doncaster,
and you can get word there of the king's procession. If they
have already ridden on to Doncaster, or even Pontefract, you
must ride after them. If they have not yet reached Bawtry,
take the forest road toward Nottingham until you meet them.
I think they will have gone on ahead, though, for Sir Nicholas
was to have met the Tudor at Barnsdale several days ago."

"Come on," Madeline said. "We must not linger here."

"No, we must not," Alys agreed, "but I hope you have no
immediate need for the garderobe either, my girl, for we
have no time left for such indulgence. We must get back to
the hall before that villainous knave comes to look for us."

Madeline nodded, her mood clearly lighter now that they
had a course of action. Ian went ahead of them, disappearing
almost at once in the dim light of the tower, and by the time
they returned to the hall, he was back by the fire, adding
logs to the blaze while one of the other menservants passed
pewter mugs of burnt claret to Sir Lionel and his men.

Alys picked up her lute again and played for some time,
and Madeline took her stool to sit near Jonet and Elva, helping Jonet sort the thread in her workbasket. An hour later,
Alys yawned and said, "I hope you do not mean for us all to
sleep here in the hall, sir, but even if you do, I must beg
leave to retire. It has been a long, exhausting day."

"Where are your rooms, mistress?"

"On the floor above this one, sir. If you look up there"—
she pointed halfway up the high wall opposite the fireplace—
"you will see yet another gallery like the one outside this
room. My chamber is in the south tower at the end of that
gallery. And if it please you, sir," she added, rising, "I should

like my things taken up, and my manservant to sleep on a pallet outside my door as he is accustomed to do. We should all feel safer thus."

"What makes you think my men would not merely spit the lad on their swords to reach you, mistress? You are a prize worth the taking, as I have said before." He leered at her over his wine, and several of his men laughed.

"The fact that you would visit your wrath upon them if they did, sir," she replied dulcetly. "Though you have changed sides for expediency's sake, I know you for a Yorkist knight at heart."

"Do you now? Well, by all that's holy, girl, I vow 'tis true enough that you may trust them to fear me." He glared fiercely at those who had laughed, then turned back to her and said, "Take your lad then, and your belongings, and on the morrow, we will talk, you and I. You have spirit, wench, and I doubt not the pair of us can make something of this place in time. 'Tis in a dismal state at present, but that will change."

"Aye, sir," she replied, nearly choking on the words. "Come, Ian, and you others. 'Tis time and more we were abed."

Upstairs, with Ian conspicuously placed on a pallet outside the door to the large bedchamber she had chosen—not because it had ever been her own but because she had remembered it was spacious enough for them all to stay together without tripping over one another—Alys explained to Jonet what they had planned.

Jonet was helping Elva set out thick pallets for themselves and Madeline near the fireplace. The room had been sparsely furnished as a guest chamber, and since Madeline preferred to sleep alone, Alys was to have the only bed to herself. " 'Tis to be hoped Ian finds the master quick," Jonet said, shaking out a quilt. "That Sir Lionel is no gentle knight, mistress. The more I see of him, the less I admire the late King Richard's judgment of men if he could think that one a suitable match for you!"

Alys sighed. "He did make some fearful errors of judgment, did he not? But Ian will find Sir Nicholas. He must."

"If he can get out of the castle," Madeline said doubtfully.

Alys rounded on her. "I don't know why you insist on making difficulties," she snapped. "First you challenge Gwilym at every turn. Then you spit at Sir Lionel when it can do us no good at all. And now you cast doubts on the only plan that can help us."

"Now then, mistress," Jonet said soothingly, "she meant no harm by it. 'Tis a pity, I'm thinking, that that gormless gowk, Hugh Gower, cannot be here when he might prove useful for once."

Madeline smiled ruefully at Alys. "She is right, although I should prefer a whole troop of Hugh Gowers to put these fiends properly in their places. Instead we have only Gwilym, who puts himself at risk for no good cause, but only to . . . to . . . and here I thought he did not care a whit— Oh, I talk nonsense. Pay me no heed!" And before Alys could think of a word to say to her, tears began streaming down Madeline's face, and she said, sobbing, "Oh, Alys, do you think they are safe?"

Alys knew now that she was thinking of only one man, and saw nothing to be gained by pointing out that she knew no more about the condition of the men in the dungeon than Madeline did. Soothing her as best she could, she persuaded her to make ready for bed. Madeline obeyed but said she would sleep in her smock since, once Ian had gone, Sir Lionel's men might come in. Alys considered following her example but decided she would not give Sir Lionel the satisfaction of intimidating her. Before climbing into bed, she wrapped her robe around her and opened the door onto the gallery to see how Ian fared.

He smiled at her. "All's nesh, m'lady. 'Tis as if they think I'm setting guard here on their ain account. I took a peek doon yonder stair tower, and there be not a sign of armor betwixt here and the wee gate. 'Twill be a miracle, I'm thinkin', if they e'en miss me wi' the dawnin'."

Alys hoped he was right, but the hope lasted only until she was rudely awakened the following morning to find not only Sir Lionel's soldiers in the chamber but Sir Lionel himself. He stood watching from the threshold while his men searched every inch of the room, overturning coffers and spilling the contents onto the floor. Madeline, Jonet, and Elva were yanked roughly from their pallets, and when Sir Lionel ordered Alys to arise—with only a quilt wrapped around her to cover her nakedness—the mattress on her bed was torn off and shaken as if the men expected to find someone hidden within it. Sir Lionel was livid, and the men holding the women were not gentle. When Elva cried out with pain, Alys said sharply, "Make them stop!"

"Where is he?"

Alys nearly asked whom he meant, but the look on his face deterred her, and she said, "Far away, I hope. You said you wanted a word with Sir Nicholas Merion. I have only put forward your meeting, sir, though I doubt it will go as you planned."

"Oh, it will still go the same," he growled, "but you will not enjoy the waiting as you seem to think you will, my girl." He made a gesture toward the others. "Take them below and throw them in with the men."

"No!" Alys cried. "You cannot do such a thing!"

"Do you not trust even the men who brought you here?"

"Oh." Alys breathed a sigh of relief and moved to follow the others.

"No, no, little heiress," he said, barring her way. "You do not go with them. You will remain here with me for a spell."

She stepped back, fully aware of her nakedness beneath the quilt, aware that he was moving aside to let the others pass him, that in too short a time she would be completely alone with him. They were gone. Glancing around hastily, she noted the poker near the fireplace and wondered if she could get near it without his discerning her intent. But his gaze followed hers.

He chuckled. "So you would crack my skull, would you?"

"Aye, if I could," she retorted.

"Well, you cannot, but I've a notion to strip you of that quilt you clutch so tightly, just to teach you the consequences of such defiant talk. What think you of that?"

She longed to tell him what she thought of him, but she remembered her own words to Madeline and forced herself to reply calmly, "I hope you will not, sir. I am at your mercy, as I know full well. I did speak hastily, but if you can find it in your heart to be merciful now, I will guard my tongue in future."

"Prettily spoken, my dear, but I should be a fool to believe you, and I am no man's fool, nor any woman's."

"What will you do?" He had come no nearer, but the way he looked at her made her cringe inside and she had all she could do to conceal her revulsion.

"You are a choice piece of goods, madam, even without your inheritance. Little did I realize it, but when Richard fell, he did me a greater disservice than I knew. Even after I'd arranged for you to come into your own, I thought only of the chattel, not the bedchamber benefits that would accompany our union. God refuse me, all I remembered was a wee chit of a girl, all teeth and hair, with a body little more than skin and bone—not even a good armful for a man. But seeing you now, grown—" He broke off, staring at her, sweat breaking out on his brow. "Just look at me! Not more than ten of a morning, and already my body is craving yours. Tell me why I should not indulge the craving."

She took another step back, but the mattress they had pulled from the bed was behind her and she nearly tripped. Steadying herself, she said, "You would not dare."

"Don't be a fool. God refuse me, but I should be a greater one to delay. The lad went to fetch Sir Nick, did he not? He'll not best me, I vow, but a taste of your charms can only spur me on to win them for mine own!" Grinning, he stepped toward her. He was between her and the door now with less than a dozen feet separating them. "That mattress will accommodate us nicely where it lies. Drop the quilt, lass. Show me what I would fight for."

Terrified, she watched him approach, one slow step at a time, as though he understood her terror and would draw it out, as though her very fear aroused him. He was tall, nearly as tall as Nicholas, and she knew that fighting him would be futile, for he would overcome her most strenuous attempt with ease. He would take her, possess her, and he would demean her, too. She could see the last in the way he looked at her.

In the few seconds it took him to take three steps toward her, her mind seemed to have frozen, but with the fourth step it snapped to life again. Straightening her shoulders, she looked him in the eye and said, "You wish to see me, sir? By heaven then, since I cannot fight you, I have no choice but to obey."

He stopped where he was when she spoke the first words, and when, with the last, she opened the quilt wide, his eyes nearly popped from his head. Seeing his mouth drop open as well, she cast the quilt hard away to the left, and when his startled gaze followed it, she leapt to her right, snatching up the poker and whirling to face him with it held out menacingly before her.

His right hand flew instantly, automatically, to his sword hilt, but it halted there, and his countenance hardened. "Drop that, wench, or by the bones of Christ, I will thrash you till your buttocks are afire before I take you."

"I will not," she said. "Use your sword if you will. Kill me if you must! I will never submit to you, Sir Lionel."

"Oh, you will submit," he said. "And afterward, in the hall tonight, you will kneel to me before them all and swear an oath of fealty to me as if I were your king."

"I will not!"

"You will, and by Christ's bones, you'll kiss my feet after, or I'll strip you naked before them all and thrash you again till you beg to serve me."

He grinned then, lewdly, and she felt her courage fleeing,

but she forced her thoughts away from the spectacle she must be making for him, and the one he was creating for himself in his lurid imagination, and fixed her attention on his eyes, watching for him to leap at her, wondering if he was so certain he could best her that he would come at her barehanded. If he did, there was a chance she might step out of his way long enough to bring the poker crashing down upon his head. He was tall for such a maneuver, but if he lunged it might be possible. As the last thought crossed her mind, she saw, just at the edge of her vision, a movement of the chamber door.

Though she tried not to look—a certain furtiveness in the movement made it plain that it was not one of his own men who entered—she had all she could do to keep her eyes on him. When she caught a glimpse of an arm sleeved in familiar light chain mail over leather, and a dark leather-gloved hand pushing the door wider, she nearly cried aloud her blessings upon Ian.

Just then Sir Lionel leapt, his hand clamping like a vise around the poker, and Alys's scream drowned all other sound in the room. One moment, Sir Lionel Everingham was leering down at her, his hand twisting hers unmercifully as he wrenched the poker from her grasp; the next moment, with a horrible bubbling cry in his throat, he collapsed at her feet. She stared down at him for a long moment, watching his life drain out of him, hating what she saw yet grateful that he was dead and could not threaten or torment any of them again. Then, wanting only for Nicholas to hold her tight, his chain mail notwithstanding, she took a quick, impulsive step toward her rescuer before she looked up and stopped in her tracks, her mouth open, her eyes wide with shock.

" 'Tis always a pleasure to see you, Lady Alys," Viscount Lovell said with his mischievous grin, "but I'll warrant your husband would dislike my seeing quite so much of you."

# 19

Alys had forgotten she was naked, and looked down at herself with greater dismay than ever, while Lovell, still grinning but ever gallant, strode across the room, snatched up the quilt, and tossed it to her. "Cover yourself, madam, and then perhaps you will tell me how you managed to get hold of that poker." Bending to wipe his blade on Sir Lionel's sleeve, he returned the sword to its scabbard and shot a last look at his victim. "They told me below that the covetous snudge had you here alone with him," he said, "so I expected to find you ravished and needing comfort. I discover instead that my assistance was scarcely required."

"Oh no, sir," she replied, drawing the quilt tight about her, welcoming its warmth but wishing for skirts and a bodice in its stead. "Your entrance was a timely one. I had put him briefly off his guard, but as you saw, I could not hold him. Though perchance," she added, "I might have managed to snatch his sword from its scabbard and then killed the villain myself."

"Nay, madam, for his scabbard hangs free. Even had you managed to lay hands upon the sword, it would have resisted your efforts, but it were no threat to me even had I not taken him unaware. Look at mine own weapons"—he gestured toward his sword and dagger—"lashed to my thighs, so that I can draw each with but a single hand. That scoundrel must needs have had both free to draw his. 'Tis a pity, though, that he had not the chance to do so. I should have liked to kill him in a fair fight."

"I am glad you did not try, sir."

"No time for it," he said simply. "Chivalry is all very well, but I've men below who depend upon me to lead them. We did not think to find this castle occupied by more than a scattering of servants, whom I had hoped would prove loyal to our cause. 'Twas so once before, when we did require sanctuary."

"Roger showed you the secret of the gate," she guessed.

"Aye, and I learned only recently of his death," he said quietly. "I am sorry for your loss."

"That villain murdered him," she said, nodding toward the corpse on the floor. "In London, they said only that his death was mysterious, but Sir Lionel gloated that it was not mysterious at all. His meaning was plain, and he meant next to murder Sir Nicholas, and take me and mine inheritance for his own."

"Such a plan might have prospered," Lovell said, frowning, "but look here, lass, we have little time. I had thought to escape the worthy Sir Nicholas's notice by hiding where he would least expect to find me, but with you in residence—"

"God save us, I sent for him!" she exclaimed. "My servant left in the night to search for him, to bring him to our rescue."

"And he will come hotfoot, I make no doubt." His expression was wry. "Almost you put me out, lass, but needs must when the devil drives, and Sir Nicholas has been driving us hard."

"Your insurrection did not succeed, then?"

"No, thanks to your husband. The man fights like seven demons, and that black monster he rides is nearly as dangerous as he is himself. I prefer not to mention at all the ugsome giant who rode so close beside him as to be mistaken for his shadow. God grant me strength! With such men as that, even a soldier as poor as Harry Tudor is might keep his throne."

Pride in Nicholas vied in Alys's breast with her disappointment that the Tudor had won yet another round. "Was it dreadful?" she asked sympathetically. "Were many killed?"

"Not so many, but we failed to capture the king, as we had hoped to do. Harry knew he was in danger, and rallied supporters to meet him at Barnsdale. Sir Nicholas was but one of many who answered the call. By the banners we saw, not only had Lincoln and Northumberland joined him but a disgusting array of Yorkshire knights, as well. 'Twas a sad sight, since many had fought for Dickon at Bosworth. The worst was Lincoln, his nephew and heir!"

"I am surprised he does fight at all," Alys said. "He was always so cautious, so carefully gallant."

"Aye, the man never talks straight, always with an 'if it were so,' or an 'it has been credited,' never just saying, 'it is.' But today he did fight, and without a single caveat." He sighed, then went on, "The army we encountered was larger than we had anticipated, but we might have won still, for they thought we were but knights newly come to join them. We took advantage of the error by riding straight at Harry Tudor and the men nearest him, hoping to snatch the king off his horse and be away with him before anyone else had gathered his wits to think what to do. 'Twas the very devil of a ride, but if we'd taken Harry hostage, we'd have been in an excellent position to name our terms."

"Aye," she agreed, "so why did you not take him?"

"Because Sir Nicholas and that giant beside him were more awake than the others. I doubt that they recognized me. How could they when they saw me only that one time, with my pretty locks hanging over my face and my motley clothing all awry? But something warned them, and we nearly lost more than our dignity. Happily, Harry himself got in Sir Nicholas's way, slowing him sufficiently so that many of my men and I were able to scatter and disappear into the forest whilst he was diverted."

"So you did not fight him," Alys said, relieved.

Lovell shook his head, his expression grim. "I am thankful

to say I did not, and thankful, too, that he is not a murderous man. When I looked back, they were taking captives, not simply dispatching them. Harry Tudor's habit is to punish half his captives and pardon the other half. 'Tis a disconcerting quirk, since one cannot know in which half one will find oneself."

"What will happen now?" Alys moved to sit on the bed, her bare feet tucked up into the quilt for warmth.

Lovell shrugged, watching her. "I make no doubt that Harry will ride on in great splendor to York, where the mayor and aldermen will welcome him with feasting and speechmaking."

"I wish they would bar the gates instead," she said. "That would teach him. York was Richard's city."

"It was, but despite their grief at Dickon's death, the city fathers have no wish to be martyrs in his cause. Their prime concern is the defense of their corporate privileges, and they want only to ingratiate themselves with the new king. But, look here, lass, we must not waste time with such chatter. Your husband will be here only too soon, and there are matters—"

"Indeed, sir, you must fly. I cannot think what keeps Gwilym so long. I had thought he would come up at once. If he discovers who you are, even the fact of your having rescued us—"

"Who is Gwilym?"

She stared at him. "But, surely, sir, you said it was the men below who told you I was here."

"Aye, the covetous snudge's men did tell us. But they are in the hall still, all trussed up like Shrove Tuesday birds."

"Sir Lionel's men sent you to protect me from him?"

"Ah now, let us say more properly that one of them was encouraged to chat with us of everything he knew."

His eyes twinkled, but she had no wish to ask for details. Instead, she said, "Then Master Gwilym Merion—my husband's brother—and Mistress Fenlord, and the others are still locked up in the dungeon and do not even know you are here. That is just as well, sir, but you must leave before Nicholas arrives!"

"Aye," he agreed, "but first, lassie—"

"Hark!" She slid off the bed, hastened to the window, and opened the casement to hear more clearly the sound she had heard even over that of his voice. "A horn, sir! They come!"

"The gates are closed, lass, so they will not be immediately upon us. They will wait to see if there is resistance first. Now, before they do come, tell me if you are well acquainted with the lad in the Tower, the one called Edward of Warwick."

Surprised by the question, she said, "You know I am. Neddie was at Sheriff Hutton with Elizabeth and me."

"You are certain the lad in the Tower is the same as the one you knew at Sheriff Hutton?"

"Aye, sir, I saw him, walking on the green. Why?"

"Only that I should be distressed to learn that any harm had come to him," he said. "We intend to make a little mischief."

"With Neddie? But what about Richard of York? Oh, sir, do not tell me he has come to harm. I have feared so. You cannot know what a trial it was to me to be so near in Wales, and yet I might as well have been in Scotland for all the good I could do, for I could not get across the Brecon Beacons into Glamorgan."

Amusement lit his eyes. "What would you have done, lass?"

"Why, I do not know, but something. Even to have discovered for myself that the prince is safe with Sir James Tyrell would have been a good thing. I cannot credit it for truth, sir, for Sir James appears to be at one with the Tudor."

Lovell's countenance grew unusually stern. "Do not meddle, Lady Alys, for you may do harm. We trust the prince is safe. In the next few months, the whole truth may well be revealed."

"How?"

"I am for Flanders, to seek sanctuary with Margaret, the Duchess of Burgundy."

"Richard's sister." Alys nodded. "Aye, she will help."

"She has done so already. I was with her on your wedding day, lass, on Simnel Sunday." He grinned, adding with a knowing look, " 'Twas but a brief visit to set certain matters in train, to see what manner of real support we can muster here, but her sympathies are certainly with us, and with her nephews."

"There have been rumors that both princes are dead," Alys said with a sad sigh, wondering how he could be so cheerful.

"Rumors set about by Harry himself, I do not doubt. He cannot shout them from the rooftops, for he does not know the truth and cannot chance a reappearance of either lad to make him a liar. He put off marrying Elizabeth, after all, whilst his men searched high and low for them, for he could scarcely declare her legitimate, or declare that his marriage would bind him to the throne, if they lived. Had he discovered them then, they would have disappeared forever, or he would have imprisoned them and abandoned the marriage. Neither course suited us then."

"And now?"

"Now Harry hopes, with these vague rumors, to flush the boys from cover. But we've learned to ignore rumors. I once heard the Duke of Clarence had searched for a babe to exchange for his newborn son, so that he might send Neddie to Ireland, to protect him. Then it was rumored that Dickon had murdered his nephews, a rumor set about by men who, had they found them, would have used them to draw others to rebel against Dickon. But such ruses did not succeed when Dickon was alive, and they will not now. Not till we want Harry to know that a Plantagenet prince lives will we tell him so. Perhaps, however, we can have a game with him in the meantime to learn more about how the Tudor mind does work."

Alys glanced nervously toward the window, her curiosity about what he meant to do warring with her rising trepidation. "Sir, you must go, but I do not know how you can get away now."

"We go nowhere, lass. I confess, I'd like to look into a certain grave to see what its resident wears around his neck— Do not swoon! I know I cannot. Not only Mother Church but the sweat that killed him does forbid it. We'll be safe until our way is clear, for I know places in this castle that I am certain your husband does not. We cannot leave with his men outside the gates, and no doubt Sir Nicholas knows the secret of the bolt."

"Aye, perhaps," she said with a sigh, knowing Ian might have told him, "but will those men below not tell him you are here?"

"They have no cause to know me, and my lads will not speak my name. Moreover, we will make them believe we have gone away. Or, we could kill them," he added a little absently.

Alys did not care about Sir Lionel's men. Her concern, with Nicholas so near, was the corpse of Sir Lionel on the floor, for how she would explain its presence in her bed-chamber she did not know. A sound from the courtyard sent every other thought from her head. "They are inside! Quick, sir, take the privy stair at the other end, for he will come up the tower steps."

"I know. You will not tell him I have been here."

"No, of course I will not. I am loyal to York, sir."

"Aye, but husbands demand loyalty, too, lassie."

"Of a different sort, sir. This is politics!"

He chuckled and turned to leave, then looked again at the corpse. "How will you explain that?"

She thought swiftly. "Give me your sword, and I will tell him I killed the knave myself, and that servants, or mayhap tenants, overcame the men below."

"Never my sword, lass, but take my dagger and welcome, and may the falsehoods rise easily to your tongue. Oh, and, lassie," he added with a delighted grin, "I recommend you put on something more becoming than that quilt to greet your lord and master."

Not even waiting for the door to shut, she flew to search her coffers for something to wear, and without bothering with smock or petticoats, dragged on a wool skirt and bodice, lacing the latter with trembling fingers while she strained her ears for sounds from the gallery. Remembering the dagger, she snatched it up and knelt by the body to smear blood on the blade.

They came silently, and when the door crashed back on its hinges, she looked up with a start to see her husband, his sword drawn, his face rigid with fear at what he might find, and Hugh close behind him on the threshold. All other matters vanished from her mind. Casting the dagger aside, she leapt up and ran to Nicholas, crying out his name. She saw his face relax, and when he put his free arm around her, she could feel his relief. Not till that moment did she realize how desperately she had yearned for his coming.

His soldier's instincts swiftly reasserted themselves, and his gaze swiftly scanned the room. Hugging her close, he said crisply, "Hugh, search about. I cannot believe the whole place is empty. Alys, where is Gwilym? Where are the soldiers Ian warned us of? And who the devil killed that bastard Everingham?"

"Please, sir, one question at a time," she begged, trying to gather her wits. Snuggling closer to him, taking comfort from the warmth of his body, she said, "I do not know what happened to his men." That was the truth. She had thought they were trussed up in the hall. "There were servants. They might have overcome his men while he was here with me. As for him, why, he . . . Oh, Nicholas, he killed Roger, and he was going to kill you! And he . . . he tried to force me . . . to . . . to ravish me!"

"Ah, sweetheart, no!" He looked grimly at the corpse, and she knew from his grim expression that if Sir Lionel were somehow to rise from the dead he would be struck down again and right swiftly. Then she saw Hugh's face.

"Mistress Hawkins," he said with dangerous calm. "Where is she, my lady? Did that villain dare to harm a hair of her head? Or any of the others?" he added as an obvious afterthought.

"I do not know, sir, but I think not. He ordered them all taken below and locked in with Gwilym and the other men when he discovered that I had dared to send Ian for help."

Nicholas released her and went to the corpse, examining it perfunctorily before stooping to pick up the dagger. Alys held her breath and watched him closely when he examined it.

"This is no lady's weapon," he said, looking over its twenty-four-inch length. "How came you by this, *mi calon*?"

"It . . . it was his," she said hastily, without thinking, gesturing toward the corpse. Then, wildly, she looked at Sir Lionel, unable to recall if he carried a dagger of his own. His right side was uppermost. There was no sheath. She sighed with relief and shifted her gaze more confidently to Nicholas.

He was frowning, looking at the dagger's gilded hilt, then back at the dead man. "Odd," he said. "I thought Everingham's device was a bear. This engraving looks more like a wolf."

Alys stiffened. Lovell's device was a dog. How like the viscount, she thought, to have the stupid thing engraved on his weapons. Giving thanks that he had not decided to have his arms engraved there as well, she kept silent, unable to trust her tongue, and was glad when Hugh's voice broke the silence.

"I will go below," he said, "and see to freeing the others."

"Take men with you," Nicholas said, "and send a pair to get that corpse out of here. He did not lay siege to this place alone, Hugh. Where the devil are his men?"

Hugh shrugged and left, but Alys realized with shock that Lovell's men must have taken their trussed Shrove Tuesday birds to their secret refuge. She prayed that if they had done so the action would not prove their own undoing. Nicholas, in searching for the men, might well flush out Lovell.

Fighting to keep silent, not wanting to lie to him again, or stir suspicions that might otherwise lie dormant, knowing there was no way she could keep him from searching the castle if he chose to do so, she still prayed he would not. Her relationship with him had grown stronger, but she knew the discovery of Lovell at Wolveston could only weaken the fragile bond between them.

He was thinking, turning the dagger over idly in his hands. She hoped he would not cut himself, and the thought reminded her that she had not been the only one recently in danger.

"I am glad you came home safely," she said. "Must you return soon to the king, or can you linger here for a time?" Her emotions in the brief moment before he replied were in a tangle. She wanted him there, beside her, sleeping in her bed. But the danger to Lovell with Nicholas at Wolveston was unbearable to contemplate. For the viscount to get away would be nearly impossible while Nicholas and his men remained.

Nicholas said, "The king enters York in two days' time, and we have had word of trouble rising in Birmingham—the Staffords, just as the rumors we heard suggested. When I leave here, my men and I will join the royal forces there. The king will remain in York through St. George's Day. He is skeptical of the city's loyalty but means to accord its citizens all honor. I'd like to be there, but I doubt I can return soon enough. Harry remains in York only a few days, then retraces his path southward. I am promised to meet him at Nottingham Castle the end of the month."

"But you will return here first!" she exclaimed. "In faith, sir, you cannot mean to abandon us here."

His look was direct. "I do not know what I intend, madam. Originally, I had meant to take you back to London, but now I am not so sure. There is unrest throughout the kingdom, and I do not know that I can be at hand in the capital to keep my eye on you. God knows, you show a distressing talent for landing in the briars when left to your own devices. You have given me no cause to believe I can safely leave you with the court."

"But I—"

"We won't discuss it now," he said, looking toward the door.

Footsteps could be heard from the gallery, and a moment later, two of his men entered and began to attend to Sir Lionel's corpse. Alys was glad to see it removed.

"We will have a proper service for him," she said grimly, "though I doubt if his soul has sped its way to heaven."

Nicholas's expression was rueful. "It must have been a terrible experience, *mi calon,* to have been assaulted by him as you were. How did you manage to lay hands on his dagger?"

The question was put casually, and she had opened her mouth to tell him she had taken it during the struggle when she remembered that Sir Lionel had not worn a sheath. Having said the dagger was his and then not seen another on his person had seemed providential. Now that same lack of a sheath took on new, and ominous meaning. She could think of nothing to say.

"He was not carrying it unless, perchance, he had it in hand and was threatening you with it," Nicholas mused, shooting a quizzical look at her from beneath his brows.

She shook her head, knowing that to accept that suggestion would only take her into more perilous territory. He waited with patience, but she could offer him no acceptable alternative.

"You did not find the dagger here in your bedchamber."

"N-no, sir." She licked lips gone suddenly dry.

"And servants never routed his armed soldiers, did they?" he asked in a gentle tone that did not comfort her in the least.

"I do not know what happened to them," she said, annoyed that her voice sounded weak, telling herself firmly that the words were true—for the most part.

"There have been other soldiers in the area today," he said as if he were thinking aloud.

"H-Have there, sir?"

"I think you know there have been, madam. Mayhap you will cease this charade now and tell me what really took place here. I weary of your game. In faith, I am weary to the bone."

"Of course you are," she exclaimed, seizing on the diversion. "Poor Nicholas. You have been in the saddle for days and must want nothing so much as to rest now."

"Aye," he replied, looking at her narrowly, "it has been a tiresome business, looking after our Harry, but 'tis no more than my duty, when all is said and done."

"But you saved him! You are a hero, sir. Why, he must have been terrified to see them riding straight at him like—" Breaking off, realizing she had let her tongue rattle too long, she said swiftly, "The king must know you would give your life for his, sir. He will no doubt be most grateful to you."

"Will he?"

"Aye." She took a step back, suddenly anxious to be farther away from him, and once again, just as she had earlier, she kicked against the mattress on the floor. Looking down briefly, she snapped her head up again to find him distressingly nearer.

He said, "I meant to ask you how that mattress got there."

That was safe. "They tore it off the bed, looking for Ian."

The answer made him smile. "They thought to find him in your bed? Everingham must have been insane."

"He was, sir," she said, paling again at the memory of the man's fury, and at the horror that rose anew when she thought of what he had wanted to do to her. "He was so angry."

"I do not doubt that," he said gruffly. "You have a knack for angering men." He held out his hand. "Come here."

"What are you going to do?"

He sighed. "I suppose the very question means you deserve to feel my hand on your backside, if not more, but I have no such intention, *mi calon*. All I want now is to hold you and to hear no more of your falsehoods. You are not skilled enough at devising them to fool a babe in arms."

He beckoned with the index finger of the hand he held out to her, and she went to him. "I did not want to lie," she said when his arms held her tight, "but I cannot tell you all the truth."

"I know. I suspect the ragged lot who attacked our Harry and rode away, came here in search of a hiding place and ambushed Everingham's little army. Mayhap, I ought to be grateful."

"There was no army, sir. He lied about that."

"Perchance he did, or perchance, having learned from Sir Lionel's fine example, his army decided to turn tippet and join the king. It matters not. Who was their leader?" he asked in the same deceptively casual tone he had used before.

But she had expected the question and knew a simple claim of ignorance would not do, so she said fiercely, "I would not tell you if I knew him. I am too grateful to have been rescued."

He nodded. "I, too, *mi calon,* am grateful to your rescuers, and glad that they were not captured before they reached you."

She shivered at the thought of what would have happened to her in that instance, and Nicholas held her tighter, soothing her. Moments later, without a word, he scooped her up and held her close, then turned and, shifting her weight, bolted the door.

"I like this dress, madam," he said, looking down at the gap in her bodice where the lacing let her breasts show through. "There is little to interfere with a man's touch. Do you prefer the mattress where it lies, or shall we put it back on the bed?"

Smiling, she laid her head against his shoulder and said she did not care. Nor did she, even when he chose the mattress on the floor. The door was safely bolted, and though she had never made love with him outside the seclusion of the bed curtains, she was too relieved to have him safe home again, and too delighted to see his desire for her so openly expressed, to care where he took her. Giving herself up to her own passions, she attacked his clothing with even more eagerness than he did hers.

"Such wantonness becomes you, *mi calon*," he said, laughing, and beginning to tease her naked body with his hands, his hot breath, and his agile tongue.

Moaning with delight, she returned his caresses until her body quivered beneath his and her thighs opened wide to receive him. The first peak was quickly reached, but they continued to make love far into the afternoon, undisturbed, until both fell fast asleep.

Alys awoke to find Nicholas smiling at her, and the glow she felt lasted through the evening, when they joined the others in the hall for supper. She decided her pleasure was contagious, for she saw Gwilym smile and Madeline blush, and Jonet was even civil to Hugh, though the giant scarcely took his eyes off her all evening, behavior to which she usually accorded short shrift.

A proper bedchamber had been prepared for Nicholas and Alys, and when they retired, he proved he had not yet slaked his thirst for her, but the next morning, mounted and preparing to lead his men to Birmingham, he seemed suddenly distant again, almost as if their intimacy had never occurred.

The change in his demeanor no longer surprised her, and she was prepared to play her own role before the men with proper dignity, but suddenly Nicholas looked down at her and said, "I shall return here before joining the king, madam, and we will decide how you are to proceed to the capital. In the meantime, I have that dagger with me. Should I chance to encounter its owner, I shall return it to him with my thanks."

With that, he raised his hand in a signal to his men, and the courtyard was soon clear except for those men at arms who had been left behind to guard the castle. Nicholas was not a man who made the same mistake twice.

Alys watched until the last man was gone, her countenance rigid from the effort not to betray the shock Nicholas's parting words had given her. So wrapped up had she been in their growing intimacy that she had forgotten Lovell's presence in the castle. But now, mixed with sadness at seeing Nicholas ride off again was a strong sense of trepidation. She had hoped to return Lovell's dagger herself. It had never occurred to her that Nicholas would keep it, let alone that he would decide to search out its owner. She was certain that he would discover only too soon whose device graced the gilded hilt, and when he did . . . She shuddered at the thought and it haunted her for the next fortnight.

She saw no sign of Lovell or his men, and assumed they had got away; and the days flew swiftly, for there was much to be done to set the castle to rights. But never a day passed that she did not wonder if Nicholas had learned the truth, and when he and his men rode into the courtyard fifteen days later, she saw at once that he had done so.

Scarcely taking time to give orders for the housing and care of his men, he bore her off to their chamber, where he lost no time in making his feelings plain. "You are fortunate," he said grimly, "that you were nowhere nearby when I learned that what I thought was a wolf was the head of a damned dog! Where is he?"

"I do not know," she answered, glad she spoke the truth. "He said he would go to Flanders." When he did not respond at once, she said quietly, "You said you were grateful to my rescuer, sir. Does it make a difference that it was he?"

"Aye, it makes a difference. The man is an outlaw, a traitor. I have no wish to be beholden to him!"

"He is no traitor," she said stoutly. "He is loyal to his liege lord. You should admire that quality in him, for you expressed contempt when you thought Sir Lionel's men had run off to join the king—turn-tippets, you called them. Would you have admired them more had you known they were still here? They must have been here somewhere, and might actually have been glad to see you, considering their circumstances, but—"

"By God, madam," he roared, "do you mean to tell me that that damned outlaw was still on the premises then? Beneath my very nose? And you protected him!"

In the face of his fury, she quailed, but she answered nonetheless firmly, "I did, and would again. I could not stop Sir Lionel. I tried to hit him with the poker, but he just took it away. And when he fell dead at my feet, I thought you had come. I cannot tell you how relieved I was, but when I saw that it was Lovell, the relief did not die, sir, merely because he was not you." Feeling her face flush at the memory, she rushed on, saying, "He saved me, Nicholas. I could not give him over for punishment! Even you must see that."

"What makes you think I cannot understand?" he asked.

"Oh, do not turn what I say! If you do understand, then you ought not to be so angry with me."

He took a deep breath and said, "Would you have told me the truth if Everingham had never come here, if Lovell had simply sought refuge at Wolveston after his attempt to kill the king?"

"He was not going to kill him, only to abduct him!"

Nicholas said nothing.

She glared at him. "In truth, sir, I doubt that I would have betrayed him even then. If you mean to punish me for supporting a cause in which I believe, then there is naught I can do to stop you." But despite her brave words, she put her hands protectively behind her and watched him warily.

He did not move, but there was nothing in his expression to comfort her. He said, "I leave for Nottingham Castle at dawn. Hugh and a party of men will remain here till Monday to provide escort for Mistress Fenlord and her woman to rejoin the court, which is now at Sheen Palace."

"Aye," she said, "we can be ready to depart by then."

"You are not going." When she began to protest, he snapped, "You will remain here until I decide you deserve to rejoin the court. Not only have you shouted your support for Henry Tudor's enemies to anyone who would listen, but you cannot even see how foolhardy you have been in giving aid and comfort to the worst among them. Add to that the fact that you find it impossible to be friends with his queen, and you make it impossible for me to allow you to join her at court. I have made up my mind, madam. Debating the matter will avail you not."

Alys did not give up so easily, of course, but though she argued and pleaded, if not to accompany him, at least not to lose Madeline's companionship, he was adamant that the loss should be part of her punishment. Nor did he linger to discuss the matter. He and his men were gone the following morning, and two days later, when Hugh and the others departed, Alys found herself a prisoner in her own home, with Gwilym a surly jailer.

She had noted a new rapport developing between the quiet Welshman and Madeline at Wolveston. Gwilym had begun to smile occasionally, had even voiced his approval from time to time of things Madeline had done to help set the castle to rights. And in return, Madeline had lost much of her puppylike clumsiness and seemed to have acquired more assurance in her manner. Alys thought that if Nicholas still contemplated a match between the two he had made a grave error by removing Madeline from Wolveston just when matters were improving. Once she was back in London, among gallant courtiers who were well practiced in the art of flirtation, Madeline was likely to forget all about the Welshman who was still more prone to criticize than to praise her.

# 20

"Right trusty and well-beloved friend," Madeline's letter from Sheen began, "I greet you well. There is not much news, but the king, having been at home for a month now, looks forward to the time when her grace, his wife, will be delivered of his son and heir. They are both most confident of a boy. The court goes to Winchester for the occasion, Alys, and you must try to join us there, for I miss your conversation and your laughter. I miss Wolveston Hazard, too. 'Tis a fine place, and pleasant withal."

" 'Tis a tiresome place," Alys interjected, looking over the page at Jonet. She had been reading the letter aloud while they sat together by the hall fire after supper. "Even Nicholas does not want to be here, and has only written to me the one time."

Jonet had turned her work to attend to a knot in her thread. She looked up and smiled. "You were not grateful when he did write, as I recall, mistress, and did not reply to his letter."

Alys grimaced. "He feared I might decide to run away again, and only wrote to warn me of his displeasure if I did. As if I had not already considered that," she added with a forlorn sigh. "He did not deserve a reply to such a letter, but it has been three months since they left. I thought he would relent by now, but he does not write, nor does he come to see me."

"He has been too busy," Jonet said placidly. "Though Lord Lovell has gone abroad, we no sooner learn that a riot has been quelled in Sussex than we hear of another in Norfolk. No doubt the master and his men are needed wherever there is unrest, but he will come home when he can, and he would write if you did. What else does Mistress Madeline have to say?"

Having skimmed several paragraphs while Jonet was speaking, Alys said, "She also mentions the riots, but she writes that the king believes Elizabeth's babe, if it is a boy, will put an end to disorder because all factions will accept him as a proper heir to the throne. I hope she has a daughter," Alys added sourly.

When the only reply was a look of disapproval, she sighed. "Do not heed my sulks." Scanning more of the letter, she said, "This is odd. Listen. 'Many men have sued for peace and general pardon, and the Tudor has shown much mercy. In sooth, in the case of a man named Sir James Tyrell, he has shown what some think to be an overabundance of it, for he has granted the man a general pardon not once but twice, with barely a month between the two.' She adds that it was no doubt done in error."

Jonet nodded agreement with that assessment, but Alys paused thoughtfully. For men to sue for general pardon had become quite common, and meant that individual infractions were not examined closely, nor even specifically written down. Since Sir James had been a follower of Richard's, it was not odd that he had asked for a pardon, but to have received two of them only a month apart must mean that he had done something new in the meantime, something not covered by the first pardon. She could not believe in a casual error of such magnitude. What could he have done?

Her tumbling thoughts frightened her, but she thought it unwise to discuss them with Jonet, and there was no one else in whom she could confide. She was getting along with Gwilym but only because they rarely saw each other. When he was not busy with the estate, he occupied himself with training men or horses, and she was kept busy with the domestic details. As a result of their efforts, Wolveston was thriving as it had not done for years. The castle was now comfortably furnished, the farms had tenants planting crops again, and the villages, their populations once ravaged by the sweat, had begun to thrive anew.

Gwilym had moved rapidly into the vacuum left by the deaths of her father and brother, and was well regarded by the tenants for his generosity and evenhanded stewardship. He understood the military resources of the region too. Not only could he be depended upon to have numbers and names at his fingertips should Sir Nicholas need to mobilize more men for the king but he encouraged men to practice their skills, even handing out gold coins to boys he saw practicing with their longbows. Alys could and did admire Gwilym's skills, but he seemed gloomy again, and unapproachable. They took their meals separately, and she would not, in any case, have confided her worries to him.

With Madeline's letter in hand, her yearning to be in the center of things again was overwhelming, and when Jonet prompted her to go on reading, she said, "Oh, she writes little more, only that Nicholas is at court now. Methinks I shall write to him, as you suggest, Jonet, and remind him that Elizabeth might take offense if I am not in attendance when her child is born."

But the response to her request for permission to join the court came with unexpected swiftness, and was a flat negative. Nicholas himself followed soon after it, however, and despite her frustration, Alys was glad to see him. She was in her solar with Jonet, counting linens, when he strode into the room. Casting aside an armful of hand cloths to throw herself into his arms, she scarcely noticed that Jonet's face lit up then fell again when he came in alone; and her own delight lasted only until he told her he could stay less than a week.

"But you have been gone nearly three months!"

"I had duties, lass, far from here."

"And an erring wife who required punishment," she snapped, pulling away, making no effort to contain her flash of anger.

"Aye." He signed to Jonet to leave them, and she did so with an alacrity that astonished Alys. "Come back here," he said then, "and soften your temper. I do not want to brangle."

Seeing desire in his eyes, she felt her body respond, and said impulsively, "Take me back to London with you, Nicholas. You cannot know how much I have missed you."

"Had you mentioned me before London, I'd believe you."

"Oh, you enrage me!" She whirled from him, and would have stormed from the room, but he grabbed her and pulled her back.

When he kissed her, she melted against him, and when he scooped her into his arms and carried her to their bed-chamber, she made no protest. In truth, she had missed him sorely, but if she hoped to find him more agreeable to her wishes once he had slaked his thirst for her, she was disappointed.

"Elizabeth's temper is uncertain, lass," he said, stroking her hair. "She is attended constantly by both her mother and Lady Margaret, and 'tis said the pair of them are driving her mad. And although everyone insists that the child will be a boy, she must be terrified of having a girl, for she is unpredictable and moody. You'd soon find yourself in the briars again."

"I can take care of myself," Alys said.

"Nonetheless," he replied, "she has not asked for you and you will not go." He shifted his position to look at her and said gently, "It is not safe. The court goes to Winchester soon to await the birth, and Harry has ordered transcripts made of the papal bull that both confirms his title and marriage and threatens excommunication to anyone who impugns either one. The contents will be read from pulpits across the realm. The bull has even been set in type, printed like the new books, so it can be posted everywhere for men to read for themselves. Under the circumstances, 'twould be unwise to allow you to go where you might annoy Elizabeth. Now, no more chatter, *mi calon*. We have better ways to spend our time."

Agreeing with his last statement, if not all the others, she recognized that further argument would not move him, and decided to make the most of the short time he was able to spend with her before he returned to his duties. They had only one other dispute during his visit, when she learned the fate of the Stafford brothers, whose rebellion, like Lovell's, had failed.

"The leaders fled into sanctuary," Nicholas told her, "but they were soon dragged out again by the king's men—"

"The Tudor ordered them taken from sanctuary!" Alys exclaimed, unable to believe her ears.

"Aye," he said. "Humphrey Stafford was hanged, drawn, and quartered at Tyburn in London, though Thomas was pardoned."

She remembered what Lovell had told her about the Tudor policy of pardoning and punishing, but the tale horrified her. "How can you bear allegiance to a man who would break sanctuary?"

Nicholas said calmly, "He did what he had to do. Traitors claim immunity wherever they can find a cross, and Culham is not a proper sanctuary. Harry is a wise man, and I bear him allegiance because I believe he is good for the country."

"For Wales, you mean!"

"Nay, *mi calon,* for England too. We need a proper king, a man, not a youth or a child over whom men wanting the power of the throne would continue to fight. Now, enough. I would go riding with you today to see more of my land."

And so she rode with him and dined with him, debated with him and slept with him, enjoying his company and his attention so much that when the time came for him to leave again, tears welled into her eyes and spilled down her cheeks.

He paused to kiss them away, murmuring, "It will not be so long now, and you have plenty to do here, although methinks you have done little to please my brother. The poor fellow is more dour than ever. Must you brangle with him all the time?"

"I do not, sir," she said, mopping moisture from her cheek with his handkerchief. "He has been like that since you sent Madeline away. I cannot think how you ever imagined they might make a match of it. She did seem a little attracted to him for a time, but if he heeded her at all, it was only to criticize her."

"At first," Nicholas said, "he saw only that it would be a good match, but now I think 'tis the lass he wants. I warned him that she was accustomed to be much admired and flattered, and that she paid little heed to any amongst her many admirers."

"But he makes no effort to please her. He cannot want her."

"As to that," he said, twinkling at her, "you have never watched him coax a wild horse to take sugar from his hand. He stands and waits until the animal becomes so curious it cannot stay away from him. Now, Hugh tells me the wench was a rare handful for him on the road to London, and I can tell you she has not been in good humor there, either. Her father has presented a string of suitors to her, all willing to praise her beauty and woo her dowry, but she will have none of them."

"She insists she means never to marry any man," Alys said.

"Aye, and my answer to that is 'baldarddws.' Her father is a doting fool. Had he sense, he would thrash obedience into her as any other man would, but he does not. He says only that she is a wench with a mind of her own." He sighed. "Gwilym says, and in truth, I agree, though you will not, that such indulgence has done her little good. She will be the better for a husband's stronger hand; and there *will* be a husband, lass, one day." Then turning before she could argue the point he shouted to Hugh, "The lads are ready to ride. Have you said your farewells?"

"Aye," Hugh shouted back with a grin, "and would have

got my face slapped, could she but have reached it. The wee minikin's got a right limber tongue though. Called me a prick-eared maggot-pate and said I was bound for the devil. What a woman!"

Chuckling, Nicholas turned back to Alys, gave her a hug, and then with one last kiss, he was mounted and gone. He had promised to write, and he did so, but though she looked forward to his letters, they continued to disappoint her, for not one included an invitation to join him or to return to the court.

Madeline's letters, though haphazardly written and carelessly blotted, were far more satisfying. When she wrote to share the court's delight after Elizabeth was safely delivered of her son in September, Alys felt as though she and Jonet might almost have been there in attendance with her.

"Lady Margaret, thinking the queen too inexperienced to handle such matters," Madeline wrote from Winchester, "did devise all the plans for the lying-in, the furnishing of her grace's chamber, the cradle, the christening, even for the nursing of the prince. It was she, not the king, who decided the baby should be born here at the legendary home of King Arthur; and Alys, they have christened the baby Arthur! The Earl of Oxford was to stand godfather, and we waited three hours in the cathedral for him to arrive, but at last the service began without him. Torches were lighted, the grand procession to the high altar was made, and two hymns were sung before Oxford galloped in like a destrier blown, right into the midst of it, in time to see the dowager queen lay the baby on the altar for the long ceremony. Elizabeth lies abed still, and there was another magnificent candlelit procession to take him home to her again. He is a fine laddie, Alys, and makes me yearn for one of my own. We go downriver to Greenwich soon, so do beg Sir Nicholas to permit you to come to us. I am become maudlin, for life at court is tiresome without you."

Alys found herself wishing that Nicholas, not Madeline, had written the last line. Thinking about Greenwich with its green parks and open vistas across the Thames, she could almost hear the lapping of the water against the banks and the cries of the gulls overhead. But Nicholas never wrote such lines to her, nor did he grant permission. Her moods soon became as unpredictable as Elizabeth's had been, and her health began to deteriorate.

At first she thought she was truly ill, once even fearing a recurrence of the sweat, but then, with Jonet's help, the reason for her capricious bouts of sickness became clear. Both elated and alarmed, she wanted one moment to tell the world and the next to tell no one, for she was certain that if Nicholas learned of her delicate condition, he would never allow her to travel to London. In point of fact, she was a trifle concerned herself about the journey, but by the time he did grant his permission, in December, she was feeling perfectly stout, and thoroughly delighted with her interesting condition.

Gwilym brought her the news, saying in his blunt way, "I've had a letter from Nick. We're to join the court for Christmas."

"At last!" she exclaimed. "But where are they now? When Madeline last wrote, they had removed to Sheen again."

"Westminster be where we're headed," Gwilym said, "and our family will be there, as well. Nicholas has hired a house in London for them. But here, the lad brought you a letter, too. We can be ready to depart in three days' time, I'm thinking."

She snatched at the letter he held out, but even before she opened it, her heart began to sing. They were returning to court at last, a fact confirmed in the first line of Nicholas's brief letter. The rest was only a carefully worded warning that she behave herself, a warning upon which she felt no necessity to dwell. She rushed to take the news to Jonet and to begin preparing for the journey, hoping the weather, which had been threatening rain for a week, would remain dry enough to travel.

It did not rain, and Sir Nicholas, riding from Sheen, met

their party at Waltham, where they put up for the night.
Though the order at Waltham Abbey was much poorer than
their brothers at Burton, they provided excellent accommodations for travelers, and lay brothers to look after them.
Nicholas was in a festive mood, and he snatched Alys up in
his arms in the guest hall and gave her a great, smacking
kiss, his eyes alight with laughter and delight at seeing her
again.

His mood was contagious, and she grinned at him. "Put
me down, sir. You will shock the good brothers, should any
so far forget himself as to peep out at us from the cloister."

He chuckled, setting her on her feet. "You have become
demure then, madam. Why, I recall, not so long since—"

"Hush," she said, putting a finger to his lips. "I am determined not to quarrel with you, but if you are to cast up all
my past mistakes for the world to mock, I shall not be held
responsible for my actions."

He squeezed her hand, then turned to greet his brother,
clapping him on the shoulder and demanding to know if he
had left the estate in good hands. "I was torn," he said with
a smile, "between my need for you there, and my lady wife's
requirements on the road. I hope she has not led you a
wicked dance, Gwilym."

"The trip was uneventful," Gwilym replied with a smile.
Alys had seen his mood improve almost hourly on the road,
as had Jonet's for once, though Jonet's comments upon her
palfrey's paces did not bear repeating. Gwilym said, "No
doubt, Nick, we have you to thank as much as anyone for
the peaceful journey we had. The land is quiet for once."

"Thank the weather," Nicholas said. "There has been little
snow, but the sky threatens a storm every day. There is thunder brewing even now. I hope we can get safe to Greenwich
tomorrow without being struck by lightning. It can tear at
the land all it wants once we are safe within the castle walls."

"We've little enough distance to cover," Gwilym said, adding with a brisk nod when Hugh entered the hall, "Ah, man,
'tis good to see you." He held out his hand, and Alys watched

it disappear into Hugh's great paw, conscious of Jonet stiffening beside her.

Hugh glanced at both women and said cheerfully to Gwilym, "I see you managed to bring our *meistr*'s lady safe to us, and that lovely but peevish butterbox of a maid of hers as well."

"Peevish butterbox, is it now?" Jonet muttered indignantly. "The blathering, totty-headed gowk!" Making a small, dignified curtsy, she said in a louder but much more polite tone, "How delightful to see you again, Master Gower, and to hear more of your pretty compliments. My lady was just saying we had naught to entertain us here, and here you are to put her to the lie."

Hugh bowed deep from the waist, saying, "Now, now, my sweet igniferent bawd, much though it goes against the hair with me to find fault with so toothsome a wench as thyself, thou must not call thy mistress a liar. 'Tis downright disrespectful."

"Igniferent bawd! Disrespectful!" She stared at him in amazement. "Why, I've never heard the like. How dare thee rebuke me in such terms, tha' great clubfisted clenchpoop!"

"You miss the cushion there, sweet cosset. I am no clown but the truest penny going, albeit a trifle woman-tired."

"Daffish dogbolt," Jonet said provocatively.

"Popping doxy," he retorted.

"Dizzard!"

"Giglet!"

"Giglet? Tha' wouldst name me doxy and giglet? Why, tha' pesterous, gorebellied lobcock—"

"Gorebellied?" Hugh cried, stung on the raw at last. "By God's sanity, lass, I am not fat, just well favored. It fair topsy-turns my brain to hear thee say such a thing of me." In an aside to the other two men, he said, "She's a filly as bites on the bridle now and again, but you watch. I shall soon have her as tame as her own palfrey, and eating out of my hand."

"Tha' wilt not, tha' cankerish, cocksure, pigeon-livered

hoddypeke," Jonet snapped. "Tha' hast nerve enough, and size, but nowt save a wee pea for a brain, and—"

"Now that was very good," Hugh interjected to the others in a tone inviting agreement. "A man likes a minx to hold her own." Smiling at Jonet, he said, "I cry creak, lass. Once more hast thou belabored me with thy tongue till I be fair crow-trodden."

"Tha' looks it, tha' great gowk," she retorted gruffly, but this time she blushed and looked at her feet when she spoke.

Putting an arm around her shoulders, Hugh said gently, "Snick up, lass. Put up thy sword, and come away with me to the fire. I've more compliments to impart, to be sure, but I'd as lief make a gift of them to none but thy lautitious self."

To Alys's astonishment, although Jonet looked up at him warily, she walked away with him without another word.

Sir Nicholas shook his head. "Hugh has fallen harder than we knew, Gwilym. 'Tis a thing I never thought to see."

Gwilym nodded, but his thoughts were clearly elsewhere.

Alys said slowly, "I can see that despite her manner with him, Jonet likes him, Nicholas, and 'tis clear that Hugh likes her, but how can they be happy if they can never be together in the same room without slinging verbal stones at each other?"

"You must learn to read passion where you find it, *mi calon*," he said, smiling at her in such a way that her skin began to tingle and her blood to run more warmly through her veins.

She wrinkled her nose at the Welsh phrase. "It does spoil the pretty sound of those words to know you are merely calling me 'wife,' as you frequently do when I have vexed you."

Gwilym, diverted from his thoughts by her words, shook his head. " 'Tis scarcely the same thing, madam, for he calls you his heart. The Welsh word for wife is simply *call*."

Nicholas smiled ruefully but shot a look at Gwilym from under his brows that boded no good for that gentleman's future, and said brusquely, " 'Twas a slip of the tongue.

Henceforth, I shall simply call her 'sweetheart' in the English manner. Now come to supper, both of you, for I mean us all to be abed directly after compline, with the holy brothers."

Hugh, overhearing him, shouted with laughter. "How now, Nicholas! You, with such a winsome wife as my Lady Alys, would have us believe you do prefer an armful of praying monks!"

Nicholas laughed then, and Alys, who was slowly coming to understand the Welshman she had married, realized that, in his mind, to be caught by his comrades in a moment of tenderness was equal to being caught in a moment of weakness, while being teased by them, or willfully misunderstood, was a perfectly normal state of affairs, and something to be cheerfully tolerated.

Later, in bed beside him, having feared he might notice the slight changes in her body after four months of pregnancy and not sure if she was glad or sorry when he did not, Alys contemplated the future. She would have to take care. Nicholas would be more than a little vexed if she displeased Elizabeth again, or spoke words that could not be repeated to the king. She hoped she would do neither. She had faithfully practiced her lute, at least, and she did not doubt that her playing would be acceptable now, unless Elizabeth chose to be difficult.

Elizabeth did not. It was evident almost the moment Alys saw her the following day in the queen's presence chamber at Greenwich that she was extremely pleased with herself for having produced an heir to the throne, and was of a mind to be gracious to everyone who came near her. The storms had struck as Nicholas had said they would, but the palace walls were thick and no one heeded them, not even the small prince, who was carried in by his nurse while Alys was there. She soon learned that he was looked after by three such nurses who had each sworn an oath of loyalty to him, and that his personal physician attended every feeding.

Elizabeth had regained her figure and looked as beautiful

and serene as ever, and she was so gracious that for the first time Alys considered confiding some at least of what she had learned in the past year. Surely Elizabeth would want to know that one of her brothers still lived. Though she did not speak about them, Alys did not think she could be indifferent to their fate. What would she say if she learned that one at least was not dead, as she believed they were? But the presence chamber, in the company of her women, was not the place for confidences.

Not all of the women were present. Alys still had not seen Madeline, and did not see her until that evening, at supper in the great hall. Then, catching sight of Alys, Madeline rushed up and flung her arms around her. "I had nearly given you up!"

"Madeline, my dear," said the man behind her, a pensive-looking older gentleman in a short black velvet robe trimmed with gold thread, and a flat hat with a golden plume, "before you knock Lady Merion over, perhaps you will present me to her."

"Aye, sir," she said, laughing, "to be sure I shall. This is my father, Alys, Sir Walter Fenlord. He and my brother Robert are to remain in town through the Christmas festivities."

" 'Tis to be a family Christmas then," Alys said when she had properly greeted Sir Walter. "Nicholas has taken a house on the Thames near Queenshithe for his family."

"His *whole* family is in London then," Madeline said, a note of innocent query in her voice.

"Gwilym brought Jonet and me to town," Alys said, answering what she knew to be the real question first. "The others arrive in a sennight. Gwenyth was distressed that her sons' duties prevented our going to Wales, and so they will come to us instead." She smiled at Sir Walter. "I know that my mother-in-law will be pleased to make your acquaintance, sir. You must visit them when they arrive."

"I will certainly do so," Sir Walter agreed with a nod. "She and her family were most kind to our Madeline at Merion Court, and I would thank her properly for her hospitality."

"We will, Father," Madeline said cheerfully, "but you go and talk to someone else now, sir, for I have much to say to Alys." He went, smiling fondly, and Madeline, taking Alys by the arm, said, "Come and tell me everything you have done and everything that has happened since I left you. I missed you dreadfully!"

Just as anxious to exchange confidences as she was, Alys went to Madeline's chamber. So delightful was it to have someone to talk with other than Jonet, someone who was as fond of her and as interested in her activities, that Alys soon found herself telling Madeline more than she had intended.

"A baby! By our Lady, how exciting! I warrant Sir Nicholas has been strutting about like one of the king's own peacocks."

"He does not know, and you must not tell him!"

"Not tell him?" Madeline frowned. "But you must. You cannot think he will be displeased. No man would be!"

"Except for the small fact that I did not tell him before," Alys said. "I was afraid he would not let me come to court. And he might yet forbid my taking part in the Christmas festivities, for he is likely to fear that I shall harm the babe."

"Men," Madeline said with a sigh. "They think they know everything. Very well, I will not tell him, but you must take care all the same. Perchance you will find that you can confide in his mother when she arrives. I think her very kind, and not at all the sort to make a fuss."

"I could not tell her before Nicholas," Alys said firmly.

The point did not arise, however, for by the time his family arrived in London, the Christmas festivities at court had begun, and though the family members were invited to enjoy much of the feasting and entertainment at Westminster, there was little time for Nicholas or Alys, who still had their rooms in the palace, to spend at the house near Queenshithe. The king enjoyed Christmas, and for once he spared no expense. By the twelfth day of Christmas, Alys, accustomed as she was to keeping household accounts, was certain that he must have spent a fortune.

The feast of the Epiphany saw as many as sixty dishes of confections alone on the groaning boards. Alys and Madeline tried counting all the courses but soon became more interested in eating and talking with friends and relatives, and lost count. The religious services in the chapel afterward were accompanied by glorious music, including pipes and trumpets, and after the services came the pageantry, the entertainers vying to outdo one another, portraying chapters in the story of Christ's birth.

After the pageants, the activity continued with dancing in the great hall. A Lord of Misrule mimicked many of the great lords present, and there were minstrels, traveling jugglers and acrobats, a dog act, and even a man with three hawks trained to fly high above the crowd and then swoop down through flag-decorated golden rings the man held out in his hands.

Prince Arthur was present, wrapped in scarlet velvet and lying in a canopied, gilded cradle on the dais near his mother's armchair, with his own yeomen and squires at hand to rock him if he cried. And Alys, who had been admiring the queen's elegant purple velvet robe, caped with ermine and sable, and the way the bright lights of the hall glistened on her gold crown and jewels, was watching when she bent over her son and reached out a slim hand to smooth his coverlet. The doting look on Elizabeth's face put an end to any lingering thought of confidences. Clearly, she would be no happier now than the king would be to learn that a prince of York still lived. By the look of her as she gazed at Arthur, she would fight much harder to see him on the throne of England than she ever would to see one of her brothers there.

"May I have the pleasure of leading you into this dance, Lady Merion?"

Alys whirled at the sound of the familiar voice, to find herself face to face with Henry Tudor. She had observed earlier that he was no longer on the dais beside the queen, but she had never expected to find him standing before her, slim, tall, elegantly clad, and smiling. There was even a perceptible twinkle in his pale blue eyes. He waited for her to reply.

Stunned and not a little embarrassed after the turn her thoughts had taken, she made her curtsy, wondering how she would get through the next few minutes without saying something foolish or unwise. But, palm to palm, they danced the stately dance, and she soon found herself conversing easily with him, responding to his smiles and pleasantries. Before the music ended, she truly was enjoying herself, and she saw her mood reflected in the faces around her. The whole court was relaxed and happy, basking in the warmth of Christmas and delighted by the presence of Prince Arthur, whom many believed was their hope for a peaceful future.

Alys saw Madeline dancing with Nicholas, and Jonet smiling up at Hugh Gower. Even Ian MacDougal was dancing, with a rope dancer from a minstrel troop. Only Gwilym was not smiling. He did not show to great advantage among the splendid courtiers, and he stood to one side, watching his brother and the laughing Madeline with a quizzical, rather enigmatic, glint in his eyes.

When the music ended, Alys saw that Elizabeth had descended from the dais and was walking toward them on the arm of the Earl of Lincoln. The queen smiled at something the earl said to her, and beside Alys, the king chuckled, a sound she had never expected to hear from one she had long thought of as her chief enemy. She looked up at him in surprise.

He said, "Lincoln is trying to cut me out with my lady wife, I believe. I shall have to speak sharply to him."

Alys said, "He means no harm, your grace. He is but—"

"Make yourself easy, madam," Henry said wryly. "I was speaking in jest. The earl has such an aptness for never saying or doing anything for which he might be censured that I know well I have naught to fear, not at least where my wife is concerned."

Something in his tone made Alys look closely at him, but there was nothing to be discerned from his expression.

Just then there was a touch on her arm and Nicholas said, "I have come to claim my wife, if you will forgive me, noble highness. The hour grows late, and she has been enjoying herself rather too much these past twelve days, as have we all. With your permission, we would have leave to retire."

The twinkle reappeared in the king's eyes. "I shall allow you to pretend you have concern for this radiant lady's health, sir, because it is a time for joy, and thus do I willingly grant permission for you to...to see to her comfort."

His words were the closest Alys had ever heard the king come to making a spicy remark, and it was all she could do to make her curtsy without betraying an unladylike awareness of his meaning. But she had sensed tension in Nicholas's voice, and so she was unsurprised when, waiting only until the king had turned away, he grasped her arm and urged her toward the stair hall. He did not say anything at once, however, for the castle was still very much awake and its halls teemed with merrymakers.

Inside their chamber, Nicholas nodded at the maidservant who jumped up from a joint stool in the corner, and said to Alys, "Jonet will soon be here also to help you remove your finery and prepare for bed, but I wish to speak with you before you retire."

"You are not staying?" She stared at him, bewildered.

"I will return shortly."

His tone told her she would be unwise to question him, but she stood gazing thoughtfully at the door after he had shut it, wondering what had vexed him. The maid helped her take off her headdress, but despite what Nicholas had said, it was some time before Jonet hurried in. Alys had intended to tease her about dancing with Hugh, but she swallowed the words after one look told her that Jonet was big with news.

Dismissing the maid, Alys demanded to know what had

occurred, adding, "Something has certainly put Nicholas out."

"Not this," Jonet said, her eyes gleaming with happiness and some other, less easily definable emotion. " 'Tis only our Davy, mistress. He came up to me in the hall, as brazen as you please, and gave me a grand hug. He even made his bow to that gowk, Hugh Gower, and would you believe it, that wretched man had the impudence to demand Davy's permission to marry me. On the spot! Said he knew not when he'd get another chance to ask him."

Alys grinned. "And what did Davy say?"

"The daffish fool said he was welcome to me, but that he'd not be able to attend a wedding till the spring."

"And what did you say?"

"Not a word. I was that stunned that they thought the matter so easily settled, and then that Hugh kissed me, and I couldn't say a thing. Why, Davy just laughed and—"

"Fetch Davy in," Alys commanded. "I would speak with him, for I warrant he will have word of Lord Lovell."

"Oh, he was not so daft as to linger, but he did bring you a letter." Jonet reached into her bodice, and Alys heard a crackle of paper before a grim voice from the doorway startled them both.

"I will take that letter, if you please," Sir Nicholas said.

# 21

For a moment there was utter silence, and Alys wished she were the sort of woman who could simply collapse at the first threat of adversity. But, having a notion that Nicholas would either leave her lying where she swooned, or shake her to her senses, so that he might more thoroughly berate her, she stood her ground, watching Jonet reluctantly hand him the letter.

"Leave us," he said, and Jonet went without a word. He broke the seal without looking at it, but shot a fierce look at Alys before he unfolded the single sheet and began to read.

Watching him, she was surprised to see shock as well as increasing fury in his expression. When he finished, his face was drained of color, and for a moment he seemed unable to speak. Then the color flooded back, and Alys, her nerves stretched nearly to breaking by the tension in the silence between them, demanded before he could begin shouting at her, "What does he write? It is my letter, sir. I would like to see it."

To her surprise he handed it to her, then turned and walked toward the hearth to stare down at the dying fire. Knowing he was containing his temper only with great effort, she quickly scanned the letter, her hands shaking so that she could scarcely read it, but it took only a glance to understand a portion at least of his outrage.

"Oh, if that is not like him!" she exclaimed. "To call me Godiva and never consider the consequences! But, Nicholas, it is not what you think, truly! 'Tis only that he had need to conceal his true identity, and mine, and decided to tease me a little."

"You do not know what I think," he retorted, not turning.

"But I do! What else can it be, particularly when he signs himself 'Dauntless Tom Peeper,' but that he has seen me naked?"

"And has he?"

"Aye, sir, he has," she replied honestly. "He saved me, Nicholas. I told you that before, but not the whole. I will tell you now if you will let me."

He turned then, but he did not look particularly appeased. He said dully, "Is it not enough that you were naked with him?"

"In faith, sir, 'twas on account of Sir Lionel that I was naked. I told you he meant to ravish me, and he would have, had Lovell not killed him. I told you, too, that Sir Lionel murdered Roger, and meant to kill you. He meant to have me for his own, Nicholas, for the sake of Wolveston. Once he learned its value, he felt cheated, so he did it all for the land, the wealth. You should understand that. You married me for those same things."

The last words came forlornly and without thought, and she instantly wished them unsaid when she saw his face tighten, but all he said was, "Fate turns the dice, madam. We can but read the numbers and take our winnings, or suffer our losses. I am sorry that yours have been so hard."

"But they have not!" she cried. "Oh, why do you say such a stupid thing to me?"

"You still believe yourself wed to an enemy, do you not?"

She shook her head. "You are not my enemy, Nicholas. To be sure, I once thought you so, for you do fight for the wrong side, but I stopped thinking of you as an enemy the first time you did sing to me. I think of you now only as my husband."

"An unfortunate circumstance for you," he said, "since it allows me to forbid you to see his lordship again."

His grim tone enlightened her, and for a moment her eyes lit up, but knowing he was still angry, she controlled her feelings and said evenly, "You need never be jealous of Lovell, sir."

"Need I not?" he snapped. "Not even when he is most likely father to a child I shall be expected to claim as mine own?"

Thunderstruck, she stared at him while the echo of his words pounded at her mind, shouting them at her until she had to accept that he had really said them. He took a step toward her, and she could see in his eyes that he had little control left over his temper. He meant at least to shake her, and what else he might do did not bear thinking about.

"You are mistaken, sir," she said steadily.

It was the wrong thing to say. He stood directly before her and put his face close to hers. "The devil I am! Madeline told me you are with child, and since you have not seen fit to tell me yourself, and since he has been sneaking about ever since I first laid eyes upon you, what else am I to think? The man is a—"

"The man saved my life," Alys cried, "and the child is yours and no one else's. Do not touch me," she added, losing her own temper at last and whirling away when he reached for her. "By heaven, you will listen for once, and heed what I say!" Glaring at him, daring him to move again, she said nothing more until she was certain he would come no closer. He did not look any the less dangerous, but he did seem willing to let her speak.

" 'Tis a matter of honor," she said, gathering her dignity and speaking more gently. "I would never have let another man touch me once I had become your wife, cared I ever so much for him. I was taught, sir, by people who held honor and loyalty most dear. And never would Lord Lovell attempt to seduce me. Even his worst enemies have never accused him of dishonor. He is a gallant man who still believes in the dying codes of chivalry, just as our late king did, and just as yours—who could break sanctuary to capture his foe—does not."

"By God—"

She spoke quickly. "I should not have said that last bit, Nicholas, but Lovell does believe in the code and follows it. He is the most loyal of all Richard's followers, and thus, sir, you may believe that he would no more take advantage of one like myself, who had been protected by his liege lord, than King Richard would have murdered nephews entrusted to him by his. Moreover, Lovell would never betray a man who, even unknowingly, had granted him shelter in his time of need, as you did."

He had been glaring at her, his expression that of one who listened only because he was forcing himself to do so, but when she mentioned Lovell's loyalty to Richard, that expression sharpened to an arrested look, and by the time she fell silent, to her astonishment, a gleam of amusement lit his eyes.

"You dare to laugh at me?" she demanded, hands on her hips.

He shook his head. "I am not laughing, madam, but you ought to thank heaven that I can find some small humor in your daring to suggest that Lovell's having taken shelter *from me* in mine own castle is reasonable cause to believe he would not betray me."

She smiled, recognizing the irony, but watched him warily, uncertain whether he believed her yet or not. He remained silent, however, until she could stand it no longer and blurted, "The child is yours, Nicholas. I did not tell you before of my condition because I feared you would not let me travel and I wanted more than anything to come to London. And Madeline, the witch, had no right whatever to tell you!"

He came to her then and put his hands gently around her, drawing her close as he said, "She did not intend to tell me, but you know how she is, sweetheart. The words just tumbled out when she least expected them to do so."

"I knew you were angry when you spoke to the king," she

said, leaning her head against his chest. "I did not know what was wrong, but I am learning to know your tone of voice, so even though you spoke calmly, I knew something was amiss. And when you took that letter, your outrage reminded me of that dreadful night at Burton when you lost your temper with me. I thought that tonight I would not be able to . . . to . . ."

"To tame me with your woman's wiles?" He held her away and looked down into her eyes, and for a moment she saw tenderness, but then he said, "My fears about Lovell and the child were brief and only part of the whole, for however gallant he may be, he has no business to be communicating with you. And you ought not to be accepting his communications, madam, let alone harboring him whenever the opportunity arises. By the rood, I find it hard to think why he would endanger himself so. Why does he confide in you if he has no affectionate interest?"

"But he does not! I give you my word, Nicholas."

"And I believe you, so mayhap you will explain to me how it is that, having no such interest in you, he writes to say you need not expect to hear from him again for a while, since he is presently with Margaret and means to take a little journey to Ireland soon, to stir up mischief guaranteed to annoy the king."

His tone was dangerous again, and she said carefully, "I do not know what mischief he means. He has written nothing else to me, and all he said before was that he meant to go to Flanders, to Richard's sister, Margaret of Burgundy."

Nicholas frowned. "If he were here in England now, I should believe him responsible for certain rumors we have heard, that the young Earl of Warwick has escaped from the Tower."

"Neddie? But he has not done any such thing, has he? In faith, I should have heard of it if he had."

"No, he is still there, but my men have encountered the rumors in more than one county. And," he added, giving her a shake, "I do remember those so-called other brothers of yours. Your explanation, when I taxed you for one, was glib enough, and I have never spoken of them to anyone, but it occurs to me now that I have never asked you to give your word of honor that you do not know more about the matter than you have admitted." When she stiffened in dismay, he added dryly, "I will not press you to do so now, madam. I, too, honor loyalty where I find it, but these little intrigues of yours are dangerous. Leave such matters to the queen dowager and her ilk."

Relieved, she said faintly, "Is she plotting again?"

He shrugged. "Elizabeth Woodville has a reputation for plotting. That was all I meant. I am told she cannot keep her fingers out of any intrigue that drifts within her orbit."

"But surely, sir, with her own daughter already called queen, and expecting at any time now to be properly crowned—"

"The lass will enjoy no coronation until Harry is convinced that he holds the throne by his own right. He does not want his people ever to believe he holds it by right of his wife, only that he chooses to unite his red rose with her white one."

"But the people will clamor like they did before, until he grants her a crown of her own, and even if he does not, Prince Arthur is the queen dowager's grandson. She would not plot against him, or against his mother."

"I hope you are right." His tone was somber. He turned away. He had already distanced himself from her emotionally, and though Alys was sorry for it, she could not abandon her beliefs merely to please him. She tried to take heart from the fact that he had said he honored her fidelity, but the sudden physical separation left her feeling bereft. Then he turned, and the look in his eyes was different from any she had seen there before. "I was a villain to frighten you tonight, sweetheart. I could never really hurt you. I don't expect you to trust me so soon after my own failure to trust you, but mayhap one day you will find strength enough to believe that I will not betray you."

It was so quiet in the room that the sudden collapse of a log in a shower of sparks startled them both.

Alys felt tears at the back of her throat. The only time after that first day that he had ever questioned her about the mysterious boys, he had accepted her suggestion that they might have been sons of some other Yorkist family. She knew he was not stupid, that it was possible he had believed all along that she knew, or at least suspected, more than she had admitted. But no more than she doubted her own loyalty could she doubt his to Henry Tudor; and, while she knew instinctively that she could trust him, that in many ways she had trusted him for some time, too much was at stake to trust him with a secret that was not hers alone to share. She knew she could depend upon him to do all in his power to protect her, and their unborn child, from the king's wrath, but she was just as certain that his strong loyalty to the Tudor would compel him to reveal the existence of any living prince of York who might threaten the Tudor crown.

He had not moved. She swallowed her tears and held out a hand to him. "Nicholas?"

He took her hand. His was warm and strong. He drew her close and folded her into his arms, kissing the top of her head.

She tilted her face up. "You do believe the child is yours, do you not?"

"Aye," he said, kissing the bridge of her nose, "I do. Had I not been caught off guard by Lovell's addressing you as Godiva, I doubt I'd ever have thought otherwise. One day I shall thank him properly for murdering Everingham. You did not tell me the villain had ripped your clothes from you."

She blushed and would have looked away, but he held her chin. "It . . . it was not quite that way," she said.

"Tell me."

"You will be angry."

"I have been angry before and will likely be so again," he said, kissing the tip of her nose again. "Tell me."

Sighing, she leaned against him. "Take me to bed, sir. I am so weary, I am nigh to dropping where I stand."

With a wry smile, he scooped her up in his arms and carried her to the bed, helping her undress, and tucking her in. Then, snuffing the lights and stripping off his clothes, he got in beside her and lay back against the pillows. Slipping an arm beneath her, he drew her closer, and when she had snuggled her head into the hollow of his shoulder, he said, "Tell me now."

She began at the beginning, but he hushed her, telling her he had heard about that and to get to the part that had come after she had sent Ian to fetch him.

"They came the next morning to search for him," she said. She went on glibly enough until she began to explain that when Sir Lionel had ordered her from the bed so that his men might search beneath the bedclothes, she had wrapped one of the coverlets around herself. "I . . . I had nothing—"

"I understand, sweetheart," he said gently. " 'Tis as well that Lovell killed him, or else I should have to go now and do it myself. Everingham ripped the quilt away, did he?"

"N-no," she said. "He was coming to do so, I think, but I dropped it—nay, flung it aside—and leapt for the poker. That gave me time, you see, for it startled him and made him pause."

To her astonishment, he chuckled. "I'll warrant it did. But you are too small, sweetheart, to face a swordsman, armed with no more than a poker."

"He said the same," she admitted. "He said, too, that I would kneel to him in the hall before them all, and swear an oath of fealty to him as if he were my king, that if I did not, he would strip me naked and thrash me until I begged to serve him, and. . .and that was when I saw the door move behind him. I thought it was you, Nicholas, and I had all I could do to keep from crying aloud my relief that Ian had found you so quickly. I kept my eyes on Sir Lionel, but when he leapt at me, I was not strong enough to keep hold of the poker. Then he collapsed at my feet and I looked up to see

Lovell grinning at me. I had nearly flung myself into his arms before I saw it was him and not you."

"I do owe him a debt of gratitude," Nicholas said grimly, "but you must forgive me for asking why he came to you."

"He had taken shelter at Wolveston before," she said, "after Bosworth, with Roger, and he thought to do so again. He knew you had not yet taken residence, and even when he discovered I was there, he had no cause to believe . . ." Her voice trailed away. She knew she was plunging into deep water again.

"You need not explain. No doubt my tenants are as loyal to his cause as you are."

"No longer, sir," she murmured. "They are grateful to you and to your brother for setting things to rights at Wolveston. They would still be reluctant to betray me, I suppose, but you are my husband, and I warrant that if you asked them for answers, even about Lovell, you would get them."

"Then mayhap you had better tell me the whole truth now, to disarm me in the event that someone decides to confide in me."

"I had not considered that a possibility," she admitted.

"There is a more dangerous one," he said quietly. "I have accepted your reluctance to trust me, knowing that it grows out of your fealty to the cause of York, but you can scarcely expect Harry to respect that explanation if he were to discover that you are somehow linked to Lovell's mischief."

She was silent, staring at a point on the bed curtains where the glow from the dying fire set shadows dancing. Nicholas was entirely unpredictable when his loyalties conflicted with hers.

"I can feel by your reaction that I have hit the mark," he said. When she still said nothing, he went on in that same quiet voice, "I can protect you better, *mi calon*, if I am forewarned. I point out, for what it is worth, that I have not yet lost my temper tonight, though the temptation has been strong. I am perfectly calm now and prepared to hear the worst."

"I believe the boy who died at Wolveston was Prince Edward Plantagenet," she blurted, wanting the worst over quickly. She felt immediate tension in his body. "I am not certain, Nicholas, but I did think it might be he, and when I told Lovell—"

"You told him! When? At Doncaster?"

"Aye, I did not go there for that purpose," she said, "but when Davy Hawkins said he was near, I sent Davy to fetch him so that I could tell him what I'd seen and ask him what he knew. He admitted Richard had sent both boys north, like Elizabeth, only not to Yorkshire, where they would have been sought by men who wanted to make trouble for him. My father was loyal to York, and not a combatant. Lovell said Father agreed to take the boys only if Richard would send me to live away from the court, to protect me, so that I might never be thought part of any plan."

"Then Edward Plantagenet is dead," Nicholas said. "What of the younger one, Prince Richard of York?"

"I do not know for certain," she said. "You told me someone had taken him away—for fostering, you said."

"Do you know who that was?" he asked, very casually.

"I think I do, but I doubt I would be wise to tell you."

She waited for the explosion, but it did not come. Instead he said, in that same quiet, murmuring tone, " 'Tis true, you would not. I am still loyal to my king."

"And I, to mine." She sighed. "I doubt that Richard of York still lives, sir. I had doubts before, and since summer I have been certain he must be dead."

"What happened then to convince you?"

"The man who most likely took him from Wolveston submitted to Henry Tudor and received a general pardon," she said, choosing her words carefully, "but he sued for a second one before a month was out. One has to assume he must have done something perfectly dreadful in the meantime. I think he killed the prince."

Nicholas sat up, grabbing her and lifting her to peer intently into her face. "Tyrell? You believe Tyrell had him!"

Her gasp gave her away, and she knew it, but she did her best to recover, saying, "I did not mention any such name."

"His pardons were much talked of, madam, but he has sworn fealty to Henry Tudor, and has served him well in Glamorgan." He stopped. "By our Lady," he said, staring at her, "that was why you asked about Glamorgan when we were traveling to Merion. Did you think to visit the man and ask him flat out where Richard was? Well, did you?" he demanded, giving her a shake. Even in the dim glow from the hearth, he must have seen the answer in her expression, for he released her with exaggerated care and leaned back against his pillows, shutting his eyes as though he feared what he might do if he continued to look at her.

Sitting up, facing him, she said, "I did think some such thing then, Nicholas, but I realized when I saw how treacherous your Welsh mountains were that there was no way I could go."

" 'Tis fortunate that you could not," he said, opening his eyes and looking at her in such a way that she shivered, "for if I had caught you trying to do such a perilous thing . . ." He did not finish, nor did he have to.

She swallowed. "I know, Nicholas. I saw at once that it was impossible, and in faith, I know not what I would have done if I had found him. I could scarce ask him if he had Richard of York hidden away in his castle."

"He cannot have him," Nicholas said firmly. "He swore allegiance to Henry. If he had control of a Yorkist prince, he would never have done so, not without telling Henry he had him."

"But he might well have had him and *told* the Tudor so. They still could not announce it to the world without putting Henry's position on the throne in jeopardy. And Henry could not kill the prince, for if it ever became known that he had, he would have had more trouble than he had already. And if he simply locked him in the Tower with Neddie and me and the others, a host of conspiracies would have erupted to get him out again."

"If Richard of York is still alive, then why has no one come forward to say so?" Nicholas asked.

"If he lives, 'tis because his keepers still do not know the fate of Edward Plantagenet," she said, "and even if Henry and Tyrell have dared to kill him, they cannot speak lest the news cause Edward to step forward with an army at his back to claim the throne. But there have been rumors that Richard murdered his nephews, Nicholas. You mentioned them yourself. Henry can have no proof that they both are dead, or he would have told whatever tale he liked to explain their deaths, but I think that when the rumors failed to bring Prince Edward out of hiding to challenge him, he decided it was safe to kill Prince Richard. When he gave the order, Sir James insisted upon the first pardon as an act of good faith, then sued for the second when the deed was done."

Nicholas was silent, and Alys was grateful. She recalled Lovell's insistence that Sir James Tyrell had been as loyal to King Richard as Lovell himself was, that he would never have harmed either prince, and it suddenly occurred to her that there might be another reason for Tyrell's second pardon. What, she wondered, if Sir James had taken the same expedient step that her brother, Sir Lionel, Lincoln, and so many others had taken, of submitting to the Tudor in order to protect his lands and titles? What if he had sued for general pardon, as so many others had done and then, afterward, had arranged for Richard of York to get safely out of England to Flanders? Had he hoped a second pardon would protect him from the Tudor's wrath? Was it possible that the crazy rumors of Neddie's escape were meant to cover the movements of another, and far more important, Yorkist prince?

She was glad that Nicholas appeared to be deep in his own thoughts, for she knew that if he had been watching her, he would suspect she knew still more than she had told him. She would have liked to share her ideas with him, but the old fears returned to haunt her. She knew he would protect her as well as he could, but if she confided her new suspicions, she was certain that his duty would be even clearer to him than it was to her.

"You may have the right of it," he said at last, and for a wild moment she thought he meant she was right in what she had been thinking, and she had to struggle to remember what she had actually said to him. Before she could comment, he went on, "It does not matter, however, because from this moment you are out of it. No, do not argue with me," he added, reaching out to place a finger on her lips. "I will, if necessary, exert every right my position as your husband grants me to see to your safety. I ought to have Gwilym take you straight back to Wolveston—"

"No! Oh, Nicholas, I promise—"

"Make yourself easy," he said, straightening and pulling her close again, drawing the bedclothes up over her. "I am not such a fool as to insist that you travel such a distance in this uncertain weather, let alone in your present condition. You will, however, leave the court and move to Queenshithe, where my mother can see that you take proper care of yourself. It cannot be good for you to continue in attendance upon the queen now, particularly in view of your precarious relationship with her."

"We get on well enough now," she said, holding her resentment in check, knowing that to lose her temper now would do her no good. "Since Elizabeth has presented the Tudor with his heir, she is well satisfied with herself and gracious to all of us in attendance on her."

"No matter, you will be better off in Queenshithe. Once this weather settles, I must be about my duties again, and will feel the better for knowing you are safe with my parents. And do not think you will be able to work your wiles on them to let you have your own way, sweetheart," he added, "for I will make my wishes clear to them, and they know that I have not only the right to command you, but the will to enforce my commands."

She did not doubt him, and she was too glad to have got through the past hour without having been banished to Wol-

veston again to resist him further. She murmured that she
would do her best to behave, but her sigh of resignation
made him laugh.

"You had better see that your best is enough," he said,
"or be prepared to face my wrath." Then, sobering, he said,
"Don't think that because I do not scold you, I am not displeased by all this, madam. You tread too lightly upon the
threshold of treason to suit me, and if either Elizabeth or
Henry should catch you at your tricks, I doubt I could protect you. Now that you carry my son, it is more important
than ever that you behave."

"Your son, is it? It might as easily be my daughter, sir."

"Aye, and a right little baggage she would be. In either
case, madam, you will take care."

"I will," she said. "Kiss me, Nicholas, so that I know you
truly are not angry with me anymore."

"You would bewitch me," he said, pulling her into his arms
and kissing her thoroughly. His hands began to move over
her body, and his breathing deepened and quickened, and
soon she knew he would speak no more that night of her
misdeeds.

That she could stir him so easily was an increasing delight
to her. She gloried in the pleasure that he gave to her body
and in what she could do to him with no more than a touch,
a kiss, or a caress. She exerted herself to please him, reveling
in each lusty groan and gasp of pleasure, tantalizing and teasing him until he could stand no more, and took command
of the proceedings in such a way as to leave her breathless.
Stirred to heights she had never explored before, Alys abandoned modesty to follow her instincts, murmuring endearments, responding to his every touch and stimulus with new
ones all her own, and crying aloud her pleasure at the end.
By the time the two of them fell back to their pillows, exhausted, there were only ashes left of the fire on the hearth.
But in Alys's heart the glow of love for Nicholas burned
warmly, making her wish that she had the power to keep

him near her always, safe, to love her and to be loved in return.

But the next morning Nicholas took her to stay with his parents in the house at Queenshithe. He was kind and loving, and he stayed there with her for the first two nights, but on the third morning he left the city at the head of a troop of his men, bound for Somerset, to look into incidents of mischief-making. Sadly, Alys watched him go, feeling her child stir, and wondering if these new incidents had aught to do with the mischiefs Lovell had promised to stir up to annoy the king.

# 22

The house at Queenshithe occupied a whole block between Thames Street and the river. From the street, one entered a walled court; from the river, one used the private landing terrace and went up through the garden. The house itself, built of brick and timber, and boasting a tower, a large oak-paneled hall, four bay-windowed parlors overlooking the Thames, and vast expanses of glass and tiled floors, was extremely comfortable.

By comparison with other places Alys had lived, the house was modern and convenient, and Nicholas's family made warm and pleasant company for her. But she missed her husband sorely.

Gwilym had already begun to chafe at being so long away from Wolveston, and decided to return. The night before he left, Sir Walter Fenlord and his son came to call, with Madeline; and while Alys and Gwenyth entertained her near the fireplace in the great parlor, the men talked of hunting and politics some distance away. The ladies paid little heed to them, although once, when Gwilym had drawn Sir Walter to one side and was talking earnestly with him, Alys saw Madeline stiffen, give them both a long look, and then turn away and put her nose in the air.

Alys did not see her again for several days. Nicholas had not forbidden her the court altogether, but his parents were not people who believed life centered about the activities there. They took part only when they were invited to attend a function, and since Madeline's duties kept her in attendance on the queen, it was not until the following week, when the family were bidden to supper, that the two young women saw each other again.

"We are to take barges to Sheen tomorrow," Madeline informed her, "and 'tis more than time, for I swear that not all the ashes in London can refresh the jakes at Westminster, the court has been here so long. We did think the king would order the remove last week, but he did not. He has been too much taken up with all the rumors regarding the young Earl of Warwick. Have all the men at Queenshithe not been talking, like everyone else?"

"Rhys and Dafydd ab Evan have spoken of them, to be sure," Alys said. "Gwilym left for Wolveston the day after your visit. Did you not know?"

Madeline's face fell, but she recovered at once and said airily, "I do not care what that man does. Marry, I had thought at one time he meant to join the host of others begging for my hand, but evidently he had the good sense to decide against it."

"Marry you? Gwilym?" Though Alys had Nicholas's assurance that that was Gwilym's exact intention, she still had her doubts.

"I saw him talking to my father that night at Queenshithe," Madeline said, "and I have seen other such conversations before, you know. In general, they do herald a request for my hand."

"Did your father tell you Gwilym had made such a request?"

"No, but I think he would not believe him suitable. He must want a more indulgent man to marry me. Moreover, I do believe he is beginning at last to believe I want no part of marriage."

Alys shook her head in amusement. "Madeline, I have seen how you flirt with Gwilym! And two minutes ago, when I said he had gone, you were upset. Confess now, you do care for him."

Madeline lifted her chin. "He is different from other men, that is all—more exasperating, if you must know. Why, I never knew another who made no attempt to please me. Only look at the difference between him and the men of the court! I did think once that he cared, a little, but I must have been wrong, and now, when he has the opportunity to know me better, he leaves! So you must not think I have changed my mind about husbands, Alys. Only look at what happens to one! Here are you, in train with your husband's family, and no husband. Where is he now?"

"Gone hunting those who would make mischief for Henry Tudor in Somerset," Alys said.

"And when will he return?"

"I do not know."

"Well, there you are."

Alys could not debate the matter, for she missed Nicholas very much. He did not return to London for nearly three weeks, and when he did return, it was mid-February, the king's great council was in session, and Alys was feeling un-attractive and too fat for her clothes.

The rumors regarding the whereabouts of the young Earl of Warwick had multiplied so that one of the first decisions of the council had been to parade the boy before the pop-ulace, to prove that he was indeed still an inmate of the Tower. Alys had not been allowed to view the procession because of her condition, and when it was over she won-dered what purpose it could have served.

"How can it help?" she demanded of Nicholas at supper with his family afterward. "Scarcely anyone in the crowd can claim to know Neddie. They know only that the king says he is Warwick."

"True enough, but the parade accomplished one thing we did not expect," he said in a tone that warned her she would not like what he said next. "Lincoln has fled the city."

His announcement startled everyone at the table.

"Where did he go?" Rhys demanded.

"*Why* would he go?" Gwenyth asked.

"He goes to join rebels in Flanders, I believe," Nicholas said, watching Alys. "It is clear now that whatever they meant to accomplish with the rumors about Warwick, Lincoln is the true pretender. 'Tis thought he goes now to lead them, to claim the crown unto himself. I should hate," he added, looking at Alys grimly, "to think that you knew aught of these plans before now."

"But how could she?" his mother asked gently. "The poor girl has scarce stirred from this house in a month's time."

Alys was shaking her head. "I cannot believe it," she said. "Lincoln has never shown any interest in the crown."

"He was Richard the Third's heir," Nicholas reminded her.

"Oh yes, named when Richard's own son died, but no one, including Lincoln himself, expected him to inherit. Even the Tudor saw no need to lock him up. Lincoln is not a man to rally others or commit himself to causes. He . . . he sidesteps them."

Nicholas shrugged. "He is not sidestepping this one. And, what is more, he seems to have some important backers. The queen dowager has this day forfeited her dower rights again and withdrawn across the Thames, to the abbey at Bermondsey."

This announcement brought more cries of astonishment from his audience. Bewildered, Alys said, "Are you telling us the Tudor took back her dower lands and banished her from court?"

"Aye," he said, adding pointedly, "and on the very eve of Lincoln's flight."

She shook her head again. "That makes no sense at all, sir. Elizabeth Woodville would never support her husband's nephew's claim against that of her own daughter and grandson!"

"Nevertheless, the dowager queen has been plotting. I do not know the details, except it is said she did receive letters from the conspirators—at Christmas." His gaze was stern.

Alys flushed but was careful to hide her consternation

from the rest of the family. If Davy Hawkins had visited Westminster chiefly in order to deliver letters to the dowager queen, it was easier to understand why Lovell had made the effort then to write to her. Had Davy been caught, he had only to say he had come to visit his sister and Alys, and they would have supported that declaration. She said quietly, "I still cannot credit it, sir."

"As to that, 'tis rumor only," he replied in the same tone, "but not the part that took place today. Lincoln is headed for his father's lands in East Anglia, where he can easily get a boat for Flanders. His father, the Duke of Suffolk, is still loyal to the king, and Harry wants to keep it that way, so I go to East Anglia in two days' time." He looked ruefully at Alys. " 'Tis to be a show of force only; we won't catch Lincoln. Harry means to follow us soon—to begin a second spring progress at mid-Lent, like last year's—but I'll be back before the child is born."

His mother cried out in dismay, but Alys was silent. She had lived her life watching men ride off to their duty while women remained at home to await their return. Listening to Nicholas placate Gwenyth, then go on to discuss details of other news from court with his father and younger brother, she felt only sadness that he would leave again so soon. She understood, she thought, her mother-in-law's consternation, for Gwenyth's husband and at least one son were content to remain at home with her, to oversee their farms and tenants, to look after their own. Nicholas was different, a soldier first, a husband only because he had deserved reward for service to his liege lord.

Nicholas did not care for the land the way his father did, nor even the way that Gwilym did. And, though he found pleasure in his wife's company, he did not care for her the same way his father cared for Gwenyth. She watched Dafydd ab Evan whenever he spoke to his wife, and she longed to see that same deeply tender look in Nicholas's eyes when he looked at her. She had seen kindness and laughter, exasperation and anger, and certainly lust, but never that same sweet unspoken tenderness.

There was naught she could complain of in his behavior while he remained at Queenshithe, for he was attentive and kind. He even played his lute and sang to her when she could not sleep; but he showed no interest in bedding her after his first night home—for which she blamed her ballooning figure—and his kindness was casual and easygoing, rather than lovingly tender.

In the weeks following his departure, she had several letters from him but little news of what was happening in the counties. And in London, there were more rumors regarding the Earl of Warwick. Notwithstanding the fact that Neddie had been paraded through the streets, many still insisted that he had escaped and meant to lead an armed invasion from Flanders, backed by his aunt, Margaret of Burgundy.

Despite the rumors, Madeline reported a relaxed atmosphere at Sheen, lasting into Lent. And despite the king's intent to show strength on his progress—and thus, deter strife—with a large, well-armed retinue composed mostly of gentlemen from Lancashire, the comments at court, according to Madeline, had more to do with the comeliness of the women in East Anglia than with any possibility of rebellion there. She had even overheard one stout courtier tell another that he believed they could drink Norwich as dry as they had left York the previous Easter.

When the men had gone, Madeline visited the house at Queenshithe as soon as she could manage to do so, and informed Alys with a long-suffering sigh that the court had become entirely too restless. "Of those left behind, nearly all are women," she said, "and Elizabeth, who is perfectly healthy this year, chafes at being left at Sheen, although the king did assure her that he left her only because he feared for her safety."

Alys, remembering something Nicholas had said, wondered if it were not more likely that Henry wanted to make this show of strength on his own account and not remind anyone that his position was any the stronger because of his marriage. "What rumors are there?" she asked, not really wanting to discuss Elizabeth. "What do they say at court now about Neddie?"

"That he is in Ireland," Madeline said with a chuckle, "stirring up the Irish. Marry, but most people do discount the talk. They fear instead that Lincoln will lead an invasion. A grown man, they say, backed by Margaret of Burgundy, is a much more serious threat to Henry than any boy could be. Questions are asked, too, about why Henry seems so loath to crown his wife. And some even suggest that Warwick is dead but that Edward Plantagenet or his brother Richard is living now in Burgundy."

Alys seized on the safest topic. "Lincoln is not a man to lead armies, Madeline. You have met him."

"Aye," Madeline said, smiling. "When he asked me to dance, he said, 'If there be space enough, mayhap you will dance with me.' Marry, he is a careful man, but my father said that with Richard for an uncle, it paid him to be careful. And you must know that the king has ordered beacons set up along the coast. That sounds as if he believes Lincoln is a threat."

Alys could only agree that it did. Not long after that it became known that Henry had ordered his uncle, Jasper Tudor, and the Earl of Oxford to gather forces and prepare for invasion from both Flanders and Ireland. And once more, the papal bull was read throughout the land, recognizing Henry's marriage and his right to the crown, and cursing with bell, book, and candle all who did anything contrary to his right and titles. But by then, Alys was past caring about politics, for the pangs of her labor had begun, a fortnight before they were expected.

Gwenyth and Jonet were in attendance with several maids, and Ian was sent in haste for a royal physician, whom Elizabeth, in her graciousness, had recommended to attend the lying-in. Alys, who had never known such pain as she was feeling with each new contraction, called down every curse she could think of upon Nicholas, both for getting her into such a predicament and for leaving her to suffer it alone, but the pain was ended at last, and to her extreme astonishment, she had not one child, but two, the first a bouncing baby girl, the second a tiny boy.

She stared at the two small bundles presented by Jonet for her inspection. One was screaming lustily; the other watched her quietly through his wide blue eyes.

When the doctor, a somber, untalkative man, had gone at last, Jonet said in a tone carefully devoid of expression, "We had better send at once for a priest to christen them, mistress."

"Oh, tomorrow or the next day will do for that," Alys said, reaching out to touch first one tiny face and then the other.

Gwenyth said, "Do you not know what you mean to call them, my dear? You and Nicholas ought to have discussed the matter before he left. 'Tis most important."

"Aye, but he did say he would return before their birth," Alys said. She knew he wanted to name his son after the king, but she had not agreed, and now, looking at the small, quiet baby, she knew she could never agree to call him Henry. Firmly, she said, "I shall call them Anne and Richard."

There was silence, but to her surprise, no one debated her choices. She looked up then, and caught an exchange of looks between Jonet and Gwenyth that sent a chill sweeping through her. "What is it? Why do you look like that?"

Both women hastened to reassure her, telling her she should sleep, that wet nurses were at hand to look after the babes.

"I want to see them both. Every inch! Unwrap them."

After brief hesitation, they did as she asked, and she could find nothing wrong with either child. Anne, though small, had fuzzy light hair and was pink and bright-eyed. Her tiny limbs waved, and her cries were strong and lusty. The little boy was not so pink, but he moved his arms and legs, and had all his fingers and toes. She stroked one of his thin arms, pleased when he seemed to look in her direction.

"Wee Dickon," she said to him softly, "you will grow."

Firmly, Jonet took both babies and gave them into the care of their nurses, insisting that Alys sleep. And finally, she did, but when she awoke, she demanded to see the children at once. Once again, Jonet was unnaturally hesitant.

"They need their rest, mistress," she said gently.

"Fetch them," Alys commanded.

Small Anne was awake and cooing, but Dickon slept, not waking even when Alys held him and tickled his cheek.

"What is wrong with him?" she demanded.

"We do not know," Jonet whispered. "He will not feed. He does wake from time to time, but in between, we cannot wake him."

"Bring his cradle here, and put it beside my bed. I will keep him with me. He will thrive then. I know it!"

"Tha' mustn't," Jonet said. "Let me take him now."

But Alys refused, tears spilling down her cheeks. And all that day she held the little boy, her heart gladdening when his eyes opened, her tears falling harder and faster when they shut again. Gwenyth added her entreaties to those of Jonet's, but Alys would not let them take the baby. And when Madeline, summoned from Sheen in the hope she might soothe her, added her arguments to theirs, Alys lost her temper.

"He is my son! He will stay with me. Fetch the physician if you want to help us. I do not know why he does not come."

Gwenyth said sympathetically, "He will come, my dear, but he has already seen the baby, and he tells us there is naught he can do if the child will not feed."

"Then get another wet nurse, or I will suckle him myself." But though she tried, the baby would not suck. They soaked a sugar tit in breast milk, and held it in his mouth, but even then he did not respond.

Finally, Alys sent them all away, becoming hysterical when they were reluctant to obey her. She settled against her pillows with wee Dickon nestled in her arms, fighting sleep when it would come, fearing that if she slept the baby would die.

When the door to the bedchamber opened, she snapped without looking up from her charge, "Get out. I will hear no more of your foolish prattle. Dickon will stay with me."

"I have come to see my son, and he is not going to be called Dickon, but Henry Arthur, to please our king."

She looked up then, sharply, and cried ecstatically, and with overwhelming relief, "Nicholas, you are here! Oh, Nicholas, they say he will die. He cannot. He must not!"

Nicholas moved to stand beside the bed, looking down at the two of them. His face was white, and she realized that the others had already told him what to expect. "Let me hold him," he said, and his voice was tight.

"You will not take him away from me!"

"No. Move over." He sat on the bed beside her, plumping pillows behind himself before he took the tiny, silent bundle from her. "I have sent for a priest," he said.

"No!"

"He must be christened, sweetheart. The lass too."

"I will not have my son named after the Tudor."

"He is my son, too, Alys."

A rap at the door announced the priest, and she knew then that Nicholas had been in the house longer than she had thought. She looked at him accusingly and with despair, and he put his free arm around her shoulders, drawing her close.

Anne was brought in by her nurse, and when the family and Madeline had joined them, the priest began the brief ceremony. When, with a hand poised over the little boy's head, he asked, "Who names this child," Rhys, standing godfather, said, "I do."

Alys gazed bleakly at Nicholas.

He looked back at her with understanding, and the tenderness in his eyes that she had longed to see there, and said quietly, "There has been a change, Father. He is to be called Richard ap Nicholas ap Dafydd of the Welsh house of Merion."

The priest nodded, and Rhys repeated the names without comment. When it came time to name the little girl, Madeline, who was to stand her godmother, looked at Nicholas. "Is her name to be in the Welsh fashion, too, Sir Nicholas?"

He looked at Alys and smiled. "One Welsh lad, and one English wench—is that not the way, sweetheart? I have no objection to calling her Anne. What say you to Anne Madeline?"

Alys looked past Madeline's pleased smile to see Gwenyth nodding in agreement, and said, "We will use three names, if you please, sir, for I do favor Anne Madeline Gwenyth."

"A large name for a child," Nicholas said, "but so be it."

The ceremony, without the usual trappings and long service, was soon over. When the others were leaving, Jonet bent over the little boy, still asleep in his father's arms. "I ought to take him to the nursery now, sir."

Before Alys could protest, Nicholas said, "We will keep him with us. Bring my lady wife some food, if you will. I think she has not eaten as she should. She must restore her strength."

They took turns eating, so that one of them might hold the baby, and when the afternoon turned into evening, Nicholas got out his lute and played for them. Alys was exhausted, and while he played, her eyelids grew so heavy, she could no longer keep them open. The bundle in her arms was so light that when Nicholas took the baby from her she did not notice.

When she awoke, she missed Dickon instantly, and sat up in a panic. The room was dark except for the glow of firelight from the hearth, and above the crackling of the fire, she could hear music, a low humming sound. Nicholas was sitting in a chair beside the fire, hunched over, singing softly to their child.

Slipping out of bed, she crept nearer, not wanting him to stop, but he saw her. When he looked up, she saw the pain in his eyes and the tears on his cheeks, and she knew before he spoke what he would say.

"He is gone, sweetheart, only moments ago. I . . . I thought he might still hear me, so I did not stop the singing."

Crying out in anguish, she collapsed to her knees by his chair, put her arms protectively around the still bundle in his lap, and gave way to her grief.

Nicholas let her weep until Jonet, coming in silently a few minutes later, took the dead child away to prepare it for burial. Then Nicholas got up and lifted Alys from the floor, cradling her in his arms and carrying her to bed. He was crying again by then, too, and he crawled into the bed with her, boots and all, and drew the quilt up to cover them, holding her tightly until they both fell, exhausted, to sleep.

When Alys awoke, he was still holding her, and he was awake, watching her, his eyes red-rimmed, his face gray with sorrow.

She said the first words that came to her, without thought. "I never thought to see you weep."

"I am not made of stone, sweetheart."

Her own tears welled again and spilled down her cheeks. "I lost your son, Nicholas. How can you ever forgive me?"

He said steadily, "It was not your doing, my love, but the will of God. There will be other sons—and daughters, too, may heaven help me. That is better—a smile, albeit a watery one."

"There is little to smile about, but I am glad you came."

"I wanted to come before, but Henry demanded as great a show of force as we could muster till we left East Anglia behind. I left him at Huntingdon. He goes to Coventry, where he wants the queen and Lady Margaret to join him at Kenilworth Castle."

"You must leave again!" She would not beg him to stay, much as she wanted him to. She could not expect him to heed her needs when his king made demands of him, but she could not stem her tears. They ran down her face to her neck, into her bed gown.

Nicholas tried to mop them away with the edge of the quilt. "My handkerchief is sodden, sweetheart, so you must make do with this, but do not weep. 'Tis Hugh who goes with the queen. It will mean postponing his wedding, too, for as soon as you are fit to travel, I mean to take you and our daughter to Wolveston, and I doubt that Jonet will let the pair of you go without her."

"You would take us yourself?" She was not anxious to leave, but neither was she much interested in staying in London or in going with the queen, especially if Elizabeth moved to Kenilworth and took Arthur with her. Thinking of the royal prince brought a fresh rush of tears, and Nicholas responded with dismay.

"You weep at the thought that I will take you myself! Would you prefer that I send Hugh with you?"

"No, no." She tried to explain that she was glad he was going with them, but was surprised as well.

"I thought you would object to going at all just now," he said, "but there are things about to happen in this country, and I would as lief you and wee Anne were well away from the court and safe at Wolveston with Gwilym and a host of armed men to protect you. My father wants to return to Merion Court soon."

"Will you stay at Wolveston with us?"

"As long as I am able, sweetheart."

"Good, for it grows lonely there without you."

"It will not be lonely this time," he said. "I mean to take Madeline Fenlord with us."

She was grateful. "I hope her father will allow it."

"He will. Can you keep a secret, sweetheart? Gwilym means to have her, just as I said he would, and he has received her father's blessing, if he can only get the wench to agree."

"Then she was right! But she thought Sir Walter had refused him." She explained that Madeline had seen the two men talking, and had suspected the subject of their discussion. "She thinks her father looks for a more indulgent husband for her, not one who is interested only in her fortune."

Nicholas smiled. " 'Tis not only the fortune, sweetheart.

Gwilym said he knew he had strong feelings for the wench the instant one of Everingham's men dared to touch her, but he said, too, that she must come to want him as much as he wants her. She has been too much indulged to appreciate a husband, he said, and he cannot go through life with a wife he must coax and coddle. His chances look dim at the moment, but I believe his patience will prevail, and in any event, a few skirmishes between the two will make life at Wolveston more interesting for the rest of us."

Alys could not doubt that, and when the time came to leave London, found herself looking forward to the journey with more interest than might otherwise have been expected. The bleak sadness she felt at seeing her tiny son laid to rest was a little compensated by the joy she felt each time she held Anne in her arms or watched her sleeping in her cradle, and when the great gray castle on the hill first came into sight, she experienced a sense of homecoming that she had never felt before. Wolveston was her home now, more than it had ever been, for she had been the one to set the house in order, and she could even take pride in the freshly plowed fields they passed as they made their way up the hill, and admire the new lambs in the green pastures.

The journey had been slow, for the baby, her nurse, and at times even Alys herself, had traveled in a litter, but today Alys was riding beside her husband, with Jonet, Elva, and Madeline riding behind them. Glancing at Nicholas, astride Black Wyvern beside her, Alys saw a look of pleasure in his eyes, and when he turned toward her, he was smiling.

"It is a fine place," he said, "especially in the spring with the hills so green—like Wales."

"Would you rather it were in Wales?" she asked.

"No, sweetheart. In Wales, it would soon be cut up in parcels, for my sons and their sons. 'Tis better here, where it can stay as it is to support all who dwell within its borders."

"Mayhap the king will change England to make it more like Wales," she said.

"He is more like to change Wales. The English way leads

to power and stability, the Welsh to parcels and dissension. Then, too, men who struggle to make a small holding feed and clothe many dependents cannot provide men-at-arms for their king. But there is Gwilym now, coming across the courtyard to greet us."

In the bustle that followed, while they dismounted, servants came from within to attend the sumpter ponies and to assist the nurse with the baby. Alys watched Gwilym but could detect no difference in his attitude toward Madeline, and she began to suspect again that Nicholas must be mistaken. Madeline seemed to be oblivious to Gwilym, but Alys was not fooled. Madeline cared, but if the man truly wished to wed her, Alys thought he would have to show at least a modicum of interest, or else Madeline would remain obdurate if only to prove she knew her own mind. At the moment, she might have been air for all the heed he paid her.

"A good journey?" he asked Nicholas, seeming not to notice when Madeline, in passing, carelessly trod upon his foot.

Nicholas grinned at him but replied casually, "Aye, not a sign of invasion or rebellion did we see."

" 'Tis quiet enough," Gwilym said. "We shall be safe here, I think, despite the rumors. You'll want to look over the place."

Nicholas did, and for the next fortnight, he enjoyed being lord of the manor and spent his days riding with Gwilym, visiting the villages and the tenantry. Sometimes Alys and Madeline rode with them, and as the days passed, Alys noted that Mistress Fenlord was beginning to take greater offense at being ignored.

"He is worse than ever," Madeline said with a sigh, as she and Alys watched Gwilym and Nicholas show a pair of small boys how to nock arrows to bows that were nearly too long for them. "He is as like to walk past a lady as to wish her a good day."

"Goodness, do you wish him to speak to you?" Alys chuckled.

"It is of no significance to me," Madeline said, lifting her chin. "He can have nothing of interest to say. Why is he giving that child a coin? It is for Sir Nicholas to reward his tenants' children if he sees fit to do so. Will he not take offense?"

"Not Nicholas," Alys said. "Gwilym gives a coin to every boy he sees practicing, believing that soon the men-at-arms from Wolveston will be amongst the finest in the land, and Nicholas approves. He says Gwilym always knows exactly what he is doing." She could not repeat all that Nicholas had said, for she had promised not to do so, but she saw Madeline stiffen alertly at her last sentence, and hoped she would take warning.

Gwilym had ceased to criticize, or to note her clumsiness, which seemed to Alys to have increased since their arrival, but more than once Alys had seen the Welshman's jaw tighten at some bit of carelessness or an ill-chosen word. She had surprised a look of amusement in his eyes once also, and once, when Madeline had scraped her arm through her clumsiness, a look of tenderness. Alys did not think he would remain impassive much longer, and two days later, when Madeline, having helped her wash her hair by the great-hall fire, suddenly took it upon herself to carry away the rinse basin instead of calling a servant to attend to it, Alys, warned by her expression that she had mischief in mind, watched with amused trepidation to see what would happen.

Nicholas and Gwilym were sitting comfortably at the other end of the hearth, absorbed in a game of Tables. Neither had paid the least heed to several conversational gambits made by the women, and Alys had hidden more than one smile at hearing Madeline raise her voice in a clear attempt to elicit at least a comment in return, but the men's concentration on the roll of their dice and the movement of their tiles was too great.

Jonet, wrapping a towel around Alys's head, said quickly, "You need not carry that basin, mistress. Call a ser—" She broke off with a gasp when Madeline tripped, seemingly over her own feet, and threw the entire basin of water over Gwilym.

He leapt up, sputtering, and Madeline said, "I *am* so sorry, sir. You must forgive my clumsiness."

He replied as calmly as though he were not dripping all over the hearth, "Such carelessness, madam, is something that we shall discuss at painful length if it persists after we are wed."

"Wed? How dare you, sir! I have never said I would marry you, nor shall I ever do so."

"We shall see. I cannot understand why your father allowed you to make such a game of a simple matter. Your consent is not needed, only his, and that I have, sweet vixen, in writing. I had hoped you would know your own mind before you learned that fact, but since you persist in denying your feelings whilst you flirt like a spoiled child demanding attention, I've decided that as soon as Hugh Gower arrives to marry Mistress Hawkins, we, too, will be wed. 'Twill save us all the bother of two ceremonies."

"Oh," Madeline cried, "of all the—" Swiftly her hand came up and she slapped him, hard.

Gwilym made no attempt to evade the blow, but afterward he said grimly, "Do not ever do that again, mistress, unless you want to be soundly cuffed in return."

"But you never even asked me!" she cried, arms akimbo.

"I told you, asking is unnecessary. You've enjoyed yourself very much, tossing suitors to the right-about like so many discarded gowns. It has become such a habit with you that you do not even pause anymore to look them over beforehand, or to search your own feelings. Thus, I did not ask. And thus, my love, when Hugh Gower arrives, we shall be married, without argument."

"Never!" she cried, raising her hand again, then swiftly snatching it back and putting it behind her. Leaning forward, she put her flushed face close to his pale one. "I will never marry you or any man. You don't even care about me!"

"We will discuss that subject in private," Gwilym said,

scooping her up into his arms and bearing her from the room.

Not much to Alys's surprise, though Madeline kicked, there was less fury than frustration in her ranting; and when they met later, she was subdued and did not want to talk, but she glowed. Her mood changed daily after that, however, and Alys, certain that her friend wanted nothing so much as to marry Gwilym, came to agree with him that she was simply too proud to admit it. As a result, Madeline worked herself into such a state that when Hugh Gower strode unannounced into the great hall the following Wednesday, she fainted dead away at the sight of him.

# 23

Hugh paid no heed to Madeline, and spared only a single glance for Jonet, who had rushed to her side. He went straight to Nicholas, who, having ridden in late for his midday meal, was ordering food for Gwilym and himself. When Nicholas turned with a smile of welcome, Hugh did not wait for his greeting.

"The rebels have landed," he said, "in Lancashire, from Ireland. 'Tis said they're led by the true Earl of Warwick, whom they crowned King of England in Dublin. They mean to take the throne, Nick. They've a host of Irish mercenaries, and German too, no doubt, since 'tis said they march to fife and drum, which the Germans always do. They are nearing Yorkshire as we speak."

"Where is Harry?" Nicholas demanded.

"At Coventry, last I saw, but meaning to ride to meet them. He sent his family back to Greenwich. Harry makes for Nottingham Castle, Nick, certain the villains will come south, and we're to meet him there at once with as many men as we can muster."

Gwilym came in just then but paused in obvious dismay at the sight of Jonet kneeling beside Madeline, who was attempting to sit up. Then he saw Hugh and understanding lit his face. He grinned. "Well met, Hugh! Shall I send for the priest?"

"We've no time," Nicholas said grimly. "Lincoln and Lovell apparently have banded together to put their false Warwick on the throne. They landed in Lancashire, and are nearing York."

"Will they take the city?" Gwilym demanded.

" 'Tis possible, I suppose. Many in the North are still loyal to the late king." He glanced at Alys, but she was too intent upon learning the news to pay heed to any underlying meaning in his words. "No matter to us now if they do take York," he said. "We ride at once to join the king."

"No!" Alys cried before she even knew the word was forming itself on her tongue. She ran to Nicholas and grabbed his right arm with both hands. "You cannot go. We need you here!"

"Madam, control yourself," he said sharply, pushing her hands away. "You know I cannot stay when the king summons me. Now, calm yourself and take Madeline and Jonet up to your solar. I have important matters to discuss with Hugh and Gwilym."

"I do not care about your important matters," she snapped. "I make no demands for myself—'twould be pointless—but you've a daughter whom it is also your duty to protect, and I will not allow you to ride off with every soldier on this estate to defend Henry Tudor! If the rebels win, as they surely will this time, for even you have said your king is no soldier, you will have lost your daughter's inheritance, and mine, by defending him."

Grabbing an arm and hustling her toward the gallery, Nicholas called over his shoulder, "Give me a moment, lads. Hugh, get something to eat, and Gwilym, fetch that list of men-at-arms for me to study after I have attended to my wife."

Too late did Alys remember that her husband's temper would not stand for her to call him to account in front of others. She did not resist his grip, but the moment he pushed her into their bedchamber, she whirled to face him, wincing when he slammed the door, then exerting every ounce of strength she had over herself not to put up her hands as if she thought she must fend him off.

"Nicholas," she said quickly, "I am sorry I spoke hastily below, but I was frightened and . . . and I just did not think. I fear for you. I do not want you to go."

"I know," he said, leaning back against the door and wiping the back of his hand across his sweating brow. "You have a rare talent, lass, for making me lose my temper. Two minutes ago I wanted nothing more than to put you across my knee, but I won't. I do know you are frightened. I must go, and you know it, though I don't doubt that you would prefer to hold me here to give your rebel friends a better chance. Do not pretend that your fears are solely for me. I will not believe you."

"You should believe me," she retorted, "but you care only for your stupid king and his false claim to England's throne. If Lovell and the others really do have Neddie with them, even you must admit his claim is greater than Henry Tudor's."

"I do not believe it is Neddie we have to fear," he said. "No one would strive so hard now to put a boy on the throne. If we do not find Lincoln at the head of this army, I shall own myself astonished. It is his claim that Lovell and the others are fighting for, and no one else's."

"Lincoln is also a more proper heir," she said stubbornly.

"This rebellion is doomed to failure, madam," he retorted. "In the meantime, I warn you, have no traffic with the rebels. I am leaving men to guard you and the babe, and I am leaving Gwilym in command, with orders to lock you in your room if necessary to keep you from doing anything stupid. I know you detest Harry Tudor, but he is your king as well as mine, and your foolish words today are naught but more treason. When will you learn to consider first, before you shout your feelings to the world?"

He left her then, and she made no effort to follow him. Even in her own ears her arguments had sounded weak, and she did not want to fight anymore with him. She knew he had to go. She could not even fault him for leaving the castle unguarded, for clearly he had never had any such intention, and had she given the matter thought, she would have known he would not leave his family unprotected. She had argued impulsively, snatching at straws in the futile attempt to dissuade him from leaving.

She realized then that she would have snatched at any argument that might sway him, that she had spoken the absolute truth when she had said she feared for him. She cared more for Nicholas than she cared about anyone's politics. Suddenly she began to wonder if she, like Madeline, had held to a conviction out of habit long after events had begun to erode her beliefs.

It was hard to hate the king, having danced with him, having come to see him not as a monster but as only a man, and a quiet, practical man at that, who had no taste for war. He wanted peace and prosperity for England, objectives that no sensible person could despise. Even her feelings for Elizabeth had changed. She was certain that the queen would never become a favorite friend, but she understood her better and no longer hated her.

She watched from a tower window as the men rode out through the tall gates and downhill to the south, until she could see them no more. At the last moment Nicholas turned to smile and wave at her. She knew he did it to reassure her that his temper had cooled, and the gesture brought an ache to her heart, and a sudden longing to hold her daughter. Hurrying to fetch the baby herself, she struggled to contain her emotions. Nicholas was gone. He might be killed. Holding Anne in her arms, her eyes awash with unshed tears, she paced the floor of the nursery until Madeline found her and gave Anne back to the nursemaid who had hovered nearby, waiting, too timid to speak to the pacing Alys.

"They will come home safely," Madeline said. "Hugh has sworn to Jonet that no harm will come to himself or to Sir Nicholas, and Jonet says Hugh never lies to her."

Alys collected herself and managed a smile. "Never lies? Does she accept all the things he said about her at Waltham?"

Madeline smiled too. "I was not fool enough to ask her. Are you? She does seem resigned to marrying Hugh, even cheerful about it. I was not certain if she really would; however, it has been an age since I last heard her speak ill of him."

"Oh, she still does so," Alys said. "In truth, I think she held men at a distance on purpose—mayhap out of devotion to me; but Hugh persisted despite her sharp tongue, and odd though it might appear to others, she does seem to love him very much."

"It does not seem odd to me," Madeline said gruffly, turning away and pretending to be busy stirring the fire with the iron poker. "Some women love the oddest men."

Alys did not press her to explain herself, but she was not surprised to see Madeline become even more subdued than before. The danger around them put an end to her sporadic protests. She displayed a new sense of purpose, and made it clear that she was as anxious as any of the others were for the men to return.

Alys saw, too, that Gwilym no longer ignored Madeline, nor did he criticize her. There was a gentleness between them now that betokened a truce at least, if not something much deeper.

Gwilym had sent men to watch the boundaries of the estate, and not content to remain inside the castle and wait for reports, he frequently rode out to look things over. Word came that the rebels were moving fast. They had not tried to take York but had passed the city and were following the Great North Road, which meant they headed toward Doncaster. Gwilym tightened the guard.

After that news came with alarming frequency, of clashes with the rebels at Tadcaster and then at Stainforth, which was much too close to Wolveston for comfort. The women gathered in Alys's solar that evening. They had seen little of Gwilym all day, for he had ridden out early to meet with his watchers.

Madeline said anxiously, "Do you think they will come

here, Alys? It is possible that Lord Lovell, at least, still thinks this estate loyal to the Yorkist cause."

"No," Alys said flatly, knowing that, like herself, her friend was more worried about what could happen to Gwilym and the men if the rebels came than she was about danger to the women. Alys also had been thinking the rebels might come, not so much because Lovell would expect the estate to be loyal, as because he might decide to use Wolveston as an assembly point. Word was that men loyal to the king were fleeing south of the Trent as fast as they could go, that the rebels controlled Yorkshire and were swiftly moving into Warwickshire and Nottinghamshire. Alys did not fear Lovell or Lincoln—and certainly not any boy they might have with them—but she did not want them at Wolveston. She did not want men and horses trampling the newly seeded fields or slaughtering the spring lambs for their food. Thus, when she entered her bedchamber the following Thursday night to find Davy Hawkins sitting at his leisure before her fire, conversing with his sister, she nearly shouted for a guard.

He leapt to his feet and made his bow, saying, "Forgive me, m'lady. 'Twas not my intention to startle you."

"Well, you did," she said tartly. "Where is his lordship, Davy? Have you got him hidden behind the window curtains?"

"Nay, m'lady. He be far from here. Leave us, Jonet," he said brusquely. The fact that she left without argument told Alys that they had talked for some time before her arrival.

"How did you get past the guards?" she demanded.

He shrugged. "There be many still loyal to the cause, mistress, but I did have to give my oath that no harm would come of it, and none will."

"You cannot quarter here."

"We will not. His lordship sent me to calm any fear you might have, and to give you this letter to show to any rebel soldier who might come in error, now or later." He handed her a folded note, and she recognized Lovell's writing. Davy said, "Our army lies west of here, close to the London road,

so there will be no fighting near here, no danger to you or
to yours. 'Tis by his lordship's and my Lord Lincoln's absolute command."

"Then Lincoln *is* at the head of it," she said, tucking the
letter into her bodice. "My husband thought as much."

Davy shrugged again. "He leads, the lad leads, my lord
leads. Who is to say who is at the head, one day to the next?"

Alys stared hard at him, shaken by his words. "What are
you saying, Davy? Speak plainly, or by heaven, I *will* call a
guard."

"Nay, mistress, do not. I cannot say more, but my Lord
Lovell did give me a token to give into your hands. 'Tis to
be kept till all is done. If we win, it matters not, but if the
fighting goes amiss, then you must carry the token to the
queen."

"To Elizabeth?"

"Aye. No, no," he amended quickly, "not the lass—the
dowager queen, Elizabeth Woodville. Lord Lovell did not
trust her with it before, but she does deserve to have it if
the matter falls awry. She will know what to do, and you are
to say to her that all is well, even then."

"If you fail?" Alys shook her head. "I do not understand,
Davy. How can I say all is well if the rebellion fails? And
how can I get this to the dowager queen? She is at Bermondsey now."

"Her daughter visits her. There will be no hurry, mistress.
You will arrange it an you can. Tell her the date upon which
you received the token, and that it were but a week old at
the time. She will understand. Things will be in a great stir
by then, no doubt, for no matter what transpires, great
changes lie ahead."

"Not if Harry Tudor wins," she pointed out.

"Harry Tudor will not win, though his armies may," Davy
said grimly. "By this time Saturday, the usurper will be dead,
hide where he may. 'Tis the first purpose of this little exer-
cise." Then, before she could question him further, he held
out his hand and said, "Take it, mistress, and guard it well.

My Lord Lovell dares not keep it longer, lest it fall into the wrong hands."

Her curiosity overriding all else now, Alys opened her hand and watched as he put into it what looked like a gold coin with a hole drilled in it for a chain. She looked at it closely, and recognized, etched into it on one side, the sun in splendor, King Edward's device. Turning it over, she found a single rose on the reverse. That was all, but it was enough. She had heard about such a medallion once before, and she looked up in dismay to ask how Lovell had come by it. But the door was just closing behind Davy, and she dared not run shouting after him.

When Jonet returned, she found her mistress huddled on her bed, her knees up, her arms folded around them, deep in thought.

"I could not warn you, mistress," Jonet said apologetically. "He came upon me in the gallery unawares."

"There will be fighting," Alys muttered. "If not tomorrow, then Saturday at latest. All for the power of the throne."

Jonet nodded. "Davy told me that his lordship expects to meet the king near Nottingham Castle, mayhap at Newark crossing. Lord Lovell has a house nearby and knows the land full well. More men will die, mistress, men we care about on both sides."

"Davy said the rebels will win; Nicholas said not. Nicholas claims to know his business. By heaven, Jonet, I hope he does."

Jonet frowned. "Davy said not so many English had joined as they'd hoped, but he said, too, that there be more than enough, that all Yorkshire is theirs, all the land north of the Trent."

They continued to speak their tangled thoughts aloud until Madeline entered, whereupon they fell silent so suddenly that she demanded to be told what they had been talking about.

Jonet looked to Alys, but Alys did not hesitate. "Davy was here, Jonet's brother. He rides with Lovell, and he managed to get past the guards to assure us that there will be no fighting here. They move south, toward Newark and Nottingham Castle."

"Now, by my faith," Madeline said with an imp of amusement in her eyes, "wait till I tell Gwilym his defenses were breached so easily. He thinks he has made this castle impregnable."

"You must not say anything to him," Alys said fiercely. "There is no danger here, for Davy gave his word, but if you tell Gwilym that I have spoken with one of the rebels, he will lock me in my bedchamber. Nicholas warned me that he had ordered him to do so. Moreover," she added, suddenly deciding what she had to do, "if you tell Gwilym that someone managed to get in, he will make it a great deal more difficult for someone to get out."

"Has Davy not gone then?"

"Certainly, he has. I was speaking of. . .of someone else." Too late did she recall that Madeline's loyalties had no doubt shifted, that she might well consider herself bound to speak to Gwilym. Madeline's next words confirmed that fear.

"Look here, Alys," she said, plumping down upon the bed and staring into her face, "I recognize that look. You are up to some devilment or other, and I will not have you playing your tricks off on poor Gwilym at such a time as this."

"Poor Gwilym?" Alys said, gently mocking her, but when Madeline blushed and looked self-conscious, Alys straightened and said much more seriously, "I have long known that you cared for him, but do you love him, Madeline? Tell me. It is important."

Madeline nodded. "Aye, I do."

"And you will not refuse to marry him?"

The answer came in a whisper. "No, but do not tease me, for I have only just come to see the truth myself. I was so stubborn and stupid, Alys. When I saw Nicholas and Hugh ride out through the gates, and knew they might not come back—that, even here, Gwilym could be killed before this business is done—I could deceive myself no longer. I cannot imagine life without him. You will think this silly, I know, but I think I love Gwilym most because I like myself better when I am with him."

"We have all been waiting for you to know your own mind," Alys said, hugging her, "but I am glad for more reasons than you know. I fear for Anne. Swear to me on your oath, Madeline, that if aught happens to me, and if Nicholas is killed, you and Gwilym will look after Anne as if she were your own. Swear it!"

"By our Lady, I do swear it," Madeline said, looking at her through narrowed eyes, "but why should I? You have said that no harm will come to any here, and if that is so—"

"Can I trust you not to betray me?"

"Marry, what a question!"

"To Gwilym?"

Madeline hesitated, then said grimly, "I owe no duty to him yet, Alys, and you have stood my friend. Tell me."

"The rebels mean to kill Henry Tudor," Alys said quietly.

"Well, I suppose they do. 'Tis natural, if they win."

Alys looked at Jonet, then back at Madeline. "Davy said the king will die no matter what, and Nicholas once told me Henry is so poor a soldier that he had vowed never to ride at the head of his army again, but to stay at the rear. What if the rebels plan to seek him out, to kill him and thus declare the battle won?"

"But Henry has a proper heir," Madeline protested.

"Arthur is a babe in arms," Alys said, "and no army will fight for him. Richard, too, had heirs. Indeed, Nicholas believes the true pretender now is Lincoln, but when I asked Davy, he would not say. It struck me then that the proper heir does not matter. Only the power of the throne concerns them. The victor will control it, and I think the rebels mean to declare victory by battle just as Henry Tudor did at Bosworth."

"But do you not want them to win?" Madeline asked.

"Do you?" Alys countered. "Do you want Lincoln to rule

England—a man who cannot speak without pausing to choose every word—or do you prefer a boy king who will have men fighting on forever over who will control him?" Seeing the answer she sought in her friend's eyes, she turned to Jonet. "And you?"

"I want an end to war," Jonet said. "The cause matters much to Davy, and I love him, but my loyalties have got mixed for I do love that great gowk, Hugh Gower, even more. I wish harm to no one, but if I had to choose, God help me, I would choose Hugh."

Alys said quietly, "The times have changed, have they not? Henry Tudor is liked by the people who know him and respected by many who do not. He has ruled well and fairly, and he has worked to bring stability to his realm. With him to lead them, men look to see such prosperity in England as we have not seen in thirty years. If the rebels win, there will be more and more fighting. The only way to lasting peace is with the Tudor."

"What must we do?" Madeline asked.

"I must try to find Nicholas," Alys said. "He has got to be warned that they intend to kill the king."

Madeline said sharply, "Then tell Gwilym, Alys! He can send men to warn them."

Alys shook her head. "They might not get to him, or be believed if they do. The rebels will have men on the watch all over Nottinghamshire. They would kill anyone riding to warn the king. But I will be safe from soldiers on either side. None would dare to harm me."

"If they know you," Madeline said. "But they will not all know you, Alys. You could be killed."

"No, I won't. I have a letter from Lovell himself. It is not a simple safe-passage that can be given to Gwilym or anyone else, for I have read it and it specifically names me, as Lady Alys Wolveston, and protects me, my lands, and people. I will be safe, but Gwilym must not know. Not only would he refuse to let me, but he would want to go himself, and he is needed here all the more if the letter is with me. I won't go alone, I promise you, but will take Ian and two others. We can leave in the morning after Gwilym rides out with his men. He does so each day, so he will do so tomorrow. And Ian will know which other men to take and how to get us horses and gear. Once we are gone, Madeline, I leave it to you to prevent Gwilym's riding after us. He must stay here to protect Anne and the rest of you."

"He will murder me," Madeline said, grimacing.

"No, for he will understand that you could not stop me. I must go, Madeline. I can convince them of the danger to the king more easily than any men we could send. I will be believed."

"Mistress, we cannot allow it," Jonet said. "By rights, we ought to tell Master Gwilym at once what you mean to do."

"If you do, I will never forgive you," Alys said fiercely. "My husband has already lost his son. If I can help prevent the death of his king, I shall feel that I have compensated him, at least in a small way, for that loss."

They did not argue anymore after that, and Alys hoped she could trust them not to speak. She had not told them that she feared even more for Nicholas's safety than for Henry's, for the feeling made no sense to her. She was no soldier and he was one of the best, but she was certain that she would not want to live if Nicholas were killed. She knew now that she loved him with a passion much greater than she had ever felt for the Yorkist cause, and that she would suffer more if she lost him now than she had suffered at the death of her son.

Not until she and Ian and the two men he had found to accompany them were safely away the next morning could Alys be sure that her friends had not betrayed her, but the escape proved easier than she had expected. The guards had been posted to keep people out, not to keep the residents within. Nevertheless, when they rode away down the hill toward the river, she was deeply grateful for the thick fog that prevented anyone seeing them from the castle ramparts.

An hour later Ian was not so grateful for the fog. "We

dinna need it now," he grumbled. "The road be difficult tae
see as it is, and 'twill tak' us days tae reach Newark at this
pace."

"How far is it?" she asked, trying to remember how long
it had taken them before.

Ian grimaced. "Aboot thirty mile tae Nottingham Castle.
Five-and-twenty till the river bends sharp west at Newark."

She nodded. Her palfrey was fresh and could go a great
number of miles without having to stop for long rests, but
she was not sure about the men's horses. The best had been
taken by Nicholas's men-at-arms, and Ian and the others had
had to make do with what was left. Still, Gwilym did not
keep any but the best horseflesh, she reminded herself. They
ought to manage at least four miles to the hour once the fog
lifted and they could see where they were going. She did
rapid sums in her head, grateful for her experience with accounts. Even if they rested frequently, they ought to manage
the distance by nightfall.

They did not try to cross the river. The other side of the
river was Lincolnshire, and with its fens and marshes, as
unknown to any of them as a foreign country might have
been. Alys knew there were several towns there, but they
did not know who held them; and, not until the fog began
to lift at noon and they found themselves with the forest on
one side and the river on the other—not far from where
they had been attacked once before—did it occur to them
that they might have done better to cross.

"Do the master's men be south of the river, like what that
fellow said they was, they will be on the other side from
where we be now," Ian said to Alys. "We havena seen a soul
as yet, but I'd as lief the first we see be royal forces."

She was not so sure. Conscious of the letter crunching in
her bodice as she rode, she realized that what meant safe-
passage to one side might, if it were found on her, mean
something else to the other. She had thought only of getting
safely past the rebels. She had not thought that she might
have to deal with royal forces to whom she would be a

stranger. She thought about it now, and realizing that she might not be able to prove her identity to anyone who did not know her, let alone force him or them, to take her to Nicholas, she decided to remain on the west bank, but to keep near the river, where she would be the least likely to meet any soldiers until they were close to their goal. Then at least, if convincing someone took time, she would be near enough to find Nicholas quickly afterward.

The sun was shining now. Birds were singing and squirrels chattering in the forest. It was hard to believe that danger lay ahead. The air was fresh and clean, the river murmured its own song as they passed, and the steady clippety-clop of the horses' hooves along the dirt road was nearly hypnotizing. They stopped briefly at one o'clock to rest and water the horses and to make a meal of the bread and meat they had brought with them, and then they were off again, their progress more rapid than it had been, but still well paced and, in Alys's opinion, with her tension increasing by the minute, nerve-wrackingly slow.

When the sunlight dimmed suddenly, she looked up to see a scattering of fleecy white clouds overhead. She heard the two men riding behind Ian and herself talking quietly to one another, but other than the river's song and the occasional rustle of leaves in the trees, stirred by the gentle breeze, there was no sound. Even the birds and squirrels were quiet now, and when the men behind her fell silent too, Alys felt a prickling of unease. She peered apprehensively into the dark shadows of the forest, then across the river, where the land was also forested, though not so thickly as it was on this side. Was that a rider?

Even if it was, she told herself, the river ran swiftly here; there was no ford. Her little party was safe enough.

Then, with a burst of shrieks and screams that terrified the horses, a band of heavily armed, half-naked savages leapt out of the forest at them. Her palfrey screamed and plunged, and Alys, caught unaware, was thrown to the ground. By the time she had picked herself up, the skirmish was over. Ian and the other two had reached for their swords, but they were outnumbered and easily outmatched. They stood still now, watching their captors.

Brushing herself off, angry rather than frightened at having her journey interrupted, Alys snapped, "What do you want?"

One man spoke for the others with exaggerated politeness. "We are for the taking o' yer horses, an it please ye, madam."

"You cannot have them. We need them."

"Well now, but I think we must have them," he replied. "We'll not be for discussing it here, however. Take them on into the woods, me lads."

She protested, but the raiders were not interested, and so they were taken into the woods at swordpoint. In a tiny clearing Alys pulled the letter from her bodice and held it out to the man who had spoken before. "Read that, sir, and you will see that we have safe-passage granted us by Lord Lovell himself."

"Do y' now, me darlin'? What a pity it is that I cannot read it. I'll be having to take yer word for what it says."

"Then do so."

"Aye, I will that, but e'en his lordship would agree that our need for the horses be greater than yer own. And I see by the packs tied to yon saddles, ye've got a bit o' sup. We'll be for having that, as well. Build us a fire, lads. We've a squirrel or two by us we can roast, and by heaven, we shall have a fine meal. Some of you lot, into the trees wi' ye! We've not seen a sign o' Harry's lads, but it don't do for to be careless. Ye'll be forgiving us," he added, grinning at Alys and the others, "if we truss ye up a bit. Ye wouldn't want to be losing yerselves in this blessed forest whilst we sup, now, would ye?"

Alys sat stiffly while her hands were tied behind her, and when they were alone, Ian muttered beside her, "Devilish heathen Irish. What a mon can want wi' sich tae fight for him, I dinna ken. 'Tis unnatural. An they dare tae touch you, mistress—"

"They will not," she said wearily. "They are much too interested in food, and I think he did believe me about Lovell. I had not thought about them not being able to read."

"They ken his device, e'en an they canna read his letters," Ian pointed out.

"Aye." She watched them making their fires, and eating. In the gloom of the forest, she was uncertain how much time passed, but she knew that even if somehow they got away, they would not make Newark now by nightfall. She was leaning against a tree, paying scant heed to the activity in the clearing, when suddenly she was aware of a stillness around her, and glanced quickly at the place where she had last seen the leader. He was talking earnestly with one of the others, who was gesturing toward the woods. The leader said something, and the men all disappeared into the trees and undergrowth. Alys straightened alertly, only to feel the sharp prick of a dagger against her back.

"Ye'll all of ye be having the goodness to keep silent or the wench'll be spitted," the man muttered loud enough for Ian and the other two to hear. They could not have spoken anyway, for as Alys could see now, a second raider was gagging the last of the three. Her gaze was caught just then by movement across the glade. There were riders among the trees, and one, on a huge black horse, was riding straight toward her. Above his head, the branches of a tree began to quake.

"Above you, Nicholas!" Alys screamed, flinging herself to one side, but expecting the sharp thrust of the villain's dagger to follow her, to spit her as he had threatened he would.

# 24

Alys saw Nicholas twist in the saddle, his sword out and up to thrust. The savage who had jumped at him from the tree crashed lifeless to the ground, and in minutes the fracas was over. Nicholas leapt from his horse and ran to untie Alys, while the other horsemen herded the surviving Irishmen back into the clearing. The leader glared at her.

"I doubted ye was at one with his lordship, papers or no."

"What papers?" Sir Nicholas demanded, pulling her upright.

Alys waited to be sure she could stand before she replied, "I came to find you, Nicholas. I must speak privately with you."

"What papers?" he repeated implacably.

"The darlin' wench bears one wi' our blessed Lovell's own device on the seal," the helpful Irishman said, sneering.

Imperatively, Nicholas held out his hand.

"Please, sir, I came to find you," she said, standing her ground. "I have news that I cannot give to anyone else. I swear to you, the letter I carry was not given me as a safe-passage."

For a moment, she feared he would insist that she explain herself then and there, but at last, with a glance at the men around them, he grunted and took her by the arm. "Come with me," he said, "but this tale of yours had better be a good one."

Alone, away from the others, she showed him the letter, explained how she had come by it, and expressed the fears that had possessed her as a result of what Davy had said about the king. She did not tell him about the medallion she carried, tucked inside her bodice, for whatever else he might accept, she knew he would not tolerate the news that she was to take it to the dowager queen if the rebellion failed. To her surprise, Nicholas believed everything she did tell him, and did not question or scold her. Instead, he called to Hugh to join them.

"I thought the battle might have begun already," she said as they watched Hugh's approach. "I never expected to encounter you so far from Newark."

"I am believed to know more than most about this part of the country," he said with an ironic smile. "The king sent us to guard the east bank of the Trent hereabouts, and one of my lads saw you taken. He did not know it was you, only that a party of riders had been attacked, and we had to find a ford before we could get to you. Hugh," he said when the giant joined them, "my lady has cause to think the rebels will make killing Henry their first task. Lovell's messenger told her they meant to find the king no matter where he hid. Sounds as if they know he means to keep to the rear." Alys noted that Nicholas had not named the messenger, although she had told him the man was Davy Hawkins.

Hugh nodded thoughtfully. "By what we make out, they are heading south, so Harry was right that Newark is the most likely place to meet them. What will we do with this lot?" He glanced uneasily at Alys. "We've no way to look after prisoners."

Nicholas also looked at her. "Set them loose," he said, "without their weapons. If this is the best that Lovell and Lincoln have to command, a few more will not worry us. As for you, madam, you go straight back to Wolveston."

Alys opened her mouth to protest, but Hugh spoke first. "There are like to be more of these louts betwixt here and there, Nick, and we cannot spare men to accompany her. As it is, we can use the three she brought with her."

"What would you have me do, man, present her to the king? I can scarcely leave her on her own somewhere along the way."

Hugh chuckled. "Why not take her to Harry? Appears to me that she could not be anywhere safer now that we know the danger, and she will be much better off with us than with only young Ian and those other two lads to look out for her."

"I shall have something to say to them," Nicholas said.

"Ian did only what you told him to do, sir," Alys said. "You told him to serve me, and he has served me well."

"I will show you what well served means once this business is over and done, my love. Your information may save the king, but Harry himself won't be able to protect you from me after this escapade. Of all the damn fool things to have done—"

Hugh interrupted him. "Ought we not to be going, Nick? The lord knows when the fighting will begin, but I'd not count on having more than the night to see us to Newark."

Alys was grateful for the interruption, but it did not spare her from hearing all that Nicholas meant to say to her. She had cause in the next half hour to regret all the times she had wished he would speak to her more when his men were around.

"You might have been killed by those villains," he snapped once they were mounted.

"But I was not," she replied, "and had I not screamed when I did, you might have been killed."

"Had you not been there at all," he retorted grimly, "I would never have crossed the river."

"Now, Nick," Hugh said behind them, "the mistress has no good cause to love our Harry, and yet did she come, all on her own, to warn him of the evil afoot against him."

There was a murmur of agreement from the company behind them, which consoled Alys but did not seem to affect Nicholas.

"What she did was reckless," he said to Hugh, "and I mean to make certain she never does such a damn fool thing again!"

A man shouted from behind, "Takes a brave lass to risk her life to save her king!" Cheers followed, and more shouts.

Alys glanced at Nicholas. A muscle twitched in his jaw. He said no more, but she thought he still looked ominously grim.

They crossed to the Lincolnshire side of the river, where they encountered royal forces, but they saw no more sign of the enemy, and it was late when they approached Newark. They could see the glow of myriad torches and campfires on both sides of the river, and well into the forest. There were signs of men and horses as far to the south and west as the eye could see, for it was at Newark that the river Trent changed its course, flowing from west to east now, instead of south to north. Nicholas ordered his men to make camp in an open space that proved to be a newly harvested crocus field north of the town.

"I've no notion where we might find Harry tonight," he told Hugh. "He could be anywhere betwixt here and Lough-borough. We will see the royal banners more easily at first light, and we will fight better, when we must, if we have rested." Turning to Alys, he said, "I've no tent for you, lass, but I have furs and blankets. You will sleep with me."

The men tended their horses and made a hasty, cold meal before making up their beds on the ground, where Alys found that the matted remains of crocus plants provided a soft mattress. She knew that only the flowers were harvested for their saffron centers, used for dyes and the flavoring of foods.

Nicholas still seemed forbidding, and watching him in the light from a scattering of stars and a waning moon, Alys wondered what he was thinking and if he was still angry. She had felt no fear, even when he had promised retribution for her recklessness. His reproaches had lacked their customary sharpness. While she munched cold meat and bread, and drank the ale he gave her in a horn mug he carried with him, she caught his gaze upon her more than once. When he saw her watching, he looked away, but the expression in his eyes before he did made her spirits rise. His demeanor seemed stern, but the look was not. She could not define the expression exactly, but there was no harshness, only tenderness and curiosity—an odd combination, she thought.

By the time she crawled into the camp bed beside him, with her heavy cloak and his brigandine spread beneath the covers to protect them from dampness, she was encouraged enough to speak to him. "Nicholas," she whispered.

"Aye, sweetheart?"

Sweetheart. She breathed more easily, hearing the word. "I feared you were still angry."

"You frightened the wits out of me," he said, sliding an arm beneath her shoulders and drawing her close to him. "Did you expect me to thank you for it?"

Her head rested in the hollow of his shoulder, and she turned her cheek so that it lay against the rise of his chest. "I am frightened, too," she murmured. "So many men I know will be fighting. I was scared before, but I have been terrified since the moment Davy told me the king would die."

"I should have thought you would not miss the Tudor."

"I have come to like him," she said. "I do not like all he has done, but I cannot wish for his death. I . . . I could not stop your son from dying, Nicholas, but I hoped I might stop the death of your king. You can prevent it now, can you not?"

"Aye," he said. "Wherever he is tonight, he will be well guarded, but in the heat of battle, knowing himself well to the rear, he might not have taken care. He will want to send all his best men to the vanguard, and if the rebels planned the business well ahead, as you believe, they might already have a party of men this side of the river, behind us and small enough not to be noted by the royal army. Such a force would be deadly if they come from behind to strike without care for their own safety."

"And if I had not come?"

"Gwilym could have told us," he said gently.

"But first I would have had to convince him there was danger, and even then he might have said you could deal with it, that he was needed more at Wolveston. And . . . and . . ." She could think of nothing more to say.

"And you wanted to come," he said.

She tried to see his face, but she could not. "I cannot explain how I felt," she said. "I did not want to tell anyone but you. I knew if I spoke to Gwilym, he might decide to send someone else, and they might not find you, and moreover, once he knew I had spoken to Davy, he would . . . he would have made it impossible for me to get away if he did not go himself. I was afraid you would be killed, Nicholas. I had to come."

"I have it now. You did not trust me to look after myself, let alone to look after the king."

"No, no, it was not that!" she said hastily, fearing she had offended him again.

He chuckled, hugging her, and said, "Oh, sweetheart, how quickly you rise to the bait. I understand how it feels to believe that no one can do a job as well as one can do it oneself, but one does not expect a woman to put her life in jeopardy because she does not trust men to do a thing properly."

"Well, I do not see what being a woman has to do with it," she said indignantly.

"Very likely not," he said, hugging her again, "but you will promise me something now, or by heaven, I will bind and gag you when I leave you with our Harry."

She did not believe the threat for an instant and grinned at the thought of what the king would think of such treatment, but she affected a deep sigh and said in a long-suffering tone, "Very well, sir, I will promise whatever you want. What is it?"

"That no matter what you hear or see, you will stay with him until I come for you, or until he bids you otherwise," he said.

The thought of why the king might bid her to do otherwise was too dreadful to contemplate, so she said hastily, "I will stay with him, Nicholas, I promise—if you will be careful."

"I will," he said, "and, sweetheart, about what you said before—you didn't let our son die. I have never blamed you."

"I know you said you did not, but—"

"I said what I meant," he interjected fiercely. "It was God's will. I understand your feelings now, but you need never have believed you must aid my king because our son was lost."

"That was not my only reason," she said. "I just wanted to explain it all to you. You were so angry before, and—"

"I was not angry. I told you that seeing you in that clearing with those savages frightened me witless, and that was true, but afterward, I said the things I did because . . ."

"Because you were furious with me, Nicholas. Even your men thought you were too harsh."

"Aye, they did," he said, chuckling.

She leaned up on her elbow and peered into his face. "You are pleased with yourself. You wanted them to speak up for me!"

"They would not have liked having a wench in their midst on such a day," he said. "Some think it bad luck even to have one near a battle. I thought there would be less resentment if they felt a little sorry for you, and I did not think it would hurt you to hear what I had to say. I could not cosset you, my love."

"Oh, Nicholas, say those words again. I am never certain whether you mean them or if they just spill out unnoticed."

"I mean them," he said quietly, pulling her down and folding his arms tightly around her. "Kiss me, wife."

She chuckled, happier than she could remember ever being before, and said, "Surely you do not mean to ravish me here in the midst of all your men, sir. What would they think?"

She saw his delighted grin. "They would think me a fool for draining energy I will soon need on the battlefield. But I mean only to hold my wife and cuddle her a bit, and maybe there will be a few kisses, and maybe"—his right hand slid down to stroke her backside—"maybe a bit more than that."

Alys did not reply. He had pressed his lips to hers, and his tongue was seeking entrance to her mouth. She welcomed it with her own, and she welcomed his hands on her body, and his kisses as well, and later, when he slept, she snuggled close to him, though her body was heated enough by then to sustain them both, even had it been a cold winter night and not summer.

They were up again and mounted before the first light of dawn, and less than a quarter hour afterward entered the silent streets of Newark. Normally a bustling place, even at such an early hour, the town appeared to be deserted that morning, its citizens no doubt cowering behind bolted doors and shuttered windows, hiding their valuables, saying their prayers, in fear that the coming battle would take place on their doorstep.

There was light enough to see more easily when they passed through the market square, past well-appointed inns, to the high-towered church. Calling a halt, Nicholas ordered Hugh to find a way up the tower. "See what you can see from up there," he said.

Hugh returned a short time later. "You might like to look for yourself, Nick. 'Tis an awesome sight."

"We have no time. Could you spy the royal banners?"

"Nay, but I saw what must be Lincoln Cathedral to the east and Nottingham Castle on the western horizon. The forest and long stretches of the Great North Road are teeming with movement, Nick. When the sun rises, it will see thousands of steel helms and pike-heads winking back at it. The king's main army is moving up from the southwest, and the rebels look to be heading for Fiskerton, that place we crossed the first time we took Lady Alys to London. From here, the crossing looks narrower and more shallow than it was then—fifty feet across, maybe two deep, for it's down a foot, maybe two, from when we last crossed there."

"Have they begun the crossing?"

"Not yet," Hugh said.

"Then we ride. We must be past that point on the road—Stoke, is it not?—before they arrive, or we will have to veer west, and we will lose time if we do. Kick that palfrey of yours to a lope, Alys. We have no time to lose."

Alys was not sure her palfrey knew how to lope, but with the example set by so many other horses, it managed such speed that she was hard-pressed to stay in her saddle, and finally resorted to clinging to the palfrey's mane. The wild ride was a short one, for they began to meet horses and men coming toward them, and heralds, weaving their mounts through the others, seeking news of the rebel positions to carry back to their leaders. It was from them that Nicholas learned the king's whereabouts, but in the midst of what had begun to look—to Alys, at least—more and more like a sea of riders, it was nearly nine o'clock before they found him in a churchyard, nearby in the village of Elston.

Nicholas dismounted quickly and went to kneel before him, speaking as he went. Alys saw Henry frown when Nicholas gestured toward her, but when Hugh lifted her down and the two of them took a few steps forward, then hesitated, Henry beckoned them on.

Making a deep curtsy, Alys looked up to see the king's eyes twinkling. He said, "I am told that you exerted yourself greatly on my behalf, Lady Merion. I am out of stirring speeches, for I have just delivered one to an immense gathering of men-at-arms, so I hope you will accept a simple thank you."

Nicholas cut in, saying, "With respect, your grace, we would ask you to go above, into the tower, where you can be better protected. I will remain here, with my men—"

"No, Nicholas," the king said. "I am sending you forward

with the majority of your men to warn Oxford and the vanguard that there are rebels about whose only purpose is to
slay me. You may leave ten men to augment my yeoman
guard, but only because I know you will not trust the thing
to be done properly if some of your own are not here."

Nicholas nodded and turned. "Hugh?"

"I will stay," Hugh Gower told him.

Alys reached out her hand to her husband but said
nothing.

Squeezing her hand, Nicholas gave her a teasing look, as
if he knew the effort it cost her to hold her tongue, not to
say she did not want him in the vanguard, which would bear
the brunt of the fighting. He kissed her lightly on the cheek,
and turned toward his horse. When he mounted, she saw
that the dagger he carried was not his own. On the hilt,
shining clearly in the sunlight, was the engraving of the head
of a dog.

She closed her eyes in sorrow, and said a prayer. Moments
after he had ridden away, she found herself high up in the
church bell tower with the man she had once thought her
worst enemy. Henry moved to the far side, to the open parapet, and without a thought for his rank or her own, Alys
moved quickly to stand beside him. "Goodness, we can see
for miles," she said.

The two armies looked almost toylike below. The massive
royal force was drawn up in battle order, its banners resplen-
dent and its armor shimmering in the sunlight. The vanguard
alone looked formidable, and behind them waited the rest,
at least twice as many men as the rebels, who could be seen
taking their stand on a hill above the river, near the village
of Stoke. Over the steady din of hoofbeats, upraised voices,
horses' cries, and clanking metal, Alys suddenly heard the
sprightly, unnerving sound of the rebels' fife and drum.

The royal advance was slow, deliberate. It seemed forever
to her before arrows and crossbow bolts began to fly. In all
the din and flurry of motion that followed, she could scarcely
tell what was happening, but before long, even she could see

that the rebels had little chance. Their casualties were dreadful. Their forces were boxed in, sitting targets. Once Henry had pointed them out to her, she could tell the Germans from the Irish, for the former moved with steely discipline, the latter with a shrieking frenzy. The Irish, without any armor at all, were falling everywhere that she could see them. For a short time she tried to pick out banners, looking for the golden wyvern, but it was too horrible. She turned away, unable to watch anymore.

At a burst of sound from the churchyard below, she hurried to the other side of the tower to look down, but the angle was wrong, and she could see nothing. Exchanging a wary look with the armed yeoman who stood below her on the stairs, she listened anxiously for footsteps coming up the steps, but when they came, they were those of a single man.

The yeoman lowered his pike and stood aside to let Hugh pass. The king turned then and spoke quickly. "Rebels?"

"Aye, your grace, but we set a little trap, and they are no more danger to you."

"Prisoners?"

"Aye, not one lost."

"Good. Keep them safe till the battle is done. God willing, I shall deal with them then."

"How goes it?" Hugh asked, moving to the parapet.

The king grimaced. "Had we not been at Bosworth, I might worry, for they are pressing the vanguard hard, but we have men in reserve today, so our position is stronger. We shall overcome them easily enough, but I tell you here and now that this is the last time I shall attend a battle. Having made the decision to keep to the rear, I ought to have known better than to come even so close as this. And do not think," he added gravely, "that this decision is taken out of cowardice."

"I do not," Hugh said mildly.

"Others might, but we won the crown through being fortunate enough to slay the opposing leader. We must not give any more of mine enemies a similar opportunity."

Alys was listening with but half an ear. The moment the king had said the vanguard was having a hard time, she had rushed to look, to try to find Nicholas. She could not do so, however, and though the battle was short, lasting but three hours in all, by the time it was over, she was nearly frantic with worry. She had thought it ended when the king announced that a great many common soldiers and quite a few knights and gentlemen were taking flight across the river, but after that there were bursts of fierce fighting that seemed to go on forever.

Finally, with a sigh of relief, Hugh said, "They've planted your banner, your grace, and there is Nick's golden wyvern, my lady. Yonder, coming toward us."

"They would not wave his banner if he were dead," Alys said, as much to hear the words as to invite reassurance. She strained her eyes to see him, but even finding him, she could not make herself believe him safe until he came up the tower steps and she could fling herself at him and feel his arms close around her.

"You'll get blood on your gown, but 'tis none of mine," he said, hugging her. Then, recalling the king's presence, he set her aside and added, "We took few losses, your grace, and the boy-king was captured. It will not surprise you to learn that he is not Warwick but a youth who confesses to being known by many names, including the unlikely one of Lambert Simnel."

"It matters not how he is called if he is not noble," Henry said. "I shall make clear to one and all that he is no enemy of mine. Methinks I shall put him to work in the royal kitchens."

Nicholas nodded but did not smile. "I have other news, your grace, that will not please you so much. Lincoln is dead."

The king swore. "I wanted him alive. By the rood, I gave orders that he was to be taken alive so that we could get to the bottom of this conspiracy. Now, by God, we may never know it all. What of that rascal Lovell?"

Alys had not been able to take her eyes off Nicholas, and when the king asked the question, her gaze shot to the dagger at her husband's side. The dog's head was clearly visible. Amazed, she heard Nicholas admit that Lovell was not dead.

"He escaped, your grace, swam the river with a number of others, but most of the rebel force has fallen. At a guess, I would estimate four thousand dead, and many so full of arrows they look like hedgehogs. 'Tis not a pretty sight."

"We will catch Lovell," Henry said, "but now I want to see Lincoln's corpse. My yeomen will arrange it. You see to your wife. As for Hugh Gower," he added, "I mean to knight him when this is over, for Lady Alys's warning was on the mark, and he was able to trap a few rebels who may prove useful to us."

A roar from below startled them all before they realized it was the army cheering Henry. He turned and waved from the parapet, then moved toward the stairs, shouting for his yeoman guard and scarcely giving the others a chance to make their bows, but Alys did not wait for him to disappear around the first turn of the stair before demanding to know if Nicholas had really seen Lovell cross the river to safety.

"Aye," he said with a guilty look, putting a hand to the dagger's hilt. "We nearly had him. There were men who would have chased him down, but in their heavy armor, I feared they might drown in the river, so I called them back. In sooth," he added carelessly, "there was such a crowd of them taking flight that he might have drowned before he reached the other side."

Alys did not need the stifled snort from Hugh to alert her. Giving her husband a straight look, she said, "Your men?"

"Aye, others might not have heeded me so quick."

"The river is but two feet deep at the ford, sir, and your men wear only brigandines and other light armor."

Nicholas shot a rueful look at Hugh, but the big man said, "He was a worthy foe, Nick, true to his liege lord."

"Aye," Nicholas said, looking at Alys, "and there were other reasons, as well." The warmth in his eyes left her no doubt that he had let Lovell escape because of his love for her. Then the warmth faded suddenly, and he turned back to Hugh with bleak sadness in his expression. "Hugh," he said, "Davy Hawkins fell defending Lovell's retreat. He is dead."

"Oh, no!" Alys cried. That news, added to all that had gone before, was too much too bear. She burst into tears, hugging herself, scarcely heeding when Nicholas drew her into his arms.

He said over her head to Hugh, "Take a couple of stout lads and see to his burial, will you?"

"We'll take him back with us," Hugh said. "My lass will want him buried at home." He shot a measuring look at Nicholas from under his brows. "There is naught to be gained by making a song here about the man's loyalties, I'm thinking."

"I agree," Nicholas said. He smoothed Alys's hair from her damp cheeks, and bent to kiss her eyelids, for once not caring whether anyone else was near. "Do as you think best, Hugh."

"Then I am for Wolveston when we are done here."

"We will both go," Nicholas said quietly. "I will commit my lady to the king's care. She will be safe with him."

"No," Alys said, straightening abruptly. "I go with you."

"You cannot," Nicholas said. " 'Tis far too dangerous. Every rebel who escaped death here today will be fleeing back to the north. Go on ahead, Hugh, I will be with you shortly."

Alys paid no heed to Hugh's going. "I will be safe with you," she said, giving Nicholas look for look. Seeing by his expression that he still meant to forbid her, she said in fierce desperation, "My daughter is at Wolveston, sir. I will not stay away a moment longer than I must, do what you will. If need be, I will ride there alone after you have gone on ahead!"

"By God, madam," he snapped, "do not try me too far. I swear to you now that if *my* daughter ever shows a fraction of her mother's impudence, I will know my duty!"

"If you ever lay a hand on her, Nicholas, so help me—"

"I do likewise swear, my love," he added much more gently, stilling her protests with a finger against her lips, "that if she ever shows a similar fraction of your courage, I shall reward her with gold coins, just as Gwilym rewards our young archers."

Relaxing, touched by his words, Alys kissed the finger pressing against her lips, then smiled at him through her tears and said, "I do love you so much, Nicholas ap Dafydd. One day, I promise you, I will give you another son, no matter how many daughters we must have in the meantime."

He grinned. "I do not doubt you, sweetheart, but I confess I find the thought of so many daughters downright terrifying."

"Aye, it is," she agreed, letting her gaze drift toward the river again. She was sorry that she had, for the sight of all the carnage below brought the tears to her eyes again. "Oh, Nicholas, what a dreadful world to bring children into!"

"Not so dreadful, sweetheart," he said calmly. " 'Tis a fine, bright world, and growing finer by the day. We've a king on the throne who means to stay there. As to plots and counterplots, we shall soon see an end to them all."

Slowly she drew the medallion from her bodice and showed it to him. "Davy brought this, Nicholas, from Lovell. He said I was to give it to the queen dowager if the rebellion went amiss."

He said quietly, "And will you take it to her?"

She stared at him in surprise. "You do not forbid me?"

"You must choose for yourself, my love."

"But that is a dreadful choice," she whispered. " 'Tis proof he lives, Nicholas. That is why Elizabeth Woodville supported the rebels, and why Lincoln never declared himself the heir. Simnel was but a puppet, sir, a token, so they need not risk exposing the prince to danger. I think, from what Lovell once said, that they named him on our wedding day, on Simnel Sunday. And now he is to serve in Henry's kitchens, poor little boy."

"At least he won't lose his head," Nicholas said dryly.

"But what am I to do about the medallion?"

"You need not make your choice all in a moment," he said. "There is time to ponder it before we return to London. So come now, sweetheart, no more tears. If you rust the plates of this brigandine, I shall never get out of it, and I promise I mean to do that as soon as I can, so I can show you how much I love you."

She gave a watery chuckle. "You had better wait until we get home, sir, if you do not want to display your weakness for me before your men. Oh, Nicholas," she added with a rueful sigh, "you must think me mad to have rushed to the Tudor's rescue and yet be sobbing now for rebel losses."

"No," he said. "You have learned to care about individuals, my love, not merely to support one cause blindly over another. 'Tis a good lesson, I think. Would that others might learn it."

"In faith, sir," she said, brushing the tears from her cheeks, "I believe you learned that lesson before I did."

"I have learned many lessons, *mi calon*," he said, putting an arm around her and urging her toward the tower steps. "I have learned that one may value true loyalty in one's enemies as much as in one's comrades-in-arms, and I have learned that love is a strength, not a weakness. And in truth, my love, I do trust that over the years that lie ahead of us, there will be many more such lessons for us both to learn. But for the present, the battles of the white rose against the red being over, I want nothing more than to find Hugh and the others, and take you home to bed."

Putting her arm around his waist, Alys smiled up at him, and they went down the stone steps of the tower together, and out into the sunlit churchyard.

Right Trusty and Well-beloved Reader:

An outbreak of sweating sickness in the north that occurred before Henry VII's troops landed in England provided Lord Stanley with his reason for not joining Richard III when he was first asked to do so. The disease was new to England and virulent, striking down young men in particular by the thousands. It is entirely possible that one or both of the princes fell victim to it if Richard had sent them north for their own safety, which possibility is suggested by more than one authority.

Francis, Viscount Lovell did swim away after the Battle of Stoke and was never heard from again. Many authorities believe that he took refuge in a secret room in his house at Minster Lovell, where a body was discovered centuries later. The body disintegrated in a puff of dust when the room was opened.

For those purists who also speak Welsh, I confess that certain liberties have been taken with the two endearments used most frequently in this tale. The words for girl (*geneth*) and heart (*calon*) are correct, but the proper usage of the time for "my girl" (*fy ngeneth*) and "my heart" (*fy ncalon*) left a good deal to be desired in context. One does not wish soft language to choke a reader trying to imagine the pronunciation. I tried to make the words sound more as they do when spoken today.

*Amanda Scott*